Grave

CW00400356

Phillip Strang

BOOKS BY PHILLIP STRANG

DCI Isaac Cook Series

MURDER IS A TRICKY BUSINESS
MURDER HOUSE
MURDER IS ONLY A NUMBER
MURDER IN LITTLE VENICE
MURDER IS THE ONLY OPTION
MURDER IN NOTTING HILL
MURDER IN ROOM 346
MURDER OF A SILENT MAN
MURDER HAS NO GUILT
MURDER IN HYDE PARK
SIX YEARS TOO LATE
GRAVE PASSION
MURDER WITHOUT REASON

DI Keith Tremayne Series

DEATH UNHOLY
DEATH AND THE ASSASSIN'S BLADE
DEATH AND THE LUCKY MAN
DEATH AT COOMBE FARM
DEATH BY A DEAD MAN'S HAND
DEATH IN THE VILLAGE
BURIAL MOUND
THE BODY IN THE DITCH

Steve Case Series

HOSTAGE OF ISLAM
THE HABERMAN VIRUS
PRELUDE TO WAR

Standalone Books

MALIKA'S REVENGE

Copyright Page

Dedication

For Elli and Tais who both had the perseverance to make me sit down and write.

Chapter 1

Brad Robinson was about to break the law, not that he knew it, and he was in too much of a hurry to worry anyway. He was a bright child, his mother would say, but then she had a soft spot for him, seeing that he was the only one of her three children who wasn't taking drugs, incarcerated in prison, or, in the case of her daughter, selling herself. To the sixteen-year-old's mother, it looked as though he might make his way in the world without resorting to crime, even becoming a worthwhile member of society, which she had aspired to but had failed to achieve.

Jim, the eldest of her three children, had at twenty-two seen the inside of more than a few prison cells. He had had to grow up hard; his father was a criminal as well as a drunk, and on many a night, he had beaten his mother senseless.

At the age of fourteen, Jim, strong for his age, had taken on the bane of the Robinson household and thrashed his father mercilessly with a cricket bat. The upshot was that Jim, the saviour of his family, spent time in a young offender's institution, and his father, once the wounds had healed, had briefly returned to the family home, a squalid council house with little charm, picked up his clothes, packed them in a suitcase and had left; not a word of farewell to anyone in the house, other than a pat on the shoulder for the eight-year-old Brad.

The second eldest, Janice, was an attractive blonde-haired child until puberty hit. After that, she had discovered boys, and then men, and then drugs. She was now twenty-one and living a transient life, moving from one place to another, eking a living by selling herself, injecting when she could, eating whatever food she could afford.

Brad tried to see her every couple of months, but it wasn't easy. He was sixteen, and his life should have been a time for exams and sport and chasing girls. Not that he tarried on the latter, as he had grown up a good-looking lad, and the genetic traits that had made Jim violent and Janice a tart hadn't touched him. He was more like his mother, except that he had tried alcohol on a couple of occasions and never found a love for it. He was glad of that.

The house wasn't somewhere you took Rose Winston. Brad didn't want to destroy her impression of him. She lived not far away in a better house and her parents owned it; her father was a professional man and her mother was a schoolteacher.

Rose had made it clear that sex was the next step in their relationship; after all, they had passed through passionate kissing and heavy petting. The next stage was the final act, where he, the over-eager Brad, and Rose, the expectant female, would come together in a crescendo of drums, the sound of waves lapping on the shore, an abandonment of themselves as they became one.

That was how Rose, an avid reader of love stories, saw it. Brad, sensitive as only a sixteen-year-old male could be, knew that wasn't how it was, but he wasn't about to tell her the truth, not just yet. It was messy, he could have told her, over far too quickly, and if she wanted banging drums and the music, then she'd better take a radio with her.

The best he could hope for was a balmy summer's night, a secluded spot in Hyde Park. He had purchased a cheap bottle of wine and taken a blanket from home, the cleanest one he could find. His mother wasn't strong on cleanliness, although she was on vodka.

Brad, in his reflective moments, wondered about his parentage. His mother was a short woman, whereas he was tall for his age and slim, although her facial features showed in him, as they did in his brother and sister. But Janice was as short as her mother, and Jim wasn't much taller, and the father of the three had been short as well. His mother, who had read about it in a magazine, her usual window on the world, apart from the incessantly-on television, said his height and physique were a genetic throwback to an ancestor. Not that he could see it, as his grandparents on both sides were equally short, and at family gatherings, not held since Janice had taken to prostitution, he had stood head and shoulders above the rest.

Jim's all too frequent brushes with the law were regarded as an occupational hazard, as the Robinsons regarded petty thieving and crime as a vocation, and the occasional incarceration as an inconvenience. However, Janice's fall into degradation had stunned them all, and her name was never mentioned by her mother, who in between drinking herself into a stupor was a regular churchgoer.

3

The evening was balmy, the love that Rose felt for Brad was that of a fifteen-year-old, which was what she was. The age of consent was sixteen, although Brad wouldn't have known that, and so what, everyone was having sex at the school they both went to. Rose had been feeling the pressure from her peers for the past year after she had inadvertently blurted out that she was still a virgin.

Rose had always felt that intimacy with another should be within the bond of marriage, and if not that, then part of an intense interdependency of one human on another, a person she could trust. And Brad was that person, she had decided five weeks previously when they had first gone out together. He had been the perfect gentleman, not once grabbing at her breasts or trying to put his hand up her skirt in the back row of the cinema; not like some others that had tried and been rebuked. The reason some at the school had accused her of being a prick teaser. She wasn't; she was just a good girl, about to become a woman, about to give herself to Brad.

The plan was in place. Brad was to leave his house in Compton Road at Kensal Green at 9.45 p.m. It was a Saturday, and there was no school to worry about the next day, not that Brad's mother would have been concerned, although Rose's would have been.

Rose was to tell her parents that she was sleeping over at her friend Steph's house that night, which was fine by them, as Rose chose her friends well, and Steph was a person they liked and trusted. It wasn't the real person that they saw, Rose knew that, as Steph was well ahead of her in the losing virginity stakes, and had been with half the boys in their class at school, including Brad, not that Rose was concerned. With Steph it had only been lust, as Rose's best friend was of easy virtue.

It had been Steph who had given Rose instruction in the more exquisite art of lovemaking, which wasn't how it was in the novels she liked to read. Rose was convinced that Steph had experienced the physical act without the emotion, something she was not going to do.

***

The two young lovers met outside Kensal Green Cemetery on Harrow Road at ten in the evening. Brad was on time, Rose was two minutes late. They held each other tight and kissed.

It was Brad who suggested they take a short cut through the cemetery to Kilburn Lane where they could catch a bus down through Ladbroke Grove and Notting Hill. And once they had reached Holland Park Avenue, they could walk up Bayswater Road and into Hyde Park.

Brad had chosen the spot, suitably romantic and secluded, but he wasn't sure how he'd last until they got there. He also wasn't sure why it had taken five weeks for him to get to this stage with Rose. He thought it was love, but he couldn't be sure. But whatever it was, it was important to him and to her.

They were, as he saw it, two people embarking on a life together, not a fumble in the dark, not like it had been with Rose's friend, Steph, nor with the others. After all, he wasn't a virgin, six women to date, and Rose was to be the last.

His brother, Jim, would have said he was a fool, and that women were only good for one thing, not that his advice was required, nor would he be commenting, as he was doing three years in prison for holding up a newsagent, the proceeds totalling just three hundred and twenty pounds, and even then he'd left his fingerprints on the cash register, and they were held in a police database.

Janice, his sister, another romantic, would have seen the gallantry in her young brother, recognised herself in Rose. Although at the time that Brad met up with Rose, she was about to be flat on her back for the seventh time that night, and it was no sixteen-year-old with sweet intentions; it was an obese, sweaty man in his late forties.

Rose felt some trepidation about walking through the cemetery, not because she was squeamish, but on account of having first watched a horror movie at Steph's before venturing out, knowing full well how distressed her parents would be if they knew of her deceit. The film, a dystopian zombie frightener, long on darkened scenes and violent deaths, devoid of a discernible plot, had not interested her, but it was Steph's bedroom, and she had been polite and had watched it.

'It'll be fine,' Brad said. 'Save a couple of minutes.'

He took her by the hand, and the two of them walked through the imposing entrance. It reminded him of a scaled-down version of Marble Arch, not that he knew why a cemetery should have such an entrance, nor that Marble Arch had been built in the nineteenth century, a triumphal arch that had initially been built as the state entrance to Buckingham Palace and had been moved in 1851 to its current location at the junction of Oxford Street, Park Lane, and Edgware Road, at the north-east corner of Hyde Park.

Rose felt a cold chill as they walked through. Some of the graves were maintained, most weren't, and the occasional one had flowers on top of the headstone, or laid on the grave. Brad would admit to not feeling as brave as he had, as it was dark in the cemetery, whereas out on Harrow Road it had been bright with the street lights and the traffic. Even though they were only halfway through, only two hundred yards from where they had entered, the ever-present noise of the bustling metropolis of London had dimmed, replaced by a low hum in the distance.

'I don't like it,' Rose said as she grasped Brad's hand tighter.

Neither did Brad, but he wasn't about to say that there was something that was freaking him out.

A man walked hurriedly by, his hat down low, his coat collar turned up high.

The two young lovers quickened their pace; the exit of the cemetery on Kilburn Lane visible not more than fifty yards distance.

Rose let out a scream. 'Over there,' she pointed.

Brad, feeling calmer once again, thinking to the night's event, especially after they had drunk the wine, didn't react at first.

'Brad, over there, on that grave.'

Brad looked briefly before averting his gaze; after all, his mind was elsewhere. He looked again. 'It's a body,' he said.

Rose ran out of the cemetery; Brad stood transfixed.

Slowly, realising the situation, Brad walked closer to the grave. He pointed the small light on his smartphone at the body, saw that it was a woman and that in her body there was a knife.

Once out of the place of death, the two of them hugged each other, the street light shining on them, a bus passing by on the other side of the road; the bus they would have caught. Rose crying and Brad shaking like a leaf.

It was Rose who spoke first. 'We have to call the police.'

'Your parents?'

'It's a dead body, we have to tell someone.'

Brad took out his smartphone from his pocket, and shakingly dialled the emergency number. 'There's a body, Kensal Green Cemetery, the Kilburn Lane entrance,' he said.

After three minutes, the sound of a police car.

'Do you want to stay?' Brad said, conscious of Rose's parents' reaction.

'They've got your phone number, and yes, we must stay.'

Brad knew that she was right. So much for a romantic evening, he thought but did not say it to Rose.

Chapter 2

Detective Chief Inspector Isaac Cook, the son of Jamaican immigrants to England, had hoped for a quiet night at home with Jenny, his wife, but it was not to be. As a DCI in Homicide at Challis Street Police Station, as well as being the senior officer in the department, it was up to him to take the lead after the phone call from his second-in-charge, Detective Inspector Larry Hill, a man too fond of drinking beer, although after the last run-in with Isaac, and another ultimatum from his wife, he was now on his best behaviour.

Isaac had been surprised when he arrived at the crime scene to find Larry sober. He hoped it would stay that way, but he wasn't confident. His inspector, Isaac knew, had a regular habit of falling off the sobriety wagon. Larry was a functioning alcoholic, and one beer didn't stop there. They continued till he was barely capable of standing, and on one occasion he had attempted to drive home, only to be stopped after twenty seconds by a patrol car that had been waiting outside the pub.

Also at the crime scene was Detective Sergeant Wendy Gladstone, the most senior member of Homicide, in terms of her age and her time in the police force, not in rank.

'What do we have?' Isaac asked. Even though he had been casually dressed at home, he had changed into a suit; Larry had not. Another bone of contention, Isaac knew, but it was not to be discussed that night. Tonight was for murder.

'Female, white,' Larry said. 'A knife wound to the back.'

'Anything else?'

'We've not disturbed the body, and it's still warm. We'll leave that to Gordon Windsor and his team.'

Isaac could only concur, as Windsor, the senior crime scene investigator, would have reacted badly if an inexperienced police officer or a seasoned detective inspector had disturbed the body. As he would say, 'If the body's clearly dead, then leave it to us.'

On a previous murder case, two wet-behind-the-ears and overzealous police constables had almost destroyed vital evidence, although, by the time they had reached the body, they had had the good sense not to touch it.

Wendy left them and went over to where the two who had discovered the body were sat. She could see they were young, a couple out for a night, minding their business, looking for a little romance.

'Rose's father's going to be angry with me,' the young man said.

'And you are?' Wendy asked as she sat down beside them on the bench at the side of the street.

'Brad Robinson. I live in Compton Road with my mother.'

'Your age?'

'Sixteen, almost seventeen.'

'Let's take this from the beginning,' Wendy said, looking down at the bag to Brad's side, seeing the bottle of wine, the two plastic glasses. 'And be honest with me. You two are in trouble, aren't you?'

'We didn't kill the woman,' Rose said.

Wendy saw a pretty young woman, similar to her at that age.

'How old are you?'

'Fifteen. I'll be sixteen in two months.'

'Brad would have been in trouble if you hadn't found the body. Lucky in one respect, although you probably won't agree. First time for you?'

'We've done nothing wrong,' Brad said.

Wendy, not unfeeling, could see that Brad and Rose were decent enough, although Rose's clothes were more upmarket than Brad's pair of blue jeans and dark blue shirt.

'Don't worry, I'm not going to say any more about it, but the law is clear. Rose is underage.'

Over to one side, a crowd was forming, a man pressing forward, trying to get under the crime scene tape.

'Your father?' Wendy said, looking at Rose.

'I had to phone him. He doesn't know I'm with Brad.'

'At a girlfriend's? A sleepover, watch a few movies, but instead finding a quiet spot with Brad and settling down for a spot of romance, is that it?'

'We're old enough,' Brad said, remembering his mother's lectures on the subject when he'd been younger, not that she could talk. What with the unfamiliar face at breakfast occasionally, his mother insisting that he was a friend of his father's and he had spent the night in the spare room.

'Before your father gets here, Rose. Legally you're underage, and Brad would have been guilty of a crime. Not the most serious, seeing that he's young too, but he would have had to answer for it.'

'We didn't do anything.'

Wendy removed the bottle of wine from Brad's bag and put it inside the large bag that she always carried.

11

'You two are in enough trouble already. It might be better if neither of you mentions the wine,' she said.

'Thank you,' Brad said. 'Rose's father?'

'Wait here. I'll go and talk to him.'

Wendy moved away from them and walked over to the crime scene tape and the irate father. She told the constable to let him through.

'Rose is helping us with our enquiries,' she said.

'She should have been at her friend's house, not here,' Rose Winston's father, Tim, said. He had obviously been in bed when he had received the phone call, and under the tee shirt and an old pair of jeans Wendy could see his pyjama top.

'There's been a murder in the cemetery. Rose and her friend are witnesses,' Wendy said, conscious of the man's concern and undoubted anger. The crime would take precedence, but she could be sensitive as to the situation.

'I know who he is. He's no friend, just another rampant male, wanting to brag about it in school the next day, put it on social media. I've seen it all before.'

Wendy knew he probably had. The man was in his mid-forties, and his teen years were before social media and instant communication. He was, however, a good-looking man, hair greying at the temples, and judging by his physique, he was an active sportsman, and in his youth, another Brad Robinson. The man's memory was selective because it was his daughter. How many daughters of equally concerned men had Winston in his youth tempted and succeeded with? Wendy knew the answer, also thought that he wasn't the sort of man to talk about it afterwards. And if she was a judge of character, she suspected that Brad Robinson wasn't either.

'Mr Winston, your concerns aside, I need to interview them first. How you deal with it afterwards is up to you, but we may need to speak to your daughter after tonight. She's had a fright, and there may be delayed shock. I would advise against you and your wife talking to her tonight. Get her home, put her to bed and let her sleep it off.'

'I'll take your advice, Sergeant. As long as she's at home. She's a good girl, but she's still young, and the Robinsons are known in the area. You're aware of his brother and sister?'

'I am, but young Brad seems decent enough.'

'A difficult age,' Winston said.

Wendy walked the man over to his daughter; neither spoke, only hugged tightly. Brad tried to talk, only to receive a look of disgust from Rose's father.

'Now, Mr Winston, if you don't mind, could you please leave me alone with the two of them,' Wendy said.

Winston took Wendy's advice and walked over to a shop across the road; he purchased a bar of chocolate and a hot drink out of a machine.

'My father, he's angry, isn't he?' Rose said as Wendy sat down beside them again.

Wendy, her two sons now grown up and married with children, could sympathise with the father and with Brad and Rose. She had been young once, and she had done what these two had; and then, older and not necessarily wiser, she had had to be what her parents had been, doting and concerned, attempting to instil wisdom and experience into teenagers, with their hormones, their peers, their belief that the older generation was out of touch.

'He has every right to be, and you're likely to get an ear-bashing.'

13

'Not from Dad, he's a softy really, but he doesn't like Brad, not any boy.'

'You're both finding your way in the world. You'll both make mistakes, tonight for instance. Let's start at the beginning, and what you were doing in Kensal Green Cemetery.'

Brad told how they had been going out for a few weeks; how the two of them felt about each other. Wendy thought it was sweet that the young man had intended to take her to Hyde Park and to find a secluded spot. She wasn't about to tell them that you didn't buy the cheapest bottle of wine if you intended to wake up the next morning without a throbbing headache and a parched throat.

'You're outside the cemetery, on Harrow Road,' Wendy said. 'It's a shortcut, I know that, but what else?'

'I didn't want to, not at night,' Rose said. 'All those gravestones.'

'Do you believe in ghosts?'

'It was Steph; she wanted to watch a zombie movie, I didn't, but it was her house, and she was covering for me.'

'I watched *The Exorcist* when I was your age. I slept with my light on for two nights after that. I know how you felt.'

'I've walked through there before late at night,' Brad said, calmer now that Rose's father had been appeased for the moment.

'I'd agree with you,' Wendy said. 'There's nothing to be frightened of, only your imagination. You're through the gates, then what?'

'We walked through. It's dark and eerily quiet. I'm frightened, holding on to Brad. We can see the gate out onto Kilburn Lane, the lights, the sound of the traffic.'

14

'You're less frightened now?'

'A little.'

'Then what happened?'

'A man rushed past us.'

'You got a good look?'

'He had a hat, a coat, his face concealed,' Brad said. 'We were more interested in catching the next bus.'

'And then?'

'I looked over to my left. That's when I saw a body on the grave,' Rose said.

'But it was dark.'

'The street light was shining onto it from over the wall. I don't know why I looked; maybe I relaxed a bit, seeing that we were nearly out of the place. I screamed, but Brad couldn't see it at first. After he looked again, he could see it and the knife in the person's back.'

'It's a woman,' Wendy said. 'Any idea who she is?'

'We didn't look that closely, but no,' Brad said.

'The man rushing by? Do you think he was the murderer?'

'We wouldn't know. How could we?'

'You can't. However, a man who concealed his face, dressed for a cold night, is suspicious,' Wendy said. 'Or don't you think so?'

'He could be,' Brad admitted.

Wendy realised that asking for the opinion of a sixteen-year-old youth who had more on his mind than murder, or at least he had had earlier, did not seem the wisest thing to do, but the consensus from the crime scene investigators and the attending police was that the man they had seen was probably the murderer. Not only had the impression of a man's size 9 shoe been found near to the body, but there had also been scuffing on the

15

gravel path where the man had left the grass and moved away.

According to the dead woman's body temperature and the state of rigor, death had been ascertained as being five to ten minutes before Brad and Rose had walked past, which meant that the murderer may have been startled by them and that he could possibly see them as a threat.

'Your descriptions are vague,' Wendy said. 'Any more you can give us?'

'It was dark. It was only on the grave that the light shone, and he wasn't there.'

Wendy left the two bewildered would-be lovers and walked over to Rose's father.

'Take it easy,' she said. 'They've had a fright. It's not every day you see a dead body; see a murderer.'

'She's doing well at school, is our Rose. It's not like her to do something like this,' Tim Winston said.

'The first flush of womanhood? What did you expect? A vestal virgin?' Wendy realised that she was being harsh with the man, but she didn't need either Brad or Rose intimidated by her father, or nervous of the police. In time, they would remember small fragments of what they had seen, but it wasn't to happen that night.

'My wife and I, we're liberal people. We understand the modern generation, been there ourselves, but when it's your daughter…'

'We all react to type, isn't that the truth? Anyway, take it easy for a couple of days, and I'll be in touch again. The eyes see, but the mind doesn't always register.'

'I'll not do anything. Brad Robinson?'

'He's not been in trouble, not according to us.'

'His family?'

'The sins of the parent, or in his case his brother and sister, are not visited on the youngest member of the family.'

'If she had waited, chosen someone more suitable…'

'She's chosen him, and from what I can see, he's a normal teenage male. We can't blame him for his older brother.'

'His sister?'

'Nor her. She's been at the police station for soliciting, but that's all.'

'Is she…?'

'Is your daughter still pure and chaste, is that what you're about to say?'

'It was.'

'According to her, she is, but you'll not stop her, just hope that she exercises good judgement.'

'We know, but Brad Robinson. She's such a timid soul, forever reading mushy romance novels.'

Wendy left the father and walked over to where DCI Cook and DI Hill were standing.

'Any luck?' Isaac said.

'Two young kids getting up to mischief, nothing more.'

'But they saw the murderer?'

'It looks that way. We'll get what we can from them tonight, but it's dark in there. At least it was till the CSIs set up their lights. They wouldn't have seen a lot, and besides, murder wasn't part of their plan for tonight.'

'We've all been there,' Larry said.

'Not with a fifteen-year-old, I hope,' Wendy said.

Larry thought back to his youth. 'I might have.'

Wendy had to admit it was an honest answer.

Gordon Windsor came over. 'You'll want a brief report,' he said.

To Isaac, Windor's verbal report was as good as a detailed one from the pathologist. The salient facts would be given, enough to commence the murder investigation, to start to bring the perpetrator to justice.

'We would,' Isaac said.

'Very well. Female, Caucasian, brunette, between thirty-five and forty-four years of age. Pathology can confirm that better than me.'

'Identification?'

'Nothing that we've found, and apart from the knife in the back, no other sign of violence.'

'A random killing?' Wendy asked.

'No sign of a struggle would indicate that the woman was there voluntarily, which means she would have known her killer.'

'A romantic tryst?' Isaac asked.

'In a graveyard?' Windsor's response.

'A sense of the macabre.'

'If it is, then you'll need to prove it. We can't see any signs of recent sexual activity, certainly not rape. Yet again, I'll defer to Pathology on that. Whatever the reason, the only identification is an inscription tattooed on the woman's right leg.'

'What does it say?' Wendy asked.

'I'll send you a photo. You can figure it out. We'll remove the body in the next hour and take it for autopsy. I'll need the area secured, and we'll be back tomorrow morning to look through the place, see if we can follow the shoeprint, not confident that we can.'

It was close to two in the morning, and the traffic on Kilburn Lane had reduced. Across the road, Wendy saw Rose getting into the front seat of her father's Jaguar,

Brad getting into the back seat. Rose was correct that her father was a good man. The folly of youth, she thought, only to be thrust front and centre into a murder investigation. Whoever it was that they had seen, he had to be regarded as dangerous, and she hoped the two young lovers weren't to become more inextricably involved.

Wendy remembered a time long ago in Yorkshire, up on the moors. She had been fourteen at the time, well developed for her age, and precocious. It had been her and a fifteen-year-old boy from the next farm and a haystack. They'd only been heavy petting, not that her father understood when he caught the two of them. She didn't sit down for two days afterwards; the boy, she couldn't remember his name now, had taken his punishment like a man, attempted to defend her honour. However, it didn't stop her father laying him out cold with a punch in the stomach and a fist, hardened by manual farm labour, in the face.

Times had changed for the better. Tim Winston, upset and disappointed by his daughter, angry with the young Brad, could at least act rationally and treat the two teenagers with the civility and sensitivity required.

Chapter 3

The crime scene yielded little more. The CSIs went through the place extensively, and even though the shoeprints found alongside the body were confirmed with a high degree of probability as those of the murderer, no more were found on the footpath that cut across from Harrow Road to Kilburn Lane.

Pathology confirmed certain facts about the dead woman, including agreeing with Gordon Windsor about her age. It was also confirmed that she was not a drug addict and in good health. No sign of sexual activity at the time of her death, which precluded sex as a motive. A notice had been placed at both entrances of the path that Brad and Rose had traversed, with officers questioning those passing by – the cemetery was closed to pedestrian traffic – as to whether they had walked through in the last couple of days, and if they had seen anything suspicious, anyone loitering, in particular in the vicinity of the grave that the woman had died on.

The only piece of luck to come from the questioning was that one man confirmed he had walked through at 9.36 p.m. and had seen nothing. The time had been checked against the bus he had alighted from, found from the bus company to be on schedule, and confirmed that the bus stop was next to the Kilburn Lane entrance. The man, a salesman in a menswear shop on Oxford Street, had admitted to having had a few drinks after work and feeling slightly tipsy, but was adamant he had seen nothing, although he would have if there had been any noise, or anyone hanging back in the shadows. A timid man, Larry thought, when he was interviewed at Challis Street later in the day, the sort of man who'd jump out of his skin if someone said boo to him. However, his testimony was regarded as sound, which narrowed the stabbing of the woman to between 9.38 p.m. and 10.14 p.m., the latter time based on Rose arriving two minutes late at Harrow Road, and the time it took to walk through the park.

Pathology agreed with the time of death, more accurate than usual, but it did not help with who had murdered the woman. She was marginally overweight, with poor muscle tone which indicated little exercise, white, presumed to be English, but with the recent wave of new arrivals in the country, that couldn't be stated with more than a ninety per cent accuracy. The clothes she wore, a blue skirt, a white top, sandals on her feet, could all have been bought in a hundred high street stores in London, as well as on the continent. It was an avenue of enquiry to follow up on, and a couple of uniforms were given the task: an eager policewoman in her early twenties and an unattractive policeman in his thirties who Wendy didn't like, believing the man had a chip on his shoulder and an unhealthy attitude to women, on account of his condescending manner when she had instructed the two police constables on what they were looking for, and how to go about the questioning.

'We might get a quicker result if we go online,' Constable Kate Baxter suggested before she and Constable Barry Ecclestone walked out of the door. Ecclestone, judging by his face, Wendy could see, was not pleased to be held back in the office for any longer than necessary. He was a slovenly man who would just do his duty, Wendy surmised, never rising above the melee, not

amounting to much in life and in the London
Metropolitan Police; definitely not a man for Homicide.

Wendy left the two of them to it, and they went
to the back of the office, found themselves a couple of
desks. Kate Baxter opened up a laptop, Ecclestone
checked out the coffee machine and what he could buy
from a vending machine in the hallway outside.

What was of more interest than the clothing was
the inscription on the dead woman's leg, found to be a
Buddhist chant in Sanskrit that translated to 'Strength
through adversity', which meant that the woman had
experienced hardship, or she adhered to a belief in
Buddhism, or she just liked the inscription. It had been
professionally tattooed, which would help in identifying
the tattoo shops that were capable of such detail and
quality. Yet again, pounding the streets, but Wendy would
undertake that herself.

Bridget Halloran stayed in the office; she dealt
with the paperwork, prepared the prosecution cases,
coordinated the support staff who dealt with the
collecting of evidence, the filing of it, the documentation,
the peripheral activities. She was a great friend of
Wendy's, and they shared a house now, since the death of
Wendy's husband, and after Bridget had kicked out her
last live-in lover, although Bridget, younger by seven years
than Wendy at forty-eight, still had the occasional man to
the house; not that Wendy was concerned, as she was
always discreet. The only consternation to her was that
she didn't have the success that Bridget had, although at
fifty-five and suffering from arthritis and now high blood
pressure, she knew that she had not maintained the same
vitality as her friend, the spark that men found attractive.

And besides, Wendy had to admit that it didn't worry her either way, not that much, not anymore, but still…

***

Apart from the clothing and the inscription, no further indications as to the woman's identity were found. As Isaac Cook saw it, that was the primary focus, and if the man had killed once, a seemingly premeditated crime as the woman had apparently been at the graveside willingly, he could kill again.

The grave's occupant had died on 15th September 1873, which seemed unrelated, but it did raise questions as to why that grave, did it have a significance, and why that night at that hour.

In his office, Isaac sat in his chair. It was eight in the evening of the second day. Across from him, Larry, Wendy and Bridget. They were the core team that he had moulded; they were the best there was. Wendy could find people who wanted to stay hidden better than anyone else; Larry's contacts out on the street invaluable, but his propensity to drink too much still of concern; and finally, Bridget Halloran, who had joined Homicide on Wendy's recommendation. The woman was a genius with a computer and an internet connection, able to find information that others preferred to keep hidden.

Bridget was an office person, whereas Larry and Wendy were glad to be out of it as much as possible, although Isaac, a self-professed workaholic, always insisted on a daily end-of-day wrap-up meeting to discuss the day's results, to plan for the next.

'Larry, what have you found out?' Isaac asked.

'The woman's not on any criminal database, and until we have a positive identification, we're flying blind, asking questions, not even sure they're the correct ones either.'

'Did anyone see the woman on the night?'

'No one we've found, which isn't surprising. She had no distinguishing features, average in terms of height, weight, blood type, hair colour. Apart from the tattoo on her leg, that is.'

'Bridget, you've been researching it, any luck?'

'I can give you a dozen places within walking distance of the police station that could have done it,' she said.

Isaac felt he was asking questions to which he already knew the answer. However, when everything has been exhausted, asking again can sometimes uncover a hitherto hidden fact, a not previously considered possibility.

'Any luck with the inks used?'

'I'll visit the most likely places tomorrow,' Wendy said. 'It's unlikely they'll know who she is; a lot of women, some men, have Buddhist chants tattooed on them, but usually on the shoulder.' Wendy thought back to the holiday in Greece with Bridget, the effects of too much ouzo, the small stars tattooed on their left ankles. They still laughed about how silly they'd been back then.

'Strength through adversity. It could be significant,' Isaac said.

'Or it could mean nothing. It's attractive to look at, not that I'd do it myself,' Wendy said, looking over at Bridget.

'Check on inks, batch numbers, samples of the most likely inks used and when. It could help.'

'I'll get what I can and get it over to Forensics, see what they can make of it.'

'Larry, let's focus on where you're at.'

'As I said, no criminal record and nobody seems to know anything about her. A Jane Doe at this time.'

'Unless she took public transport or drove there, she would have to be a local.'

'I'm looking. Give me a couple of days. I should turn up something.'

'That's the problem, we don't have the luxury of time. It's a clear case of murder, a woman in a cemetery, a man she had obviously known, a knife in her back. Any luck with the knife?'

'Any department store in London, the cutlery section. An eight-inch knife, the sort that most houses would have; it's not a name brand, generic Chinese, but sharp.'

'Sharp enough to have killed the woman with one stab? Not even a frenzied attack.'

'How could he be sure that she would be dead within a few minutes?'

'The blade pierced the left atrium of the heart. The chances of survival are rare.'

'Does that mean it was luck that he stabbed her in the right place or he knew where to direct the knife? The latter would indicate medical knowledge; the former, more than likely.'

'Or he could have had military training. If he had killed under orders, he could have been trained in how to take out a man without making a noise,' Larry said.

'We're postulating here. The man saw the two youngsters walking through.'

'He could have got a good look at them, even if they hadn't seen him,' Wendy said.

'Dependent on the man's state of mind, professional or gifted amateur, he might not want loose ends,' Isaac said. 'We need to follow up on the young lovers.'

'I'll go and see them, tell them to be careful, find out what more I can.'

'Before you go tonight, phone them both up, make sure there's a uniform outside each house until tomorrow.'

'I've got one person already,' Wendy said, thinking of Constable Ecclestone who had been absent most of the morning, following up on a lead he had said. The man was on night duty, sitting downstairs, taking it easy. He'd not like it, but she didn't care. To her, people who didn't pull their weight got what was coming to them. She'd find another constable for the other house, but not Kate Baxter, who was doing a sterling job.

***

The following day it started to rain, an English rain, the type that overseas visitors to London remember only too well. At the cemetery, the crime scene investigators had gone as far as they could, and apart from the tape around the grave and the small patch of grass surrounding it, people were starting to walk through again and to begin visiting the graves, although few did.

Larry went with Wendy to the first house for that day, the Robinson residence. Brad Robinson and his mother lived in a nondescript row of red-brick houses; not the upmarket terraces of Holland Park and Bayswater, more downmarket than that, as far removed from the wealth of the area as could be.

On the next-door neighbour's front lawn, a motorcycle with its engine removed. Looking at the rust, Larry could see that it would never run again. A dog barked from inside another house, a yapping sound that grated on the nerves, a street where the animal would meet an unfortunate ending, poisoned bait.

Two knocks at the door and Brad Robinson's mother opened it. She was a woman who had seen better days, Wendy conceded, but she had a cheery disposition and an easy smile. A woman, Wendy thought, who had been dealt a cruel hand by her upbringing, her lack of education, a family that skirted the boundary between legal and illegal, slipping over into the latter on more than a few occasions.

Larry knew Jim Robinson, the woman's elder son, in passing and had spoken to him a few times, the man not averse to a beer and a fifty-pound note in exchange for information; not that it had ever been any good.

'You'll be wanting Brad,' Gladys Robinson said. 'He's expecting you, but he's got school later.'

'We'll make sure he gets there,' Wendy said.

'Not in your car. People are sensitive around here, recognise a police officer from a mile off.'

It was true, Larry knew. He drove a regular car, dressed as others, but in an area where crime abounded, they always knew he was the police.

The house was clean enough, although there was an air of decay, not necessarily on account of its occupants, but because the local council had through experience realised that if you gave something too pristine to those who could only afford the low rents that they paid, they wouldn't respect what they had been given. The Robinsons had clearly tried, but even so, one of the drawers in the kitchen was broken, a windowpane was cracked, and the cooker had seen better days.

Larry shook Brad's hand as he came into the kitchen wearing his school uniform.

'We've a few questions,' Larry said.

'Her father's been on the phone,' Gladys Robinson said. 'None too happy. Accused Brad of seducing his daughter, and her only fifteen.'

'He dropped Brad home on the night,' Wendy said.

'He did, and I grant you that it was the right thing to do.'

'Your son and Rose Winston?'

'I've nothing against it. I've seen her, not spoken to her, but she's a pretty little thing. I can see why Brad likes her, and if they want to go out, then it's fine by me.'

'She's underage, not at the age of consent.'

'I've known her father almost our entire lives; grew up with him, went to the same school. He wasn't so posh back then, and as for his wife…'

'A reputation?'

'Stuck up, nose in the air, looking down at us, even at school. She's done well for herself, so has he. Brad could do worse than their daughter.'

'This may take a while,' Larry said, aware that the mother wanted to talk. She had lived in the area all her life and was a good source of local knowledge, someone who might know something.

The four sat down at a small table, the mother having dragged a damp cloth across its surface first.

Wendy had no objection to the mother being present, as she was clearly not obstructionist.

'He doesn't want me to see Rose again,' Brad said. 'Blames me for what happened.'

'You can't blame the man,' Larry said. 'It was his daughter.'

'He's right, I know that, but I want to see her again. He reckons our family is bad news, more than our being out together late at night.'

'Tim Winston's right,' Gladys Robinson said. 'But Brad's not like the rest of us. He's never been in any trouble, not likely to be. He'll be the one to save this family.'

'Your other son?' Larry said.

'He takes after his father. He'll be in and out of prison till the day he dies, which won't be too long, not with his drink driving record, and the people he goes around with.'

'Local gangs?'

'Violent individuals. Cross them, and you're dead. Jim's a good-hearted man, give you the shirt off his back, but trouble and he go together, and then there's his and Brad's sister, my daughter.'

'Janice?' Wendy said.

'I was wild at her age, but back then, it was alcohol more than drugs. A few pills, uppers, downers, but never the hard stuff, but Janice, she had this boyfriend that was dealing drugs, not that you'd know it, smooth as he was, used to bring me flowers. He talked her into injecting herself, instantly addicted. I read somewhere that some people don't get addicted, but she did soon enough. Pretty as a child, close to Brad and to me, but she changed, hardened, and now she's out on the street selling herself. How do you think that makes a mother feel? Knowing that her daughter is prostituting herself.'

'Not good,' Wendy replied, although they were there to discuss murder, not to solve the Robinson family's problems, not that they could if they wanted to.

Jim Robinson was known to Larry, and Janice was known to Wendy. The mother had only spoken the truth.

'As sensitive as we are to your situation, Mrs Robinson, it's Brad we need to talk to,' Larry said, turning the subject back to the reason for being in the house.

'We saw nothing,' Brad said.

'We realise that, but it's the minor details that are important, the details that are only remembered sometime after the event. The woman was killed not long before you and Rose walked by, possibly five minutes, maybe less. You said that you saw a man walk by.'

'Just before Rose screamed, not that we could tell you anything about him.'

'We believe he was the murderer, not that we can be one hundred per cent.'

'It was dark; we didn't see him, not in detail, not that we were looking either. Rose was freaking out, so was I, but I never admitted it to her.'

'We haven't been able to identify the woman other than to age her at between thirty-five and forty-four, white, probably English, with a tattoo on her leg.'

'They've all got them around here, even Janice, but then, she's got more of almost everything,' the mother said.

Neither Larry nor Wendy felt the need for the mother to elaborate on Janice. If the woman was doing it rough, that was for social services and others more skilled in bringing fallen women back from the brink. It was outside the scope of Homicide, and Wendy, sympathetic to the woman's plight, knew that well enough, although Larry knew she would do something when she had an opportunity.

'Here's our dilemma,' Larry said, looking directly at Brad. 'You and Rose saw the man, the only two who did. We've not found anyone else, not yet, who can remember either him or the woman.'

'Dilemma?' Brad said.

'We don't want to be alarmist, but the man who committed the crime could be a local, the same as the woman probably is, or he was a professional brought in to kill her because she knew something. Which brings up another problem: how did he manage to get her in the cemetery and by that grave of her own free will?'

'We don't understand, or at least I don't,' Gladys Robinson said.

'What Inspector Hill is saying,' Wendy said, 'is that there are inconsistencies in the woman's death. The most common reason for a murder in such a place is rape, especially when a female is killed, but that wasn't the case, and a knife in the back is usually accompanied by violence, a tussle, but there had been none, which means the woman knew her killer, and if she's local, then that means he's probably local too. And Brad and Rose are the only two who could possibly identify him.'

'But we didn't see him,' Brad said for the second time.

'He doesn't know that,' Larry said. 'We need you to be careful, to go to school, to come home. We'll keep a uniform outside the house at night for the next few nights, but whatever you do, don't go out at night, attempt to meet up with Rose.'

'I want to see her.'

'At school,' Wendy said.

'Not there. I need to talk to her, to apologise for the trouble she's in.'

'Chivalrous,' Larry said. 'We're meeting with Rose later. We'll put you forward as a man of good morals and decent to a fault.'

'Don't overdo it,' Gladys said. 'He was still up to mischief. Tim Winston's not going to go for it if you paint Brad as a saint; he's not that, never has been, never will be, but you'll not see him in trouble with the police.'

'Describe the man,' Wendy said. 'Distinguishing features, the way he walked, a smell of aftershave, of sweat, of alcohol, of anything.'

'I can't. We told you all we could.'

'Enter our numbers into speed dial on your phone. Phone us at any time, day and night, if you remember anything, see anyone suspicious,' Larry said.

'A ride to the school?' Wendy said a smile on her face.

'Not with you. Sorry, more than my life's worth,' Brad replied.

Chapter 4

Tim Winston was not in the mood to hear that Brad Robinson was a fine young man; it had been his underage daughter that the sixteen-year-old was attempting to lead astray.

The Winston family home wasn't far away from the Robinsons', only five minutes by car, but it was a vast improvement. No discarded motorcycle next door, no look of decay, but a two-storey semi-detached house, freshly painted inside and out, the aroma of air freshener throughout.

Winston's anger was palpable, which both the police officers thought under the circumstances to be understandable.

Even so, Tim Winston and his wife invited Larry and Wendy into the living room, offered them tea and asked them to make themselves comfortable.

'You can't understand how disappointed we are with Rose,' Maeve Winston, the young girl's mother, said.

Wendy looked over at Rose, and although she had spent time with her at the murder scene, it was the first time she had seen her in the light. A fresh-faced and pretty fifteen-year-old; no one would have thought her to be older.

'I'm sorry, Mum,' Rose said. 'It won't happen again.'

Maeve Winston looked across at her daughter, managed a weak smile. 'I hope not, scared us half to death when you told us where you were.'

'I can appreciate that the situation in the house is not the best,' Larry said. 'However, we need to follow through on the events at the cemetery.'

'I told you all I know,' Rose said. She looked as though she had been crying, lecturing from her parents most likely the cause. Not that it would help in the long run, Wendy knew, although it might make her think twice.

'We've met with Brad Robinson,' Larry said. 'He's not been able to help us much more. We need to see if you can help with anything, no matter how insignificant.'

'That name is not to be mentioned in this house,' Winston said, a man quick to anger.

'Unfortunately, it's a murder enquiry,' Wendy said. 'We must conduct our investigation, regardless of your dislike of the young man.'

'How is he?' Rose asked timidly.

'He's fine, sorry for what happened.'

'Dislike is not the word I would use,' Winston said. 'Not only was he with our daughter late at night, but he was also planning something that we disapprove of, especially at Rose's age.'

'I don't think we should talk about this in front of Inspector Hill and Sergeant Gladstone,' Maeve Winston said.

'Don't worry about us,' Wendy said. 'I've been there, know the anguish that you both feel, Rose's awkwardness. However, it doesn't alter the fact that she and Brad Robinson probably saw the murderer.'

'We only saw a man walk by. I can't tell you any more than that,' Rose said.

'Let's focus on him,' Larry said as he sipped his tea and helped himself to a biscuit from the tray in front of him.

'Do we need to go over this now? Rose is still traumatised,' Tim Winston said.

'You gave the two of them a ride back last night. Did they say anything to you?'

'Neither of them spoke, which was as well. I was relieved to have Rose in the car, and as for the other one, it seemed the right thing to do; not sure why as he didn't live far away.'

'I understand that you knew his mother?'

'We both did, Maeve and me, went to school with her, friends once.'

'So you know of the family?'

'Trouble, all of them,' Maeve Winston said.

'I'd agree that his mother hasn't fared well,' Wendy said, 'and the eldest children have fallen on hard times, but the youngest hasn't been in any trouble, nor has his mother.'

'We hoped for better for our daughter,' Tim Winston said.

Judging by the Winstons' apparent affluence, Wendy didn't understand why their daughter was at the same school as Brad. The area had more than enough schools for those who could pay, and most parents would seek an alternative to government-funded education if they could.

'That can be debated at another time, Mr Winston,' Larry said. 'What's important is what Rose can tell us. Now, Rose, you're walking through the cemetery, not looking around, graves to each side, and a man walks by.'

'We were almost out of the park, and we could see the bus stop on the other side of the road. He was wearing a hat, the collar on his jacket turned up.'

'Jacket or overcoat?' Wendy asked.

'I can't be sure. He wasn't much taller than Brad; I can remember that.'

'Anything distinctive about the clothing?'

'Not that I could tell. I wasn't looking that closely, and it was only afterwards, when you were asking, that we remembered him.'

'Anything else?' Wendy said.

'He may have limped.'

'May or did?'

'Did. He nearly bumped into Brad, although he didn't say anything.'

'Does it help?' Tim Winston asked.

'It could,' Larry said.

'Is your day busy at school today?' Wendy asked Rose.

'After two o'clock I should be free, although I've got homework to do later. Why?'

'We need you and Brad down at the cemetery. We need to recreate that evening, for the two of you to walk through with us, no shyness on your part, none on his.'

'I can't allow this,' Tim Winston said. 'Rose has suffered from this. I don't think she wants to be reminded.'

Rose looked over at her father. 'It's fine, Dad. I can handle it, if it helps.'

The love of a daughter for her father, a father for his daughter, apparent in how they spoke to each other, how they caught each other's gaze.

'Very well. Either Maeve or I will need to be there,' Winston said.

'Make it your wife,' Larry said. 'We need Rose to act naturally, exactly as she did last night. We don't want you there intimidating her.'

36

'I can't say I'm happy about this, but we'll go along with you.'

'We still don't know who the dead woman was, no identification apart from a Buddhist chant tattooed on her leg. All indications are that she was there with the man voluntarily, no sign of a struggle. Which means one of two things: she was a local, and the man is possibly a local as well, or, and the most unlikely, the murder was an assassination, although why she was with her killer is unclear. So what we have is a local who has killed once, and may well kill again, and could be nervous that he was seen, or a professional who doesn't want loose ends.'

'Is that a convoluted way of saying that our daughter is a possible target?'

'We don't think there is any reason for concern. Needless to say, we're anxious to wrap this case up as soon as possible.'

***

Kate Baxter worked late the first day she had been tasked with finding out what she could about the clothes and the footwear the dead woman had been wearing. Constable Ecclestone, who had been assigned to work with her, had lasted less than fourteen hours before he found himself outside the Robinsons' house the first night. He'd not be coming back into Homicide, other than as a minor player, if that, and Kate preferred to work on her own. She was, it was soon discovered, almost as much a computer geek as Bridget, and the two women had hit it off almost immediately.

Kate Baxter had been duly pleased with herself when she had narrowed down the sandals the dead woman had been wearing to a discount shoe shop.

Wendy, on her return from visiting Brad Robinson and Rose Winston, picked the young constable up from outside the police station; a special dispensation for Baxter in that she wasn't to wear her uniform. An ambitious woman, she recognised the trust that was being placed in her, the chance for advancement, the impetus it gave her to complete a degree that had been proving difficult due to a faltering romance and the time she had been spending to keep it alive.

'I checked out Forensic's report,' Kate said. 'They had checked the clothing and the shoes, nothing special with them, except they said the sandals had little wear and were new. That was the lead. If they were last year's stock, which I found out they were, then where had the woman purchased them? I buy clothes and shoes in the discount stores myself.'

Wendy didn't reply, not wanting to interrupt the constable, although she always checked out such places herself, sometimes bought there.

'I've spoken to the manager. She's waiting for us, so it's a good idea I'm not wearing a uniform.'

'Factory seconds, old stock, stolen, is that what you're thinking?' Wendy said.

'Could be. Who knows where it all comes from. I suppose most of it's legal, the same as in a pawnbroker, but you can never be sure, can you?'

'Never, but that's not what we're interested in today. Focus on the sandals, not where they came from, and try not to look like a policewoman, if we ever can.'

'I'll try, but I love my job; I'm proud of what I do.'

Wendy parked the car down a sidestreet. She placed a sign inside the windscreen identifying the vehicle as police. Nobody would give it a ticket.

Brompton Road, Knightsbridge. The most prominent building was Harrods, the department store that Wendy sometimes walked around with Bridget of a weekend, buying little apart from a coffee and something to eat in the cake section. Opposite it on the other side of the busy road was *Shoe Seconds*, a threadbare store with the merchandise stacked in boxes, a couple of sales assistants, a concrete floor and six chairs for customers trying on the shoes. It gave the appearance of having just opened or being about to close, but the website for it and a chain of six others with the same name, spread out across the city, was professional.

The closing down sign, all stock must go, the giveaway prices painted in bold letters on the shop's window were an illusion, as were the prices, Wendy could see that when she picked up some of the merchandise. The first shoe, the bargain to get people into the shop, literally falling apart, the sole separating from the upper, a sales assistant on hand to show another shoe, this time much better, the price indicative of that. It was, Wendy knew, a ploy to get people in the door with whatever means they had at their disposal and then the hard sell. The sales assistant, pushy and mildly annoying, spoke with a strong accent, Spanish, Wendy thought. It was the sort of place that blew out the customers as fast as it could if they weren't spending, the sales assistants even quicker if they didn't make the grade, and Wendy's sales assistant wasn't going to last long, too ready to leave her alone after she had said she was only looking.

Kate Baxter, undeterred, made it through the locals and the tourists – always looking for a bargain that wasn't – and out through the door at the rear.

'Can I help you?' An indignant woman sat there, her feet up on a chair, her shoes cast to one side of her on the floor.

'Constable Kate Baxter. We spoke.'

'I could have sent you what information we had, and besides, one of our other stores could have sold the shoes.'

'Not the colour, I checked.'

'Seeing you're here, pull up a seat. I've been on my feet all morning, and the concrete floor may be a breeze to clean, but it does play havoc on my ankles.'

Wendy walked through to the back, saw the two women sitting there. She introduced herself and took the third chair.

'A madhouse out the front,' Wendy said.

'That's the quiet time,' the manager said.

Wendy judged the woman to be in her forties, thinner than was healthy, a wedding ring on her left hand, a dramatic tattoo on her upper left arm, not as professionally inked as the chant on the dead woman's leg.

'You've worked here for a long time?'

'Over two years. No one else would stick it, not with the money they pay, nor what we have to put up with from the customers.'

It was clear that the manager didn't have to put up with anything. She was a hard woman, her function to cycle the sales assistants, to make sure the profit margin was adhered to, to do whatever was necessary.

Wendy didn't like her. The sort of person who pretended to care about the store and its workers, but didn't for either. It was typical of an attitude all too common in the overpopulated metropolis. There was always someone more desperate, willing to put up with working under such conditions, used to being cheated, not expecting any different.

Kate Baxter handed over a photo. 'Is that the sandal?'

The manager lifted her feet off the stacked shoe boxes and put them on the floor. She took out a pair of glasses from her handbag and put them on. Then she studied the photo for longer than was necessary.

'We sell a lot of shoes here, but yes, they came in a week ago. We put some of them in the window, sold out in two days.'

'Good value?' Wendy asked.

'Better than most. Old stock, last year's fashion statement. Nobody will pay top money for them now, but if you're on a budget, or just tight, they'll do fine for the weekend, or in the office.'

'Who did you sell them to?'

'Not everyone pays with a card; some still prefer to pay cash, although for the life of me I can't see why.'

Wendy did. Impulse buying with a card was dangerous; cash was the moderator to prevent the purchaser from transitioning from wise to foolish; the reason she left her card at home, apart from Saturday. One day of temptation out of seven was better than seven out of seven.

'Those that paid cash?'

'Not a chance. You've seen it outside, chaos, and the sales assistants have a high turnover.'

'How long do they last?'

'Most only stick it for three to four days. Those that are any good soon find somewhere else paying better. Can't blame them, something I should do.'

The manager was someone who complained a lot, treated the employees abysmally, and siphoned money off the top as she discounted stock to maintain the cash turnover, probably with the de facto blessing of senior management, who wanted results, not scrupulously honest people.

'Those that paid with a card?' Kate said.

'I've already sent them. Check the emails on your phone.'

One thing the woman was, she was efficient, Wendy conceded. She checked her phone, Kate checked hers. The email with the attachment was there.

'What's so important about them, anyway,' the manager asked.

'One of the women who bought them from your store was murdered,' Wendy said.

'Takes all sorts,' the manager's reply. She had no interest in a dead woman, only the money she had handed over.

Chapter 5

Kate Baxter, her work done, returned to her regular duties. She had proved herself, and Wendy was determined to put her name forward as a possible member of Homicide when the opportunity presented itself.

At the station, Bridget followed through on those who had bought sandals in the same colour as the dead woman's. It had been a popular line, and the list contained over forty names. The process of elimination would take some time which suited Bridget as long hours and computers were her forte. Isaac knew she would be working late that night.

The day had not been without progress. There was Rose Winston, confident that the man who had hurried by had a limp, and one of the names from the shop could well be the murdered woman's. Whether she had been a local was still open to question, as no one had come forward, even after her face had been displayed on signs outside the cemetery. Usually, the next of kin would have been informed before taking such a step, but without identification, the decision had been made to circumvent standard procedure.

Isaac's concern as the senior investigating officer in Homicide was that the woman's death had been calculated and calmly executed, which suggested that the man was used to killing, or he had no compunction about what he had done. The probability of another murder remained, and if he was local, then he had to be apprehended quickly, and if it was professional, then why, and who was the assassin.

Larry and Wendy had had a busy day, not that it was over, and at eight in the evening, while it was still light, they were outside the cemetery at the Harrow Road entrance, Brad on his own; Rose with her mother.

The mother, Wendy could see, was not as firm as her husband, and the two intended lovers spoke to one another. It was sweet, Wendy thought, young love, innocent and pure, unsullied by the realities of the world, the cruelty, the degradation, the hurt, the disappointment. Although, on reflection, she knew that Brad had experienced more than his fair share, although Rose had not.

'Why the school?' Larry asked Maeve Winston.

'Why we don't pay, is that what you're asking?'

'If you want to protect your daughter, surely you would give her the best opportunity.'

'Tim and I, we came from humble stock, working class. We could afford better, but we're not snobs, nor do we want Rose to be. Committed Labour voters all our life.'

Larry wasn't sure of the woman's rationale. It seemed that Tim Winston's middle-class aspirations and his working-class beliefs were out of kilter, and how could the father then complain when his daughter went out with the brother of a criminal and a woman who sold herself. To him, even though he was a detective inspector, and not able to afford the best school where he lived, he intended to place his children where it would be to their best advantage.

And even if Tim and Maeve Winston weren't cloth-capped Labourites, him driving a Jaguar for instance, it still made no sense to deprive their daughter.

Both gates at the cemetery had been closed off, and entry had been restricted at two other entrances, although they were further away, and not many people would be walking through. However, there were sufficient uniforms present to keep the curious onlookers at a distance.

Isaac arrived, not to take an active part, but with his inspector and sergeant at the cemetery he had cancelled the evening meeting at the office.

'Detective Chief Inspector Isaac Cook,' he said as he shook Maeve Winston's hand.

Wendy was sure she swooned on meeting the tall black police officer. He was an attractive man, a ladykiller in his youth, not the murdering type, and he had seduced a few in his time. Now he was married to Jenny, as white as he was black, and a child was on the way.

The group moved inside the imposing gates of the cemetery. Wendy called them to order. 'Rose and Brad, we need to recreate this accurately. No being coy because we're present, and Rose, disregard your mother. If she doesn't like it, she'll have to close her eyes.'

'Mum's alright; Dad wouldn't have been.'

'I'm not that comfortable,' the mother said. 'But I'll not interfere. After tonight, you and I will need to sit down and have a good talk.'

Rose whispered to Brad, 'They're just worried about me, that's all.'

'Something I never had. A violent father who thankfully left us; my mother's decent enough, but she drinks.'

Rose, even though she was young, felt motherly towards Brad, although she didn't understand why.

The instruction was that Brad and Rose were to act as they had on the night when she had pretended to be staying at a friend's house.

Brad had no difficulty in putting his arm around Rose and kissing her, although Rose kept looking over at her mother.

It was always tricky when dealing with children; the need for a responsible adult to be present, a parent.

'Mrs Winston,' Isaac said. 'If you don't mind, can I have a word with you.'

Wendy could see that her DCI had sensed the situation, and he could play a part in taking the mother away, letting the daughter relax.

'Okay, Rose, your mother's not looking now,' Larry said. 'Show us what happened on the night.'

'I didn't want to walk through,' Rose said. 'Not after the movie that Steph and I had watched.'

Brad put his arm around Rose; she responded and puts hers around him, leaning over to give him a kiss.

'We walked down the path, over to Kilburn Lane,' Brad said.

A member of Gordon Windsor's crime scene team was present as an observer. The area had been checked and heavy rain had removed the possibility of further evidence.

The group moved forward, Brad and Rose in front. Allowances had to be made, as it wasn't dark and Rose wasn't scared, just embarrassed; Brad Robinson appeared to be enjoying himself. Over in the distance, Isaac and the mother walked.

'It was here,' Rose said, 'when the man walked by.'

'The limp?'

'I didn't see it,' Brad said.

'If you were to the left of Rose, you would have been looking ahead or towards her,' Larry said. 'She would have been looking in your direction, the direction of the man and the grave. That's why she saw the body and not you.'

'Why the limp?' Wendy asked. 'How can you be certain?'

'I can't, not really. Other than what I saw.'

'A limp isn't always noticeable, not in the dark.''

'I saw him before Brad. I saw him over near where the woman was.'

'You've not mentioned this before.'

'I don't know. Maybe I just forgot.'

It was understandable, Wendy conceded. A young woman disobeying her parents, late at night, a scary movie. Too many issues for a young mind to comprehend.

'What did you see?' Larry asked.

'I think I saw the murder. I can remember something. I thought it was a statue or something like that, but now I think it was the man and the woman.'

Wendy messaged for Isaac to bring the mother back; if Rose was going to get emotional, hysterical even, the result of the realisation, delayed shock, then it was for Maeve Winston to console her daughter.

'Can you remember any more than that?'

'Nothing more, only that he moved away and onto the path. It was just the way he walked, as though he had hurt one of his legs.'

'We never found any indication of a limp,' the CSI said.

'A kick to the shin?' Larry said.

'The woman fought back, is that what you're saying?'

47

'It's possible. Any sign on the woman's sandal or on her feet to indicate that she did?'

'Pathology might be able to tell you, but as for the sandal, it wasn't the best quality, new as has been recorded, but one wear and there would be scuffing. Nigh on impossible to be certain, but she could have reacted.'

Maeve Winston arrived, took one look at her daughter and put her arm around her.

'I saw the woman die,' Rose said to her mother. She was tearful but bearing up.

'No more tonight,' the mother said.

'No more,' Wendy agreed.

'We'll give Brad a lift,' Maeve Winston said.

'Thanks, Mrs Winston, but I don't live far. I can walk.'

Brad Robinson walked away in the direction of Compton Road and his mother, almost certainly the worse for wear after an encounter with alcohol. He was sad, but he didn't know why.

***

Isaac would have said that the day was over and that the team would meet at Challis Street in the morning at six, except that as the activity at the cemetery was winding up, Bridget phoned from the office.

Larry was too hungry to continue without sustenance, and Wendy was too tired, but both issues were resolved by Larry buying a McDonald's cheeseburger, and Wendy joining him, taking the opportunity to rest, closing her eyes for five minutes. Isaac, younger and definitely fitter than the other two, drove straight back to the office, grabbed himself a coffee, a biscuit out of the tin that Bridget always kept filled. Bridget would want an audience for what she had discovered. He didn't intend to steal her thunder.

Twenty-five minutes later, Larry and Wendy walked into the office.

Bridget handed folders to the three police officers once they were all in Isaac's office. 'Of the credit cards that were used, I've eliminated virtually all of them.'

'How?' Isaac asked.

'It's not conclusive, and we may have to go back over some of them if what I'm giving you isn't sufficient, but if I have a name, then there is Facebook, as well as the purchases made with cards issued overseas, Chinese, Japanese names, others I can't pronounce.'

'Those remaining?'

'One lives in Hammersmith, probably too far if you hold to the local angle. Another lives south of London, twenty miles.'

'The others?'

'Two in Notting Hill, one in Bayswater, another in Paddington, and two close enough to the cemetery to walk to, to even walk through.'

'Have you tried phoning?' Larry asked.

'Not yet. I phoned you as soon as I had something tangible.'

Bridget was right, Isaac knew. She had done her work; now it was over to him and the other two.

'Tonight?' Isaac said.

'The two close to the cemetery,' Wendy said, not that she wanted to as she was ready to go home, but she had known her DCI for a long time, from when he had been a constable in uniform. She knew he'd not agree to leave it till tomorrow.

'Larry, you take one; Wendy, you take the other. Keep me updated.'

Isaac opened up his email and read those that needed answering, deleted those that were either unimportant or spurious. Jenny was waiting for him, wanting to tell him about her visit to the gynaecologist, although she would understand, she always did.

He wouldn't leave the office until Larry and Wendy had phoned in.

Bridget shut her laptop, stood up, said goodbye to Isaac and left the office. She was going home, her work for that day complete.

***

Larry knocked on the door of a house very similar to Brad Robinson's, only two streets away and built at the same time, monuments to the working class and to successive governments attempting to make society encompassing, not shuffling those less fortunate out to suburbs so far from their places of work that some of them would spend two to three hours a day travelling.

The door was opened by a child of five or six, dressed in pyjamas and with bare feet. 'No one's here,' the boy said.

Larry, not easily deterred, was aware that the child delegated at such a tender age to lying for a parent had been sent to deal with unwelcome visitors.

'I saw them in the upstairs window,' Larry said. 'Tell your mother to come down here now. Tell her it's the police.'

The child walked away and up the stairs. On the top landing, he shouted out, 'It's the police.'

It was a house of crime, although what sort of crime Larry didn't know. The address and the name on the card weren't known to him.

'Tell him to come back with a warrant,' a woman's voice said from the front bedroom. 'We've done nothing wrong.'

Larry wasn't concerned whether they had or not, not that night. Back at the station the next day, he'd ask someone to check out the address where a child was forced to lie, and a mother locked herself in her bedroom. He walked into the house, shouted up the stairwell.

'Pearl Harris, Detective Inspector Larry Hill, Challis Street Police Station. I'm not here about a crime. One question, that's all.'

The door upstairs opened, and a woman of African or Caribbean background descended the stairs. 'I'm Pearl Harris,' the not unattractive woman said. Larry thought her to be in her late twenties or early thirties. She was dressed in a pair of old jeans and a shirt too large for her, clearly belonging to the man upstairs, put on in a hurry.

'The child?' Larry said.

'Nothing to do with me. He belongs to him upstairs.'

'Who's he? Someone special?'

'Ben, Ben Swinson. He's my de facto.'

'Where's the child's mother?'

'She took off, left Ben with him. I do the best I can with him, not a bad kid, not really. Why are you here?'

Apart from finding out that social services would need to visit, which he did not say. 'Did you purchase a pair of sandals at a store in Knightsbridge?'

'They weren't much good, the strap broke after two days, and they won't give you your money back. There should be a law about it,' the woman said. 'Good money for rubbish.'

51

Larry could have said buyer beware, *caveat emptor*, as Wendy had said the no return policy was clearly stated in the shop's window, but did not. 'Do you have the sandals? Can I see them?'

'What's so important, disturbing people at night?'

'The sandals first.'

Pearl Harris opened a cupboard under the stairs, showed them to Larry. Upstairs a husky voice: 'Haven't you got rid of that copper yet? A man's got needs.'

'Horny,' Larry said, judging that crudity wouldn't be amiss.

'Always, not that he's much good.'

'You've had better?'

'Much better, but I better get back up there. You never know…'

'He hits you?'

'Not Ben. He's a decent man, looks after me, looks after the kid. Do you want me anymore?'

'Not as long as you're alive, I don't.'

'What's this about?'

'Another woman who purchased the same shoe as you was murdered. One door we'll knock on, and the woman won't be there. I'm glad it's not you.'

'You're not bad for a policeman,' Pearl said.

'All heart, that's me,' Larry said.

She was a pleasant woman, he decided, trying her best, although Ben upstairs was probably skirting on the edge of illegal, and Pearl's history could well be suspect. He'd let others deal with it, although the child was well looked after, clean and well-fed, but where was his mother?'

'Best of luck with your search. Sorry about the woman, too much of that these days,' the woman said as she closed the door.

As Larry walked away, he could hear Pearl talking to the child, asking if he wanted a glass of milk, a visit to the bathroom. The child may not have been hers, but she still cared in her own way.

***

Wendy's address, even though it was walking distance to the cemetery, was further away than Larry's, almost five hundred yards.

The house appeared empty, no light on inside, not even a sound when she placed her ear against the front door. To her, it looked more promising than Larry's address.

A white-painted house with a bay window, it was in good condition, and the street was well maintained, although there were roadworks at one end of it, a house being renovated two doors away.

Wendy knocked on the front door four times, each time harder than the previous one. Eventually, a stirring, a light at the rear of the house. The door opened, a woman dressed in black stood in front of Wendy. Whatever it was that she had disturbed, she didn't like the look of it.

'What is it?' the woman, in her fifties, jet-black hair combed straight and down to her waist, said.

'Sergeant Wendy Gladstone, Challis Street Police Station. I need to speak to Flora Soubry.'

'Don't know why. I thought it was someone from down the street complaining, no idea why, but people can be difficult when they don't understand.'

'If you have problems with them, it's nothing to do with me. It's Flora Soubry that I need to see; one question.'

'Come in. We're odd, that's what you'll think.'

A house in total darkness, heavy curtains closed, a woman in her fifties, her hair jet-black and down her back. Yes, Wendy thought, it was odd, but no different than some other houses she had been in over the years: devil-worshippers, mad all of them, and then those who were dressed as characters out of nursery rhymes, not forgetting the house with swingers, the couples pairing off with whoever. She had been younger then, following up on a complaint, the swingers not only inviting her in but asking her to join them. She had beaten a hasty retreat, arranged for a couple of policemen in uniform to sort it out. They had returned to the station after a couple of hours to a rousing cheer from the others; Wendy had updated her colleagues on what she had seen there, and whereas there was no proof that the two had succumbed, one of them a lay preacher at his local church, it hadn't stopped the ribbing.

In the back room where the light had first appeared, five women sat around a table, a Ouija board in the middle.

'A séance?' Wendy said.

'We communicate with the dead,' one of the women said.

It seemed more benign than some other situations she had seen over the years, although Wendy didn't like it. Summoning spirits, attempting to communicate with the dead, didn't sit well with her. She'd do what she had come for and then leave.

'I'm looking for a Flora Soubry,' Wendy said.

'That's me,' a woman with a high-pitched voice said, her hand on the board. Wendy found it hard to imagine that this woman, clothed in black, the same as the woman who had answered the door, could wear colourful

clothing and footwear, although out of the house all of
them would have been indistinguishable from the
majority, and London was awash with the eccentric, the
mad, the weird, and now, one murderer.

'You bought a pair of sandals from a shop in
Knightsbridge?'

'A week ago, a good price.'

'Do you have them with you?'

'I do. In the other room.'

'Can you show me?'

The woman got up from the chair, taking her
hand away from the board, and opened the door to her
right. In the other room, the women's everyday clothes on
hangers. She knelt down, picked up the sandals.

Wendy took a photo as proof and went back to
the other room. 'Do you believe in this?' she said, looking
down at the Ouija board.

'We do,' one of the other ladies said.

'Why are you here?' Flora Soubry asked.

'A woman who bought the same sandals as you,
the same size, was murdered. The sandals are the only
clue we have.'

'How tragic. Can we help?'

'Communicating with the dead, hardly
investigative, not sure it's even admissible as evidence,'
Wendy said.

'Everyone is sceptical until they have proof.'

Wendy left the house. The five women had a new
focus for that night; finding out the identity of the dead
woman. They couldn't fail any more miserably than
Homicide.

Chapter 6

An impasse. That was how Isaac saw it. As the senior investigating officer, it was his responsibility to deal with the murder investigation, the reason that Jenny was mildly annoyed that night.

She had been excited to tell him about her day and how they were going to decorate the baby's room, or whether they should buy a house instead of staying in the two-bedroom flat in Willesden.

He was distant, although he had tried to be interested, a woman's death troubling him. Eventually Jenny, tiring of the stilted conversation, left him and went to bed.

He went and sat in the living room, picked up a book, scanned the first few pages, tried to read it but couldn't. From the other room, the sounds of Jenny asleep. It was where he should be, where he went. 'Sorry,' he said. 'Rough day, not getting any better either.'

Jenny rolled over, looked at him through semi-closed eyes and gave him a kiss. 'It's what I signed up for,' she said.

And it was, they both knew that when she had first moved in with him. The long hours, the weekends away cancelled at the last minute, the romantic candlelit dinners in the flat, just the two of them, disturbed on more than one occasion. The lot of a police officer's wife was difficult, and Isaac had had more than one broken romance when a lover had said she could deal with the long hours on her own, the uncommunicative nature of her man at the end of a long day, his indifference to violence and world events, but then couldn't.

It had only been Jenny who could; he knew that, and for that he was grateful.

'A house,' he said. 'It'll be better for the baby.'

Another kiss, this time more passionate than the previous one. Isaac looked over at the clock on the bedside cabinet. It was after one in the morning, but sleep eluded him. He got up and went into the other room, opened the fridge, put on the kettle.

A cup of coffee in his hand, a problem to ponder. He phoned Larry.

'Sorry about the late hour,' Isaac said. 'I couldn't sleep.'

'That's alright,' Larry replied, even if it wasn't. After a couple of months of tension between the two men on account of Larry's drinking and slovenliness, he was pleased that his chief inspector was looking to him for help, rather than telling him what to do. The disciplinary still hurt, and if Larry had been more ambitious, he knew it would have had some bearing on his promotion opportunities, but he wasn't.

Sure, he had tried to knuckle down and study for the requisite qualifications, but his brain wouldn't kick in, not only because of the demands of Homicide but because he had been no more than a moderate student at school, invariably receiving a could-do-better end of term report. He had come up through the ranks from uniformed constable to sergeant to inspector, the same progression as his DCI, but Isaac was a smart man, intellectually gifted, and he was going places, whereas Larry knew his race was over, and he'd see the rank of inspector alongside his name until the day of retirement.

Larry went and made himself a cup of coffee too.

'We're clueless,' Isaac said.

'I know. Apart from a Buddhist chant and a man who may or may not have limped, we've got nothing.'

'The limp?'

'The CSIs will go over the place again, but don't expect too much. They're only watching their backs, worried that the young woman might be right.'

'Discount it for now. What can we do?'

'A name for the woman, otherwise the case is dead and buried, unsolvable.'

An ignominious outcome, Isaac knew, and not something he'd want to explain to Chief Superintendent Goddard. How would he go about it if he had to? A dead woman, a knife, two witnesses, one who had possibly seen the murder, and we're stumped, he thought. It made him shudder: the first murder case in his career where he had failed. And he knew how it worked, the same as in life. A multitude of successes, one failure. Which of the two would they remember? He knew the answer.

'Tomorrow,' Isaac said. 'Forget the early-morning meeting, focus on the other names you have.'

'I was going to phone you early tomorrow and suggest it. I've already spoken to Wendy about it,' Larry said.

'Great, go with it. Do you need assistance?'

'Leave it to Wendy and me. If we need someone, we have a name.'

'Kate Baxter?'

'She's competent.'

'Tomorrow, a result,' Isaac said. He hung up the phone and went back to bed, Jenny briefly acknowledging his presence. He was asleep within five minutes; Larry wasn't. The coffee had woken him up; it wouldn't let him go to sleep, not for some time.

***

Janice Robinson sat on the bed in her squalid bedsit. The darkened street corner where once she had sold herself now replaced by the mobile phone at her side. And besides, soliciting on the street was illegal, selling herself from her phone was not, nor was bringing the client to where she lived.

If she were cognisant, she would have said that her life was on a downward spiral with only one end, but she was not, having just injected herself with heroin, a momentary calm settling over her.

It had been almost a year since she had seen her mother, three months since Brad and she had met. She missed him, cheerful and cheeky, able to make her laugh; her mother she did not miss.

If the house had not been the way it was, then she would have not succumbed to debasing herself, but her mother's live-in lovers, not all of them, but most, had seen the mother as acceptable when she was sober, her daughter when she was not.

She had been fourteen the first time one of them snuck into her bedroom, held her down with his weight; she remembered it as if it was yesterday, but it wasn't. It was seven years ago that first time, and Jim, her elder brother, had beaten the man senseless, kicked him out of the house when she had told him, but then he wasn't there much, as he was invariably on an anti-social behaviour order, migrating between incarceration and freedom, and now he was in prison.

A good student in her early teens, a broken young woman at the age of sixteen, she had moved from smoking marijuana to harder drugs in a short time; then to selling herself at seventeen to feed the habit. Twice she had weaned herself off, but memories came flooding back, the lost times of her youth, the wasted education, the futility.

The bedsit she reasoned was better than the street. She was smart enough not to expect too much, not to assume that the man who had phoned would be any better.

A knock on the door, a voice telling her to open up.

Regaining her senses, Janice lifted herself from the bed, adjusted her bra strap; no need to overdress for what the man wanted. She opened the door, saw the man was dressed better than most; not overalls straight from work, smelling of manual labour and sweat, covered in grime. This man was dressed in a neatly creased pair of trousers, a blue open-necked shirt, a jacket. Even his shoes were leather and polished.

Janice, if she cared, would have said that he was a better class of man than those that pulled up alongside her on the street, asked her how much, indulged in friendly banter, called her a hag as they drove off, not willing to pay her price.

But this man hadn't argued about the price, more than on the street, because of the cost of the bedsit, owned by a grubby immigrant who spoke poor English and took part of the rent in services rendered by Janice.

The cost of the bedsit was only one factor in her higher prices. Having to service the landlord who was foul in his demands, aggressive in his lovemaking, was a payment that she did not make willingly, but did.

'Janice,' the man said.

'Come in.'

'I've been looking for you,' he said as he sat on a chair by the side of the bed.

Janice, accustomed to the procedure, removed her underwear. 'This is what you've come for, isn't it?'

'In time. We can talk first.' He made no attempt to move closer to her, to touch her.

Janice, unused to such behaviour, sat up and pulled the sheet across her.

'I prefer you naked,' he said.

'Are you one of those who like to watch?' she asked. She didn't care either way, only that they paid. The idea of sex no longer appealed to her; it was purely mechanical, the groaning on cue, pretending that the man on top or under her was satisfying her, whereas all he was doing was filling her with disgust. She felt nothing for any of the previous men, hundreds of them, nothing for this one.

'How long have you been doing this?'

Not another one trying to reform her, she thought. Not someone about to spout on about Sodom and Gomorrah, fallen women. She'd had enough of them, some even praying, but all of them taking her, and then crying afterwards, blaming her, hitting her for tempting them with the pleasures of the flesh, but this man appeared different. He didn't look at her with wanton eyes, wanting her but incapable.

There had been one, she remembered, who had been impotent, but it had been his wife belittling him that had been the problem. That had been in the past, when she had been prettier, when her face had been fuller, her lips rosier, not that she ever let them kiss her, her body firmer, her breasts rounder.

Now, at the age of twenty-one, her skin was sallow and pitted, the colour of alabaster. It had been eight months since she had been to a doctor, as she knew what would be said. The lecture about her killing herself, the diseases she might have, the damage to her vital organs. It wasn't what she wanted, but what did she care. Her life had run its full course, the only joy in her life was Brad.

'I've another appointment,' Janice said, which wasn't true. The room was cold, not enough money to pay for heating, only for drugs and the occasional bite to eat.

'I won't need long,' the man said as he sat on the bed. She arched her body in anticipation. Men liked that, she knew, believing that somehow paying for a woman was pleasurable for her, not understanding that it wasn't, would never be.

He ran his hand lightly over her body, his expression emotionless.

'It's a shame,' he said.

'Aren't you capable?'

'Once so pretty, but now, look at you lying there, waiting for me to take you.'

'That's what you paid for.'

The man opened a small case that he had been carrying. He withdrew a towel.

'You don't need to shower first,' Janice said. The man was clean enough as he was, even if his manner was unusual. But some were slow starters, while others were ready, barely in the door, and yet others had sulked away without doing anything, racked with guilt at impure thoughts, looking for a priest to confess to.

'It's not a towel. It's what's inside it that's important.'

Sensing that something was amiss, Janice drew herself up further. 'I think you better go,' she said. 'You're scaring me.'

'There's no need to be scared,' he said. 'It's quite painless.'

The bed was up against the wall, the only way out was over the man or the bottom of the bed. Janice Robinson, sister of Brad, sister of Jim, chose the latter.

The man grabbed her as she attempted to get away, thrusting her down onto her back, the sheet falling away.

'You would have been attractive once,' he said. 'Now you're just a whore.'

With one hand holding her down, he unwrapped the towel with the other. He picked up the knife inside and thrust it into Janice's body four times in rapid succession, holding the towel over the knife and the body.

He then took a shower before walking out of the room.

***

Six possibilities remained to identify the woman in the cemetery, assuming that a card had been used to buy her sandals. If not, then Larry and Wendy knew that they were in for a wasted day.

Larry understood Isaac's predicament, the reason for the late-night phone call, the coffee keeping him awake, the two glasses of whisky dealing with the problem.

The plan was for them to fan out from Kensal Green Cemetery, focussing on the nearest addresses first, discounting the two they had dealt with the previous evening, and then widening the circle, eventually ending up at the last address twenty miles to the south.

The first house, a mews close to Portobello Road, the haunt of the bargain shopper, not that there were many bargains, not after the daily deluge of tourists, the prices upping at first sight, and the antique shops were always pricey.

'Can I help you?' an old man said as he opened the door of the mews house.

Larry did the introductions, both he and Wendy showing their warrant cards. It was still early in the morning, not yet seven, and most people would be asleep or thinking about work, the ideal time to catch them at home.

After the houses in Notting Hill, the two of them would separate, aim to check every address by midday, hopeful of a result, although it would mean a very long night. Larry had to admit to still feeling tired after his disrupted sleep and his wife sending him off without breakfast for sins committed.

It was the excuse he needed to visit his favourite café for breakfast; he was sure that Wendy would join him.

'We're looking for Deborah Landis,' Wendy said.

'That's my wife. I hope it's not anything serious. We don't drive, don't go far these days, broken no laws.'

'It's not that,' Larry said. 'If we could talk to Deborah, I'm sure we can resolve it very quickly, leave you alone.'

'I'm Deborah,' an elegant and upright woman said. In her seventies, yet looking younger, whereas her husband, crippled by age and ailments, looked close to eighty.

The four sat down.

'What can we do for you?' the husband said.

'Mrs Landis, you bought a pair of sandals at a shop in Brompton Road, Knightsbridge, opposite Harrods,' Wendy said.

'For our daughter, a present.'

'And your daughter, where is she now?'

'I gave them to her the day I bought them. Such good value and I know that Megan loves the colour.'

'Can't resist a bargain, my wife,' Landis said.

'Your daughter?' Wendy said, more than a little alarmed.

'We've not seen her for a few days, not since I gave her the shoes. She goes to university, up north. We told her to find one nearer to here, but she was adamant.'

'We need to contact her.'

'I could phone her if it's important.'

'It is, very,' Larry said. 'Now, please.'

The woman picked up her phone and dialled. 'Hello, dear. Two police officers here that want to talk to you, no idea why.'

Wendy took the phone and spoke. 'Megan, Sergeant Wendy Gladstone. Your mother gave you a pair of sandals?'

'One size too small, but don't tell Mum.'

'I won't. Can you take a photo of them and send it to your mother's phone number now.'

'I can, but what's this about.'

'I'm pleased that you're fine. We're trying to identify a woman. The only clue we have is that she purchased sandals similar to yours at a shop in Knightsbridge.'

'I've certainly got mine. Two minutes and you'll have a photo.'

'Thank you,' Wendy said. She ended the call.

'That's it,' Larry said as he got up from the chair; breakfast was on his mind and soon.

'We have a right to know why you're asking,' Landis said.

'It's not a good story. Are you sure you want to hear?'

'We're over the age of twenty-one, not old fossils.'

'No offence intended. A woman was murdered in Kensal Green Cemetery. The only clue we have is that she was wearing sandals the same as your wife purchased for your daughter.'

'And you thought…' Deborah Landis put her hands up to her face, 'our daughter?'

'It's a process of elimination. We didn't assume anything, just eliminating the possibilities.'

'Bad news for someone then.'

'Thankfully not for you and your husband.'

'But someone else. How sad.'

'Unfortunately, we see it all too often,' Wendy said.

***

Larry phoned the café, told them twenty minutes and a full breakfast, heavy on the bacon and sausages. Wendy knew he'd be in trouble that night when he got home, but she wasn't his keeper, not even his senior, and she wasn't about to say anything, considering that he ordered for both of them. What's good for one is good for the other, she thought, and besides it was to be a long day, with, as Deborah Landis had said, a sad ending.

The other address in Notting Hill, St Marks Road, close to the railway line, wasn't as good a house as the

Landis's; however, it was neat and tidy, even though it was a busy road and the traffic was noisy.

Not even a police sign on the vehicle would allow them to park on the street; instead, they parked in the forecourt of a petrol station directly across the road, Larry showing his warrant card, saying that he'd be back in ten minutes for the vehicle.

'You purchased a pair of sandals in Knightsbridge, is that correct?' Wendy said. There was to be no sitting down in the house. It was clear that the woman they were talking to was the grandmother from the Indian subcontinent who had been brought over to England to look after the children while their parents were out at work.

'I don't speak good English,' the hindi-speaking sari-clad woman said.

Larry picked up his phone, dialled Challis Street, asked to speak to Jasmine Chandra, a sergeant at the station. He explained the situation to her, then handed the phone to the woman.

A beaming smile lit up on the woman's face, animated gestures with her hands before she disappeared into another room. After a while, she returned, handed the sandals over to Larry, and then the phone.

Larry spoke to Jasmine, found out that the daughter had bought the shoes, but she was at work. Also, the old lady could give them a phone number if they wanted it.

Wendy took the number, but it wasn't needed. The sandals had been seen, and the dead woman was not of Indian extraction.

Two checked, four to go. A breakfast first, though.

As they left the house, the woman thrust a bag of home-made cakes into their hands. They were sweet, more to Larry's palate than Wendy's, but they would finish off the breakfast nicely.

Chapter 7

An anonymous phone call to emergency services was regarded with suspicion – prank
calls still occurred, but not as much as in the past thanks to call identification technology and virtually everyone using a mobile phone.

Regardless, a patrol car had been dispatched to the address. Every call to 999 had to be followed up, documented and filed.

The house had long since been converted into small flats and bedsits, with paper-thin walls. It wasn't their favourite part of London for the two officers assigned to check it out. It was, however, a place where people minded their own business – too many questions could lead to a physical beating or a brick through a window, even a car with four slashed tyres.

A police car was a prime target, so much so that one officer stayed with the vehicle, the other checked out the address. No point having to explain back at the station how the car came to have graffiti sprayed down both sides, and where the wiper blades were.

There should have been three police officers, but staff levels were down, and no one was that much interested in taking the phone call seriously. Across the railway line, on the other side of the road, loomed two circular gas towers, no longer in use, but not demolished. Behind them, although not visible from where the car was parked, the Grand Union Canal, still plied by houseboats.

Another one hundred and fifty yards, the murder site of the, as yet, unidentified woman.

Sergeant Connelly, a tall man, strong and broad, stayed with the vehicle. An ominous quietness in the area; he didn't like it. And he certainly didn't like the street. A couple of dogs scavenged on the other side of the road: unleashed, probably dumped by someone who didn't want to feed them anymore, an unwanted Christmas present that had passed the cute stage. He'd let the authorities know but didn't expect them to do much about it.

The two men had been a team for nearly two years. At first, it had been difficult, the plain-talking burly Connelly, a stream of expletives whenever he spoke, and Fahad Khan, a moderate Muslim who neither drank alcohol nor swore, although he'd light up a cigarette with Connelly, even share a joke with him.

Connelly would have admitted to being prejudiced against other religions, other people, especially after his brother had been close enough to a terrorist attack in Manchester to receive shrapnel to his upper body and lose an eye.

But Fahad Khan had won him over, assured him that he was as appalled as he was, and wasn't that what they had had in Northern Ireland, religious intolerance.

Connelly wasn't so sure that it was precisely the same, but he had to concede to Khan on that point. And then five months after they had teamed together, a car accident, petrol dripping down onto a hot exhaust, a woman inside screaming.

Connelly, brave and without thought, had opened the car door to let the woman out, struggled with the seat belt and the steering wheel that was pinning her down. The petrol igniting, the rear of the car aflame, unable to get the woman out, unable to leave her. He swore, as he always did, exerted himself to no avail. On the other side of the vehicle, with Connelly at his limit, just about to be forced back, his offsider scrambled into the car, releasing the seat belt, allowing Connelly to pull the woman out.

Five minutes later, the car interior was an inferno, and a crew from the nearest fire station were smothering the vehicle with foam. After that Connelly, with newfound respect, tempered his bad language, and during Ramadan, he'd make sure not to eat or smoke in his colleague's presence.

Fahad Khan knocked on the door of the building. A smaller man than his offsider, he pushed against the front door; it opened with little trouble.

Inside, a downstairs flat. Upstairs three bedsits. He knew what the building was used for. That was one of the downsides of being a police officer: having to confront the seedier side of life.

Number 3 at the top of the stairs the caller had said before he hung up. A false alarm or not, no man wanted his name associated with prostitution.

At the top of the stairs, an open door. Khan took one look inside, saw clearly that it wasn't a false alarm.

***

Isaac stood outside the room. He was wearing coveralls and shoe protectors. On his hands, nitrile gloves. It was a crime scene, and Gordon Windsor was adamant that no one unnecessary was allowed in the house. He commended Connelly and Khan on arrival, pleased that they had acted correctly and not contaminated the crime scene, other than Khan climbing the stairs, looking in the room; acceptable for an emergency call out.

Statistically, the area had a high probability that the emergency call was a false alarm; local kids pranking, nothing better to do, excited to see activity.

It was remarkable, Connelly thought, that after the body had been discovered, the street had filled again. Up the road, two women gossiping. A group of children, ages eight to ten, he guessed, trying to fix a bicycle. None of them could have known that a murder had been committed. It was as if they had sensed it, but then, it was a high crime area, a place where people learnt to mind their own business.

He knew that if he spoke to anyone in the street, he would only receive bland answers. Not that he intended to; that was for Homicide.

'Not something you see every day,' Connelly said.

'She was on the game,' Khan said, having learnt to use the talk of the street. He should have been appalled, but he wasn't, just jaundiced that so much depravity existed.

Windsor came out of the room and over to where Isaac was standing. 'Well, DCI,' he said, 'it seems that you're starting to ratchet up the count. How many this time? A new record?'

Isaac understood where Windsor was coming from. One murder leads to another. Too many recently. He had hoped for an easy solution to the body at the cemetery, but it wasn't to be.

'A name?' Isaac asked.

'Janice Robinson. Does it mean anything to you?'

'It does.' Isaac took out his phone and made a call. 'Sunbeam Crescent, as fast as you can,' he said.

'Female, twenty-one, heroin user, in reasonable health considering, possibly malnourished,' Windsor continued.

'We know who she is. What else?'

'Four knife wounds to the chest area. A prostitute.'

'Was it professional or a client?'

'Come in and look for yourself.'

Isaac, used to crimes of violence, walked over to the woman's body, looked down at her lying on her back, her face in repose as if she was asleep.

'Attractive once,' Windsor said. He and Isaac were used to murder. Neither would be phased by what they were seeing; neither would have any trouble eating afterwards, sleeping that night.

'Blood?'

'Not as much as you'd expect. Whoever did this put a towel or something similar over the top of her and the knife.'

'The weapon?'

'It's not here, surprising really. An amateur wouldn't have thought about that, and the man had the nerve to take a shower afterwards.'

'Fingerprints, hair?'

'With the number of men she's serviced? We'll do our best, and we should get something off the body. Hopefully, we can disseminate the most recent. It should help, but if the man's not got a criminal record, details on the database, then it's going to be difficult.'

'There should be evidence of him on her,' Isaac said.

'No sign of seminal fluid. He might have looked at her, but that's it. No sexual activity, not from him.'

'Professional? I asked you before.'

'I can't tell you, not from what we have here. Covering the body with a towel to restrict blood splatter indicates some forethought. But the man could have been a fanatical cleanliness freak, as can be seen by his showering.'

'A professional wouldn't have concerned himself; an arrogance on his part, thumbing his nose up at us.'

'Why is it so important. And what would a hired killer want with a woman of easy means?'

'You've read the report on the Jane Doe?'

'Yes.'

'Brad Robinson, the fifteen-year-old youth who found her with his girlfriend, Rose. Janice Robinson is his sister, or she was.'

***

Neither Larry nor Wendy saw the body when they arrived at the scene. The woman was dead, she was the sister of a witness at another murder, that was enough for them to know.

'Did anyone see anything?' Wendy asked.

'*Around here*?' Larry's answer. 'No answers, no talking, and definitely not to us.'

'The other houses? Prostitution?' Isaac asked.

Larry was the man who knew what happened in the area at street level, more than either Wendy or Isaac. 'I'm surprised she was hawking her wares here,' he said. 'Not that they would care either way what she was up to, but there are families here. There was a drug dealer up the road, he died two years ago. At number 68, there's Old Seamus O'Riley, but he's doing five years for robbery with menace. Apart from that, no one I know, and they're not likely to talk.'

'Too close to home?'

'Has a door-to-door been conducted?' Wendy asked.

'I was leaving that up to you,' Isaac said.

'You'd be wasting your time,' Larry said. 'If they had seen something, and they may well have, they'll not talk, and if they do, don't trust it.'

'An aversion to the police?'

'There's that, but they'd be scared, not sure who it is, and if the man can murder one woman, he can kill another.'

'A serial killer?'

'How would we know?'

The three moved away from the front of the house and walked up the street. The two women who had previously been gossiping disappeared inside one of the houses, two of the children following.

'See what I was saying,' Larry said. 'It'll be quiet in the street for a couple of nights. At least one benefit.'

'It's Brad Robinson's sister,' Wendy said. 'It's not a time for humour.'

'Apologies. Have they been told?'

'Wendy, do you want to do it?' Isaac asked. The most challenging part of a police officer's job, telling the next of kin. He had done it enough times, so had Wendy and Larry.

'I'll do it,' Wendy said. 'Confirmed?'

'A driving licence. It's her. The mother can identify her. Later today if you can, before Pathology's checked her out, done what they need to do.'

'Before we move on,' Larry said. 'Professional?'

'It could be. The man had minimised the blood splatter, but the knife wounds weren't precise.'

'So, it's either a professional wanting to appear to be an amateur or an amateur who had read up on the subject, had a thing about prostitutes.'

'The man showered afterwards which tells us a couple of things,' Isaac said.

'No criminal record, or none that we can prove, or else he's got a phobia about blood.'

'Or he's a cleanliness fanatic.'

'Rose Winston,?' Wendy said. 'Is she at risk?'

'We don't know,' Isaac said. 'Make sure she and her family are updated. And ensure that her house has a uniform and a patrol car patrolling the streets nearby.'

***

Due to the sensitivity of the situation, Wendy drove to the Robinsons' house in Compton Road; Larry headed to the school that Brad Robinson and Rose Winston attended.

He found the administrative office, explained the situation to a pleasant rosy-faced woman in her fifties who broke down in tears after being told what had happened.

Larry waited in the office while the woman went off to find the two of them.

The first to arrive, Rose. She looked even younger in her school uniform than when he had first met her outside the cemetery. No wonder her father was upset with Brad Robinson. On the night of the first murder, with makeup on, lipstick applied, she could have passed for seventeen, but at the school she looked no more than fourteen.

'Inspector Hill, you wanted to see me,' Rose said. Larry found that he liked her; a credit to her parents, someone who would do well in life. What she saw in Brad, he wasn't sure, other than he was a good-looking young man, but from the wrong side of the street.

'Take a seat, Rose,' Larry said.

She complied.

'Did you ever meet Brad's sister?'

'No. Never. Brad told me that he and she were close, and he sometimes saw her.'

'You know what she did?'

'Yes.'

'There's no easy way to say this. She's been murdered.'

The young woman said nothing. Tears started to roll down her cheeks. After what seemed an eternity, the door of the office opened, and Brad walked in.

Rose got up from her chair and flung her arms around his neck. 'I'm so sorry,' she said.

Brad looked bemused, not sure how to react.

'It's Janice,' Larry said. 'I'm afraid she's dead.'

The colour drained from Brad's face and he slumped, Rose holding him up. Larry took hold of them and sat them down on a couple of chairs.

'I'll get some tea,' the rosy-faced admin lady said. The universal cure in England for all ailments, Larry thought. For him, a stiff brandy would have been better, but not in a school, and not for children. And that's what they were, even if they believed they were on the cusp of adulthood.

'How?' Brad said.

'I can't lie to you, Brad,' Larry said. 'The bedsit where she lived. She was murdered.'

'Mum always thought she'd come to no good.'

'We need to go to your house. Rose, your parents?'

'I'm going with Brad,' Rose said. 'He needs me.'

'I can't allow it, not without your parents' permission.'

'I'll phone,' the admin lady said. 'Rose, your phone, the one that's meant to be switched off in school hours.'

Rose put her hand in her pocket, took out the phone.

'Don't worry, I've got the number,' Larry said.

On the other end of the line, Maeve Winston listened as Larry told her the situation. The call ended.

'Your mother will come over to Brad's house,' Larry said. 'You two can come with me.'

'We have counselling available,' the admin lady said, wanting to be helpful.

Outside the office, Rose turned to Larry. 'Mrs Montgomery, she's always fussing about, but we all like her.'

The two youngsters sat in the back of Larry's car. He had suggested that Brad sit up front, Rose in the back. It wasn't going to be, and he hoped that they arrived at the Robinsons' before Rose's mother, as she could well be upset that the police were encouraging the inappropriate romance.

On arrival, Larry was pleased to see that his fears weren't realised. Wendy's car was parked outside the house, a uniform at the door.

***

'Our Janice,' Brad's mother screamed as he entered.

Brad left Rose and went over to his mother, put his arms around her. 'I'm still here,' he said.

It was a touching scene, Wendy thought, as did Rose. Larry looked away, not sure what to think or how to react. He was always uncomfortable in intimate situations: an austere father, a mother who was not affectionate, although he had had a good upbringing, a decent education, a brother and sister who had not been in trouble with the law.

Rose, her first time in the house, looked around, not sure what to make of it. To her, it was an alien world, the decay, the smell of damp in the air. A cat lay curled up on the windowsill taking in what sun there was; a dog barked outside.

A knock on the door. Wendy opened it.

'Rose?'

'She's here.'

'Gladys?'

'Mrs Robinson is fine, upset of course. To be expected under the circumstances.'

In the front room, the two women looked at each other – one who had lost a daughter, the other who had bettered herself and didn't want to be reminded of where she had come from – rushed together and hugged, kissing each other on the cheek.

'It's been a long time,' Maeve Winston said.

'I've seen you sometimes, but you never waved.'

'I couldn't.'

No more was said by either woman. Brad sat with his mother; Rose with hers. It should have been touching, but wasn't.

After a few minutes, Gladys Robinson spoke. 'Jim needs to know.'

'It's been dealt with,' Larry replied, not sure that it had, but he was confident that his DCI would have contacted the prison, asked someone skilled to tell the man.

'I want to see her,' Brad said.

'It's for your mother to confirm identity,' Wendy said.

'I still want to see her.'

It was irregular and would not be welcomed by the staff where Janice's body was, but an exception would be made. Jim Robinson would be allowed to attend the funeral to say his goodbyes.

Wendy was sure what Maeve Winston was thinking, but she wasn't interfering, not even when Rose left her and went over to Brad and put her arm around him, kissing him on the mouth.

'Did Janice die because of what we saw in the cemetery?' Brad asked. His voice was firm, a sign that he was starting to accept the situation, or a momentary need to ask questions that troubled Homicide.

'We don't think so,' Larry said.

'Which means you're not sure,' Maeve said. 'Which means that Rose could be next. Have you considered that?'

'Please, Mrs Winston. We've just come from Janice. We don't think there's a connection, and prostitution is a high-risk occupation. Each year, prostitutes die at the hands of a client.'

'We need protection; Rose needs protection.'

'Protection will be provided for Rose and you and your husband. Also for Brad and Mrs Robinson.'

What Larry had said was true, but the protection would be a uniform at each house, but the school would present difficulties. It was a sprawling collection of buildings; easy entry in and out.

But why kill Janice? Larry thought. What use would that be to a professional? To Larry, and no doubt to Isaac and Wendy when they sat down to discuss it, nothing seemed to make sense.

The fear was that it wasn't professional, it was psychopathic, and the man they were looking for was a madman, a man who could act normally, even to his family and friends, but someone who could kill, had killed before, could kill again.

Chapter 8

For three days Rose stayed away from the school, although Brad returned after two. Jim Robinson, after a phone call from Isaac, and with Chief Superintendent Goddard's assistance, had been granted a visit to the family home, a prison officer with him, and Larry present.

Larry knew Jim, and the two had shaken hands at the front door before the prisoner had been let into the house. Violence wasn't on his criminal record, and he was an acceptable risk in that he wouldn't disappear over the fence at the rear of the house. Besides, he had only four months left on his sentence, a reduction for good behaviour.

In the house, mother and sons, a quiet moment to reflect on the family's loss; even Larry closing his eyes. He had seen the body at Pathology, although Brad and his mother had seen it before the pathologist had commenced his work, removing organs, cutting the body from shoulder blade down to the pubic region, a Y-shaped incision.

Jim would not be allowed to see the body, and his four hours were soon up. He was off back to the prison, although Larry, going out on a limb and with the prison officer's agreement, first took the three of them to a pub on the corner, gave Jim the first pint of beer he'd had in a long time.

'Drugs,' Jim said after he had downed his glass in one gulp. 'That's what it is; that's what killed Janice.'

No mention of the mother's live-ins, the abuse the daughter had suffered at the hands of one or two of them. Brad had told Larry some of it; the mother had vehemently denied it when questioned, but it was true, looking away as she said it.

A family always on a financial precipice, with a low level of education, and abuse wasn't far away. His wife would say it was self-induced, although Larry knew it wasn't that, not always. Life was tough for most people, and whereas the majority kept their heads just above the water, paddling madly under the surface to stay afloat, others weren't able to.

The Robinsons weren't bad people; just surviving, taking the rough with the smooth, enjoying the highs, coping with the lows.

Jim had been upset at the house, but he had been in prison, removed from the period of grieving that Brad and his mother had already endured, to the extent that Brad was almost back to his usual self and talking about Rose again. Not that her father would ever give his permission.

Isaac had visited the Winstons the day after Janice had died; the father upset that his wife had been with Rose at the Robinsons. He had every right, Isaac knew that, but a woman had been murdered, and not someone unknown, as the woman at the cemetery remained, but the daughter of someone he had known in his younger days, the sister of a young man he had given a lift to that night at the cemetery.

Pathology had confirmed that Janice Robinson was a drug addict and she had not had sexual intercourse with her murderer. The pathologist had also concluded that she had in all probability not had sex in twelve hours before her death. And apart from the knife wounds, delivered with a nine-inch blade and not specific as to where they were aimed, not much more could be deduced.

After this second death, visits to the other purchasers of the sandals continued. The Hammersmith address had not helped as it had been another mother buying for her daughter, the daughter proudly wearing them. Bayswater and Paddington had both drawn blanks. The only one left was twenty miles to the south of the city.

And as Isaac Cook saw it, a dead prostitute took precedence over an unknown woman, although the tie-in of the two was both puzzling and far too circumstantial to be a coincidence.

The only solution to firm up opinions on the two women was to identify the Jane Doe, to ascribe a name to her, or there would be another murder. The latter option not desired.

Isaac visited the Robinsons, found the mother busy in the kitchen. He had been told of the condition of the place, but Gladys Robinson was there, a broom in one hand, a bucket in the other.

'I've got to put on a show for the relatives. She's dead, dead and gone, never forgotten.'

The woman seemed hard to him, as though she didn't care, not anymore. Although it could be a pretence, given that a hard life takes the edge off any sentimentality.

'When she lived at home,' Isaac said, 'you had men here.'

The woman put the broom and bucket to one side. 'I never sold myself, if that's what you're asking.'

'Was Janice abused?'

'Not by me.'

'Your lovers? Was it the reason that she was mixed up?'

Isaac wasn't sure where he was going with the conversation, only that Larry and Wendy were busy trying to find the Jane Doe, and Homicide was quiet for once. He needed to get out and about, in the thrust of it. Visiting Gladys Robinson was as good a reason as any.

'I caught one of them sniffing around, caught him before he did anything.'

'The others?'

'She was always that way inclined. Always walking around in her underwear, showing off whatever she had under there. Not much I can tell you, not like me when I was her age.'

'You were a prostitute?'

'Not me. I was quality, not a cheap whore who put it on display, not like Janice; meat on a plate, take what you want.'

'Your opinion of her has changed since she died.'

'It hasn't. She took one of my men, an accountant he was, treated me nice, bought me flowers and chocolates every Friday on the way home from work, took me to the cinema and everything.'

'What happened?'

'I came home from work, cleaning houses, nothing fancy, but it paid well enough; enough to feed the kids, and Jim, he was a handful, ate like a horse.'

'You're getting away from what we're talking about, Mrs Robinson. Janice?'

Isaac had seen the vodka bottle when he had come in, and even though she had been drinking steadily, judging by her occasional slurring of words, she was coherent.

'She's there, in bed with him, only fourteen, younger than Brad's girlfriend. Can you imagine it, seducing my man in my house, in my bed?'

'You blamed your daughter?'

'Who else? Not him, a professional man, educated, treated me well.'

'She was a child, not able to understand. If she had not resisted, which you are intimating, then she had not received the proper guidance from her parents.'

'There was only me, not that her father would have done much. He used to look at Janice as she was developing; indecent it was, and I told him so.'

'His reaction?'

'He hit me. That's when Jim, growing up fast, exercising at the gym twice a week, flattened him, sent him packing.'

Isaac had heard the story more than once. The wayward child. If it was male, then crime and joining a gang; a female, and it was prostitution, at first to feed a habit, and then because there was no way back. The family home would not have helped Janice; the drugs and the lifestyle the result of her younger life.

'Tell me about Tim and Maeve Winston.' Isaac changed the subject.

'We went to school together. Maeve lived next door to me, not here, somewhere better.'

'What was she like?'

'She liked to read books, not that I could understand why. The teacher we had that last year, he said I'd end up as a cashier at the supermarket if I were lucky.'

'I thought they were meant to encourage you.'

'He was. What he had wanted to say was that I'd end up flat on my back for every hard-luck case who had the money, tart that I was.'

'Tim?'

'He was as bad as Brad, always wanting to get his leg across.'

'You?'

'I was one of them, but Maeve, she was studious, not totally innocent, but innocent enough. Why is it that men want women like me when they're younger, and then women such as Maeve when they get older?'

'You said it. When they get older, their brain rules their groin, not the other way around. Brad's got his head screwed on.'

'Rose, pretty, I'll grant you that, but what do you know about her? No virgin, not her, been around the traps a few times.'

Isaac had been willing to give the woman a chance, but it was clear that she was not a fit parent, in that she had failed her daughter, and would Brad if given a chance. Social services needed to be informed and to check out the woman, if they weren't doing so already.

'Brad and Rose, any problem for you?'

'No, why should it be? He's still young. Why should I care?'

'Because you're his mother. Whether you agree or not, it's still for you to be concerned, to guide if necessary.'

Isaac could see that he was getting nowhere, and that wasn't the reason to be in the house.

'Was Maeve told that her future was in the supermarket?'

'Teacher's pet, not her. I wouldn't have been surprised if she…'

'Stop, sit down and start making sense. If Janice was killed because Brad saw the murderer of the other woman, then it's not only Rose who's a possible target, so is your son.'

'I wouldn't like that.'

'We're in agreement on one thing,' Isaac said. He sat down opposite the woman. 'Now, let's get this straight. Janice was selling herself, not getting a lot of business from what we can see.'

'Too much of it about these days. Why pay?'

Isaac did not offer a comment, not sure what to say. He'd had his fair share in his day, he knew that, and not once had he resorted to a woman whose phone number was on the internet or, in the past, on a card inside a telephone box.

'When you weren't drinking, which isn't often judging by that bottle of vodka, did you ever see Janice? An honest answer, please.'

'I kept a watch on her from time to time, not that I could have spoken to her, broke my heart she did.'

'Don't give me that sob story. You didn't care, not much, and you knew that men were abusing her, probably took money off them as well.'

'My own daughter…'

'Answer my question.'

'Okay, I knew she was in that bedsit, and she was doing it tough. She looked old when I saw her dead.'

'Did you see men entering the premises.'

'She wasn't the only one on the game in there.'

'We know that, and we've interviewed one of the women, not that she's there now, too scared, worried that it will be her next.'

'I never saw more than three men, but it was on the way home from seeing a friend, and I'd sometimes watch from the end of the road.'

'Tell me about the men?'

'You said there was another one in there selling herself.'

'Process of elimination.'

'Tim Winston used to visit her.'

'You've not mentioned that before. Why?'

'Why what? Why I didn't mention it, or why he visited her?'

'Both; start with the first.'

'Tim was always that way inclined. When he was younger, whoever he could get, two a night, cheating on each with the other.'

'But he married Maeve.'

'Tim was bright, smarter than all of us, a man destined for better, and he knew it. And Maeve, she wanted to improve herself. A matched pair the two of them, but she could be a cold fish, saving herself for marriage. Tim, he would have liked that, but he hasn't changed, not if he was seeing Janice.'

'Could he have killed her?'

'I don't think he'd be that stupid, and why? He had it made. The loyal housewife at home; my daughter, whenever he paid the money.'

'Your daughter? A substitute for you?'

'He would have seen the humour in it. As long as Maeve didn't know, it wouldn't have worried him, and she'd have him on short rations. Sometimes, we used to tease her that she fancied women more than men.'

'Did she?'

'Just childish nonsense. She was more sensible than us.'

'Tim?'

'What does it matter? It's what men do. They can't help themselves, can they?'

'Your daughter? Tim Winston or the men you had here?'

'They're all the same. No doubt you were in your day.'

Isaac chose not to answer.

'One final question. Winston's with your daughter, then overly protective of his. What do you think of that?'

'He was doing his duty. It would have helped if Janice's father had done his.'

'Did he touch her?'

'Not him, barely able to get it up.'

'Where is he now?'

'In hell, I hope.'

'And Rose?'

'If Brad wants her, that's fine by me, not that he'll stick by her.'

'We've marked him as a decent young man, good moral values. Where do you think he got them from?'

'Not from me; not from his father, and certainly not from Janice or Jim. We're not good people,' Gladys Robinson said. 'Not evil, but none of us is like Maeve or Tim Winton and their precious daughter.'

'Tim Winton's not looking so good now,' Isaac said.

'Don't let Maeve know. She was a friend once.'

'I'll try,' Isaac said, although he knew it would not remain a secret. It was a murder enquiry; the truth is always revealed.

The relationship between Brad and Rose, Isaac knew, would be strained when it became known that the father of one had been paying the sister of another for sex. Isaac personally wished he hadn't found out; professionally, it was another line of enquiry.

Chapter 9

Gladys Robinson could not be regarded as a credible witness: the ease with which she had accused Maeve Winston of giving herself to their teacher when they had been younger, ignoring or even condoning the abuse of her daughter. However, regardless of what anyone thought of her, she had made a serious accusation about Tim Winston.

It was early afternoon the next day when Isaac and Wendy met with the man. Isaac had broached the subject in the morning with Winston, and he had agreed to come into Challis Street.

Sheepishly, the man sat across from the two police officers in the interview room.

'A disturbing development,' Isaac said. He was prepared for a reaction. Hopefully, it would not be outright denial, the man indignant and storming out of the police station, huffing and puffing, threatening legal action. Wendy hoped he wasn't involved, purely for Rose's sake.

'I'm willing to help, not sure that I can,' Winston said. He wore a suit, a white shirt and a blue tie.

'Tell us about Janice Robinson,' Isaac said.

'There's not much to tell.'

'You used to see her?'

'We don't live far from them, and sometimes we'd see them at the shops, not that I spoke to them much, just the usual courtesies.'

'No wish to associate?'

'Why? Do you keep in contact with those you went to school with?'

'Mr Winston, we have reason to believe that you have seen Janice Robinson more recently,' Isaac said, ignoring Winston's previous response, a question with a question.

Wendy sensed a feeling of panic across the table.

'Not for five or six years. The last time she was wearing a school uniform, hanging out with a group near McDonald's.'

'What were they doing?'

'The usual. Playing with their phones, smoking, flirting with the boys.'

'Incorrect behaviour?'

'We've all been there. I didn't think much about it. I only looked because I recognised Janice, the spitting image of her mother at that age.'

'You took out Gladys Robinson?' Wendy asked.

'I'm not sure I'd call it that; nothing official. We'd meet up, watch a movie, and then I would walk her home. We were young, finding our way.'

'You were a good student, hoping to improve yourself; Gladys was never going to be up to your standard.'

'We were fourteen, fifteen. I don't think I gave it too much thought, not Gladys, that is.'

'We're deviating,' Isaac said. 'The reason that you had an intimate relationship is not what we're here for.'

'Intimate? I'd hardly call it that. Gladys was putting it about something dreadful. I would have been a fool not to take advantage,' Winston said, a man too much at ease in the interview room.

'Back of the bike shed, the cinema?'

'Something like that, although I don't ever remember a bike shed.'

'If you had had sex with the mother,' Isaac said, 'why then the daughter?'

'Janice? Is this what this is about? Are you accusing me of murdering her?'

A calmer reaction than expected.

'Paying for her doesn't make you a murderer.'

'I deny it.'

'That's your prerogative. However, you've not answered the question. It could be an aspersion, a slanderous accusation made against you, but we still need to check, to know the truth.'

'Maeve?' Winston said. The previous cockiness was no longer apparent. Wendy could see the sweat beads on his forehead, the shaking of his left hand as it rested on the table.

'No guarantees. Not in a murder investigation. We need to isolate you from the murder scene, and for that we need a sample of your DNA, a strand of hair.'

'I didn't kill her.'

'We're not accusing you. To be honest, we don't think you did it. There was a lot of blood at the murder scene, and we saw you later that day. Unless you're a methodical man, a good planner, it's unlikely you could have pulled it off.'

'I wouldn't have done that. The sight of blood.'

'Germ phobia? Cleanliness freak?'

'An accident when I was a child, three days in the hospital.'

'Not good enough, but we'll accept it for now. The DNA?'

'If you want.'

'When did you start paying Janice for her time?' Wendy asked.

'I can't just deny it, and you leave it at that?' Winston said.

'If you do, then we will need to check further, follow up on your movements, talk to your wife as to whether she has any suspicion that you've been with another woman.'

'Maeve hasn't known up till now.'

'Which is yes. You did pay for Janice Robinson's services.'

'Two, possibly three times.'

'The truth,' Wendy said.

'Every week on a Thursday at seven in the evening. Maeve was always out with friends, a regular get-together at a restaurant, and Rose would be busy with schoolwork.'

'Any reason why Janice?'

'If you think it was a substitute for her mother, you'd be mistaken. Janice was agreeable to look at, and her price was reasonable. Nothing more than that.'

'Did she know who you were?'

'She did, not that we'd talk about it. It was sex, nothing more.'

'How long did these sessions last for?'

'Fifteen, maybe twenty minutes. There were no meaningful discussions. I didn't ask her about why she whored, nor did I ask her about her family. I should be regretful, but I'm not. A man's got needs. Sometimes they aren't satisfied.'

'Is this why you don't want Rose associating with Brad Robinson?'

'She's fifteen, what do you think?'

'We're asking the questions,' Isaac said.

'She's still too young. Okay, I was with her boyfriend's mother when we were both under sixteen, but that doesn't mean I would agree to my daughter doing the same.'

'It doesn't help that you've known Brad's mother and sister.'

'That's not the point. We want better for Rose, that's all. We don't want her with a family that has never amounted to much. Brad's better than the others, but he's tarred with the same brush. In time, he'll revert to type, and I don't want Rose to be dragged down, to get pregnant before her time.'

'Why not put her in a better school?'

'There are no guarantees. Young people push boundaries. It's for us to guide them.'

The man was a good parent, both Isaac and Wendy conceded. He was, as is so often the case, a hypocrite, who had taken advantage of Janice Robinson's degradation, and she had only been six years older than Rose, only two years older when she had first sold herself. Yet, he wanted to protect his daughter at all costs.

He hadn't murdered Janice, that much was known, but he was guilty of other crimes, not criminal, but moral.

Isaac was willing to give the man the benefit of the doubt; Wendy wasn't. To her, he was a typical example of selective reasoning, able to absolve himself from his wrongdoings but not to give others their chance, to see Brad Robinson as suitable for his daughter. Although he had been right on one score: Rose was still a child, even if she wanted to be an adult.

***

95

The village of Godstone in Surrey was mentioned in the Domesday Book of 1086, although it was named Wachelstede back then, and then in 1248 it was recorded as Godeston, suggesting an etymology of the Old English personal name Goda, who was the daughter of Aethelred The Unready, and 'tun', which is loosely translated as farm.

As to why a former king of England would be unready, Larry Hill wouldn't have known or have cared.

It was his third visit in as many days to the last address from the store in Knightsbridge.

Number 156 High Street, Godstone, a detached two-storey house, was well maintained, not cheap to purchase, and within commuting distance of London.

Larry had taken up his position in a coffee shop across from the house, not at the White Hart, the closest pub.

Yet again, he asked the waitress if she had seen anyone at the house; the answer always the same. 'Not for a few weeks, but then, they keep to themselves, never come in here, barely give you the time of day.'

'Describe them.'

'I'm not sure I can. He looked older than her, although I couldn't be sure. Just average, I suppose.'

The local police hadn't been able to help, nor had the estate agent who had leased the house to them; average was the most oft-quoted description. The agent, a garrulous man, told Larry that they had come into his office seven months previously, taken one look around the house, and had deposited funds into his account and set up an automatic credit for each month.

'We're managing it for them, not that there's much to do, as they're not here too often.'

The photo of the dead woman rang no bells with anyone; they had all been clear that the woman at the house had been blonde, tanned and under thirty. Either way, those in Godstone had seen the man's face, the woman shielding her face when anyone looked her way.

On his first visit, Larry had knocked on the door of the house, checked around, looked in the windows, and spoken to the local police; on his second, he had obtained a warrant and the house had been opened by the estate agent. Inside, no sign of habitation, no food in the fridge or the pantry. The beds were not made up, yet outside the house, the lawn was mown, and in the garage at the side of the house, a late-model BMW.

Larry believed that crime was the most likely reason for the place being leased. There was a forwarding address for the mail, but that had drawn a blank.

Janice Robinson was now occupying more of Homicide's time than the Jane Doe. Larry was glad of the opportunity to be on his own, to use his initiative. It was clear that the village would offer no more clues, but why an expensive car was in the garage concerned him.

Only one group of people had money to waste: drug people. Not those taking them, like the Robinsons' daughter, but those who imported and sold them, and they were dangerous, and usually none too subtle about who they killed and how.

The possibility remained that the woman in the village and the body in the cemetery were one and the same. And if she had been in the village with an older man, that suggested a relationship: adulterous, platonic, or otherwise.

Larry finished his coffee and headed back to London; village life had never suited him, too quiet. The hustle and bustle of the metropolis was more to his taste, even though the coffee he had just drunk was excellent, and the pub sold his favourite beer. Not that he would taste it this time; he had the bit between his teeth and there was something he needed to check out.

***

Winston's admission that he had paid for Janice Robinson's services hadn't advanced the murder enquiry; its only function was to cause embarrassment and a probable end to the burgeoning romance of Brad and Rose, who still met at the school, snatched moments during the breaks, whispered conversations.

At the school, a low-key police presence, two police constables aiming to blend in; failing miserably.

One of the two, Constable Ecclestone, complained whenever Wendy spoke to him. 'A rabble and they're trading drugs in the playground. In my day…'

In his day, Wendy knew, they would have been doing precisely the same, but now weapons were a more significant issue, especially knives and knuckle dusters. The miserable and negative constable was right, but that was something to deal with another day.

'Anyone strange?' Wendy said. 'Remember, we've got two murders now. We don't want a third, or you and I will be up before the chief superintendent, and he doesn't appreciate failure.'

'I heard that he and DCI Cook are friends.'

'You've heard right. However, in the superintendent's office, it's business, not pleasure. Have you seen anything?'

'Robinson's mother was here, not for long, and the girl's father waited outside for her, said a few words and left.'

'When?'

'At 2.46 p.m. today, not long before you arrived.'

'Any idea what they were talking about?'

'I couldn't get that close. It looked serious, but there was no shouting.'

'Their children see a murder, and then Brad's sister dies.'

'I knew her.'

'How?'

'Not as a client; no help needed there.'

Wendy squirmed at the man's comment. Why was it, she thought, that men wanted to brag to female police officers? What was different? Or was it shock value, the fact that a female police officer had seen it or heard it all before, and they wouldn't say anything or react? Whatever it was, she didn't like it.

'How?'

'Before she was up at Sunbeam Crescent, she used to hang out down by the canal. There's a dark stretch down there where the street lights don't penetrate. They used to think they were safe from us, but they weren't. We knew their tricks, and we'd pick up one or two of a weekend to let them know it as well.'

'Not all of them?'

'What would it achieve? Some of them were too far out of it to know what was going on, no money to pay the fine either. But Janice, she was smarter than most. She always came willingly, fronted the magistrate, fluttered her eyes, wiggled her hips, cried about her habit and a mother who didn't understand.'

'Assuming half of what you just said is true, what's the point of the story?'

'Nothing. She'd get a fine, a slap on the wrist, be back in another month or two. Sometimes we'd not arrest her.'

'A knee-trembler up against a wall?'

'Not us,' Ecclestone said. 'Nothing like that.'

If he didn't, Wendy knew, he would have been unique. She didn't believe him for one minute.

***

Isaac entered the gates of Maidstone Prison. It's main claim to fame was that its exterior had been used in the opening sequences of the TV comedy series *Porridge*. It was Category C, a closed prison for those who couldn't be trusted in an open prison but were unlikely to escape. It wasn't his first time in the place, but the first time visiting Jim Robinson.

Suspects for the murder of his sister were worryingly few. Apart from Winston, nobody else had been found, and Wendy's attempt at a door-to-door on the street of Janice's bedsit had turned out to be as Larry had described – a waste of time, in that those who knew something weren't talking, and those who didn't were only too ready to waste police time.

It was clear that Jim Robinson was regarded well in prison and where the two men met was more pleasant than the usual meeting room assigned at most prisons. They shook hands, went through the usual pleasantries, spoke about the weather. Jim was adamant that he was going straight this time. Isaac took the 'going straight comment in the manner given but didn't believe he would. Jim Robinson, for all his charm and good intentions, was a habitual criminal and not very good at that. However, that was not the reason for the visit.

'Jim, your sister. I need to know what happened in your home,' Isaac said. He had already given a carton of cigarettes to the man who didn't smoke but could use them as collateral, and a box of chocolates, Jim's favourite, which the prisoner would keep for himself.

'Our mother, you've met her,' Jim said as he opened the chocolates, took one for himself, offered one to Isaac which he declined. He could buy them at any supermarket, Jim couldn't.

'Unable to cope?'

'And some. Our father, when he was around, kept the place under control, but he was a hard man, a bastard, in that he'd drink and then start getting violent. Hit me a few times, as well as Brad, and Mum had more than a few black eyes.'

'Did he abuse Janice?'

'Not Janice. Don't believe our mother; not that she was innocent on all counts.'

'You knew?'

'Some of the men in the house weren't there out of love. Brad was too young to understand, and Janice could be naïve, even when she started to develop, but I was older.'

'What did you do about it?'

'There wasn't much I could do when I was younger, and later I ended up spending more time away, courtesy of Her Majesty.'

'Your father looked at Janice as more than a daughter?'

'I told you, don't listen to my mother. If he had looked at Janice, it would have been out of admiration, not lust. His problem was that he would get drunk and then violent. I dealt with him that night, never saw him again, no idea where he is.'

101

'No idea?'

'I'd prefer not to know, and I haven't seen him, not since that night.'

'Where can I find him? It's important.'

'Not sure why, but try Canning Town, out to the east of the city.'

'A phone number, address?'

'Ask around. I only heard that he was there, can't remember who told me and that's the truth. Why's this important?'

'Apart from one customer who's not the murderer, we haven't anyone else to pin her death on.'

'She was always going to come to an unfortunate end, our Janice. Our mother was right about that, one of the few times, though.'

'Why do you say that?'

'Janice was gullible, used to watch that nonsense on the television, get herself upset, want to do something about it.'

'What sort of nonsense?'

'The starving, the downtrodden, the needy. We were all of those three as children, not much better now, apart from Brad. He's got a chance.'

'And you?'

'Detective Chief Inspector, out there, no one's going to give me a decent job, and why should they? A prison record, no qualifications.'

'You could get qualifications, learn computers.'

'Dyslexic. I'll try to stay out of trouble, but it runs in the family. No violence, not from Brad or me; our father was the exception.'

'I'll give him your best wishes when I find him.'

'Don't bother, and what do you hope to gain?'

'I need to know who else spent time with your mother and your sister. He might be able to help.'

'DCI, leave well alone. Don't rake over old coals. The past is just that, long gone. What happened to us, what happened to Janice, won't bring her back.'

'We can't leave her murder unpunished.'

'It would be better if you did. We'll remember her in our own way, remember the young girl.'

Isaac slipped a fifty-pound note across to Robinson as he left; he hoped he would use it wisely.

Chapter 10

Kensal Green Cemetery. A hunch. It wasn't often that Larry saw things so clearly. He was a methodical police officer: follow the process, talk to people, move forward. Yet, as he had sat in the coffee shop in Godstone, looking over at the house, it had seemed more evident to him.

He walked over to the gravestone, looked at it, looked for the imperceptible. If the subterfuge of the couple who had leased the house in the village was so good, then a random killing at the cemetery made no sense.

Brad and Rose had only walked through a small part of the cemetery which was extensive, stretching almost a mile to the west and still within the cemetery boundary, sixty-five thousand graves.

Larry studied the grave where the woman had died. He hadn't had lunch, no food since breakfast at home, but it didn't seem important, not now.

He took a photo of the headstone with his smartphone; took a slow amble around the cemetery, not totally sure of where he was heading, confident that it was important.

The first clue, the numbers of the plots fronting the path painted on the kerb. The first number he saw belonged to a sadly-neglected grave dating back to the 1830s, the woman's name almost erased due to weathering over the years. Even so, a sad-looking bunch of flowers was placed on it. He couldn't believe that a descendant still remembered, although sometimes well-meaning people felt the need to remember the lost forgotten. The number, freshly painted in black on a white background – 12813.

As he walked, he observed the numbers rising in steps of three, which meant one grave fronting the path, one behind, and another behind that. An intersection, and a new set of numbers to the left and the right. He chose the last two digits, realising that they indicated the area of the cemetery; laid out in a grid, he supposed.

The area he was looking for was 73. He kept walking, eventually finding it at the western extremity, just before the cemetery gate exit onto Scrubs Lane.

From there, he chose left, the last two digits remaining the same, the other three slowly heading in the right direction.

He looked around, realised that this was the most neglected part of the cemetery and rarely visited. There were no flowers here, barely a headstone, other than those that had fallen down. He presumed that in time, and if someone was willing to pay the twenty-two thousand pounds needed to purchase a plot, some of the bodies would be coming up; so much for the dearly departed, he thought.

When his time came, a cremation, his ashes scattered on the garden where they would do some good.

An elaborate and costly funeral had been more important in the distant past, before the advent of the motor vehicle, the upwardly mobile population, post-Christianity, and the suburb of Kensal Green wouldn't have been the bustling hive of activity that it was now.

He had come this far; now wasn't the time to give in. He counted the rows in three, figured that 15973 was four rows down, the second grave in. The date that the occupant of the grave at the murder site had died, 15th

September 1873, correlating with another grave's plot number.

He could see the grave, or what little remained of it. The ground was wet and soggy; he removed his shoes, knowing that they would make a more significant imprint.

Underfoot was cold, and he regretted his decision. At the grave, he looked around. 1902, the year of burial, a man of fifty-six, of this parish., Larry was sure that Archibald Vincent wouldn't be concerned with his ferreting around, not that he could do much about it if he was.

On one side of the grave, the most neglected, the stonework broken in places, he found nothing. At the bottom of the grave, the same result.

The headstone, which had fallen over, he carefully lifted a few inches. It was heavier than he expected, and he dropped it, not seeing anything obvious, the damp soil cushioning the headstone, not cracking it. On the far side, the dampest and the least inviting, he couldn't see anything.

'In for a penny, in for a pound,' he said as he put one foot on the soft soil, sinking into it almost up to his ankle. He pulled his foot back, took stock of the situation, debated with himself as to whether he should continue or wait for another day. His wife was going to give him hell for coming home dirty.

A man shouted to him from the path. 'What are you doing?' he said. He was dressed in green overalls, a badge on his breast pocket.

'Inspector Larry Hill, Challis Street Police Station,' Larry shouted back.

'You won't find anything in there. Dead a long time.'

It was clear that the man, short and overweight, with a round face and an even rounder belly, enjoyed the humour of the situation. But then, why shouldn't he, Larry thought. Death's a sad time for most, but for a cemetery employee and a police officer, it was commonplace.

'We're investigating the body on the grave over the other side.'

'And you think you'll find something there?'

'I think that I might. Does anybody come down here?'

'People at the weekend out for some exercise, the occasional dog on a leash, not that we encourage it, always a mess to clear up afterwards. Some can't read the notices, or if they can, they take no notice.'

'Anyone else?'

'Now that you mention it, I can remember someone down here ten or eleven days ago. A rum sort of fellow, didn't want to talk, took no notice of me, not that he was causing any trouble, just walking around the graves. It was drier back then; didn't make such a fool of himself as you are.'

'This grave?'

'Probably. In fact, I'm certain that it was.'

'Stay where you are. I'm coming out.'

Larry looked where to place his other foot, to extricate himself. In one corner, at the angle between the far side and the headstone, a large rock under the soil that had been exposed by his moving around.

'I found something,' Larry said.

'I'll be over, give you a hand.'

'Stay where you are. This could be a crime scene.'

Larry carefully moved the rock to one side.

'There's something underneath,' he shouted to the man in

the overalls. 'I'd suggest you backtrack the way you came, just in case.'

'As you say, but after so much rain, you can't expect much.'

Larry did.

***

Due to the relatively low-key nature of the site, one uniform had arrived, put crime scene tape in place to prevent entry to the area of the grave, and asked the cemetery employee to close off both entrances to the path; not difficult as there were boom gates installed. It was just a case of lowering them and securing them with a padlock.

Larry had dried his feet, wrung out his socks after washing them in a basin in a hut in the cemetery grounds. A bar heater, not very safe, but efficient, managed to take the socks from sopping wet to damp and warm.

After close to fifteen minutes, the first of the CSIs to arrive, Grant Meston, a good man in Larry's estimation, removed the rock. Crime scene stepping plates had been placed from the path to the grave, and it was Meston, Larry and the cemetery employee who stood watching as the other CSI took the rock and put it into a large bag. It was evidence, even if to the layman it was just an inanimate object of no value. That was how the employee saw it, but then he was a manual labourer, not paid very much, probably didn't do very much either, judging by the general condition of the cemetery and the untidy state of his hut.

The rock removed, the CSI withdrew a box. It was metal, in good condition, and blue.

'Nothing special,' Meston said. 'What's inside is important.'

Larry knew they would not find that out at the site. Forensics would take that responsibility, subjecting the box to a drying process, water ingression was a probability. Whatever happened, it would be twelve to fourteen hours before any clues were revealed.

It was, however, excellent police work, and Isaac had been on the phone to congratulate him, as had Chief Superintendent Goddard.

Larry was pleased with himself; he only hoped his wife would be, considering that his previously black, shiny leather shoes were now a shade of mud grey.

***

In the interim, Larry returned to Challis Street. He was behind on his paperwork, the bane of any police offficer; a vital component of modern policing, Chief Superintendent Goddard would say. But then he was a political animal, careful to say the right words, anxious to let his superiors know as to how professional those under his command were, not that it helped with the Met's commissioner sitting in his office at Scotland Yard. The man had taken an instant dislike to Goddard and had tried to unseat him on more than one occasion, succeeding briefly once, careful not to repeat the mistake of having to rescind the order and to have Goddard placed back in his old position.

Goddard didn't like the man any more than he disliked him; excessively cordial when they met, buttering up each other, a metaphorical knife poised to inflict the fatal blow.

Isaac, after Maidstone Prison, had phoned Bridget. It took her no more than ten minutes to find an address and a phone number. If the Robinson patriarch had been in hiding, or just keeping away from his family, he hadn't done it very well.

Hector Robinson was not what he had expected. Isaac had tracked him down to the Durham Arms in Canning Town. Isaac rarely visited the area, known for drug gangs and violent crime, so much so that courier companies were refusing to deliver there, and the police entered in groups. The pub was on a corner site; the railway across the other side of the narrow road, a scruffy recycling plant to one side, and on the other side, down Wharf Street, a factory, empty from what Isaac could see. The pub had a website; it was in an industrial estate, make as much noise as you like, don't worry about the neighbours. Isaac didn't understand how that concept operated, nor how they had unrestricted hours, and the photo of the pub in better times didn't match what he saw, a two-storey building, the upstairs painted off-white, the ground floor covered in out-of-date green tiles.

Robinson sat in one corner; it was four in the afternoon, and the crowds that the barman had said would be in later weren't even trickling in. There was just Robinson, Isaac and the barman, and two of them didn't look to be good company, the barman obviously three-quarters of the way to being drunk and the missing father not pleased to see him.

Isaac regretted that he hadn't brought support with him. He made a phone call, an inspector at a police station nearby, a colleague from their uniform days.

'You must be mad,' the inspector had said, colourful expletives included. But that was Bill Ross, a rough knockabout type of guy who had lived up north,

110

run with a gang in his teens, realised the error of his ways, joined the police. As he said when he met with Isaac occasionally, 'Not much job security running with a gang, although we were mostly harmless, but better money. Now I've got the security, a mortgage that kills me, and not much else.'

It was the way the man spoke, but after he had called Isaac a fool a few more times, he phoned a patrol car to get out to the Durham Arms and make its presence known. It was daylight, they'd do that, but come nightfall, it would be at least six officers and two vehicles, weapons available if needed.

'What do you want?' Robinson said as he downed his pint, looked over at the barman.

'I'll pay,' Isaac said.

'There was never any dispute about that.'

Isaac could see why Jim, as a youth, hadn't laid the man out until he had been fourteen. Robinson was not tall, barely to Isaac's shoulder, but he was broad, with bulging muscles and a nose bent to one side, a street fighter or a one-time boxer.

'We're investigating a couple of murders.'

'I killed no one. If you're here about Janice, I've heard.'

'How?'

'Not from you.'

'We didn't know where you were.'

'You've found me now. What was so hard before?'

Isaac hadn't an answer. Robinson hadn't been in hiding, and with the name of the suburb from Jim, it had been easy enough to find him. If Homicide hadn't been so busy, and if the father had been regarded as important, it would have been possible to trace him. Even now, he was a person of interest.

111

'I'm here now.'

A uniform stuck his head around the door, nodded over at Isaac.

'Back up?'

'I've been told it's dangerous.'

'It is. The reason I'll be making myself scarce after you've bought me two more pints.'

'The price of friendship?'

'We're not friends, not you and I. Brad's out for a night of fun with some floozy, a good sort is she? And then, Janice is murdered.'

'You seem remarkably well-informed, Mr Robinson.'

'Only people who want money from me call me that. The name's Hector.'

'In that case, Hector, how come you know so much?'

'Smartphone. I like to keep abreast of what my family's up to, not that I see them.'

'You had an altercation with Jim?'

'Fancy word for him flattening me, a blow to the chin, another to the stomach. In Maidstone, so I'm told.'

'I've been to see him. He gets out in a few months.'

'How's his mother, still putting it about?'

'Not that we know of. Besides, we're not investigating the foibles of your family, not unless they're relevant.'

Isaac took a sip of his beer; not a connoisseur, not like Larry, but he knew it to be of the worst quality, the reason the pub could keep the prices low.

'We're not relevant. Janice went bad, but then, that was always going to happen.'

'Because of her mother?'

'She was on the game, not that you'd know it. Back then, when she was young, she was real class, dressed up nice, worked in Mayfair, a posh establishment, influential clientele.'

'She married you.'

'Her selling herself to the toffs didn't last long, and they always want fresh meat, no shortage of supply. Six months in and she's damaged goods.'

'You had no issues with your daughter prostituting herself?'

'I did with the drugs, but if she came to no harm.'

'She did. She's dead, murdered.'

Robinson was a despicable man who cared little for anyone, let alone his family. They hadn't fared well without him, but it would have been worse if he had stayed.

'She was pretty, more than her mother when she was young.'

'According to your son, you would get drunk, start hitting your family.'

'That much is true; I couldn't handle my drink, that's why I'll only have three pints.'

'Your wife accused you of ogling your daughter, but Jim said it wasn't true; that you were fond of her.'

'A good lad, is Jim, not like that hag. My own daughter? What kind of person do you take me for?'

'I don't take you for anything. I deal in facts. It's not for me to judge you or anyone else, only to get the truth. Your daughter is murdered, yet you seem unconcerned.'

'I control it better these days. If I got hold of the person who killed her, I'd be swinging on the end of a rope.'

'Capital punishment was abolished in 1969, the last execution in 1964.'

'I'd still kill the bastard.'

'Any ideas?'

'Not yet.'

'You're looking? What about the men who spent time with your wife, abused Janice?'

'In time.'

'What does that mean?'

'In time, that's what I said. If I find any of those that touched Janice, at the house or that bedsit, they'll know my wrath.'

'Premeditated murder is a life sentence.'

'Not to me. The heart's not so good, steroids when I was a serious bodybuilder. And now they tell me there's cancer.'

'I'd caution you against committing a criminal act.'

'Caution all you want. There's nothing you can do to me.'

Chapter 11

Forensics had taken the box from the cemetery, dried it out, and set up a meeting for eight in the morning. A preliminary report said that it could have been purchased in any hardware store and that it was almost new and had been in the ground for seven to fourteen days.

'It doesn't help,' Larry said, the afterglow of his discovery still resonating in Homicide.

The cemetery employee had given a description of the man who had been seen at plot 15973, and even though it could have been the man in Godstone, the man who had killed the unknown woman, it was inconclusive.

Slowly, the lab technician lifted the lid of the small metal box. Larry craned his neck to look.

'It's an envelope,' the technician said as he removed it with a pair of tweezers. 'No water on it.'

The envelope was placed on his workbench. 'I'll need to check it before we open it,' he said.

'I'll take the responsibility,' Isaac said. 'We need to know the contents.'

'On your head, DCI. There could be fingerprints.'

'They'll be there after you've removed what's inside.'

For now, the contents were all-important.

The letter was laid out on the bench. On it an address.

'What does it mean?' Isaac asked.

'We'll check it out,' Larry said. 'This is too sophisticated for drug smuggling.'

Isaac hoped it wasn't anything to do with the secret service; he'd dealt with them before, and they played dirty. On a previous case, one of the deaths had been an assassination, and he had slept with one of their operatives, only for her to disappear when he started asking questions, then phoning him a year later, wanting to take up where they had left off. He had declined the offer, much as he had liked her initially: too much baggage, too much unknown, too dangerous.

***

Isaac hadn't gained much from Hector Robinson, other than he was a surly individual who didn't like the police. Apart from a run-in with the law in his twenties for stealing a car, and later convictions for various offences, he had kept out of prison, something his son hadn't. His defence for taking the car had been that he was drunk, the keys were in the ignition, and he had thought it was his.

The judge accepted his version of the truth, as the cars were similar. The arresting officer's view when he gave evidence was that the man hadn't been all that drunk, just tipsy, and that his car was in the garage at home, and it was a different make, only the colour was the same.

It had been put forward by the prosecution that the Robinsons lived a hand-to-mouth existence. With the arrival of a child in the house, Jim, Gladys Robinson wasn't working, and Hector, the sole breadwinner, was labouring, and had been unable to explain how he could afford a two-year-old four-door saloon car in good condition – his story of a win on the horses wasn't believed.

Robinson had walked free, jumped into his car parked down a side street not far from the court, seen the parking ticket, cursed loudly, and headed off to the pub to celebrate.

Six pints later, as he drove home, a breathalyser, and his driving licence cancelled for one year.

The story had been told to Isaac by Bill Ross, the inspector at Canning Town. How he came to know about it, Isaac didn't know, but then, that was Ross's style, a man who knew the street as well as Larry Hill.

It was Ross on the phone. 'You better get over here,' he said. 'It's Hector Robinson; he's dead.'

Isaac had been preparing to join Larry and an armed response team on their visit to the address found in the box.

In Canning Town, two blocks from where Isaac had met Robinson in the pub, a body was slumped up against the old wooden gate of a derelict factory.

'No one took any notice,' Ross said. The two police officers hadn't met for over a year, not since Isaac had married Jenny, and the man had changed. Before, strapping with a bright red complexion, a cheery disposition, a beer gut. Isaac did not comment on the man he met: bags under his bloodshot eyes, and the belly, once so prominent, replaced by empty space. Bill Ross looked ill to him.

'They would have thought he was homeless.' Isaac said.

'Or drunk. Your pub has plenty of them of a night.'

It wasn't his pub, but Isaac said nothing in response.

'Staffing levels, that's why we don't get down here as much as we should. Up in the town, the hoodies are stealing whatever they can, uneducated most of them, condemned to the street, and then there are the fundamentalists who control half of Canning, and if a woman walks through with bare flesh exposed she gets verbal abuse, a cane around the legs.'

'Not your cup of tea?'

'Nor yours.'

'We don't have the problem,' Isaac said. He didn't want to get into a political or religious debate with Bill Ross, a no-win situation. He was more interested in the slumped body of the man he had met the previous day.

'What's the situation?' Isaac said.

The area around the gate smelled of urine, the patrons at the pub unable to wait for somewhere better or not caring either way; the latter the more likely.

'If anyone saw him last night or this morning, no one contacted us. Not that we'd expect them to. Mind your own business is the best policy; I'd adopt it myself if I lived here. Thankful that I don't, a three-bedroom house ten miles away. No idea why I don't get a transfer.'

'How did you find out?'

'A routine drive through the area by a patrol car, to check the pub and any lingerers. Robinson's not the first body down here, and there's often fights, a knife used more often than not.

'Anyway, they were down here at nine this morning, the safest time of the day. The drunks are sleeping it off; the fundamentalists, hooligans from what I can see, are at prayer or whatever they do.'

Bill Ross was prejudiced, Isaac had known that for a long time. It wasn't a healthy attitude for a police officer to openly display.

'Time of death?'

'According to the publican, he reckoned that Robinson left the pub fifteen minutes after you; before the heavy drinkers arrived and started causing chaos.'

'Cause of death?'

'Knife, none too subtle. The upper arm, lower torso, close to the heart, and his throat's been cut. I'd say the throat was cut after death, but I can't be sure. The CSIs will know better than me, and the pathologist will give you an A to Z, words you would barely understand.'

'It's your case, not mine. Motive?'

'He had a place not far away, a dive, cheap even for around here.'

'Bill, I need to know facts, not an opinion of the man's living arrangements.'

'It could be random, but it was early in the night. The worst of them wait for later before venturing out.'

'My visit?'

'It's the angle I would take, the most logical. I'll need an update from you.'

'I'll send you a report. That'll show you what we're investigating.'

'Something to go on. It could have been you instead of Robinson if I hadn't got a car down there to look after you.'

Isaac shuddered; Ross was right. If Robinson's death was tied in to his daughter and the Jane Doe, which looked increasingly likely, then those who were killing weren't the sort of people to draw the line at a police officer.

'Robinson's daughter was murdered, not sure why, although she was operating out of a bedsit,' Isaac said.

'Prostitute?'

'Correct.'

'Most of them around here are from the Caribbean, others from China or Vietnam, a few Thais.'

'Voluntary?'

'Those from the Caribbean are, not sure about the others. We do what we can; send a few back to where they came from, but they reappear with increasing regularity. One woman's been deported two times but ends up back in one brothel or another. It's hard to imagine why.'

Isaac thought the man should get out and about, see the rest of the world; come to realise that Canning Town was better than where the women had lived before, and they had been fed the dream, seen the movies, believed it was milk and honey, not sour and definitely not sweet.

'Janice Robinson is murdered, but there's a twist to the case, not sure what it all means yet.'

'You'll figure it out.'

'Janice's brother, before her death, witnessed a murder or nearly did. He briefly saw the murderer, as did his girlfriend.'

'Related?'

'It appears to be. But the Robinsons are not major players, nothing really.'

'Not sorely missed.'

'They've not made their mark.'

'Sometimes, people die due to association, never knowing the reason.'

'That's why we think it might be professional.'

'Whoever killed Hector Robinson wasn't.'

'Or doesn't want it to look as if it was.'

'Leave Robinson to us. I'll keep you updated and don't start driving down any back streets, not around here, and don't go visiting pubs, nor start asking questions.'

'Bill, it's all yours; you're welcome to it,' Isaac said.

***

Larry was waiting at Challis Street for Isaac to return; the address found in the box was under surveillance.

The armed response team thought it was an overreaction from Homicide, but they were ready to play their part, and they knew DCI Cook from other investigations.

The raid was to go ahead, although delayed by twenty-five minutes as Isaac had an onerous duty to perform first. Wendy removed Brad Robinson from school and took him to Compton Road.

At the house, on Isaac's arrival, Gladys Robinson, Brad and Rose.

Isaac looked over at Wendy on seeing the young Winston; Wendy lifting her eyes to indicate that the two couldn't be separated.

'Ask Rose's mother to come over here,' Isaac said.

'What is it, Chief Inspector?' Brad asked.

'I'm afraid your father has died.'

'He died a long time ago when he left us,' Gladys said.

The reaction of the mother wasn't unexpected. Rose went and put her arms around Brad's mother.

'That's alright, dear. Nothing lost, not to us.'

'How?' Brad asked.

'He was killed in Canning Town. We don't know who or why.'

'Was he living there?'

'I met with him yesterday. Jim had known about Canning Town.'

'Is this to do with the woman in the cemetery?' Rose asked.

'We have no proof, no reason to think it should be. Canning Town has a bad reputation. It could have just been a gang after his phone or his wallet.'

Isaac had wanted to discount the more obscure theories, but events were moving fast. And if they killed a woman selling herself, a father doing it tough, then no one was safe, not even the young Rose or her boyfriend, not even their parents, not even the police.

'I've got to go,' Isaac said as he stood up. 'Wendy, stay here, phone Inspector Bill Ross, arrange for Mrs Robinson to identify her husband.'

'I'll not do it, not after what he did to Janice.'

Paranoia on the woman's part, Isaac was sure.

'Very well. Wendy, get the details from Bridget, contact Maidstone Prison. Jim can do the necessary.'

'I can do it,' Brad said.

'I'm sure you could,' Wendy said, 'but you were only young when he left. It would be better if your brother identified him.'

'I still want to see my father.'

'That can be arranged,' Isaac said before he left in a hurry. He should have stayed longer, but time was of the essence, and those entering the mysterious house were ready and waiting.

***

Wendy would stay with the Robinsons, smooth the inevitable from the Winstons, ensure that security was upgraded for both families – safe houses if Chief

Superintendent Goddard would approve, which he probably wouldn't, not yet.

Isaac looked over at the imposing house hidden behind a high wall, the best part of Holland Park. Whoever they were, they had money and good taste. A police helicopter had flown over the building at sufficient height not to raise suspicion, low enough to suss out the detail. Larry remarked after he had seen the images that Google Streetview would have revealed as much for less cost. However, it wouldn't have shown two vehicles at the rear of the property; one of them a Bentley, the other a white people carrier, suitable for twelve.

The armed response team waited, poised to act, binoculars trained on the windows of the house. Isaac preferred a softly-softly approach, a knock at the door, await a response.

The inspector in charge of armed response wasn't so keen on the idea, but he had to concede. After all, it was Homicide's show, not that they could tell him much about why they were there; some conspiracy, things that go bump in the night, three deaths, apparently unconnected but probably were.

On the hour, watches synchronised, one of the armed response team, bullet-proof jacket fastened, helmet on, opened the garden gate. Even though it was locked, he had seen an exit button on the other side, four feet in. An extended rod that he carried soon dealt with it.

Inside, the armed men fanned out, some taking crouching positions, others standing behind trees. In the house, nothing changed. A light upstairs, a flickering shadow.

The front door was reached, the bell rung, an anxious pause. The bell in the house would be allowed to sound twice before the team would knock the door aside.

It wasn't standard procedure, not when there had been no proof of weapons inside the house or criminal activity, but Homicide had used influence to get their compliance.

A sound in the house, the door opening, a petite Asian woman in her twenties.

'All clear,' from the armed response team.

Isaac walked up to the front door, showed his warrant card to the woman who opened the door fully. 'Follow me,' she said.

Alarm bells rang in Isaac's mind, although so far nothing seemed out of the ordinary.

Larry slipped past armed response who were maintaining a standby position, their weapons at their sides.

Isaac followed the woman, saw Larry looking around and into the rooms on each side of the hallway, a winding staircase heading up, the sound of music.

At the rear of the house, a man sat looking out at the garden.

'Chief Inspector Isaac Cook,' Isaac said.

The man was tall and slim. In his late forties or early fifties, he had an air of breeding. 'Ian Naughton,' he said, his accent English, as he shook Isaac's hand vigorously. 'And to what do I owe this pleasure?'

'We're surprised to find you at home,' Isaac said.

'A man's home is his castle, haven't you heard? That's a mess you made outside. I hope the police force has the funds to clean it up.'

Isaac doubted if they did, but that wasn't the point. No adverse reaction from Naughton.

The man was smooth, but that was what Larry had been told in Godstone. Isaac was sure the two men were one and the same.

'Your colleague may as well come in here. If it's a guided tour you want, I'd be happy to oblige.'

'A few questions answered would be preferable.'

The young lady at the door came in with Larry. He received the same cordial welcome, asked to sit down, have a drink.

'Analyn, our housemaid, looks after the children,' Naughton said as Isaac watched the woman walk out of the door. 'Legal. I have all the papers.'

One of the questions Isaac would have wanted to ask, but would not at the present time, was whether Analyn had the papers or Naughton did and if the woman was free to leave if she wanted to.

'We found your address in a box buried in a cemetery in Kensal Green,' Larry said. 'Does that come as a surprise?'

'Why would someone do that? It makes no sense to me.'

It did to Isaac; he'd met men similar to Naughton before, men who maintained a distance, financing crime, creaming the profits off the top, never sullying themselves with the sordid details.

'Three deaths so far; all interconnected, all pointing to this house,' Isaac said.

'I don't see how. It's only my wife and myself. The children are not here at present, on holidays.'

'Analyn?'

'She's been with us for over a year. Comes and goes as she pleases.'

'Mr Naughton, we can't ignore the address in the box,' Isaac said.

'I'm afraid you must. As you can see, there is nothing of interest here, just myself and Analyn in the house at present.'

125

'Your wife?'

'Tomorrow. A trip to Paris with friends, Eurostar. You should try it if you haven't already.'

'We checked the house before we came here, never found a mention of your name.'

'You won't. My business and personal interests are structured on advice from my financial advisor and my legal team. Now, if you don't mind, I would appreciate it if you leave.'

'What is your occupation, Mr Naughton?' Isaac asked. 'Where does the money come from to afford this house?'

'Independent means. And next time you intend to make an unscheduled visit, don't.'

'We weren't sure you were here.'

'And that, Chief Inspector, is a lie. That address you found, not that I can explain it any more than you can, caused you to believe that this house was a den of iniquity, a house of low repute, a drug baron's hideout. Am I correct?'

Isaac saw no reason to lie, not to a master criminal; that was indeed what he thought the man was. 'It was either drugs or women destined for brothels.'

'Instead of a family home.'

'As you say,' Isaac said as he and Larry retreated from the house. The enthusiastic handshake on arrival was not repeated on their departure.

Chapter 12

Bill Ross phoned Isaac two days later, told him to get over to Canning Town Police Station.

Larry went with Isaac. The last resort police station, he had heard it referred to, where the least ambitious, the most ruthless and politically-incorrect police officers wound up. To him, it was his sort of place; a place where true policing could be done, instead of the fussing and fretting, the constant concerns over his drinking and his bad habits.

Bill Ross, Larry could see, had maintained some dignity, but the duty sergeant when he and Isaac entered the hallowed sanctum of the station had taken one look at them, looked at their warrant cards, looked down at DCI Isaac Cook. 'I've heard of you,' he said, not recognising Isaac's seniority, only seeing his colour.

Racism, religious bigotry and poor education weren't only out on the street; they were alive and well in the police station.

In Canning Town, a depressed mood pervaded, so sharp it could almost be sliced with a knife. Outside the station: graffiti everywhere, a lone man walking down the street, two women pushing prams, covered from head to toe in black.

England to him was fish and chips, a pint of beer, each to their own, mind your own business.

Yes, Larry thought, Canning Town was somewhere he could make a difference, not in Notting Hill or Bayswater or Holland Park, and even the gangs up there were becoming gentrified with their illicitly-gained affluence, now put into honest pursuits.

'Inspector Ross,' Isaac said.

'He'll be out in a minute,' the sergeant said.

Canning Town Police Station was equipped for twice the number of police officers, but few wanted to be there, and coercion was oft used; postings for the most miserable and disreputable, those who did no credit to the Met.

Bill Ross burst through the door behind the duty sergeant. 'A result,' he said, 'and you must be Larry Hill,' warmly grabbing Larry's hand and shaking it. 'A low-life, out back in the interview room. You'll want to see him, no doubt.'

'Certainly,' Isaac said. 'A confession?'

'Sometimes it's as easy as picking fruit off a tree,' Ross said. 'We pulled him in last night for public drunkenness, not sure why we do, as they claim a deprived childhood, discrimination, no money, and so on.'

'Then why?' Larry asked.

'We need to maintain our quota. The superintendent, he's a stickler for performance, after us every other day.'

'We've got one of our own,' Larry said.

Enough of the banter, Isaac thought. Time to see what Bill Ross had.

In the interview room, a youth of nineteen, in a hooded jacket with the hood pushed back.

'Your name?' Ross said. Isaac sat to one side of him; Larry was outside.

'You know it. I told you before,' the youth said. He was of Caribbean descent, probably Jamaican, born in England.

Legal aid had been provided. Across from Isaac, an Asian woman dressed in neat and tidy blue jacket and trousers. She looked competent.

'It's important that you answer,' the woman said.

'My friends call me Wazza.'

'It's a game they play,' Ross said, looking over at Isaac. 'Thinks it makes them look big, coming in here and wasting our time. A badge of honour, us asking them questions, the magistrate letting them off. Street cred, the only qualifications they are likely to ever have.'

Isaac could sympathise with Bill Ross, and it was true, the young man was part of a legion of unemployed, straight out of school, no chance of a job, onto the street and surviving the only way they knew. It was a failing of the government, he knew, the government that had condemned his parents to purgatory and slum landlords when they had arrived in the country before he had been born. Back then, there had been racial prejudice, and although he rarely experienced it, he knew that in Canning Town he still would.

Nothing changes. The underdog would always be there, as would crime and prejudice. The young man with the contemptuous attitude was the result of a system that had let him down, a democratic belief in equality, a fair go for all, that had gone wrong.

'Warren Preston,' the youth said.

'Mr Preston, thank you. You were in the cell cooling off after a night of drinking. Not like your people to drink, more often it's ganja or ecstasy.'

'It was my birthday. The boys took me to the pub.'

'The boys range from fifteen up to twenty-three,' Ross said, looking over at Isaac once again.

'Not older?'

'A few will end up in prison; some will die at the hands of another gang, or kill themselves with drugs. One even froze to death last winter when we had that cold snap.'

'Is this relevant?' the legal aid said.

'I'm just setting the scene for DCI Cook. He's not from around here; He operates out of Challis Street, up near Notting Hill, more your part of the world.'

'Where I live is not relevant, my client is.' A sharp rebuttal. The woman was all business, Isaac could see. No doubt efficient, almost certainly believed that Preston was of little worth, but she'd do her job.

'All of you, ganging up on me. What chance do I have?' Preston grabbed hold of his corner of the metal table, attempted to lift it in an act of defiance.

'It's bolted to the floor,' Ross said. 'You're wasting your time. Now, why don't you just sit there and tell your lawyer what you said to me last night? After you've done that we can take your statement, have you up before the magistrate and then find you a cosy cell in prison until your trial comes up.'

'I don't remember.'

'If this is badgering my client, I can't allow it,' the legal aid said.

Bill Ross took no notice. It wasn't Challis Street, and he was pushing hard, probably too hard, running the risk of a confession given under duress by a man who, if not illiterate, was clearly unable to understand the seriousness of the position he was in. Isaac had used the technique before, but he had had some evidence behind him; he hoped Ross did.

'When you were hauled into the station, and I asked you about a man being knifed down near the Durham Arms, you told me that you knew about it.'

'So what, everyone knows what goes on, and why worry? One of us dies, and you don't care. And you, the black man, are you on his side?' Preston said, looking over at Isaac.

'I'm on the side of law and justice. The only problem in this room is you. I was with the dead man not long before he was killed. It could have been me; the question is should it have been, was it me they wanted?'

'If I talk, what are you going to do?'

'Are you willing to drop charges against my client if he cooperates?' the lawyer said.

'He's here for public drunkenness. I'm willing to consider it.'

'That's a yes,' the lawyer said, looking at her client.

'Okay. It was the night he died. There was six of us. A man approached us.'

'Describe him?' Isaac said.

'White, dressed like you.'

'Well-spoken, educated? He should have been frightened. Why wasn't he?'

'He handed each of us a hundred-pound note, said there was more if we cooperated.'

'Did you?'

'Not me, but some of the others did.'

'Which ones?'

'I'll not grass, not on the gang.'

'Loyalty or fear?'

'I don't want to end up the same as that man, a knife in my gut, my balls stuffed in my mouth.'

'He was knifed, not castrated.'

'He wasn't a member of our gang.'

'Tell the police what they want, and we can get out of here,' the lawyer said. 'It's getting late, and I have other clients to deal with.'

'Canning Town?' Isaac said.

'Everyone has the right to justice, to legal representation, or don't you believe in that?'

Isaac did, so did the lawyer, but she had no intention of remaining in the area any longer than necessary. She'd do what was required, but no more.

'He said five hundred pounds to anyone who did what he wanted, no questions asked.'

'Who agreed?'

'I can't remember.'

He was putty in Bill Ross's hands. Warren Preston could have kept quiet, fronted the magistrate, received a fine, probably not paid it, but he wasn't smart enough to realise that. His legal aid lawyer wasn't about to interrupt him either. He was small fry, not worth more than a modest stipend to her. She would have more prestigious clients, those that would make it worth her time.

'What did he want?' Isaac asked.

'He said for us to check you out in the pub.'

'Which you did?'

'I didn't; they did. I wasn't involved.'

'Did you see anyone?' Ross asked Isaac.

'I wasn't looking, but someone could have looked in the window.'

'We had a patrol car there.'

'It was before that,' Preston said.

'Did he say why?'

'Not to me. Not that I cared, I wasn't going to kill anyone.'

'Because you couldn't?'

'Preston's killed, another gang's member, not that we'll ever prove it,' Ross said to Isaac.

'Is that it?' Isaac said. 'Mr Preston, you've killed?'

'My client will not answer that question. Now, if you don't mind, I suggest we wrap this up, let my client leave.'

'Not so fast,' Ross said.

'He said he wanted the old man killed; to make it look as though it was a robbery,' Preston said. 'We weren't asking questions, not with that amount.'

'Why didn't you just take it from him?'

'There was a car nearby, a man inside. He had a gun, one of those that fires lots of bullets, real expensive.'

'Pointed at you?'

'At all of us.'

'The car, describe it?'

'A BMW, dark blue.'

'Registration number?'

'I wasn't looking, nobody was.'

Larry, listening from the other room, took out his phone and called the police in Godstone.

'Describe the man with the money, the other one in the car.'

'It was dark; we only saw the gun. The other man, he wore a hat, the collar on his coat turned up.'

Ross turned to Isaac. 'You've got twenty-four hours, forty-eight at a push. We'll be holding Mr Preston here until then.'

'The charge?' the lawyer asked. Her coat was across her lap, her handbag on the table, the case file closed. She was going, regardless.

'Mr Preston will be held on suspicion of murder. You may wish to believe him, but I don't, nor does DCI Cook. It's not the first time that Mr Preston and I have crossed swords. It might be the last.'

***

It wasn't possible to provide security to the level required to ensure the safety of the Robinsons and the Winstons, not that Tim Winston hadn't been insistent, furious as he had been about Rose being at the Robinsons' house again.

The front room of the Winstons' house. On one side of the room, Tim and Maeve Winston, on the other, sitting on a hard chair, Wendy. Rose maintained a neutral position, a book resting in her lap, pretending not to be involved, but she was.

Jim Robinson was going to identify his father the next day, and Brad would be taking the morning off school to accompany him.

Tim Winston was not interested in the Robinsons, only his family, a natural reaction, and so far Wendy hadn't told him about the detention of an individual in Canning Town.

No longer regarded as a robbery or a random killing, Hector Robinson's death had all the hallmarks of an assassination.

Nobody at Challis Street could make any sense of it. It was illogical why a criminal organisation would remain secret, yet focus attention on themselves through a concerted attempt to eliminate anybody who was somehow associated with the murder in the cemetery.

Rose and Brad had only seen the body, had a brief glance at the murderer, and Hector Robinson had not been involved at all, nor had Janice Robinson. It was a modus operandi that Homicide couldn't make sense of.

'Who next?' Tim Winston said. Wendy was on her own, Larry and Isaac on their way back from Canning Town, and besides, she didn't need assistance to talk to the family, only had something to tell them.

'We have no reason to believe that you or your family is under threat,' Wendy said. It was the official line for her to take, but she didn't believe it.

Winston sat close to his wife, holding hands; Maeve listening to all that was said but saying little. It was clear she did not know yet of her philandering husband and the weekly meetings that he had enjoyed with Janice Robinson.

It was bound to come out eventually, and Wendy was curious to see the reaction, to see if Maeve Winston was as placid as she seemed, as forgiving and loving of her husband as Gladys Robinson had suggested.

'Brad's father? Random or something else?' Winston asked.

'It's under investigation. A local youth, a member of a gang, has been detained.'

'That's not the question.'

'It's all I can tell you at this time.' All that Wendy was willing to say. If it was an assassination, elimination of those close to the murder in the cemetery, then doubling the police presence at both houses, ensuring that patrol cars circled the area every hour on the hour, wasn't going to achieve much.

Wendy wanted to believe that Rose was safe, that they wouldn't harm her, but she knew that was wishful thinking.

Was it, as she had read about overseas, a breakdown in government and policing, anarchy rearing its head, as in Northern Mexico, parts of South America, America during prohibition; criminal organisations taking over the role of government, installing their own people.

It was a frightening thought. Society was becoming fragmented, with ghettos springing up throughout London and the other major cities. Violence

135

was on the rise, the court system was under strain. Was Warren Preston to go free?

The young man with no hope of a future, perpetually unemployed, not even looking for a job, just his dole payment and what he could steal or scrounge or trade: what of him and the thousands like him? Even in the area of Challis Street Police Station, there were other 'Warren Prestons', disenfranchised, looking for something, not knowing what, causing trouble.

'Do we keep Rose at home?'

'I suggest you continue as before,' Wendy said. She had no more to say; nothing that would help. The police were as powerless as the Winstons; it was in the hands of Homicide. It wasn't a comforting thought.

Chapter 13

It was, as Chief Superintendent Goddard said, a complete stuff up. The man was livid, and his DCI, Isaac Cook, was on the receiving end of the man's blunt assessment.

'Not only do you have an armed response team out to a house in Holland Park, I've had Commissioner Davies on the phone, asking me to front in the morning with a written report and an explanation about what's going on and what I'm going to do about it.'

It was the angriest that Isaac had seen his senior. As the SIO in Homicide, he had to take the blame. The investigation had been conducted correctly by the team, and they had put in the hours, filed the reports, but had always been one step behind.

'I stand by my team,' Isaac said. He could see a long night ahead of him. It was Jenny's birthday. She would be disappointed that the planned celebration would have to be curtailed. He felt bad about it, but there was no way he could substitute, not tonight.

Even if Larry had been up to it, which he wasn't, not when the commissioner was involved, he was in Godstone, meeting with the local police, trying to understand how a BMW that had sat in a garage for weeks had mysteriously disappeared.

'We had no reason to impound it,' the sergeant had said. 'No reason at all. As far as the estate agent was concerned, the payments on the house were up to date, the outside had been maintained. If the people, God knows why, wanted to leave it empty, that's their business, not ours. No law broken, no action from us.'

'You were keeping a watch. Didn't you see it was missing?'

'We kept a watch on the house. The agreement was, if I remember correctly, to phone you if we saw someone, to talk to them, find out a phone number.'

They were right, Larry reluctantly agreed. The address belonged to a woman who had purchased sandals at the shop. It didn't mean that she was dead, or that Ian Naughton was the man in the village and in Holland Park.

Larry spoke to the waitress in the coffee shop that he had frequented on past visits to the village, ordered a latte and a croissant.

'It's official,' he said. 'If you've got a minute.'

'There was someone there two days ago,' she said after she had given him his order.'

'Are you able to give me a description, and why didn't you phone me?'

'Forgot, I suppose. Or we could have been busy.'

Or didn't want to get involved, more likely, Larry thought. He'd keep his opinion to himself on the waitress, a pleasant woman, carrying more weight on her hips than she should and a bright red lipstick that didn't suit her. Apart from that she was Godstone born and bred, had never travelled, and regarded London as somewhere for Christmas shopping and the New Year sales.

'Was it the man and the woman that you saw?'

'I can't say I got a good look. It was a woman, Asian, I think.'

'Think or know?'

'Short, slim, straight jet-black hair. I wasn't close, and she never came in here. All I saw was the garage door open, the car reversing out, and then she closed the garage and drove off. Not there for more than a few minutes.'

'Asian? Certain?'

'I believe so. Does it help?'

'It does.'

***

Isaac, Larry, Wendy, and Bridget worked late into the night, going through the case so far. They had to provide a concise report for Chief Superintendent Goddard.

'Save his bacon,' Larry had jested, the one attempt at humour that night.

Isaac, who had more experience of Commissioner Davies than the others in the department, knew that their boss was going to have an uphill battle with the commissioner. The man was a no-holds-barred police officer who had earned his stripes in Wales, played the politics well, ingratiating wherever, adopting a Machiavellian approach to those who threatened him.

Goddard was an adroit political animal, but he still played fair most of the time; Davies had no time for such subtleties. The man would use the current case to unseat Goddard, to bring in the unpleasant and obsequious Seth Caddick.

Re-examination of the case had confirmed that the house in Holland Park was significant and that Ian Naughton was not an innocent bystander, and, as Larry had determined in Godstone, the description of the petite Asian woman pointed to Analyn, the woman who had opened the door in Holland Park.

Two in the morning, the report was ready. Isaac, not willing to leave anything to chance, phoned Goddard.

'What is it?' Goddard said on answering the phone. Isaac had known that he wouldn't be annoyed. He was still a friend.

'You're not going to like it,' Isaac said. Homicide was quiet, the other three had left the office.

'I'm not going to like a dressing down from Davies either. What have you got?'

'The BMW in Canning Town and Godstone are one and the same.'

'Proven?'

'Ninety per cent. We'll be checking CCTV cameras out in Canning, the ones that still work. We have the registration of the BMW in Godstone. If we get a match, then we're one step ahead.'

'Ahead or on the first rung?'

'The BMW was picked up in Godstone by an Asian woman; matches the description of the woman in Holland Park.'

'Matches or you're thinking it does?'

'There's a correlation, something we need to check further.'

'While Davies is slowing you down by wasting your time producing reports, attempting to keep me out of the dog house.'

'I think you're already there, sir,' Isaac said.

'And so are you. It's a tough case, and I appreciate that you and your people are doing your best, but we've no results, only deaths. More to come?'

'We can't protect everyone, not even us.'

'Davies doesn't understand, up in his ivory tower.'

'We need to revisit Holland Park,' Isaac said. He looked up at the clock, saw that it was 2.23 a.m. Jenny would wake when he arrived home, whatever time it was. He had a duty to the murder investigation; a duty to her.

Sometimes it wasn't easy to know which was more important.

'Armed response?'

'Will you authorise it?'

'Phone them, get hold of their inspector, take a couple of men, not the full squad, too expensive, and an overkill.'

'It's not,' Isaac said. 'I was targeted in Canning Town.'

'Don't tell your wife; she'll freak out.'

Isaac had never had any intention of doing that. He went and made a cup of tea, sat down, put his feet on the table, attempted to ease the tension in his body. It was stress, and it was unhealthy.

The next Isaac knew it was 3.56. He had slept for over ninety minutes. Slipping on his jacket and grabbing his keys, he headed for the door; Jenny would be worried.

***

The revisit to Holland Park proved to be an anti-climax. Larry had expected more, but on arrival at the house, it was soon apparent that the place had been vacated.

After what seemed longer, but was documented as two minutes thirty seconds, one of the armed response officers gave the all-clear.

Larry looked around. Nothing had changed. There was food in the fridge, a good stock of quality wine, and the television was switched on.

'How long since they left?' one of the armed response team asked.

'Long enough,' Larry's response.

Ian Naughton and Analyn were gone. Upstairs no clothes remained, only a toothbrush in one of the bedrooms, a solitary earring on the floor.

Gordon Windsor was alerted; his team of CSIs would check out the place, find out if there was anything to give a clue as to who the two people were.

Forty-eight hours after he had been held over, Warren Preston walked out of the front door of the Canning Town Police Station, raising two fingers at Ross, then thrusting his arm with a clenched fist up at an angle to make a statement: up yours, copper, it said.

Bill Ross hadn't reacted. He was used to it by now.

***

The Durham Arms was quiet, its licence temporarily revoked, although a few more days and the place would be back to normal. Bill Ross wasn't sure how, but he suspected that money, bribe money, was being handed around. The pub was a goldmine located in the centre of a garbage dump. He rarely visited it, but he had to admit to doing so once or twice when he had been transferred to Canning Town after he had roughed up a couple of suspects who had broken into an off-licence, helped themselves to a few cartons of beer, two dozen bottles of cheap wine.

Idiots, he had called them, plus a few more words that he shouldn't have. Out on the street, the language was often crude and insensitive, but a police officer was meant to keep his cool, not to offend a criminal, not to subject him to a fist in the stomach, nor a smack in the mouth. How was he to know that one of the two thieves was the son of a local councillor, high on crack cocaine.

The Winstons and the Robinsons bonded more closely, although Tim Winston wouldn't let Brad over to his house, nor Rose over to his.

Inevitably, the police presence at the school relaxed, and the two youngsters found more than enough places to get some time to themselves.

Nobody in Homicide believed it was over, and still they had not identified the Jane Doe, nor why she had died. The initial suspicion that Naughton and cohorts had been involved in drug importation and distribution had been put to one side. The sighting of Analyn had raised the spectre of sophisticated illegal transportation of women to brothels in England, but no proof had been found.

To Isaac, it seemed more sinister. And now, Jenny and their unborn child. It was starting to show, and he was worried for them as well; worried for everyone, but powerless to do any more.

Whatever the future held, it appeared that it would be Naughton, if he were the main person, to make the running. Which meant only one thing: another death.

The only positive was the BMW.

Warton Road, less than two miles from the Durham Arms, a patch of wasteland used as an unofficial car park, a refuse tip by others.

Larry took one look at the burnt-out but still smouldering shell. 'It's the car,' he said to Bill Ross and Wendy who had accompanied him.

'No one inside?' Wendy asked.

'If there were, there wouldn't be much left, not now.'

'Anything to be gained?' Larry asked Gordon Windsor when he arrived at the scene.

'We'll check it out, then put it on a flatbed truck, get Forensics to have a look. They might find something, but don't expect much.'

***

Holland Park had been canvassed, questions asked on the street outside Naughton's house. The owner, the name given almost certainly false, due to a complex purchasing route through an overseas trust five years previously, had not been found.

'We never met the person,' Agnes Hepplesworth said in the comfort of her plush office in Mayfair.

'There are still money laundering checks that need to be dealt with if it's cash,' Isaac said.

Hepplesworth and Daughter, Solicitors, was a family concern, three generations, Agnes was the first. Seventy-five at least, a pinched face, heavily lined with wrinkles, no makeup, dressed conservatively although expensively.

A hard woman, Wendy thought.

'All the necessary requirements were dealt with. As you must understand, there is confidentiality that I need to consider.'

Isaac had to concede the woman had a point.

'Have you any knowledge of an Ian Naughton?'

'The name means nothing to me. Let's be clear here, Chief Inspector, the aspersion that my client is somehow involved in – what was it?'

'Murder, three so far.'

Isaac had stated the reason for the visit on arrival and he felt the woman was being evasive, not a good sign.

'Murder, yes, I understand. However, my client is not involved. How could he be if he's not in the country.'

'Client? Male? Overseas?'

'My apologies if I've confused you,' Agnes Hepplesworth said. 'I've never met the person or spoken to him on the phone. I assume that it is a man, but it could be a woman.'

'You must have a signature on the documents?'

'A complex purchase, the name on the documents is not Ian Naughton, nor is it necessarily the person you met at the house.'

Agnes Hepplesworth had been obstructionist. Whether she had acted professionally or if it indicated an ulterior motive, he wasn't sure. After the episode with Naughton, he wasn't trusting anyone.

***

Larry spent time out in Canning Town, not that the area offered any more opportunity than Challis Street and its surrounding area. But it had been the only place, apart from Holland Park, and possibly Godstone, where one of the perpetrators had been seen.

Warren Preston hadn't been able to tell them much, other than it was two men, but even that was flawed. Why trust a man's death to a gang of poorly educated and unreliable black youths? It was a question that Bill Ross pondered.

The two police officers were enjoying a curry on Barking Road; one of the only advantages of working in the area was great foods, Ross had said. Larry couldn't disagree with him, and he intended to take advantage.

Wendy was with the two families, Isaac was in the office, and Bridget was dealing with the paperwork, attempting to get the recalcitrant Agnes Hepplesworth to open up about what she knew.

145

Checks had been made on the woman; it appeared that her company specialised in purchasers from overseas. No complaints against the solicitors, but no checking of their records had ever been carried out, although Isaac was keen for one to be done.

'Can't be done,' Fraud Squad had told him. 'Not without something solid to go on.'

Larry finished his curry, drank his tea; usually a curry deserved a pint of beer to wash it down, but not today.

Ross answered his phone; a meeting had been arranged with Preston's gang.

'Preston's not the smartest,' Ross said as the two men stood outside the restaurant, a cigarette in his hand, a look of longing from Larry. So far, he had kept his alcohol consumption under control and had given up smoking. Too much friction at home and at Challis Street had made the decision for him, but out at Canning Town, a more liberal attitude prevailed, with a superintendent who wasn't always politically correct, having said what he thought of the hoodies to Ross and Larry, and not succinctly.

Two blocks from the Durham Arms, an old Toyota. Inside the vehicle, two hoodies. Both were the same colour as Preston, the same chip on the shoulder, the same speech patterns.

'You're asking questions,' one of them said. Ross knew him to be the second-in-command. A hierarchy existed, and the smaller of the two was the person in charge.

'Are you part of the gang?' Ross said. He wasn't comfortable with where the four of them stood, the reason he had phoned for a patrol car to drive past the end of the road every five minutes.

'Dangerous, knife you as soon as look at you,' Ross had said back at his station. The black gangs that Larry knew well in Notting Hill were mild compared to those standing in front of them. The leader of the two, softly spoken, a scar across his left cheek, a tattoo barely visible on his neck, looked ruthless.

His real name, not that he'd use it, was Waylon Conroy, a local born Jamaican, more intelligent than most, capable of better, but life on the edge suited him.

Bill Ross knew it for what it was: a lost generation. And as for Conroy, a couple of GCSEs, a chance of further education, a possibility of going to university, but the youth was generationally destined for a life of crime.

'You wanted to talk to us,' Conroy said.

'Where's the Mercedes?' Ross said.

It seemed to Larry that Waylon Conroy and Bill Ross were acquainted; as he was with their counterparts over near Challis Street.

'Safe, under lock and key. Too many villains around here.'

'We're not here to bother you,' Larry said. 'It's the information that we want.'

'Who's he?' Conroy said. 'New around here?'

'He can be trusted,' Ross said.

'You were interested in the two men.'

'Help us; we'll help you.'

'Trust a copper? Why should we? We didn't kill anyone. The one in the car, not that we could see that much, wore a fancy watch on his left wrist.'

'Make?'

'Gold; it glinted in the light from a street light down the street. Expensive, probably a Rolex, but I can't be sure.'

147

'Any more? The weapon?'

'Can't help you there. Not English, not purchased locally.'

The patrol car passed the end of the road. Conroy looked around. 'You're safe with us,' he said.

'You can't blame us for taking precautions,' Larry said.

Ross lit up a cigarette, offered the packet around.

'I can sell you better, half price,' Conroy said.

'The two men,' Larry said.

'We didn't kill the old man, regardless of what you think. Nothing to be gained.'

'Where is Warren Preston?'

'Around.'

Ross nudged Larry. Both men knew that the gangs were extremely sensitive, liable to act adversely if questioned too closely.

'Are you trying to tell us that you didn't kill Robinson?' Ross said.

'Sure, we took the money. We're not fools, are we?'

'I'm not so sure about the others in your gang.'

'Warren Preston's the stupidest of all.'

'You took the money, did nothing, and made yourself scarce.'

'Wazza, he's vanished.'

'If you didn't do it, then who did?'

'I reckon those in the car did it when they realised they'd been duped. Candy from a baby, that easy it was.'

'The man who gave you the money. Describe him?'

'Posh, looked as though he came from money.'

'Look? How can you tell that?' Larry asked.

'The same way you do. The way he stood, his speech, the manicured nails, the Breitling watch, not a fifty-pound fake with a Seiko inside.'

'I hope they don't find you,' Ross said. 'You wouldn't stand a chance.'

'Around here? We're invincible,' Conroy said as he got back into the car.

The patrol car passed again. Larry and Ross settled back into their vehicle.

'I could do with a pint,' Ross said. 'How about you?'

'Sounds great,' Larry replied. 'Did they do it?'

'Probably. Life has no value to them. Robinson was a damn fool, nobody comes down here by choice unless they have little regard for their safety.'

'If they didn't do it, they're dead; if they did and got a good look at the two men, they'll still be dead,' Larry said.

Chapter 14

Isaac decided that too much time had been spent out at Canning Town, and whereas the death of Hector Robinson could be relevant, it was unclear why.

Jane Doe and Janice Robinson were close to home; Bill Ross could deal with Janice's father, spend more time with the gangs, try and understand why they would have killed Hector Robinson, money aside; denials from them were not believed, and it was a typical gang slaying.

Jim Robinson had identified his father, spent time with his brother, and had been returned to Maidstone Prison.

Tim Winston was still in the family home, just. As Maeve Winston, who had found out the truth about her husband and Janice Robinson after a late-night tearful confession from Tim, had admitted to Wendy, 'I suspected something, but not Gladys's daughter.'

Maeve said that she had always wanted Tim, but he had wanted to play the field, as all young men did. She had wished for the white wedding, not out of convention, but because she was still pure. The reason that Tim had wanted her, Maeve said.

'Pure and chaste, that's what they want, all of them. Even Hector, not that he got it.'

'You knew him?' Wendy asked.

They were in the front room of the Winstons' home; one forty-five in the afternoon. Maeve Winston had called her for a chat. Tim was at work, and Rose wasn't due home for another two hours.

'It's about Janice,' Maeve said. 'I knew she was in that awful bedsit, selling herself to any drunk or lecher who wanted her.'

'How?'

'Before Jim had started getting himself into trouble, and Janice was still innocent, I used to meet with Gladys. Not often, once every couple of months.'

'Your husband?'

'He didn't like it, but he knew. We were going through a rough patch, money-wise, not the marriage. Sure, Tim had wandering eyes, but I kept him under control.'

'You don't seem the sort of person to keep anyone under control,' Wendy said.

'There was no need for him to look elsewhere. If you think that he's the great lover, you'd be wrong. It's a pretence, him and Janice.'

'I'm not sure I understand,' Wendy said as she picked up a chocolate biscuit from the plate in her lap.

'Gladys used to confide in me, tell me about her family and her fears for Janice.'

'From her father?'

'Don't always believe Gladys. She always saw things that weren't there.'

'Janice was abused by some of the men that her mother had in the house from time to time.'

'You're aware that Gladys was an escort?'

'Is it relevant?'

'I don't know, only that Hector didn't want to be reminded of it, not when they argued, and she'd bring up as to how beautiful she had been and what she could have made of her life, the offers she received.'

'Where's this heading?'

'Tim, I want to leave him, once Rose finishes school, goes to university, but I'm not sure about her choice in Brad.'

'I thought you were alright with it.'

'I was, but on reflection, his family, their history. He can't be untouched by it. Sure, for now he's fine, but he's still young.'

'I don't think it's up to you. Rose is nearly sixteen; it's not you that she'll be listening to.'

'Up north, there's a job I'm qualified for. I could go there, take Rose.'

'Maeve, you can't take Rose, even if she wants to go, not now. It's too late for that. You should have done something years before.'

'It wasn't important, but with Janice…'

'What is it? Out with it.'

'Gladys never stopped with the men, not even when she was married to Hector. He knew that. The man would never have touched his daughter, nor would he have played around, but Gladys couldn't help herself.'

'Janice?'

'I think she was Tim's.'

'Does he believe that?'

'I knew about him and Gladys at school, and then, around the time when Janice could have been conceived, a meeting at the school for the parents.'

'Yes,' Wendy said. Not another one, she thought. Why is that every time Homicide believes that it's starting to get a handle on the investigation, another unknown comes into play.

'I was there with Tim, but I left early for some reason or another. Later that evening, much later, Tim comes in, takes a shower, and climbs into bed. I could see by the look on his face that it had to be Gladys. She was on her own that time; they had separated, and Gladys was never one to hold back, not just because he was married to me. Well, it wouldn't have made any difference.'

'Proof?'

'I never thought much about it, not until I found out that he had been visiting Janice.'

'She's not,' Wendy said. 'We've taken DNA from her and Hector. She was his daughter, but do you think your husband suspected she was his?'

'I doubt it. That wasn't Tim's style; too trusting.'

'Of you?'

'Of me. Nothing like that, but I've looked, thought about it, and if I got up north, who knows.'

Wendy wasn't there as a psychologist nor as a marriage counsellor. She wanted out of the house, back to Challis Street and Homicide. A murder made more sense than the woman's neurosis.

***

Ian Naughton remained elusive. No sight of the man since he had left Holland Park, no sign of the people carrier or the Bentley that had been at the rear of the house.

The number plate of the BMW had been changed from when it had been in the garage at Godstone to when it had re-emerged as a burnt-out shell. Forensics had checked the vehicle, found that it had been stolen two years previously, resprayed, re-registered and the vehicle identification number had been doctored.

It was a high-quality transformation, not the sort of thing a backyard operator could have done.

But it was more than that, Isaac knew. Naughton was baiting them; Moriarty to Sherlock Holmes, the master criminal leaving clues, revelling in the sport, killing as needed.

He was, Isaac could tell, a man who would be almost impossible to find.

It had come to him the previous night. It was late, and he had been unable to sleep. In the end, believing that worrying about the investigations wasn't going to help, he picked up a paperback from the bookshelf, a book he had read more than once.

Holmes had described Moriarty as the 'Napoleon of crime', a criminal mastermind, adept at committing any atrocity to perfection without losing any sleep over it.

And that was it; Naughton was playing with the police. A man so successful in crime, but boring of the game, he had thrown in clues, killed people, purely for his pleasure.

As Isaac read more of the book, of the Machiavellian criminal mastermind, the more he realised that there were no clear motives behind the deaths. Jane Doe, whoever she was, could be relevant, but Janice and Hector could be minor players and he, Detective Chief Inspector Isaac Cook, was being tested.

If that was the case, Isaac was sure he was up to the challenge.

Challis Street. Homicide. Early in the morning, the most productive time of the day, Isaac assembled the team. Bridget was bright-eyed, Wendy was struggling, and Larry looked as though he'd had a rough night.

'A curry,' Larry said as he drank a cup of tea.

Bill Ross's favourite restaurant had done the man a disservice. Enough for Larry to reconsider policing in the east of London, seeing it as nothing more than a momentary fascination.

154

The café in Notting Hill that had served him breakfast for the last three years, when his wife wasn't talking to him, or he could sneak it in undetected, had never let him down, never given him a queasy stomach.

And even though it was policing at the coal face in Canning Town, the crooks were all the same, just less intelligent, less articulate. The superintendent over there might not have been politically correct, nor Bill Ross, but it was still a thankless task, and the gangs were without exception a disreputable bunch of reprobates. Moriarty would have understood their ethics, but he would have found little use for them. Larry wouldn't have seen the analogy or the correlation. His reading consisted of the occasional magazine, the news on his smartphone.

Isaac outlined his theory; Larry couldn't make head nor tail of it. Wendy trusted her DCI; she'd go along with his reasoning, not sure how it was going to help and how she was to proceed. Bridget wasn't sure how it would affect the investigation.

'What do you want from us?' Larry asked. He looked perplexed, felt as though he should understand but couldn't.

'The woman in the cemetery is the prime focus. We keep Janice and Hector Robinson on the side; they'll resolve themselves in due course. If they're related, which we must assume they are, then we'll get the answers eventually.'

Wendy could see the flaw. 'If Janice and Hector are diversionary, a game someone's playing, then how do we know that Brad and Gladys won't be targeted, and what about Rose?'

'We've done all we can, you know that. Barring a massive protection effort, we can't do much more. And how long are we going to be in the dark? You tell me. You can't; none of us can.'

'I could revisit the cemetery,' Larry said.

'I could find out where Naughton and the Asian woman have gone,' Bridget said.

'Which is what you've been doing already, and with little success. The man's supremely arrogant, playing with us.'

'But why? He wasn't to know that I'd figure it out,' Larry said.

'It must have been for someone else,' Isaac said.

'Illogical, it makes no sense.'

'It's neither of those. Think about it. Naughton wants to draw the best criminal minds to him, which means he's a major player.'

'Like SPECTRE,' Larry said, referring to a James Bond movie he'd watched on Netflix the week before.

'Similar, but purely criminal, although it could be more. We'll not know, not yet.'

'If Naughton's playing us as fools, then he must be leaving clues,' Bridget said.

'Which means the man's nearby or somewhere we can find him.'

'I don't like this,' Larry said.

***

Isaac had known he was going out on a limb, and even Chief Superintendent Goddard thought his DCI was clutching at straws when the two of them sat down in Goddard's office, up on the third floor, a view through a large window as far as the London Eye. Isaac hadn't been up in it, not yet, as Jenny was afraid of heights, and he wasn't going to go on his own.

Larry visited the cemetery, looked at the grave, walked around the area inside the cemetery and up Harrow Road and then down Kilburn Lane. He couldn't see anything more. The cemetery employee who he had met on that day at the second grave came up to him, had a chat, offered him a cigarette.

'Not much of a day,' Larry said.

'It's about normal. You don't expect much working here; no Christmas bonus from the residents.'

'Any more?' Larry asked as the two men leaned up against one of the graves. He thought that it was sacrilegious, but the other man didn't; used to it, Larry thought. 'Late at night, scare you sometimes?'

'I've heard things, not that they worry me now.'

'What sorts of things?'

'In summer, courting couples. They can always find a way in, and once we had a coven of witches, attempting to summon the devil, not that they had much success.'

'What happened?'

'Sometimes I spend the night in my hut.'

'Sometimes?'

'Okay, every night. I don't want for much and the hut, not the tidiest I'll grant you, does me just fine. Can't get cheaper and the neighbours don't bother me, no screaming children, barking dogs.'

'The coven?'

'They were not far from the hut, not far from where you found the box.'

'Any significance?'

'I doubt it. It wasn't the same grave, and it was eight, nine years ago. I was just getting off to sleep when they started up.'

'What did you do?'

157

'Nothing, not with them, and besides, it doesn't pay to become involved, not when I'm using the hut as a home.'

'The cemetery doesn't approve?'

'As long as I keep it low-key, cause no fuss, they don't bother me. Besides, it's good to have someone here. A few vandals sometimes, although they've got better things to do nowadays, what with their smartphones and no discipline. I've not seen any of them in here for some time.'

'The witches?' Larry asked. The man was apt to deviate from what he was talking about. Larry thought that he was a lonely man who spoke to only a few people, and no doubt had a bottle of something strong in the hut. Not fit for human habitation, Larry would have said as he'd been inside it, but that wasn't his concern.

'I went outside the gate, phoned the police, not that they came quick and it was a cold night. They came into the cemetery, rounded up the offenders, not that they were doing much, not desecrating anything, and took them down to the police station.'

'What happened to them?'

'Not sure. Probably not much, a fine for trespassing; it was an arrestable offence.'

Larry doubted if the man would have been as diligent with the courting couples.

'We can't find out who the dead woman was.'

'I'm not surprised. We get all sorts in here, and that grave where she died, I've seen others.'

'You didn't tell us that before.'

'You never asked. And besides, I keep a low profile. But now you're here, scratching your head, I thought I should give you a hand.'

Larry felt like grabbing the man by the throat but knew that it would be him that would be in trouble, and the man would probably clam up.

'In summer, people like to wander around, look at the headstones, the dates, speculate who they were, what their lives must have been like. I've done it myself, not recently though. I must have seen most of them, and there's over sixty-five thousand. Did you know that Marc Isambard Brunel and his son Isambard Kingdom Brunel are buried here?'

Larry didn't know, although he could remember from his schooldays that the father had been responsible for the construction of the Thames Tunnel, and the son had been involved in the construction of the first propeller-driven, ocean-going iron ship, the largest ship in the world at the time. Also, he was responsible for building the Great Western Railway.

'Princess Sophia, King George 111's daughter, is buried here. Don't know why she isn't at Windsor Castle. Some say it was because she wanted to be buried near her brother, the Duke of Sussex, but I reckon it's to do with her having an illegitimate child. But you're a detective inspector, you'd know better than me.'

Larry didn't. History hadn't been his forte at school, and the teacher had been a boring man who rammed dates into the students, expecting them to learn them parrot-fashion: 1066, the Battle of Hastings, William the Conqueror, and a few other kings and queens. The only King George he knew of had been mad, but which number, he didn't know.

'The grave?' Larry said. He didn't need an interminable history lesson; he needed something tangible.

'It was three weeks ago, a cold day, a wind blowing through the cemetery, although it wasn't raining. I was up near there, tidying around the place, doing the best I could anyway. I see this woman, not the one that died. She's interested in the grave, so I go up to her, ask her if she needs any help.'

'She spoke?'

'Not really. She said she was fine, polite to me, but nothing more. I couldn't see any reason to hang around, so I left her to it.'

'How long did she stay there?'

'Five, ten minutes, no longer, but I thought it strange that she would have been interested in that grave, not when we've got others more famous. Not far from there we've got…'

'The woman,' Larry said.

'She was young, in her early twenties, dressed in a buttoned-up coat. No hat, but she had probably come from somewhere cold, colder than here even.'

'Why do you say that?'

'I don't know, but isn't China cold?'

'Chinese, are you certain?'

'She could have been Japanese, I suppose. Not that I'd know. Her English was fine, a strong accent, but I could understand it well enough.'

'The Philippines?'

'It's possible, not that I know much about there. Attractive, a good figure from what I could see.'

The man's evaluation no doubt gained from perving at the couples in summer, Larry thought. He was a sad specimen of a man, but his description of the woman was invaluable.

Larry took out his phone, made a call.

'I'll have someone up here within the hour. You'll work with him, try to come up with an accurate likeness of the woman.'

'Do you know who it is?'

'It's a possibility, but we don't know where she is.'

Chapter 15

If there's one thing that a cemetery employee isn't much good at, it's remembering faces. Larry thought it was something to do with the job, numbed through dealing with the dead. Regardless, the officer sent to work with the man came back with an approximate likeness.

It looked liked Analyn, the Naughtons' housemaid, but it could have been a thousand other young Asian women in the city: petite, straight jet-black hair, small-breasted, and attractive. It wasn't going to help much, not unless it was enhanced by someone else.

Wendy was just inside the entrance to the cemetery on Harrow Road and Larry took a similar position on Kilburn Lane. A booth had been set up at both locations, three junior police officers given the task of questioning those who walked through.

Neither Wendy nor Larry intended to spend the day there, that was for the junior ranks, but Wendy had been adamant that she needed to ensure that everyone knew what was required.

The early-morning rush had concluded: two hundred and forty-seven people questioned. The weather was closing in, and the junior officers weren't in a good mood, complaining about why it was them standing there.

Larry would have told them that no matter how well-educated they were – virtually all new police officers were studying for one degree or another – they still had to put in time out on the street, to do the least pleasant jobs.

'I saw her,' a schoolboy on his way home from school said. Another hour and the police would wind up for the day. It was Constable Gwen Pritchard who had spoken to him. He had looked her up and down. A fourteen-year-old on the cusp of manhood and the softly-spoken statuesque blonde.

'What time?'

'It was three thirty, three or four weeks ago, not sure of the day.'

'What do you remember?' Gwen Pritchard said, conscious of the young man's wandering eyes. He wasn't the first man that had looked, and while she could take it in her stride, a fourteen-year-old in school uniform seemed indecent to her.

He was, she knew, no different to her younger brother at that age.

'Describe her.'

'Nice to look at, not very tall, black hair, Asian.'

'Is that it?'

'She had a ring on her right hand, I could see that.'

'William, how could you see that from the path? The grave's not that close that you could see detail.'

'Good eyesight, I suppose.'

'Or you tried to see more than you could. Don't worry, I'm not judging you, but it's important. Did you fancy her?'

'She was older than me. Why should I be interested?'

'The same reason you're looking me up and down. Adolescent, the hormones going crazy. Nothing wrong in that, but it's important. You know about the woman who was murdered there?'

'I heard. Is this what this is about?'

'You know it is. Details, that's what I need. What did you see and why so much?'

163

The young man had been caught out. He was embarrassed, not sure whether to tell the truth or not.

'Look here, William, I'll make it easy for you. You see her standing there, no one else is around, so you find a quiet spot behind a headstone, maybe take a photo, something to show your friends, or maybe you want her to yourself. Am I getting near the truth?'

'Somewhat. I couldn't help myself. I snuck up close, took a photo, not sure why, but I'm keen on photography.'

'The photo?'

'I took three or four, not that she saw, and I'm not a peeping tom, nothing like that.'

'You're not being accused of anything. The photos?'

'On my phone. I've got one of those zooms that you can clip on. I can send them to you.'

Gwen Pritchard forwarded them to Wendy, who distributed them to Homicide.

Larry took one look, confirmed that it was Analyn and the time stamp on the photo agreed with what the cemetery employee had said.

It was a good result, so much so that the team met at the pub not far from Challis Street Police Station that night for a couple of drinks. Gwen Pritchard joined them, as did the other junior officers who had been at the cemetery.

Larry kept to one beer.

***

A sense of optimism in Homicide, further confirmation that Ian Naughton was critical to the murder enquiries, irrevocably confirmed by the photo of Analyn. The question remained as to who she was and what she was doing at the grave in Kensal Green. No one had any more ideas; the only option was for Wendy and Larry, now assisted by Gwen Pritchard, to get out and about again. Larry had his contacts, Wendy had the Robinsons and the Winstons, Gwen had enthusiasm.

It allowed Larry to visit his favourite café in Notting Hill and to enjoy a full English breakfast; he reckoned it gave him the energy lift to see him through the day.

Wendy could see as she sat opposite him that it gave him the makings of a double chin and an imperfect complexion, not that she was complaining as she was enjoying the same food.

Gwen Pritchard, younger than the two by more than a few years, kept to toast and jam. Larry looked over at her, approved of what he saw. She was aware that adolescent boys and grown detective inspectors were alike in that they all looked. It had been a problem when she had first joined the police force; the stalwarts of the male bastion who took her to be a bit of fluff, a hobbyist until she became pregnant and left.

However, DI Hill didn't seem to be that sort of person, nor did DCI Cook. She had done some checking, found out that Larry Hill was a man who could mix it with the less desirable, and that Wendy Gladstone was the best there was, diligent, never giving up, able to find people who didn't want to be found.

As for her, Gwen knew that the police force was where she wanted to be, not as a constable in uniform, but as a chief inspector, a superintendent in time. She intended to fast track the process, and if the occasional chauvinist got in her way, she'd deal with them through charm, professionalism, and sheer hard work, and if they

165

still persisted she'd complain about discrimination and sexist behaviour. Behind the agreeable exterior beat a determined and indefatigable heart.

Notting Hill was a good starting point for their renewed search, even though Kensal Green was the focus. After all, Holland Park was near to Notting Hill, and that was the first place where Analyn had been seen.

Larry laid out the plan after he finished his breakfast. 'Gwen, stay around the house where Naughton and Analyn were, ask questions on the street, show the photo. Wendy, ask in the pubs, the shops. As for me, I've got a few people to meet with, some not polite company.'

'Criminals?' Gwen asked.

'Businessmen, they'd tell you if asked, but yes, the usual riff-raff.'

Gwen would prefer to meet with Larry's people, real policing, rather than showing a photo.

Outside the café, even though it was early, the locals were heading to Notting Hill Gate Station, the tourists starting to flow in, looking in each and every window, others going to Westbourne Park Road to get a selfie outside the blue door made famous in the movie *Notting Hill*, some even having the temerity to knock on the door, hopeful of an invite in, not realising that behind it wasn't a rundown house, but an upmarket residence.

Larry was the first to leave. His car was parked around the corner, not far from his first meeting. Gus Vincent, a local man of limited means and a schoolteacher's pension, had been born and bred in the area. He was in his late sixties, with a grey goatee beard, a bald head, and wiry thin. Naturally slim he would say, but Larry knew about the man's incessant drug-taking. Not heroin – not for me, not the hard stuff, he would say – but anything else he was game for: ganja, speed, ecstasy, cocaine if he could get it, and his hand-rolled cigarettes contained more than tobacco.

He was a walking advert for keeping away from drugs; a man who would be dead before his time, although Larry liked him. Charismatic, well-spoken, educated and articulate, Vincent lived in a depressing block of council flats, not far from Grenfell Tower in North Kensington, where seventy-two people had died in a fire caused by a malfunctioning fridge-freezer on the fourth floor. Vincent's building was of the same era and similar construction.

There was no question that what had happened at Grenfell could happen elsewhere, and council regulations had been tightening up, not only on council-owned properties but on the owner-occupied and those with absentee landlords.

A teacher in his younger years, Gus Vincent had taught the young Isaac Cook and more that a fair share of the criminals in the area.

Larry knocked on the man's door. Inside, Gus Vincent shook his hand warmly; Larry dashing to open a window as soon as his hand was released.

'Sorry, Gus, I don't want to leave here high as a kite.'

'Look at me, not a day sick in ten years.'

'Impossible for any germ or infection to survive,' Larry said.

Vincent went into the kitchenette – too small to call it anything else. He pushed a cat that was sitting on a cushion on the kitchen top to one side, squeezed the kettle between the tap and the unwashed dishes in the sink. 'You'll have a cup of tea,' he said.

'If it's only tea.'

'English Breakfast, none better.'

Outside the window, the burnt-out tower loomed.

'Some of them want to go back,' Vincent said.

'How about you? Willing to stay here?'

'My needs are few. If not here, then I'll sleep on the street.' Which would not happen, Larry knew.

The most successful of the gang leaders, Spanish John, on account of his having been born in Spanish Town, the former capital of Jamaica, owed his success to Gus Vincent, the man who had recognised his intelligence and had given him extra tuition.

Not that it led Spanish John to get a job in an office, to become an accountant or a solicitor. However, it had helped him to use his intellect to wrest control of his gang and the lucrative ecstasy market.

Gus Vincent had a benefactor, disreputable, but still a man who would not let his teacher be without a roof over his head, some food in his belly, a ready supply of narcotics.

'I've got a photo,' Larry said, handing it over to Vincent. 'If you could take a look, tell me what you reckon.'

Vincent held it in his hand, moved over to the window where there was more light. 'Asian,' he said.

'I need to find her.'

'What do you expect me to do?'

'Eyes and ears. She's important.'

'Not so many Asians around here, although you'll find Thai women in the massage parlours, a happy ending if you pay extra, and there are others in rooms with fairy lights and soft music. But this woman,' Vincent said as he waved the photo at Larry, 'she's not Chinese, not Vietnamese, and definitely not Thai.'

'We're certain she's from the Philippines.'

'An illegal?'

'We don't know, probably not. I met her once, but now she's an important witness in a homicide.'

'There's not much I can do, and why around here?'

'She was at a house in Holland Park. That's where we met her, and before that, she had been at a murder site in Kensal Green Cemetery. Whoever, whatever, she's involved, voluntarily or otherwise, we don't know.

'You used to be friendly with Rasta Joe; he could have helped you,' Vincent said.

'A former pupil of yours, but he's dead.'

'A few are. Isaac Cook turned out alright.'

'He did, but I need to get traction, I need to meet Spanish John.'

'When?'

'Now, or in the next couple of hours. He won't talk to me, not after the last time.'

'Arresting his brother for stealing cars, two years in prison.'

'Spanish John's brother was lucky. Not that bright, driving around the area, showing off.'

'Still, it was his brother.'

'He'll not like women being murdered either, and that's what we've got, two so far.'

Vincent picked up his phone, made the appointment. 'I better go with you,' he said.

***

It wasn't unexpected, certainly not to Detective Inspector Bill Ross; he had seen it before.

An early-morning jogger, down by the River Lea in Newham, no more than half a mile from the Durham Arms, had found the body.

'Every morning, rain or shine,' Barry Bosley said. Looking at the whippet-thin man, expensive trainers, a tee shirt with a running man logo, Ross thought that he would definitely run the London Marathon every year, placing with the lead amateurs.

Rain or shine was appropriate, as, by the time he had arrived at the site, the heavens had opened up. Bill Ross was perishing cold, but steam appeared to be coming off Bosley as he jogged on the spot.

'Can't afford to cool down,' he said. 'I came down from my flat in Maltings Close, crossed the river on Twelvetrees Crescent and then took the path down by the river. Never seen anything like this before.'

'Firstly, Mr Bosley,' Ross said, 'you can forget about completing your run today. We need a full report from you, times, what you saw, who you saw.'

'The time is when I phoned you up, and as to what and who, nothing, unless you include a few ducks.'

Ross looked at the body. It was on the river bank, and judging by its condition, it hadn't been in the water, although there were concrete blocks tied to each leg.

'I'd say you interrupted what they were doing. It was dark when you got here?'

'It makes no difference to me. I know the way.'

The amount of blood could only have been caused by knife wounds. Even though he was face down, there was to Ross no mistaking the clothes the man was wearing, nor the phone in his pocket; he had rung the number on arrival.

'Do you know him?' Bosley asked. Resigned to his fate, he had stopped jogging and started to feel the cold air, exacerbated by the proximity of the even colder water.

'He was a suspect in a homicide. And why jog down here? This is a dangerous part of the world. You never know who you're going to meet.'

'Not in winter. The troublemakers are fair weather, keep gentlemen's hours.'

'I'd agree. Definitely not the hours that determined runners and police officers keep. In summer?'

'I drive out to Victoria Park, run around there. It's not as good, but safety first.'

Ross phoned Larry who phoned the team. 'Preston's been killed,' he said.

'Any reason for us to get involved?' Larry asked.

'Not yet. I was expecting it. They wouldn't have trusted him after two days in the station, no matter how much he denied. It's one thing to thumb your nose up at the police, to spend a night in the cells, but Preston got out without a charge.'

'Which means?'

'He was guilty of murdering Hector Robinson, the same as they all were. In their ignorance, they would have been certain that he had struck a deal, a plea bargain, and that he'd turn Queen's evidence for a reduced sentence.'

'Rough justice.'

'Don't look to me for sympathy. I've got to deal with the paperwork, try and find out who killed him,' Ross said.

'Who? You must know that,' Larry said.

'It's the proving that's the hard part. His so-called former friends will keep a low profile for the next week. I'll try and find Waylon Conroy, but if I do, he'll have an alibi, and he'll come the sob act, deprived childhood, absent father, the usual.'

'Evidence at the site?'

171

'I'll know later today, but I don't expect much. He was meant to go in the water, which means our jogger friend missed them by minutes. There's an APB out for them already.'

Chapter 16

The death of Warren Preston didn't phase anyone at Challis Street and few more in Canning Town. One more low-life wasn't going to be missed, although Bill Ross had to deal with a grieving mother in the station – telling him what a good child he had been, never forgetting her birthday, always looking out for her, especially after his father had done a runner.

Always the same after the event, Ross thought. Where had been the parental guidance, the discipline needed, the push for their child to attend school, to better himself? But he knew that was harsh. These were marginalised people, largely ignored by government services, dismissed by the police as a criminal element, condemned by poverty. Ross knew that you didn't need to go far to find the third world; it was close to his police station, and the violence and the poverty were not getting better. It was a losing battle.

Warren Preston had soon been processed, the victim of a gang conflict; a gang that was maintaining a low profile. Crime was marginally down on account of the gangs keeping their heads down, and any that poked them up soon enough found themselves at the police station and in the interview room.

Not that it gave the police any concern, although social services would soon be around, as would legal aid, including the female lawyer that had represented Preston before. All of the do-gooders, heads up high, vocal in their condemnation of the police and their heavy-handed tactics in dealing with the deprived and the disadvantaged.

173

Bill Ross wanted to say to them come out with me of a night, see the truth of it, where they live, but he didn't.

As if somehow it was him and the police that were to blame, not the society that left them isolated, the government that had seen the short-term gain in cheap labour from overseas, the unwillingness to resolve the mess they had created.

But it was, he knew, the human condition. The cream rises to the top, the milk settles just below, and those who don't make the grade are condemned to purgatory. That had been Warren Preston, from a council flat in a fifties red-brick monstrosity where the lifts smelt of urine, and in the area outside a few swings for the children, most of them broken, and graffiti on the building and inside the lifts and the common areas. A war zone that the police only visited in groups of four, with another two outside in a locked car, ready to call for backup if needed.

Waylon Conroy, the leader of Preston's hoodies, lived in a similar monolith honouring depravity. Bill Ross had made the climb up eight floors – the lifts were not working, no one willing to repair them, knowing that soon enough they would fail again.

Bill Ross had banged on Conroy's door, the bell no longer working. After a couple of minutes, it opened, a child of ten standing there. A pretty little girl, Ross acknowledged.

'Waylon?' Ross said.

'He's not here.'

'Your mother? father?'

'Not here.'

A child conditioned to lie. Ross picked up the girl and took her into the flat. Inside was as expected: clean, basic and unloved. He placed the child on a chair and called over to one of his constables. 'See if there's any food in the house, otherwise go out and get her something to eat,' he said as he handed over a twenty-pound note. 'McDonalds if there's nothing else.'

'How long since you ate?' Ross said to the child.

'Not today.'

'How long have you been here on your own?'

'I'm not. Mummy's in the other room, on the bed.'

Ross gestured to a uniformed sergeant to check around. He soon found the woman unconscious underneath a bear of a man. Two other uniforms went into the room and wrested the black man off the grossly-overweight woman, the mother of the small child and of Waylon Conroy.

The naked man lay flat on his back on the bed, a female constable administering assistance to the woman. 'She's not dead. Paralytic drunk, that's all.'

The young child entered the room. 'He's not my father,' she said. 'That's Ernie.'

'He lives here?' Ross said as he shepherded the child out.

'He's mummy's boyfriend. I don't like him. He hits Mummy.'

Generational, parent to child, Ross could have told social services. Waylon Conroy, beaten as a child by a succession of his mother's men; the sister of Waylon, neglected at the age of eight, inured to domestic violence, almost certain to be abused by a drunken friend of the mother once she reached puberty, the cycle repeating itself ad infinitum.

Preston and Conroy, along with the young girl and the vast majority of young criminals in the area, were not the cause, they were the symptom.

The mother, semi-conscious, sat in a chair in the living room; her gentleman friend remained in the bedroom, his hands cuffed behind his back. A couple of uniforms had managed to put a pair of trousers on him. He was bare-chested and bare-footed; he would remain that way when he was taken to the station for further questioning. The man was known to police, and Bill Ross intended to throw the book at him, first questioning him about the little girl. She would be checked out by a doctor for malnutrition, neglect and abuse, and subject to his findings, social services would take the child into care, or return her to the mother, who would be carefully supervised; not that it would do a lot of good in the long run.

A uniform handed Waylon Conroy's mother a hot drink, which the woman clasped with both hands as she lifted the cup up to her mouth.

'Thanks,' she said. 'My head, it hurts.'

She wasn't an attractive sight, even after she had put on some clothes, an ill-fitting top too tight for her ample bust, a skirt too short for her age. Once, Ross could see, she'd had a pretty face, reflected in the young daughter, but time and multiple lovers had rendered the woman haggard. Black, as were her children, although the daughter was a couple of shades lighter than the mother.

The young girl sat in another bedroom munching a hamburger, grabbing the french fries with her small hands.

'Waylon?' Ross said. 'We need to find him.'

'He comes and goes.'

'Your daughter?'

'Gladiola, what about her?'

'Neglected.'

'I do my best, but it's not easy. I can't find work, and Waylon doesn't help, other than to come here and shout at me.'

'Hit you?'

'Not Waylon, not that.'

'The man in the other room?'

'Sometimes, when he's angry, but I love him.'

Ross felt like vomiting. He had heard it before, but he never got used to it. Next, it would be how the government had let her down, never given her a chance, and as for Waylon and Gladiola… Never accepting the blame, her behaviour similar to what she had experienced as a child.

'Did you know Warren Preston, they called him Wazza?'

'I don't know. If he came here, I wouldn't have been introduced.'

'He's been killed. We need to ask your son some questions.'

'I could do with another drink, something to eat.'

'Later. Your son?'

'I've not seen him, not for two months.'

'Anywhere we might find him?'

'He's got a cousin, lives in Croydon.'

'Address?'

'I don't know. Jayden Conroy. My sister's son, he made good. He and Waylon grew up together as children before his mother found herself another man and moved away, something I should have done.'

'We have a concern about your daughter.'

'It's not the first time. I do my best, but it's not easy, you must know that.'

'Social services will advise, but I suggest you pack a bag for her, a change of clothes. She'll need to be examined, probably at the hospital.'

'I'll go with her. Waylon?'

'We need to ask him questions relating to the death of Warren Preston.'

'Not my Waylon, not him. I know he can be dangerous, but he'd not kill anyone.'

Ross knew that Conroy's mother did not believe one word of what she had just said. He felt sorry for her. It wasn't an emotion that he would hold for long; he had a job to do, and sentimentality didn't figure in it.

***

Larry Hill remembered his last encounter with Spanish John. It had been eighteen months previously, a homicide, a man by the name of Bevan Harris, a minor criminal adept at cracking safes, getting into any locked building and disabling the alarm.

Larry had known Harris by sight, a Geordie from Newcastle, in the north of the country, easily recognisable by the cartoon figures tattooed on his arms. He was neither charismatic nor agreeable, with a sour look and a foul mouth. Apart from his unique skills, he was a man that had few friends, other than Spanish John's brother and an ugly mutt of a dog.

Akoni was the brother's name. Larry had googled it and found that it meant someone who is a brave warrior and has excellent leadership qualities. Neither attribute could be accorded to the small weasely black man when he was hauled into Challis Street Police Station on a Tuesday night.

Harris and Akoni had argued vehemently in the morning, a dispute over money, although nobody who had witnessed the affray could remember the details, and if they could, they weren't about to tell them to a police officer.

Even Larry had to see the humour in the two men fighting. The tattooed white man, over six feet tall, with a long dark beard and with an accent and a choice of words that sometimes left others looking for a translation, and the five-feet-six inches Akoni, skinny and shaven-headed.

According to those that had been there, why they were fighting wasn't apparent, but Akoni had acquitted himself better than expected, getting in under Harris's guard, a flurry of punches to the stomach before retreating. In the end, the two men tiring, the anger appeased, they had embraced and gone into a pub for a pint, Harris's ugly mutt relegated to sitting outside, looking at its master through an open door.

As Akoni had sat in the interview room, stating his innocence, a dissolute friend of the deceased from Newcastle, a man who had a genuine grievance in that Harris had stolen his woman from him and brought her south, was arrested for the murder. Harris, for all his faults, could draw women to him, whereas Akoni, small and agreeable to talk to, a good patter in chat-up lines, couldn't.

Then, when Akoni left the police station, he was approached by two uniforms and asked for the registration papers for the top-of-the-range BMW that he was driving.

He was detained once again, although Larry wasn't directly involved, not that Spanish John would listen to reason, as it was Challis Street where Akoni had been arrested.

The BMW and other luxury cars were being stolen off the streets in London, put into a container and shipped off to Africa, to countries that drove on the left. With sufficient bribes, they would reappear a continent away.

Akoni acquired the vehicles, delivering them to an industrial estate to the north of the city. Spanish John was investigated, but nothing was ever proven. Larry always thought that the smarter brother wouldn't have risked dealing in stolen cars; drugs were more his style, easier to conceal, easier to sell, a higher profit margin.

The three men met at a restaurant in Kensington; Spanish John was paying, not out of courtesy to the police, but because Larry was accompanied by Gus Vincent.

Spanish John, taller than his brother, carrying more weight, not only in fat but in gold jewellery, his fingers bedecked with rings, a heavy gold chain around his neck, a Rolex on his wrist, embraced Vincent, scowled at Larry.

'What do you want, Hill?' the criminal said.

'Two women, one man murdered,' Larry said. No reason to mention Preston, he thought. A gang member in Canning Town wouldn't interest a man to whom violence came easily.

'My brother?'

'If he hadn't driven that car over to Challis Street, we wouldn't have caught him.'

'Not too smart, Akoni. I was angry, angry enough to have done something about it.'

'You wouldn't have. Spanish John, let's not pretend here. I know what you are, and you know who I am.'

'What I am is an honest businessman, just you remember that. You're right, I can trust you. What do you want from me?'

'We need to find someone.'

'The two women, the man?'

'An unknown woman at Kensal Green Cemetery, Janice Robinson and her father, Hector.'

'I knew her father, not well. He was a nobody, why kill him?'

'We don't know. We're fairly sure who knifed him, but we can't prove it.'

'Janice?'

'Did you know her?'

'I paid her the occasional visit, not in that dreadful bedsit, before she reached the end of the road, before the drugs destroyed her.'

The drugs you sell, Larry thought but did not say. He looked over at Vincent, studying the menu. Their eyes met. Vincent did not approve of what his former pupil had become, but he wasn't a man to make waves.

'I'll have fish,' he said.

Spanish John signalled the waiter, Italian by his halting English and appearance. 'A bottle of your finest red,' he said.

'Steak for me, heavy on the chips,' Larry said to the waiter.

'Make that two,' Spanish John said.

'We're not certain that the murders are over.'

'Assuming I can help, what do you want?'

'We have only one firm lead, a woman who I met at a house in Holland Park. Subsequently, we found out that she had been at the first murder site.'

'You've lost her?'

181

'Initially, we couldn't do anything when we first came across her, and we were forced to believe that she wasn't important, but now…'

'Scratch your back, you'll scratch mine, is that it?'

'I'm with Homicide, not narcotics. That's not my concern, not now, but murdering people is. Janice and Hector make no sense.'

'You reckon there could be more?'

'We don't know. I've got eyes out there looking for one woman. I could do with some help.'

Spanish John saw himself as Godfather to his community, a benevolent figure who supported the local charities, gave money to a homeless shelter, helped out the occasional family down on their luck. A man who weighed his misdeeds with the good he did, a man that the police regarded with suspicion, but little proof.

The gangster took a sip of his wine, clinked glasses with Vincent and Larry. 'Give me the photo. If she's around here, we'll find her.'

***

Gwen Pritchard stood outside the house in Holland Park, the photo blown up and on a large board secured to the front gate. It wasn't the first time that a police officer had been in the street, but before the picture had been an identikit based on Larry's recollection, and there wasn't any shortage of women who matched Analyn's description.

The first trawl of possible women from information gladly given by some, coerced from others had drawn blanks, although two illegals had been identified working in a massage parlour. Both of them were in detention and due for deportation.

It was a thankless task, and it was cold, so much so that Gwen was looking forward to a break from standing outside the house. She decided she'd stop after talking to the first twenty people, mainly retirees with nothing better to do, and school pupils off to the first lesson of the day: the females looking up at the tall constable, pleased to talk to her; the adolescent males taking the opportunity to speak to her, some of them misbehaving, one getting a rebuke for getting too close, another for a smart comment.

Nobody knew anything, which wasn't surprising as the house hadn't been occupied for more than a few weeks, and there was a rear entrance down a lane at the back, a remote control to open the sliding gate.

'I remember her,' the next-door neighbour said when Gwen, tiring of the street, knocked on the door. 'I could see her from my bedroom window, not that I could hear. I don't make a habit of looking in other people's backyards, seeing who's who, but these days, you can't be too careful, can you?'

The lady was in her seventies, obviously very well off financially judging by the antiques in the house, the oil paintings on the wall. Gwen had studied art and had once considered a career in the restoration of paintings, soon discounted as it had only been a fad brought on by her parents who saw the police force as a dead-end job, only suitable for the lower echelons of society. Her parents were snobs, she was not, but she could act the part if required.

'New money, singers, we've had them all down here. No breeding most of them and some of the parties...'

'Next door?' Gwen glanced up at a Matisse, his blue period, a caricature of a nude female. It was genuine from what she could see, worth a fortune.

'I can't say I approved of the two of them, but they were quiet, hardly ever saw them.'

The story had already been told to other police officers, Gwen knew, having read the reports.

'Cavorting?'

'The two of them in that house together.'

'Ian Naughton, the man in the house, said that his wife was away, and the young Asian woman was a housemaid, looking after the children. Not that we've ever found proof of that.'

'I spoke to her once. My dog, a sweet little thing, wouldn't harm a fly, had found a break in the wall and had gone into their garden.'

'I know that this has been mentioned by you before, but I'd appreciate it if you'd tell me in your own good time.'

'I can tell you come from breeding.'

It wasn't mentioned, not by Gwen at Challis Street, and never by Detective Superintendent Goddard, but she had had a privileged upbringing; money wasn't a determining factor in her life, but having a vocation was.

The two women sat in the front room of the house. It was warm, too warm for a policewoman in uniform.

Gwen took off her jacket, the dog in question coming over to sniff around.

It was, Gwen decided, neither sweet nor little, but a giant poodle, its coat clipped regulation style.

'What can you tell me about the woman?'

'Asian, not sure which country, but then it's not so easy.'

Gwen handed over the photo.

'That's her, a good likeness. No idea why she'd want to be with him.'

'A relationship?'

'I saw them out there. Late at night, but I can see well enough. The two of them…'

'Making love?'

'I wouldn't call it that, not him and her. He must have been in his fifties, she, just a teenager.'

'We believe her to be in her twenties. A lot of them do look younger than they actually are. When you spoke to her?'

'She didn't say much, just got hold of Boris, not that she liked dogs, held him at a distance, and handed him back to me.'

'You've got the photo. Anything else you can tell us?'

'She wasn't happy to be there. I saw her another time arguing with him in the back garden.'

'He hit her?'

'I heard him say that it was up to her, but the repercussions would be on her head and her family's.'

'Which you understood to mean?'

'They left that night. I didn't think any more about it, but that's her in the photo. Is she in trouble?'

'We don't know, but it's suspicious. What do you know about the murder in Kensal Green Cemetery?'

'A young woman. Was she involved, her next door?'

'She's a person of interest, someone we need to find before it's too late. Any help–'

The woman interrupted her. 'I'll tell you what I know, not that I was nosey, but she wasn't the first woman in that house. There had been others.'

185

'Why wasn't this mentioned before?'

'You know…'

'I know somebody who's taken more than a casual interest in her neighbours. Before this goes any further, and being nosey is not a crime, just mischievous and in bad taste, you'd better tell me the truth.'

'I saw two other women.'

'Describe them.'

'One was Asian, the other was white, not sure where from.'

Gwen opened up her smartphone, scrolled through the photo gallery, showed one of the images to a woman with an unhealthy interest in spying on her neighbours.

'That's the white woman,' the neighbour said. 'Who is she?'

'She's the woman that was murdered in the cemetery.'

Chapter 17

It seemed that Analyn, the mysterious and most important person for the team to interview, was at the Holland Park address under some duress and that Ian Naughton was involved in a shady business where women were possibly trafficked. But that assumption was flawed in that the woman on the grave was English, her DNA's genetic markers confirming her ancestry.

If Analyn and the other Asian woman seen by the nosey neighbour were brought into the country either illegally or legally, under contract or not, it didn't explain why the murdered woman had been at the grave with a man.

The early-morning meetings at Challis Street continued. Larry still struggled with his weight, Wendy with her arthritis, and Isaac with Jenny's advancing pregnancy, the morning sickness, the occasional mood change, the decision to put the flat on the market and to buy a house. It was only Bridget who seemed immune as she spent her days with her computer, the evenings enjoying a glass of wine, and watching soap operas on the television.

Chief Superintendent Goddard would occasionally be in Homicide, not that Isaac concerned himself too much, except that the man would ask penetrating questions which the team couldn't answer.

'Still no idea who the dead woman is?' Goddard said.

'Not yet, but we're getting closer,' Isaac said, realising that it was a stupid reply.

'I read the report,' Goddard continued. 'Long on detail, short on fact, but that's the problem, isn't it? You've run out of ideas.'

Isaac, as the senior investigating officer, wanted to deny, to offer up a fervent rebuttal, but he knew that it was best to let his senior have his say. The pep talk and the criticism were the way the man operated, and he wasn't a tyrant, not like Commissioner Davies.

Homicide, Challis Street, was a special focus for the man, especially after the commissioner's favourite, Seth Caddick, had been brought in to replace Isaac firstly and then, after his promotion to superintendent, Richard Goddard. On both occasions, Caddick had left with his tail between his legs, but he was still there, champing on the bit, eager to prove his worth.

Isaac and Goddard had no time for the man, an incompetent sycophant, sucking up to Davies, but he wasn't the only one in the Met. There were more than a few who succeeded through adroit manoeuvring, waiting their time, moving in to grab the accolade, retreating to the shadows when someone needed to take the blame.

On a couple of occasions, Isaac had considered leaving, finding himself a more regular job, head of security for a company overseas, but each time he had stayed, although the salaries on offer had been inviting. And as he had reflected with Jenny the night before, more money would come in handy. They had spent a couple of hours looking at their finances, the price they could sell the flat for, the mortgage they would need to take for a house.

'We'll manage,' Jenny said. 'And when the baby's old enough, I can find a job.'

The expected promotion to superintendent hadn't occurred for Isaac and wasn't likely to as long as Davies remained in control.

'We're making a concerted effort to find the Asian woman,' Larry said.

'Yes, I know all that, but why's it taking so long. Assuming she's relevant–'

'She is,' Larry interrupted the chief superintendent's flow.

Not a good idea, Isaac thought, as he cast a steely glance over at his DI: keep quiet, it inferred. Larry took the hint and picked up his mug of coffee from the desk, grasped it firmly and sat back.

'As I was saying, assuming she's relevant,' Goddard continued. 'And now we're using criminals to find her. It's irregular.'

Isaac and his team knew it wasn't, as did the chief superintendent, but others in the police force, isolated from the reality, back-room boys, politically correct aficionados, believed that criminals were to be arrested, not consorted with.

Richard Goddard had to deal with those people, as did the team in Homicide, but it was a reality that couldn't be avoided. Sometimes those you despised were the best people for the job.

Spanish John, one of the more distasteful in terms of the business he conducted, the people whose lives he ruined, was a man close to the street. He was a man that Larry trusted, and had even enjoyed his company at the restaurant.

'Without the woman, we're going nowhere,' Isaac said. 'We can place her at three locations of interest; she's the glue the brings the investigation together.'

'We do what's necessary,' Larry said.

189

'Any money to exchange hands?' Goddard asked.
'Not from me.'

'And we know this man, Spanish John, a stupid name if you ask me, but you're not, can get a result?'

'No guarantees, sir, but he can cover more territory than me. He's also checking on Ian Naughton. He doesn't want murderers in the area any more than we do; bad for business, more police on the ground.'

'So, if we find the murderer, he sleeps better at night.'

'He does.'

'I'll accept that you're doing all you can, but it's not good enough. It won't be long before I'm under pressure again. You got me a stay of execution last time. By the way, thanks for that, a good report that you all put together.'

'Sir,' Wendy said, 'I've still got a concern about Brad Robinson and his mother, Rose Winston and her parents.'

'You're keeping a watch on them?'

'We are, but we've pulled the uniforms, no budget, and the threat level has abated.'

'That's what they say with the idiots killing in the name of their religion. The threat is downgraded, and then another one of them pops up, kills a few bystanders, people on their way to work. Still, you're right about the budget. And besides, don't you believe that the woman died as a result of a disgruntled customer, the father at the hands of hoodies?'

'In part, failing further information. It makes no sense to kill those two just because the youngest of the family had seen the murderer in the cemetery.'

'No more than the grave and this woman,' Goddard said as he got up to leave. 'That aside, keep a watch on the two families. If anything happens, we're open to criticism and censure, and Commissioner Davies will have a field day laying the blame on this department and my handling of the murder investigation.'

Wendy understood the rationale in pulling back the protection from the two families. However, it didn't abate her concern. She hoped they were safe, but she wasn't sure, nobody could be. And if anything happened to any of them, not only would it be doom for the chief superintendent and her DCI, it would leave her with a strong feeling of guilt. If that day came, it wouldn't be her health that decided when she would be retiring, it would be her as she handed in her resignation.

***

Wendy had come into Homicide as a constable before being promoted to sergeant on Isaac's recommendation. Up in Sheffield, a junior constable, she had honed a skill for finding truanting children, some because running away had an aura of romanticism, others because of an abusive parent.

It had been a good period in her life, away from the confines of a remote farmhouse, a drudging life, a father she had loved, a mother she always felt distant from.

In her first couple of years in Yorkshire, and in uniform, a few romances, a lot of alcohol, and a broken heart after one man, a sergeant at the station and three years her senior, had blabbed about their night together.

She had heard the details from a friend, seen the sniggering at the station, not unexpected as the police back then were openly chauvinistic, no political correctness to deter them.

191

Inspector Dermot Loughlin had regretted putting his hand up her skirt in his office, closing the door with one foot and pushing her up against a filing cabinet with such force that some papers stacked high on top fell to the ground.

'Don't worry, love, you can pick them up afterwards,' he had said.

It had been late at night, an emotional time for the young constable because of a recent case. A child, Helen Moxon, she had found hiding out in a squat in Attercliffe, a suburb to the east of the city centre. A frumpish fifteen-year-old with a horrific story of how her mother beat her and her father sexually abused her.

Helen Moxon was critical of her parents in the court, glaring at them; the mother in her Sunday best, a peach-coloured dress, a smile that excited the magistrate, a sour-faced old goat, Wendy thought. And the father, dressed in a business suit, upright, distinguished military record, a local government employee, a respected man.

Social services, weak and ineffectual, represented by a woman just six months after she'd received her degree at a university in Sussex and who hadn't prepared, and in the end Helen Moxon was returned to the care of her parents.

Two days later, she was dead, the result of a beating from both parents; the sexual abuse confirmed by the pathologist.

And then Loughlin was pushing Wendy, rubbing his groin up and down her, trying to get her to relax. She grabbed the nearest heavy object, a coffee percolator, and smashed it on his head. He fell to the ground, unconscious, and she ended up on suspension.

Two months later, she was reinstated after another officer, an inspector who had more chivalrous

ideas on how to treat women, came forward in her
defence.

No apology was ever forthcoming, and the
amorous inspector had returned to the station, demoted
to sergeant. Nine months later, he was back to his old
rank, and Wendy was in London.

Even now, many years later, she would
occasionally wake up and remember the look on the
young woman's face as she got into the back seat of the
family car.

And now, Rose Winston, loved by her parents,
was at risk, as was her boyfriend, Brad. As cold as it was
outside, and as much as her legs hurt, and would more
before the day was out, she was determined to find the
Asian woman.

In Notting Hill and Holland Park, and up to
Bayswater, she entered each shop that could have been of
interest to Analyn. Gwen Pritchard was with her; she was
being brought into the department on an as needs basis,
which was most of the time, as was Kate Baxter, who
would take some of Bridget's workload.

Wendy focussed more on the area from the house
towards Notting Hill; Gwen Pritchard up towards
Bayswater.

Three hours later, the two women met for lunch;
neither had had any success. Wendy chose chicken, Gwen
kept to a salad. The restaurant on Holland Park Avenue
had a good reputation, but neither of the women had
been there before; it was also moderately priced, which
came as a surprise. The two felt they were entitled to a
brandy – purely medicinal, they joked.

The waitress, in her thirties, a pleasant smile,
tattoos covered by a long-sleeved tunic, brought over the

brandies, Wendy and Gwen thanking the woman who stayed transfixed to the spot.

'What is it?' Wendy asked.

'The photo.'

An enlarged photo of Analyn was clearly visible where Gwen had put down her copy.

'I know her,' the waitress said.

'You better take a seat. We've been trying to find this woman for some time. What do you know about her?'

'I'm busy, and the manager is not an easy woman, fire me in an instant, what with my background.'

Wendy left the table, went over to where an ever-smiling red-haired woman stood next to the cash register and explained the situation.

'We help where we can,' the woman said, the smile waning. 'Do our bit to bring in people who've fallen by the wayside, help them to regain their self-esteem.'

'Do you own this place?'

'I do.'

'We need to talk to your waitress; she doesn't want to neglect her duties.'

'Tell her it's fine.'

Wendy knew two things: employing the fallen, recently released felons, those deemed at risk, came with tax benefits and they were cheaper to hire, and secondly, the woman didn't care for the waitress, probably for nobody.

'It's fine,' Wendy said as she returned.

'Not here, not in the restaurant. If you don't mind eating elsewhere, I can tell you what I know.'

The food was good, so were the brandies, so much so that Wendy had a second one. The three sat off to one side of the kitchen in an area that could have been pleasant but was full of drums of cooking oil, racks of vegetables, and an industrial-sized freezer at one end. Neither Wendy nor Gwen were complaining, and the owner had made her presence known by popping in, touching the waitress, Meredith Temple, on the shoulder, telling her not to worry, and the meals were on the house, no cost, not to our excellent police.

A pretence, Wendy knew.

'Meredith, your story?' Gwen said.

'I wouldn't have told you, not if you had shown me the picture. It was just a reaction on my part, not that I have anything to be ashamed of.'

'We're sure you don't,' Wendy said. 'Maybe it's best if you start from the beginning.'

'I went off the rails, drugs and bad men, a tale you've heard before.'

'Too often.'

'Anyway, a man who I thought cared for me, but didn't, threw me out on to the street. This was four years ago, and I've never been a shrinking violet, no issues with men, lots of them, but I was willing to settle down.

'He had been a good bet, financially sound, had his own business, a restaurant. That's where I learnt about waitressing, although it doesn't take much skill, just remember the orders, don't spill the food and drink over the patrons, and make sure they're in and out quick enough, so you get more in. That's her creed, her out the front. All smiles when you're paying, as miserable as sin if you work for her, not that she pays for the overtime either.'

'You could register a complaint.'

'Not worth the bother, and besides, I'm not staying. I'm three-quarters through a degree, a local council initiative. With my background, I'll have no problem getting a job in social services, a homeless shelter, a woman's refuge, helping women to stop selling themselves.'

'You were one of them?'

'Sort of, not that I need rehabilitating; I did that in prison. As I was saying, I was out on the street, nowhere to go. I had some money, but no skills, and nowadays everyone wants computer experts or at least someone handy enough with them.'

'In prison?' Gwen said, reminding the woman who clearly wanted to give her life story that the woman in the photo was all-important.

'I had been an escort once or twice, so it didn't concern me to enter the brothel. Neat and tidy, regular medical checks, condoms, a couple of men to deal with anyone who got out of control and started roughing up the woman, half-throttling them as if it was some sexual elixir, and then there were the perverts, the deviants, who wanted you to do things that'd make your hair curl.'

Not mine, Wendy thought. Hers was curly enough, and besides, she had heard similar stories before.

'I stayed there for four months, saved up some money and went out on my own. Good money, decent men who paid well, and some of them even knew what they were doing.'

'The photo?' Gwen said.

'There were other women there. One of them was the woman in the photo.'

'Analyn?'

'She didn't use that name. She was there for a couple of weeks and disappeared, not that she ever fitted in.'

'Why?'

'She was clean, no drugs. She was popular, made decent money, but it was forced, as if she did it because she had to, as though she felt shame.'

'You didn't?'

'Never have, not really.'

'Any idea what happened to her?'

'Not after she left.'

'An address for the brothel?'

'Don't say it was me that sent you. That's the past, I'd prefer not to revisit it, and I've found myself another man. He'd not want to know the sordid details.'

Wendy scrolled through the images on her phone, Meredith looking over her shoulder.

'I know her,' Meredith said.

'Janice Robinson.'

'Yes, Janice. I was friendly with her, although she was worse than me. Drugs, that was her problem, unable to keep away from them.'

'And you?'

'It wasn't so difficult. A good place in my life and they didn't seem important, but Janice…'

Wendy continued to scroll, Meredith looking more closely than before.

'Stop. That one,' Meredith said. 'I know her.'

'We've not found anyone who has met her before,' Gwen said. 'How come you do.'

'She didn't work in the brothel, but she knew the woman in charge. Sometimes she'd come in, look around, never spoke to any of the girls.'

'Her name?'

'I never heard it mentioned. She was an attractive woman, spoke well, could have made good money, but it's not everyone's idea of employment. Better than waitressing, though. Anything's better than that.'

197

'She's dead, Kensal Green Cemetery. We need you at Challis Street for an interview. You, Meredith Temple, are an important person.'

'Square it with her outside.'

'By the way, what were you in prison for?'

'I had this client who should have known better. He starts getting demonstrative, sprouting the bible at me, Sodom and Gomorrah, blaming me for his inability to get it up. I push him off the bed, and he bangs his head on the floor, suffers internal bleeding of the brain and dies in hospital. They said I had purposely banged his head on the floor, not that I did.

'I'm sentenced for involuntary manslaughter, and then the man's estranged wife turns up at her local police station, says that she's been overseas in Nepal or some other place, explains that her husband had been diagnosed years before as susceptible to an aneurysm. No idea why it didn't come out at the trial in the first place, but then a prostitute, a lawyer for a client – what could you expect?'

'No more,' Wendy said.

Chapter 18

Wendy wasn't a fan of football, but her husband had been, the reason she had been to Wembley Stadium on a few occasions, the first time back in the eighties, and more recently on 17th May 2008, the FA cup final between Portsmouth and Cardiff City, with Portsmouth winning 1-0, the winning goal kicked by Nwankwo Kanu.

The stadium loomed large as Wendy and Sergeant Garry Hopwood from the local police station – she had informed them out of courtesy, not wanting to encroach on the station's area of operation – drew up outside the address that Meredith Temple said had been operating as a brothel.

Entering a brothel came with certain risks, and too many brothels, even those close to Challis Street, were involved in the selling of illegal drugs.

It was intended to be low-key, just the two sergeants, but Hopwood's senior, a bully of a man with pudgy hands, a tie off-centre, and perspiring, had been adamant. 'No going in there unless all bases are covered,' he had said.

He was right, Wendy knew, and Detective Inspector Con Waverton had a good reputation, even if he was unpopular.

At the rear of the premises, a three-storey terrace, two uniforms waited for those who'd be dashing out, not wanting to be caught, their names to be taken.

It was ten in the evening, the busiest time of the day.

Meredith Temple had been at Challis Street from two in the afternoon until six in the evening. During that time, she had given a statement, scanned through hundreds of photos of women of the night. Apart from a couple of women, she hadn't been able to identify anyone, other than to say that Eastern European women, mainly from Ukraine, were flooding in, and some of them were underage, and that the Asians were being pushed out to the more disreputable premises.

Larry had the address of a third English woman that had been at the brothel. He intended to visit her.

Waverton stood away from the front of the brothel, not far from a pub. Wendy knew where he would be heading afterwards, successful or not.

Garry Hopwood knocked at the door, showed his warrant card; Wendy showing hers as well.

'What do you want?' an elderly woman said. Her hair was piled high and dyed a shade of blue. She wore a frilled white blouse, a short blue skirt and tottered on stiletto heels.

'Running a brothel's illegal,' Hopwood said.

Waverton should have taken the lead, which made Wendy think that the man was willing to take a backhander to look the other way, a freebie at a house of ill repute.

Once the murders had been solved, she'd pass on her suspicions to her DCI. She wasn't at the house to make arrests, only to find out who the dead woman was and where Analyn was.

'So's lying to the police,' Wendy said. She went in the door, walking to the end of the long hallway, ensuring the back door was locked, removing the key.

There was no doubt what was going on in the building. There was a distinct rustling upstairs, the men with their peccadilloes exposed, their marriages about to blow asunder.

'I've lived here for twelve years, never a complaint,' the woman said. It wasn't true; Wendy had checked.

A man dashed out from a room to the left and made for the back door. He didn't get far, turning on the spot, aiming to get past the three standing in his way. 'I can't be found here,' he said.

'We'll need a statement,' Hopwood said to him.

'I can't.'

'If you and the others could make yourselves comfortable, we won't take long.'

Two more police officers came in through the front door, showed the madam the search warrant. They climbed the stairs; a search for drugs was underway.

'Your name?' Wendy asked.

'Gwendoline.'

'Your real name.'

'Mary Wilton.'

'Now Mrs Wilton, or is it Ms?'

'Mrs will do.'

'You had two women working here, one of them was Janice Robinson, the other was Meredith Temple.'

'There's not much point in denying it, is there?'

'None. Drugs here?'

'It's clean.'

Wendy thought it probably was. Apart from the house being used illegally, it was in good condition.

'We know of another English woman. Any more?'

'Not these days, and besides, they're bad news. Drugs, they can't keep off them. Janice and Meredith couldn't.'

'Nationalities here?' Hopwood asked.

'Eastern European, one Thai, two Vietnamese.'

'Financial refugees?'

'I don't check. All I know is that they give me less trouble than the locals. And believe me, that's the last thing we need. Enough with some of the men who come through the door.'

'You've a couple of men here if there's any trouble?'

'You're remarkably well-informed. Who was it? Janice? Meredith?'

'Neither. Meredith's straightened herself out, no longer selling herself, and Janice is dead.'

'Drugs?'

'Murdered, and don't pretend that you don't know. It's been plastered on the radio and television, and social media was full of it for a while.'

Detective Inspector Waverton entered through the front door. Any more weight, Wendy thought, and he would have had to come in like a crab, sideways.

Mary Wilton looked at Waverton, feigned a smile, changing it to a scowl. Waverton wouldn't be getting special treatment that night, nor could he avoid arresting the woman.

The four retreated to the back of the house, a small bar in one corner, two sofas where the women would wait, scantily dressed, while the men made their choice.

Waverton took the most comfortable of the sofas, Wendy sitting alongside him. Hopwood remained standing, and Mary Wilton leaned against the wall, her arms folded.

'Mrs Wilton,' Wendy said, 'you employed a woman from the Philippines, Analyn.'

'The name is not familiar.' She knew the situation was tenuous, having been there before. Denying what was obvious wouldn't assist her case, and the maximum sentence was between six months and seven years. She would be truthful.

One of the uniforms came into the room. 'No drugs, not that we can find.'

A sniffer dog would have had more success, Wendy knew, but that was up to Waverton and the Brent Police. It wasn't going to happen, and the woman would be charged with running a brothel, the women working there would be checked for their right to be in the country, their age, and cautioned. Yet again, Waverton's decision.

Wendy passed over a photo of Analyn, a blow-up from William Townsend's phone. The definition had been lost in enlarging it, but it was clear enough for the purpose.

'Not the name she used. She wasn't here for long, no idea where she is now.'

'I don't have an issue with you on that,' Wendy said. 'The woman's elusive, but we need to find her. Any idea where?'

'Sorry, pointless asking. I just don't know. Some of them breeze in, entertain a few men, and leave. Easy money, no references needed, just an ability to turn a few tricks, make a few lonely men happy for a while. Does no harm.'

'As you say, but the law's the law. The women haven't committed a chargeable offence, you have.'

'I know the drill. If I could help, I would. Assistance in a murder enquiry can only go in my favour.'

Wendy could well imagine that in the dock at her trial, Mary Wilton would not be bedecked with her hair piled high, a shade of blue, and the blouse and the skirt, along with the stilettos, would be gone; all replaced by a sombre outfit more befitting the woman's age.

'What name did she use?'

'I don't know, and that's the truth. She said she had been in the country for some time, had a British passport.'

'Did you check it?' Garry Hopwood asked.

'I took her word for it.'

'Which means,' Waverton said, obviously feeling out of it and confident that Mary Wilton wasn't going to spill the beans, 'that she could have been underage, illegal.'

'I trust my girls.'

'Hopefully, the women in the house are all legal,' Wendy said. 'Are they?'

'They are'

'I've another photo, a woman who's been in this house, not a prostitute from what we know. You must study it carefully and answer truthfully. People have died, continue to die. Why they do, we don't know, but if we're correct, you could be at risk and so could Meredith Temple and your girls.'

Wendy handed the second photo to Mary Wilton.

'Her name is Amanda Upton,' the woman said.

Wendy was so excited that she felt as though she wanted to kiss the woman, absolve her of all crimes. A name at last. She texted her DCI, ending the message with 'more to come'.

'What can you tell us about her?'

'A shrewd woman, she made her money as a high-class escort. No drugs, worked out at the gym daily, financially sound after three years. She used to travel overseas, paid for by wealthy and secretive men who wanted absolute discretion, no two-bit hooker with a big mouth and genital herpes.'

'How do you know this?'

'Is she dead? Is that why you're here? Not for the other woman, but for Amanda?'

'For both. The woman we know as Analyn, is, we believe, alive, although for how long we can't be certain.'

'Amanda?'

'You obviously don't keep abreast of the news.'

'Never watch television or look at the internet. A Luddite, I suppose I am, but what about Amanda?'

'Why are you so interested?'

'She is, or should it be was, my daughter?'

Wendy felt a lump in her throat, so did Sergeant Hopwood. DI Waverton looked into space, unable to comprehend the gravity of what had just been said.

'I'm sorry, Mrs Wilton, but your daughter, Amanda, is dead.'

Mary Wilton sat still, saying nothing. Eventually, she spoke. 'I hardly ever saw her, not for years, and then one day, she turned up here.'

'Any reason?'

'We weren't close, although I did my best when she was younger. I paid for her to go to a good school, and she was a bright student, went to university, a degree in English. I was proud of her, not selling herself at first.'

'You were a prostitute?' Wendy asked.

'Until I was too old. It's for young women, but Amanda never saw any of the seedier side. I managed to buy a small flat, and I never messed with drugs. School holidays I'd be there for her; she boarded most of the time, so it wasn't so difficult to make money, and then take the time for her.'

'Her father?' Waverton asked.

'No idea. He could have been a banker or a labourer. I never knew, although he must have been honest and decent, otherwise she wouldn't have grown up to be such a beautiful woman.'

'Escorting?'

'She had been kept away from it, as much as I could, but she knew that her childhood had been paid for by illicit earnings. Ambitious, ruthlessly ambitious, that was Amanda. I tried to talk her out of it, not that I was one to talk. She joined an agency that dealt with the wealthy and the discreet, men who wanted absolute silence and total involvement from the woman, not a five-minute screw or a blow job, but a weekend or a week, the sort of woman they could take to a function, impress with.'

'Amanda was capable?'

'I'm sure she was. And then she's here, wanting to spend time with me.'

'And did you?'

'She left after twenty minutes, and I never saw her again.'

'How long ago?'

'Janice and Meredith were here, ask them.'

***

Larry knew that Janice Robinson was dead, Meredith Temple was doing well at university, and Cathy Parkinson, the other English woman who had been at Mary Wilton's brothel, was still prostituting. She was living in Hammersmith, not far from the station, and whereas the address indicated upmarket, the reality was anything but; it was a rundown hotel, a probable place where the women on the street could bring the men, no questions asked if a percentage of the price was handed over at reception.

'Cathy Parkinson?' Larry said at the reception.

'She's not been in for a few days,' a long-haired male with a cleft chin, beady bloodshot eyes and a pointed nose, said. He looked between thirty-five and forty-five years of age, and he didn't impress, so much so that Larry took hold of the register, spun it around and looked for the room number himself. Computers hadn't made it to the hotel yet and weren't likely to if it proved to be operating as a brothel.

'You can't do that,' the man had protested. In vain, as far as Larry was concerned.

'The room's been paid for, up until the weekend.'

Larry climbed the four flights of stairs, walked down a dark corridor – the lights didn't work, not even the emergency lights.

Outside, on the street, a uniform stood, another one in the small lane at the rear.

Larry knocked on the door and waited. Inside the room, the sound of a television. It was late at night, and judging by no lights visible under the doors of the other rooms on the floor, no one else was staying the night.

According to Meredith Temple's description, Cathy Parkinson was beyond her use-by date, the first flush of womanhood long gone, replaced by a snarling woman who craved alcohol and drugs, not particular in which order, and she was usually the last one to be chosen at the brothel.

He banged on the door again, harder than the first time. The volume on the television did not alter, nor was there the sound of someone moving around. Not willing to break the door with a firm shoulder, not as easy as it looked in the movies, with their paper-thin doors and make-believe locks, and the brooding hunk of a police officer, muscles bulging.

Larry took out his phone and called down to reception. 'Up here and with a key,' he said. 'And don't take forever, or I'll have you down the station, answering questions as to why you let women screw for money in your hotel.'

A uniform brought the man up. 'He tried to do a runner, but I caught him before he got far.'

'Anything to say?' Larry looked over at the receptionist, a bruise developing just under his eye where the uniform had smacked him one. Serves him right, Larry thought.

The door opened with the master key. Larry gingerly opened it, ensuring he was wearing nitrile gloves. He stood at the door, not crossing the threshold.

'Cathy Parkinson?' he shouted once more.

With no option, he entered the room, keeping to the centre, a bathroom to one side, an open wardrobe to the other, the ubiquitous metal hangers. No doubt a Gideon Bible in the drawer, he thought, not knowing who Gideon was and why so many bibles.

The room was at least clean, probably because the woman lived there permanently, working from home.

A small fridge, the television perched on top. Larry switched it off.

A noise from behind him, the sound of a man being sick.

'The bathroom,' the constable said. Outside of the room, in the corridor, the disinterested long-haired man from reception down on all fours, getting rid of the curry he had eaten earlier.

Larry looked at the woman suspended from the metal pipe coming out of the wall, a shower fitting attached. Even he felt his stomach heave.

The constable left and walked away, getting as far as the stairs before he joined the long-haired individual in being sick.

It was a job for Gordon Windsor. And it was proof that seeing Amanda Upton at her mother's brothel was a death sentence.

Larry phoned Isaac to update him, Wendy to find Meredith, and Windsor to bring his team down. It was going to be another long night.

Chapter 19

The discovery of Mary Wilton and her house of ill repute had thrown the case wide open. Of the three English women at the premises on the day that Amanda Upton had visited, two were dead and another was frightened.

Meredith Temple had provided the first solid evidence in a murder enquiry that had dragged on too long.

The depressing hotel room where Cathy Parkinson had died had been checked over by the CSI's, the woman's body taken to the pathologist. Isaac had seen enough corpses in his time to know there had been a struggle. The hanging in the shower seemed to serve no purpose as there were also multiple knife wounds to the body, except to add to the possibility that the killer had a perverted sense of the macabre. It was a sloppy killing, the likelihood of evidence stronger than in the murders of the other women.

Gordon Windsor offered his appraisal that death had come slowly, that the woman had not been in good health, and that she, along with many who sold themselves, was a drug addict – a syringe and tourniquet had been found in the bathroom. He also confirmed that recent sexual activity was probable. Which meant that this time the murderer had had sex with the woman before killing her, whereas with Janice Robinson he had not, assuming the killer was one and the same for both deaths.

Seminal fluid contained DNA, and it could be traced if there was a record on the database or could prove conclusive at an arrest and subsequent trial.

Wendy sat with Meredith in an open area at the university. Neither woman was saying much; Wendy because she was mulling over what had happened and how to move forward, Meredith due to her fear.

Around the two women, the students moved up and down, talking to one another, some reading, others playing with their phones, one or two asleep. They were blissfully unaware that in their midst was a woman who had seen the seedier side of life, an acquaintance of two recently murdered women, and a police officer.

'I can't say I knew her that well, Cathy, that is,' Meredith said. 'She was a terrible tart.'

'What do you mean?'

'She seemed to enjoy it. After a time, or maybe it was always, you start to hate yourself and what you've become. The reason that so many become further drawn to heroin. A vicious cycle, screwing to make money to buy the drug, hating yourself, needing more drugs, screwing more, no longer caring what you do or with whom.'

'You managed to break the cycle.'

'Cathy was predisposed.'

'Janice had been sexually abused in her early teens.'

'A lot are. Cathy, when she did speak, would talk about her family; a mother she loved, a father she hated. It's the same story as Janice's, I suppose.'

'Janice wasn't too close to her mother, but she was to her brothers, especially the younger one.'

'My parents were good people; I loved them, and nothing happened to me. My only problem was that I enjoyed men too much, especially in my teenage years.'

'So did I,' Wendy admitted. 'Never drugs, only alcohol.'

211

'What about me? What now? I've given you information, and Cathy's dead and so is Janice. Am I to be the next?'

'I can't be sure. We don't know why people have died, not yet. You saw Amanda Upton, as did Janice and Cathy. There has to be a link through the woman.'

'Mary?'

'Do you care?'

'Not really. I can't say anything against her, though. She played it straight, never cheated on the money, and we did have protection from violent men.'

'Amanda comes into the house; she meets with her mother,' Wendy attempting to focus on the murders, to try and make sense of the killings so far.

'I was never introduced, and until you told me, I never knew she was Mary's daughter. An attractive woman, elegantly dressed, nothing cheap about her.'

'High-class escort. A rich man's folly,' Wendy said.

'*And* she is the dead woman in Kensal Green?'

'There seems little doubt that she is.'

'The Asian girl?'

'Any more you can tell us about her?'

'She stayed a few weeks, kept to herself, did her job, and then left.'

'After Amanda Upton had been in the house?'

'Two, maybe three weeks after. I'm not sure of the dates, time blurs when you're living on the edge. Do you think it's significant?'

'It could be. She must have spoken to you.'

'Conversations, never about the men, but then we don't.'

'A whore's code of silence?' Wendy said.

It was the first smile that Meredith Temple had allowed herself.

'Hardly. Cathy might sometimes, but we preferred to forget. It was neither love nor pleasurable; it was carnal, animalistic, dogs on heat. It was just disgusting.'

'And Analyn did what you did?'

'If she was distressed, she never showed it. Not a smile or a laugh, impassive, a china doll.'

'A seasoned prostitute? Sold herself in the past?'

'I wouldn't know, but she would ask about Mary occasionally, what her history was, where she came from, family, that sort of thing.'

'What did you say?'

'I don't think any of us said very much, and besides, what did we know? We didn't know about her daughter, not really.'

'You suspected?'

'It was Janice. She had finished with a client, a fat and sweaty man who usually chose me, but for some reason he decided on a change.'

'A keen judge of women?'

'Just a man too ugly he couldn't find one for free.'

'Janice?'

'She was curious. She told me that Mary and her daughter were talking at the back of the house; Mary smoking a cigarette, the other woman standing nearby.'

'And?'

'According to Janice, the other woman's telling Mary about her life; not in glowing terms, either. As to how it was good money, but that some of the men were dangerous individuals, secretive men, possessive, wanting her to always be there.'

'She wanted out?'

'She was frightened for her safety. No idea why.'

213

'If she overheard something, the same way that Janice had, then who knows. Powerful people have powerful secrets, facts they would not want to be known.'

'Janice would have told Cathy, who wasn't always discreet.'

'She could have told Analyn?'

'It's probable. As I said, a few weeks, and she was gone.'

***

Early the next day, Wendy picked up Mary Wilton from the former brothel. The women who had been plying their wares at the place on the day the police had first visited were long gone, some to a different brothel, others back to the street.

At the mortuary, the madam, duly charged with running a brothel, but out on bail on her own surety, and now dressed more fittingly for the solemnity of identifying the Jane Doe, looked away as the sheet was pulled back.

Wendy was the first to look, and even though it had been kept in a cooled environment, the effects of time were starting to show on the dead body. If a body had a soul at death, not that Wendy believed they did, then this one did not. An attempt to make the deceased more palatable in appearance for the next of kin to identify had not occurred this time. All that Wendy could see, as did Mary Wilton when she turned around, eyes glazed, to look at the body, was a slab of flesh and hair, the caricature of a person.

'It's Amanda,' Mary Wilton said.

With that, the woman turned around and left the room, not once looking back.

Wendy found her outside on the street, a cigarette in her mouth, a handkerchief in her hand, a look of desperation on her face.

'Difficult?' Wendy said as she put her arm around the woman who had visibly shrunk.

'I never wanted her to follow me into the business, that's why I devoted my time to her, ensured she had the best opportunities. Not that it made any difference, only that she found a better quality of man, made more money, but it's all the same, isn't it?

'A lecherous fornicating drunk on his way home from work, a labourer, a wife-beater, they're all the same, and the bastard who did that to her, influential, one of those who goes home to his wife and children of a night, has a title or infinite wealth.'

Wendy found that she had little empathy with the woman, who showed a momentary humility but was, apart from her love for her daughter, cold-hearted, more interested in the bottom line, money in her bank account, and the protection afforded the girls at her brothel was more there to protect the assets.

However, the brothel was central to the investigation, in that of five women who had passed through its door, three had been murdered, another was attempting to put her past behind her, and the fourth, an Asian woman, was the consort of Ian Naughton, who was increasingly looking to be the "Mr Big" in whatever criminal venture they were dealing with.

The madam and the police officer sat down in a coffee shop, Wendy ordering a latte, the other woman preferring a cappuccino. Mary Wilton perused the menu, choosing a slice of cheesecake; Wendy, conscious that she shouldn't, but knowing that she would, ordered a slice of chocolate cake that was in a glass-fronted cabinet on the shop counter.

'We need to find the connection,' Wendy said after she had taken the first bite of her cake, 'and Mrs Wilton, it might be you.'

'I'll accept that I've broken the law, not the first time either, and there are other convictions against my name, but I can't see how. I've always held that discretion is vital, and I've never spoken about the clientele, not to others. Sure, sometimes one of the girls would tell me about a client, even have a laugh amongst ourselves, but I chose my girls with some care. I know that a few had their problems, drugs usually, bad men more often than not, but they all had some education, the sense to know when they were on a good thing with me.'

'Tell me about Janice,' Wendy said.

'There's not much to say. She was rough around the edges, a working-class accent, not that I liked it much, but she didn't swear and she was polite. And besides, she had an endearing quality about her, the sort of person you instinctively trusted. Without the drugs, she could have got on in life. Not achieving too much though as her education wasn't the best.'

'You didn't try to discourage her from prostituting herself, to get herself sorted out?'

'Don't misjudge me. I'm still a cold-hearted businesswoman trying to make a decent living, and remember, it was prostitution that gave my daughter the opportunities, but then…'

'Flat on her back,' Wendy said, not sure if the woman was sanctimonious, giving a story for her benefit, or whether it was just an act. She felt the latter was the most likely, but at least the woman was talking.

'It's strange,' Mary Wilton said, her voice barely audible, a tear in one eye. 'I've been around prostitution all my life, my mother even, but you don't want to think that your children are going to end up making the same mistakes.'

'Mistakes? Do you see it like that?'

Wendy took another bite of her chocolate cake, signalled over to a waitress who was looking into space, made it clear that a repeat order for both women was required. The waitress, another backpacker by the look of her, smiled and slowly walked over to the counter and the coffee machine.

'Not for me, prostitution. I never had any issue with what I did when I was younger, nor with running a brothel. Men need an outlet, and if no one is harmed, then I can't see it as a crime. And why am I guilty of an offence, but the girls aren't?'

'The law can be illogical,' Wendy admitted.

'You asked about Janice.'

'There's more?'

'She was a drug addict, not as bad as Cathy Parkinson, but bad enough. Even if I had wanted to help, which I didn't. I don't say that to be callous, but I've seen plenty of women like them over the years, and whereas some of them sort themselves out, most don't.'

'The trauma of their childhood?' Wendy said.

'I was academic in my earlier life, the chance of achieving something, finding a decent man, a decent life, but that didn't happen.'

'The "Mrs"?'

'Briefly, when I was young, a few years before Amanda was born. A holiday romance, an infatuation with respectability. Three months later, we're married in a registry office, just the two of us and a couple of witnesses.'

'What happened?'

'It came out one night. We're in bed in the little bedsit that we rented. We're just talking about this and that, our plans for the future, our past history, people we had known, places we had been.'

The waitress arrived, deposited the coffees and cakes on the table, made an attempt to clear away some crumbs and sauntered away, balancing the used crockery that she had taken. Wendy thought back to the shoe store in Knightsbridge and the manager of the shop. The waitress would have been lucky to have lasted the first day there, but in the coffee shop, she had the look of someone who had worked there for a while, not concerned as she started scrolling through her smartphone after she had deposited the dishes in a dishwasher.

'You told him?'

'My mother had been a prostitute, and she had tried to shield me from it, but I knew. How couldn't you? There was no father figure in the house, and when you're young, you just don't understand, but in my teens, with the phone calls, the late-night knocks at the door, I figured it out. She admitted to it, told me that my father had taken off with another woman, not died as I believed, and that out of desperation she had turned to the only occupation that would pay enough money to look after me, give me a chance in life.'

'A different time back then,' Wendy said.

'No equality, not that I'm making a case for feminism, but a deserted wife with a child didn't have many options. It was either work in a factory making clothes or a laundry, manually scrubbing clothes and ironing, paid a pittance, allowing yourself to be treated as chattel, no more than a serf to the squire, or else you did what many others had done.'

Wendy, who was almost twenty years younger than the woman, could understand where Mary Wilton was coming from. She had experienced the injustice back then, although it was tempered to some extent by the time she entered the workforce, and growing up on a farm with a mother and father who loved and cared for her was something she was glad of.

'Your husband?'

'Before I met him, I was away from home, aiming to get a place at a university, struggling to make ends meet. Part-timing in a restaurant, studying at nights; I needed money. I placed an ad.'

'Where?'

'Not so much an ad. I had been approached a couple of times before, knocked back the offer. I just made it known to the next one who came along, a professor at the university, one of those who said he could help with my entry into the university, but couldn't. No different to the casting couch, and I, in desperation, fell for it.'

'You slept with him?'

'Not that it helped. He bragged to another professor who offered his assistance for services rendered, but I knew that academia and I were not to be close friends. I was blacklisted, thrown out with the bathwater. After that, I milked whoever had the money, was outwardly respectable, inwardly half-decent, and could pay.'

'The holiday?'

'I wasn't tainted by what I had done. I still maintained an innocence about it, and I always believed in romantic love.

'I went down to Bournemouth on the south coast, booked into a small hotel, walked along the promenade, bought fish and chips, heavy on the vinegar, wrapped in a newspaper, not the cardboard box that you get today, paddled in the sea. I was happy, just minding my own business, when Albert, that was his name, comes alongside, starts talking. He was a commercial fisherman, knew all about the tides, where was the best place to catch fish. Not sure if you would find many fishermen these days, but back then, there were plenty of boats going out to sea.'

'You spent time with him?'

'He wasn't educated, so I downplayed mine. But yes, we were inseparable, and then after the marriage, it came out, as I was saying. I thought that honesty in marriage was important, but it wasn't, not to him. He attempted to put on a brave face about it, and then one day, he goes out to sea, leaving a letter on the mantlepiece, telling me he loves me, but he can't deal with my having sold myself to other men.'

'What did you do?'

'I waited for him to return from the sea, to see if I could quiet his concerns.'

'Did you?'

'There was a massive storm that day; his boat never returned, he and two others drowned at sea. We had parted in anger, never a chance to say I was sorry. Since then, I've been Mrs Wilton, never fallen in love again.'

It was a sad story, one of many that Wendy had heard over the years, but it was the past. The present was still playing itself out, and those that had died violently had to be vindicated; those that were still alive needed to be protected.

'Cathy Parkinson?' Wendy said, not wanting to dwell on Mary Wilton's past, although feeling some sympathy for the woman, realising that everyone, rich or poor, educated or not, male or female, had a sad story to tell.

'Nothing could be done to wean her off heroin. Sometimes Janice would moderate her injecting, but not Cathy. She was not a person that I warmed to; entertaining when she was in a good mood, sullen when she wasn't. Another sad tale, but let's not talk about it. She did her job, played up to the men, wiggled the hips, got them excited, but no class about her. Although who knows, before the drugs got her.'

'Meredith Temple?'

'Classy. I didn't like tattoos, but I accepted them. She wasn't strong on the drugs, not as much as the others, and if she was in a good mood, she wouldn't inject, Maybe a bottle of wine, no more. Educated, I could tell that, but I always suspected that she was mildly schizophrenic. I'm not a doctor, so I could never be sure, but she walked away from me one day, gave me a hug, thanked me, and that was it. I never saw her again.'

'How long ago?'

'Two years, give or take a few months. She told you about my place, didn't she?'

'She did,' Wendy admitted.

'I should be angry, but I'm not. At least I know about Amanda. It's always better to know than to worry indefinitely, don't you think?'

221

Wendy wasn't sure if it was, but she wasn't about to admit that to the woman. 'Yes, it's best to know,' she said.

Over behind the coffee shop counter, an anxious-looking manager eyed the occupied table. It was close to lunchtime, and the place was starting to fill up, not to just drink coffee and eat cake, but to purchase a meal, to spend real money, more than the amount the two women had spent so far.

Wendy called the woman over, opened her warrant card. 'Two meals, your special for the day, and make sure we're left alone.'

'Of course. A special discount for our fine police service.' It was not as obsequious as at the restaurant where Meredith Temple worked, but it still read as 'better to have the police on our side than against'.

Another place probably underpaying the backpackers, Wendy thought, but it was only too common in the city. She would do nothing about it; she had bigger fish to catch.

'What connects the five women?' Wendy said, looking directly at Mary Wilton. 'Why is your daughter the catalyst for the deaths, and why was she in the cemetery? We have a direct connection from there through a man to Analyn. What is it? Is it you, Mrs Wilton? Is there something you're not telling us, something that got your daughter murdered?'

'All I know is that Amanda was scared of something or someone, but that's it. I just don't know. I wish I could help, I really do.'

Wendy was sure in part that the woman was genuine in her desire to assist, and sad that her daughter was dead, but there still remained the nagging sense, an intuitive belief that the woman was holding something back. Whether it was out of fear, the same as her daughter, or for another reason, there was no way of knowing.

The manager reappeared, two plates of chicken and rice, a salad in a dish to one side. 'A couple of glasses of white wine,' she said. 'You look as though you could use it. Bad news, is it?'

'Thanks,' Wendy said. She didn't need someone being nosey. She cast a glance over at the manager who was moving over to tidy the table next to them, ears pricked. 'Privacy, as well,' Wendy said.

A look of disinterest from the manager as she walked away. 'I was only doing my job,' she said as she passed Wendy.

The food was good, and for a while, nothing was said. Eventually, it was Mary Wilton who spoke.

'If Analyn was trafficked, I'd not know, and the others are all English, so it can't be that.'

'It would be the most logical reason for the deaths, the secrecy of the organisation, but we're not convinced that it is, not yet. Analyn appears to have free movement and not to be under duress. We know that she was in a village to the south of London on her own and that she was in Kensal Green Cemetery on one occasion. Apart from that, we don't know a lot about her, other than she was also in a house in Holland Park masquerading as a nanny to the children or a maid, but was probably neither; more likely the live-in lover of the man at the house. The name of Ian Naughton mean anything to you?'

'Not to me, but then, most of them don't give their names, a first name sometimes, and cash still reigns supreme in the world of prostitution. A few have used credit cards, but the bank account name I use is innocuous enough not to raise suspicion.'

'You seem calm about Amanda's death,' Wendy said.

'Life hardens you, and I've seen more than my fair share. As a police officer, you must feel the same about death, inured to the inevitable, no matter how tragic.'

It was true, Wendy thought. She gave scant regard to those that had died, not even her husband. Sure, she was upset for a few weeks, but he had been suffering for some time, barely recognising her at the end. They'd had a shared history stretching back over many years and two sons from their union. If anything happened to them, she was sure that she wouldn't be able to distance herself from the grief with the ease that Mary Wilton apparently could.

But then the self-confessed madam was a conundrum, one moment caring and sweet, the next, hard as nails. Wendy left her at the table after paying the bill, offering a compliment to the manager on the quality of the meal, appeasement for the harshness she had subjected her to before. It wasn't the woman's fault; it was purely a natural inquisitiveness, the need to know other people's business. It was the same with a car accident, the dead and injured lying around, the medical teams tending to them, the crowds forming, anxious to see what was going on, to believe that however bad their lives were, others had it worse.

It was mid-afternoon, and she was needed in the office. There had been developments, as now the woman at the grave had a name, and there were connections, however circumstantial or coincidental, between Brad Robinson and the young and still innocent Rose, Brad's sister and father, and the two other dead women.

Whatever it was, it wasn't over yet, and were they coincidences? Wendy didn't believe in them, no more than her colleagues at Challis Street Police Station did. She was confident that on her arrival at the station, her DCI would be ready and waiting, and probably Detective Chief Superintendent Goddard with his obligatory compliment for excellent policing, his need to stir the pot, to tell them they could do better. But then the chief superintendent had someone to answer to, Commissioner Davies, a man unloved by most, sucked up to by a few.

The heavy workload was not about to reduce but to intensify. Wendy knew she was ready for it; she only wished her legs didn't ache so much.

Chapter 20

Bill Ross closed the lid of his laptop, straightened the loose papers on his desk, looked outside at the rain, and decided that he had had enough for the day. It was just after four in the afternoon, a miserable day in the office at Canning Town Police Station wrapping up the paperwork on the death of Warren Preston.

He cared little about how the man had died, but Pathology had confirmed that he was bodily intact and that the jogger had probably disturbed his killers. His gang, almost certainly the people responsible for his death, were not to be found, having gone to ground in one hovel or another.

Ross knew that policing, more a vocation than he would admit, was important, and taking the attitude of 'couldn't care less' about who had murdered the verminous hoodie Warren Preston wasn't correct. He vowed to lift his game, get a transfer to somewhere else, to be more politically correct. Those that knew him would say it was impossible, but he was determined.

He put the laptop in his backpack, grabbed an umbrella from behind the door, looked around the office, and said his farewells. There was a warm fire at home, a warm wife as well, and it was still early enough to spend time with the children before they went to bed. He had to admit feeling pleased with himself.

The death of Hector Robinson still concerned him, but the paperwork wouldn't be completed until the team at Challis Street found out who was orchestrating the murders of the Robinson family members, another prostitute and a Jane Doe, if not actually committing them.

Hector Robinson had been killed by the gang that Preston had belonged to, no doubt about that. Murdering one of another gang's members was regarded as a rite of passage, the same as a three-point turn when you're learning to drive; an occupational hazard when you're the one who's murdered. But Robinson was a different issue, and if the man was integral in some way, although how was unclear, his death could not be put down as a man down on his luck, in the wrong place at the wrong time.

Still, Ross was adamant: today he was leaving early.

He got as far as his car before one of the officers in a patrol car rang. 'We've just found another one of your hoodies,' he said.

So much for an early night, Ross thought, annoyed at the inconvenience of another low-life impacting on his family life. Disgruntled, angry, but still a police officer, he shrugged his shoulders, got into his car, started the engine, and drove out to the location given. No need for the GPS in the car, the area was well known to him, as it was to the other police officers at Canning Town Police Station.

Three blocks from the Durham Arms, the patrol car waited. They had already set up a preliminary area with crime scene tape, listened to invective from a drunk sitting on the ground nearby, been jeered at by a car of local hooligans driving by, the two-finger salute and foul language their limitations.

Bill Ross got out of his car, made sure he had gloves on and shoe protectors and made his way into the factory compound long since vacated, not due to the economy but because it just wasn't viable to continue trading in the area. It was a case of vandalism, theft, or pay the extortionists for protection.

The body, face down, was clearly visible in a corner of the forecourt.

'It's one of your hoodie friends,' the patrol car officer, a sergeant formerly from Liverpool, still with a strong scouse accent, said.

At least I'll be home early after all, Ross thought. No point in worrying too much about who killed this one. It wasn't the first that he had seen, nor would it be the last if he stayed in the area much longer. It was a gang conflict, either a fight between the dead man and one of his hoodie gang for leadership or a battle between rival gangs.

Ross had three duties to deal with before he left. First, he had to phone the crime scene team, make sure that they would be down in due course to conduct their investigation, and second and most important, he would need to phone Isaac Cook to tell him that Waylon Conroy, the gang leader, was dead. He knew that he wouldn't be phased that the man had died of multiple knife wounds.

There was a third item to conduct, but he wasn't going to do it, not that day; family life was more important. He phoned a sergeant in the police station, informed him of the facts, gave the address. Someone else could inform Conroy's mother that her son was dead.

As Ross had told Isaac, no one gets old in a gang. They either move on or they die. Tomorrow he would deal it, round up the local gangs if they could be found, question them, listen to their excuses, receive a lecture from a legal aid lawyer about police victimisation, and no doubt, at the end of the day, release them back out on to the street.

As he got into his car, he knew of one certainty: tomorrow would be quiet, and criminal activity would be low, the one good thing that Waylon Conroy had done in his short life. In death, not in life, he had provided some cheer and goodness, but it wouldn't last long.

***

The team at Challis Street Police Station took the death of Waylon Conroy in their stride. As far as they were concerned, it was a local matter for the police in Canning Town, as was the death of Warren Preston, and whereas Hector Robinson's death was still integral to their case, it was Conroy and his gang who had killed him.

The reason for Robinson's death was important, more so than who had committed it, and for that they had one name, Ian Naughton, and regardless of how much they tried, the man remained elusive.

Larry met with Spanish John at a pub in Notting Hill. He knew he would drink more than he should and he would be confined to the sofa that night, but as he had explained to his wife, who was not sympathetic to his dilemma, and to his DCI, who while understanding the problem still had to deal with it, he drank not only to loosen the tongues of the local villains but also because he enjoyed the taste of beer too much.

However, regardless of his trepidations and the flak that was coming his way, Larry sat down in the corner of the pub. On the other side of the table, the frightening presence of Spanish John. Akoni, his brother, sat close by. He was cordial, Larry conceded, but he wasn't an impressive figure, not in comparison to his brother.

'We've been looking,' Spanish John said.

'And?' Larry's reply. When dealing with men such as Spanish John, Larry knew not to push too much; it was best to let them talk first. After all, the man was a criminal who should be in prison for his activities, but was not, due to ensuring that others did the dirty work, and if challenged by the police, he'd retreat, allow his lawyers to deal with it.

Spanish John's original focus had been on the body on the grave, now identified as Amanda Upton. The phone call forty-five minutes earlier from the gangster, asking Larry to meet with him, had been unexpected.

'I've got an address for you,' Spanish John said as he downed his pint of beer; his brother looked into space, kept sipping at his drink. If it hadn't been for his smarter brother, he would have survived through petty crime, largely friendless, ignored by most. But to those in the pub and out on the street, being the brother of an important man came with its perks, and long after Spanish John and Larry had gone, the brother would continue to receive free drinks and the cordiality of others. One thing Larry knew was that it didn't pay to get on the wrong side of a major crime figure, nor did you upset his family. Retribution was swift, and although this time they had Conroy's body in Canning Town, bodies weren't always found, or if they were, the state of decomposition, the condition of the body, made identification virtually impossible, other than by DNA.

Early in his time at Challis Street Police Station, there had been a dismembered, headless torso in the water at Little Venice on Regent's Canal, a barking dog alerting its owner to it, much to her consternation and the interrupted ardour of a man and his wife in a houseboat alongside.

'Whose?' Larry asked. 'We've found out the name of the victim at the cemetery, although not a lot more, and certainly no idea as to why she was there.'

'Cathy Parkinson dead?'

'A question or do you know the answer?' Larry said as he started on his third pint. He was still sober, careful with his speech. But the opportunity to drink more than his usual two pints was pleasurable, and he wasn't sure if he could stop before the inevitable end of night debacle where he'd stagger out of the pub, hail a taxi and receive curt words from his wife.

'Confirmation. I knew her, not well, not as well as Janice. The same person that killed Janice?'

'Different modus operandi. Janice's death was clean, no sign of sexual activity, no usable evidence from the CSIs nor Forensics; Cathy Parkinson's death was messy, not that we've got a lot from it yet. If it's the same person, they're playing us for suckers.'

'And Amanda Upton's was carefully done. No amateur there,' Spanish John said. Larry could see that he was enjoying sparring with him; a game of one-upmanship. Leverage a probability, to ensure that the police looked the other way from certain activities.

Larry wasn't in a position to either give or deny the man what he almost certainly wanted. That was the problem, not only at Challis Street Police Station but throughout the country. The villains had influence and power, and they couldn't always be ignored. Sometimes the more immediate gain outweighed the greater good, and the recent deaths were definitely immediate.

'Either it was a professional or someone who knew where to place the knife. You seem remarkably well-informed.'

'I keep my ear to the ground, and besides, I've got you further information on the woman.'

'Amanda?'

'Yes.'

'What is it?'

'Firstly…'

Larry was ready for the favour. He wasn't sure how he would respond, but Amanda Upton was only second in importance to Analyn and Ian Naughton.

'I've got an address,' Spanish John said. 'More than you have, I assume.'

It wasn't the rub, not yet, or was the gangster baiting him, Larry thought. Whatever it was, he needed to ease back on the alcohol. He needed his wits about him, and strangely, after the first two pints, he had found that the flavour wasn't as good as he had expected. He hoped it was because his need for alcohol was abating, but he thought it was probable that as a connoisseur of the fermented hop, he was not enamoured of the beer dispensed in the pub.

Akoni, Spanish John's brother, swayed on his seat, oblivious to the conversation, only making the occasional guttural sound to indicate that he was listening. He was on his sixth pint, and the need to leave the table and circulate was foremost on his mind. He was a sociable man with little charisma, but an easy drunk's friend, and the pub was rapidly filling, the general hubbub of people talking and laughing, some arguing over near the bar. It was a place that Spanish John liked, he would have admitted if asked, as it afforded him a degree of anonymity, a chance to mingle, to not look over his shoulder all the time. Although close to the entrance of the pub, in the bar, a heavy, a club bouncer when he wasn't looking after his charge, and out on the street, a late-model Mercedes, a couple of men lounging nonchalantly on the bonnet smoking cigarettes and perving at the occasional dolly bird that walked by, making inappropriate comments, receiving scowls from some in return, a smile from others.

Spanish John looked over at his brother. 'Leave us to it,' he said.

Akoni walked away, headed for the loudest group, those drinking the most.

'Inspector Hill, I'll level with you. You're not a bad sort, not for a police officer, but normally people like you and I don't get on well.'

'We can't ignore each other, your people and mine. Sometimes we need to come together for the common good.'

'I know you were friends with Rasta Joe and he trusted you, and Isaac Cook was at the same school as me, one year above.'

'Where's this leading?'

'Someone's killing people for no apparent reason, and it brings focus on the area, something that neither of us wants or needs.'

And definitely not an increased police presence, Larry knew that.

Spanish John continued. 'What did Mary Wilton tell you?'

'She's critical to the investigation in that all the dead women were involved with her establishment at one time or another.'

'Except for Amanda, who never sold herself there.'

'Amanda? The first name suggests that you knew her.'

233

'Not personally. Did you find out where she lived?'

'Not yet. Apparently, confidentiality was a prerequisite of her line of business.'

'High-class whore, intimate friend to the rich and famous, to the secretive and the infamous.'

'At least that's what Mary Wilton believed she was. Apparently, Amanda was frightened, probably in too deep with the wrong people,' Larry said.

'Amanda Upton had a place in Marylebone,' Spanish John said. 'No idea why you haven't found it, but then maybe you and your chief inspector aren't as smart as you think you are.'

Larry wasn't going to bite. 'We're smart enough to have found someone who would for us, aren't we?' he said.

'Touché.'

'The address?'

'Akoni's in trouble again.'

'You want a favour?'

'He's an idiot; that's confidential, between you and me, but blood is thicker than water, even if I think he's as thick as two short planks.'

'What's he done?'

'Don't worry, it's not important. I can deal with it or a smart lawyer can. Just remember, you owe me one.'

'I can't break the law, just put a word here and there if I have to, but don't expect me to overlook your more serious criminal activities.'

'An honest cop. Do you get a medal for that?'

'I sleep easy at night, but apart from that, just a modest salary, index-linked superannuation.'

'Sometimes, I wish I'd taken the easy road, but I didn't. Of all those at that school, some are dead, one's a politician, another's a chief inspector, the majority are slaving away in menial jobs, and some are important men in their community.'

'Which one are you?'

'The latter, and I don't like to be crossed. If you've got anything on me, anything that can stick, you let me know, and I'll back off.'

'Don't ask me to interfere if it's too serious to ignore.'

'Number 256, Glentworth Street, Marylebone. On the second floor, an apartment. She lived there in London. Do you know the street?'

Larry did, a two-minute walk from the Sherlock Holmes museum on Baker Street.

'How did you find the place?'

'Someone I know.'

'And the other women, Hector Robinson?'

'Plus a couple of hoodies in Canning Town.'

'Yes,' Larry said.

'I can't help you there. The hoodies are perfectly capable of killing each other, no help needed there from outsiders. As to Janice and Cathy, they're probably tied in with Amanda.'

'Mary Wilton?'

'She's been around a long time. No doubt she knows more than she's letting on, but you can never be sure.'

'There are two others that need finding. Ian Naughton and Analyn, no surname for her.'

'Sorry, can't help. I've done as much as I can,' Spanish John said as he got up from his chair and walked out of the pub, the heavy following him. Over near the bar, the man's insignificant brother was propping himself up with one arm on the counter, holding on to a glass with the other.

Larry picked up his beer, took one sip and put the glass back on the table. He'd not be sleeping on the sofa that night.

Chapter 21

Even though it was after eleven in the evening, and Larry hadn't made it home, such was Isaac's enthusiasm to act on Spanish John's information that he, Wendy, and Larry found themselves outside Amanda Upton's residence. It was definitely upmarket, but then again it was Marylebone, and the name came with a premium if you were buying property there. A row of elegant red-brick apartment blocks, each storey interspersed with a layer of white stone, rose up five floors. A local estate agent had been roused from his sleep. As the managing agent, he had a set of keys, and though reluctant, he had listened as he was told of the circumstances of the late-night visit and had arrived at the address five minutes after the police.

At the windows of the adjoining properties, a rustling of some of the curtains, as well as a couple of residents standing outside asking questions. Wendy had spoken to them, asked if they knew the woman on the second floor. None did, and as always, she received the obligatory response that it was a quiet neighbourhood, never any trouble, no wild parties.

Any further information Wendy could give to the locals regarding Amanda Upton would wait until they had confirmation that it was her place of residence, and then the following morning a door-to-door would commence.

The estate agent opened the imposing two-doored entrance to the building, Isaac and Larry following him in. All three were wearing nitrile gloves and shoe protectors. So far, the crime scene investigators were not at the scene but would be notified if and when their presence was required.

Inside, a lift, but the three walked up the stairs, keeping to the middle of the stairway, which was also a thoroughfare for the other residents in the building. At the door of the apartment, the agent, a man fatter than any man had a right to be, and attempting to catch his breath, knocked on the door. After a couple of attempts, he turned the key and entered, setting off the burglar alarm.

Isaac found the alarm's control panel soon enough, and entered 000 onto a keypad, disabling the alarm. So much for security, he thought.

The agent held back, as he had been told. It was an impressive residence, Isaac had to concede. Three bedrooms, the first with an en suite, a designer kitchen, upmarket furniture, the lair of a successful woman, which Amanda Upton had been.

Larry, unable to curb his interest, joined Isaac in the apartment and looked out of the front window. He could see Wendy talking to a group of locals.

By the time Isaac and Larry left the apartment, it was after one in the morning. Two crime scene investigators had arrived in the interim and would continue their work. A fingerprint on a wine glass in the kitchen had been matched to the woman at the grave, confirmed as Mary Wilton's daughter from a photo that she had of her and Amanda Upton, and the handwriting from a letter that the mother had handed over and a diary in the apartment would be compared, although it looked to be a formality.

On the street, a uniform stood, and a sign had been placed outside the building stating that it was a place of interest to the police.

Wendy had a list of people who had some recollection of the woman from a photo she had shown them, although no one could remember speaking to her. She phoned Kate Baxter, checked on her movements for the next couple of days. Competent and in demand, she was working with Fraud, although she expressed a desire to be with Homicide if she could. Gwen Pritchard was free, and even though she had been woken from a deep sleep, she was excited at the prospect of once again working with Homicide.

If, as seemed probable, Amanda Upton had made sure to keep her activities secret, it would come as a shock to some in the building that the woman had been a high-class prostitute.

***

Larry arrived at Amanda Upton's apartment at eight in the morning, the agent having supplied a key. Inside, as the night before, or more correctly, earlier that day, nothing had been disturbed. The CSIs had completed their work, so Larry only needed to wear nitrile gloves.

In the main living area, a photo on display of a young girl and an older woman; without question, Amanda and her mother in happier times. Larry methodically walked through the apartment, casting his eyes around, aiming to understand how the woman had moved, what her nature was: tidy, obsessive, casual about where she placed her things. In the bedroom, the probable place for secrets to lie hidden, he took a seat close to the door. He then moved over to the wardrobe, slid one of the mirror-fronted doors to one side. The labels on the neatly hanging clothes were all designer labels, and not all of them had been purchased in England.

He pulled open the drawers of an antique chest of drawers, only to find the woman's underwear neatly folded, some of it wrapped in tissue. This was a methodical person, he knew, not the sort of person who would leave sensitive information visible, not the sort of person to have died for an indiscretion.

Ian Naughton figured large in the mind of Homicide, and he was seen as a strong possibility for the murder of the woman. But that brought issues. Firstly, Rose Winston had said the man had a limp, although that was being discounted for the present. It had been dark, and both she and Brad Robinson had romance on their minds, and it could have been that the murderer had just stumbled.

It did not assist in the death of Janice Robinson either. Her murder had been carefully done, with little blood and no evidence, and the man had not had sex with her. After all, Isaac reasoned, if Naughton could act as cool as a cucumber when the police were ready to break down his door, then he was a controlled man, an impassive personality, offering a veil of blandness.

However, Cathy Parkinson's murder had been anything but. For one thing, she had been knifed repeatedly, the blood splattering on two of the walls in the hotel room that doubled as her home and her business. And then she had been strung up from the shower pipe sticking out of the wall. Why the woman had been hanged made no sense as she would have already been dead. It was as if a statement was being made, but there was no way that the man could have left without his clothing having blood on it, and he had had sex with her. Two diametrically-opposed murders: one neat and tidy, the other messy and bloody. Which brought in the unresolved question as to who was sitting in the back of the BMW when one of the two white men arranged the death of Hector Robinson with the now-deceased Waylon Conroy and his gang.

Inside a bedside cabinet he found a passport in the name of Amanda Upton, a good likeness of the dead woman, close to five thousand American dollars, an equivalent amount in Euros, and a plane ticket for Paris, dated two days after she had died. Which meant that someone had been waiting for her in the French capital, a man most likely, someone that she would have provided with her services: accompanied him to the opera, wined and dined with him, bedded him.

Apart from that, Larry could find no secret compartment, no safe behind the books on a shelf, no notebook taped to the underside of a drawer.

Chapter 22

On the second floor of the building in Marylebone there were two apartments: Amanda Upton's and another that was owner-occupied. From the street, the building looked small to have two apartments on each floor, but it stretched down the narrow block, an extension that had been done forty years previously, before the tightening of building regulations.

Wendy knocked on the door of the other apartment, and it opened immediately. All the residents in the building had been previously informed by a couple of constables that they would be interviewed. Over the five storeys, there were eight two-bedroom apartments and a couple of studio apartments at the top. Three were owner-occupied, four were leased, and three were vacant.

'I was expecting you,' a smartly-dressed woman in her thirties said. 'I hope this won't take long, busy day at work.'

'Not too long,' Wendy said as she showed her warrant card. 'Can we come in?'

'Please do. I've got the kettle on, a cup of tea?'

Both the police officers acknowledged they were fine with tea, Gwen saying that she preferred hers black, and Wendy asking for two sugars.

The apartment, they could see, was not as good as Amanda Upton's, and the furniture and fittings were worn. In short, it needed renovating.

'You are Sally Fairweather?' Wendy said after the woman returned with three cups on a tray.

'I am. I work in the city, financial analyst.'

'You've been told about your neighbour?' Gwen said, anxious to make her mark, to impress her sergeant.

'I only ever knew her as Amanda, never her surname. I was told she is involved in a murder enquiry, is that true?'

'It is. Did you know her?'

'She wasn't here often, but when she was, we'd talk, sometimes go out for a meal nearby. She was keen on Indian, not that I was, too spicy for me, but I went anyway.'

'Good company?'

'Always, and I went over to her place once or twice, shared a bottle of wine.'

'Did you ever meet anyone else there?' Wendy asked.

'Never. I asked her once about her family and friends, but she always changed the subject. Surprising really, as she was pleasant, attractive, and confident. No idea why she preferred not to talk about herself, but then, some people are loners.'

'Are you?' Gwen asked.

'Not me. I've got a steady boyfriend, and sometimes he's here, sometimes I'm at his place. Low-key romance, taking it slow, see if we're ready to take it to the next level.'

To Wendy's parents, the first level would have been marriage and then sleeping together. But Sally Fairweather belonged to a different generation.

'Were you told that Amanda Upton was dead?'

'I was. I asked one of the police officers, not that he was too keen to tell me, not sure if he knew too much about it.'

'He wouldn't have. Were you upset?'

'Surprised. I can't say I was upset. We were acquaintances, and whereas I enjoyed the time that I spent with her, it wasn't that often.'

'Did she talk about where her money came from?'

'I never asked, and no, she never told me. As long as people don't bother me, I don't interest myself in their business. Although, judging by the condition of her place, I'd say she must have inherited the money.'

'And you?'

The woman looked around at her surroundings. 'Mortgaged to the hilt,' she said when she resumed looking at the two police officers. 'I'll be in debt for years with this place, the reason that it's not in good condition. I've enjoyed the increase in its value, not that it means much, only if you sell and go cheaper, which I don't intend to.'

'You could refinance, realise on your capital,' Gwen said. It was clear that the constable was on the property ladder, although unlikely to be living in Marylebone, not on her salary. Regardless, Wendy knew that was not the reason they were talking to Sally Fairweather.

'Coming back to Amanda Upton,' Wendy said, casting a glance over at Gwen, a look that said leave it to me. 'The woman was murdered. Did you know that, Miss Fairweather?'

'It wasn't explained, but I assumed she had been.'

'Why?'

'The police presence, the uniformed officer outside the front door to the building.'

'The problem is we don't know why. Did you have any idea as to what she did when she wasn't here?'

'She travelled; she told me that much, but I assumed for pleasure.'

'Amanda Upton was a high-class escort, a woman who specialised in men of wealth and influence.'

'If she was, I'm shocked. But each to their own, not that I could have done that.'

'Nor could I,' Gwen said. 'What's important is for us to find out the names of some of her contacts, and so far, we've found nothing in her apartment that helps.'

'I can't help. I'm sorry, but that's all I knew about Amanda. As I said, just an acquaintance. A nice person and I did like her, but I'm always busy, and then there's my boyfriend.'

'Will he know more?'

'I doubt it. Mostly I go to his place. He lives closer to where I work, and he's got a better place than mine.'

***

In the apartment at the rear of the building on the ground floor, a poorly-dressed man in his eighties, his straggly grey hair unkempt and uncut for a long time. He wore a jumper replete with holes, and on his hands, he wore fingerless gloves.

'Yes, what do you want?'

'Sergeant Wendy Gladstone, Constable Pritchard. We're with Homicide, Challis Street Police Station. We've a few questions.'

'If it's about her upstairs, there's nothing I can tell you.'

'Still, it's important that we interview everyone in this building. The woman has been murdered.'

'I can't say I'm surprised.'

'You knew her?' Gwen said.

'Never laid eyes on her.'

'We need to come in,' Wendy said.

Inside, the apartment did not have the pristine appearance of Amanda Upton's, nor the well-worn look of Sally Fairweather's. It smelt of dirt and damp, and there was litter on the floor. The man lived in a good area of London, yet preferred to live as a pauper, which he wasn't as he was Benjamin Yardley, a man of note in the city in his younger days, a stockbroker.

Wendy thought that he was either suffering from low-level dementia or a traumatic event in his life had changed him from dynamic to barely functioning. However, it was not of importance for the present; the dead woman was of more concern.

'You said that you weren't surprised,' Gwen said.

'Attractive, walking around in a tight skirt, showing her wares?' Yardley said.

'If you mean, was she dressing as befits a modern woman of her age, then yes,' Wendy said.

'Your constable's age?'

'More or less. Does that mean she was asking to be murdered?'

'Not from me, but there are enough people out there who would regard her dress and her manner to be asking for it.'

'Do you believe that?'

'Too promiscuous, too easy, that's the modern generation. Your constable should be more careful.'

'Mr Yardley, your personal opinion is yours,' Wendy said. 'However, it doesn't answer the question. Did you know or see the dead woman?'

'I don't go out much, not at my age, only to buy food. I saw her once. She said hello, asked how I was. How the hell did she think I was, couldn't she see?'

'Apart from that?'

'Now, if you don't mind, I've got a busy day.'

'Doing what?' Gwen asked. It was remarkable, she thought, how much he looked like her grandfather, but he was lovable and always pleased to see her, Yardley wasn't.

'Checking my money, that's what.'

Once free of Yardley and his depressing apartment, the two women walked out of the front door of the building, took deep breaths.

'Rough,' Wendy said.

Gwen did not comment, only looked up and down the street. Finally, she spoke. 'Nice area. You can't always choose your neighbours. He'd cause trouble for everyone in the building. It's a wonder he's still there.'

'More money than all of them. I can remember him when I first came to London, a financial wizard, always reading the stock market correctly, buying when others were selling. His money hasn't given him much in the way of happiness, not for a long time.'

The ground floor apartment at the front of the building was not occupied, and Wendy left Gwen to knock on the doors at the top of the building.

Out on the street there'd been little success. Amanda Upton had been sighted on a couple of occasions by some of the people, but no one had any more to say about her, and none could ever remember her in the company of anyone else, other than another woman of a similar age, identified as Sally Fairweather.

Wendy could achieve little more in Marylebone, and she returned to the police station, leaving Gwen to wrap up their enquiries.

***

Larry, although preferring not to revisit Canning Town, had to do so. The concern, not satisfactorily investigated and to some extent put to one side, was the man in the back of the car when Naughton had met with the recently deceased Waylon Conroy, a man not missed by anyone other than his mother who had wailed at the news of his demise, offering platitudes as to how she had tried her best, but a delinquent father who had taken off with another woman had rendered her motherly instincts and attempts at raising the son inadequate and of little use.

Waylon Conroy was dead, as was Warren Preston, aka Wazza, the latter the victim of his own gang, the former due to an altercation with a rival gang. Or that was what was assumed.

Larry sat in the office at Canning Town Police Station. Across from him Bill Ross, the inspector charged with solving three deaths in his area. First and foremost, Hector Robinson, killed by Conroy and his gang after receiving money to commit the act. Whether Preston had been present when the man died wasn't known.

Bill Ross picked up his mug of tea and looked out of the window, not that it was a scenic view, only a red-brick wall no more than twenty feet away. Larry could see that the man was in a good mood.

'I've got a transfer out of here,' Ross said. 'If you don't mess it up for me.'

'How?' Larry's reply.

'If you start digging for dirt, getting yourself killed. Crime's down in the area, the local hoodlums are keeping a low profile. Mind you, we've still got other villains, but someone else can deal with them.'

'Where to?' Larry said.

'Dagenham, where they used to make cars before they all went broke or had them made overseas.'

'Plenty of hoodlums there.'

'Compared to here? It's relative, and besides, it's closer to home, and the station's better equipped, a decent crew. It's not where you're from, gentleman criminals, upwardly mobile populace.'

'We have enough villains, but Dagenham will be disenfranchised, high level of unemployment. Not somewhere I'd fancy.'

'Beggars can't be choosers, and that's what I still am. It's a reprieve, in part from working with you and Isaac. It seems he put in a good word for me.'

'Then make sure you don't let him down. You harbour a few prejudices, you know that?'

'Around here? What do you expect?'

Larry had to agree, although he thought it wise not to comment. It was easy to be non-judgemental out of the area, but on a day-to-day basis dealing with people who weren't deserving of respect, it was the easiest way to deal with the situation.

'Not a lot more,' Larry conceded, aware that debate with Ross wasn't the reason he was in the station.

'You're after whoever was in the back of that car, is that it?' Ross said.

'It is.'

'I don't see how I can help. The man didn't say anything, not to Conroy and his gang. All he did was point the gun.'

'Conroy's gang?'

'One or two have been seen, not that I can do anything about them.'

'Conroy didn't kill Preston on his own.'

'The death of a hoodie gang member doesn't rate highly around here. Sorry, but that's the reality. Even if we secured a conviction, and there's no evidence that we can use with Preston's death, the prisoner would be out in a few years after suitable counselling, a do-gooder stating that the offender is a reformed person and is ready to regain his place in society.'

'He will be.'

'He may well be, but once released, what happens?'

'Social services will keep an eye on him, ensure he receives money regularly, find some work somewhere for him. But he'll not stay, too much like hard work, and then he'll be back in the same environment, the same people, the same temptations, a high probability of re-offending.'

'As you said. This man, what's the chance of finding out who he is?' Ross said.

'About as good as meeting up again with Ian Naughton or whatever name he's using now,' Larry said. It still irked him that he had had the man alongside him, even shaken his hand, and that he and Isaac had retreated from the house in Holland Park. It had been suspicious at the time, a mysterious set of clues from the grave where the murder had been committed, and then over to another grave, a metal box, an address. It still didn't make any sense, and probably wouldn't until the man was found and he explained why.

'I've got an address for one of Conroy's gang. We'll visit him, see what he's got to say for himself, but I'm not arresting him or accusing him of anything. Is that clear?'

'It's clear. Your reason?'

'Proof. And giving him the third degree isn't going to work. He knows how the system works, and he'll clam up if you push.'

Larry understood; after all, he had spent time with Spanish John and Rasta Joe before him, had met with thugs and murderers, sometimes socially if they had something that he wanted. Dealing with the criminal underclass was a fine art, and the social commentators who thought that they should all be in jail or dealt with in a draconian manner were detached from reality. There were just too many of them, and in Canning Town and other areas, the situation was worsening as technological advances were rendering unemployment levels even higher.

Chapter 23

Mary Wilton opened the door to her house. Her hair was piled up high, the makeup was back on, as were the clothes.

'Mrs Wilton, we've a few questions,' Isaac said.

'You better come in,' the woman said. 'The police on my doorstep gives me a bad reputation, starts the neighbours gossiping.'

'And when you were prostituting women here?' Wendy said.

'It was always discreet. I doubt if many knew.'

Which to Wendy was probably true. People tend to look the other way if something doesn't impact on them personally, and the brothel's clientele was usually upper middle class, men of means.

And even though Janice Robinson and Cathy Parkinson had been plagued with drugs, the photos of the two women in the brothel, arms around their madam, showed that they had once been fresh-faced and agreeable, not as the two of them had ended up, haggard, old before their time, and dead.

'We've been told that you haven't been entirely truthful with us,' Isaac said.

The three were sitting in a large room at the back of the house.

'I told you what I know. I've been honest about the business conducted here. I'll take my punishment when the time comes.'

'Which will not be severe. You know this. Is that why you've been so helpful?'

'Once this is over, I'll sell the house, find a place in the country.'

'Amanda?'

'I had hoped for better for her, I really did.'

'Mrs Wilton,' Isaac said, 'coming back to what I said before. We have it from a reliable source that you know more than you've told us.'

'I've told you what I can.'

'Can or will? There seems to be a subtle difference. One infers there is more.'

'They both do if you want to debate semantics. I admitted to knowing the three dead women, one who, if you haven't forgotten, was my daughter. What do you want me to say? That I'm sorry for their deaths? It won't make them come back, will it.'

'Are you frightened there might be more if we keep pressing? If you tell us more?' Wendy said.

'My daughter has died. What do you want me to do? Tell you more, put your lives at risk, as well as others.'

'We want and demand the truth,' Isaac said.

Wendy thought her DCI was pushing a little too hard, but she could see his point. A possible breakthrough in the murder enquiries, and the fear that the two teenagers, Brad Robinson and Rose Winston, were still targets, considering that Brad's father and sister had already died, and the two were back at school with no police protection.

'Ian Naughton?' Wendy said.

'The man in Holland Park is not Ian Naughton. He is somehow tied in to Analyn, but I'm not sure of the connection,' Mary Wilton said.

'Then who is he?'

'I don't know. Analyn spoke to me once as to how she had come to this country. I know she had not been trafficked.'

'Analyn, where can we find her?'

'I've no idea. I know of another woman, a friend of hers, where she lives. I suggest you go and see her.'

***

Bill Ross drove. A multi-storey high-rise greeted him and Larry on their arrival. Larry had seen worse not far from Challis Street Police Station, the burnt-out remains of Grenfell Tower, a reminder of similar blocks of flats.

New Barn Street was a thoroughfare connecting Barking Road and the A13 up to Dagenham, Ross's next assignment, although Larry wasn't sure it was going to be any better there; just a change of scenery, not that there was much, and a different set of villains.

Ross parked in the open area in front of the building, a patrol car close by to ensure no vandalism. As Larry looked skyward, he saw despair and squalor. Some people had washing draped over the glass-fronted balcony rails, others had attempted to create another room by blocking the balcony front from floor to ceiling with wooden boards. Once it would have been under the control of racketeers, but now it was the local council, who had clearly abrogated their collective responsibility. In the car park about forty cars, although none were old or perilously cheap. A smattering of Japanese imports, some English cars, more BMWs and Mercedes that people on subsided rents and low incomes should have been able to afford, in contrast to the building. It was high crime, low intellect.

It was good, Larry thought, that they were afforded protection by the government, both national and local, but…

A pub next to the building was closed, its windows boarded up, the outside brickwork graffitied. Larry thought it was a depressing area, the sort of place that engenders drug-taking and crime. He and Ross would do their job and get the hell out of it.

Sean Garvey lived on the fifth floor, which was just as well, as the lift inside wasn't working, vandalised by the looks of it. Larry assumed the vandals who had smashed the control panel didn't live up at the top of the building as there were at least twenty floors, but he wasn't sure of that. Vandals, youth on the cusp of crime, but still too young to be legally responsible, had probably thought it was fun. Outside, as they prepared to enter the building, a crew of local council workers arrived, followed closely by a repair vehicle from the lift company.

'Not much point, is there?' Ross shouted out.

'Not much,' the reply from a white-overalled man with a ruddy complexion and a beer gut. 'Still, it's a job. Just glad I don't have to live here.'

Larry smiled at the humour between the two men as he opened the door of the building, the lift at the end of a hallway, the stairs to their right. At the fifth floor, Ross was attempting to catch his breath; Larry had fared better, and he appreciated his get-fit regime that went with the lower alcohol consumption and his wife spurring him on.

The sound of a child crying from one of the flats, two people arguing in another flat. Ross knocked on the door where Sean Garvey lived, a surly youth answering it. 'Yeah, what do you want?'

'I telephoned. Inspectors Ross and Hill, may we come in?'

The reason for the patrol car stationed outside, Larry realised. Not just to make sure that Ross's car was untouched, but to make sure that Garvey, known on sight to the local police, didn't make a run for it.

Larry could see that Garvey had an arrogance about him, and though he was sixteen and should have been in school, he wasn't, and judging by his attitude, he wasn't concerned either way. The flat was not an agreeable sight, but then that had been expected.

'You're after our Sean?' a fat man, sitting in an armchair, bare from the waist up and holding a bottle of beer, said.

'Ganja?' Ross said, looking at the joint in the man's free hand.

'What's it to you?'

'It's Sean we want.'

'He's an idiot, I'll grant you that, but he doesn't get into much trouble, not like me when I was his age.'

'Mr Garvey,' Ross said, 'is that where Sean is heading, prison before his twenty-first birthday?'

'I was framed. It wasn't me.'

Ross looked over at the son of a man who was setting anything other than a good example to a youth well on the way to serious crime. Already, Sean Garvey had two convictions against his name, one for stealing a car, the other for illegal drug possession. He was a tall, skinny individual, able to run faster than those chasing him, although on his neck, the unmistakable scar from a knife blade.

'I haven't done nothing,' Sean Garvey said.

Other than mangle the English language, Larry thought.

'Nothing proven,' Ross said. He seemed to want to niggle the son and his father. It was succeeding, Larry could see, and the father, neither tall nor skinny, had put down his bottle of beer, rested his smoke on the edge of the armchair.

'Before we go further,' Larry said, 'you are, Sean Garvey, a member of Waylon Conroy's gang?'

'The gang's gone.'

'Warren Preston, a friend?'

'He was one of the gang. Hardly a friend, not after what he did.'

'And what was that?' Ross asked.

The father went back to his beer and turned on the television. Parental guidance and care were of little concern to him.

'Nothing.'

'Are you saying that because he spent time at the police station, he had done a deal with us?'

'He did, didn't he?'

'He never said a word, not against you and your gang, nor did he admit to the killing of Hector Robinson, the white man down by the Durham Arms. His death was pointless, but then again, none of you live for too long. Waylon Conroy?'

'I don't know what happened to him.'

'But you do know about Warren Preston, or as you call him, Wazza. Were you there? Did you see him die?'

The television went off, and Garvey Senior was on his feet. 'Are you accusing Sean of murder?' He was ready to grab Ross by the throat until Larry got between the two men.

Garvey Senior was a big man, stronger than either of the two police officers, and it was his home, and Bill

257

Ross didn't have a warrant, only a hunch that Sean Garvey could help.

'Not at all. Not at this time,' Larry said. 'What Inspector Ross wants is assistance. We're not here to accuse anyone, certainly not your son.'

'As long as we're clear.'

The father was easy to anger, easy to calm down, and he went back to his previous position, turned on the television again, took a drag of his drug, a swig of beer.

'Sean,' Larry said, 'we're not here about Waylon and Wazza. We need to find the two men who approached your gang in the street. What do you remember about the man in the car, the one with the gun?'

'Nothing, really. Waylon, he was keen to take the money, do the job, but none of us was.'

An element of truth, the two police officers realised. Bravado as a gang, a lot of talking big but not doing much about it. And as for murder, killing a rival gang member was not a crime, just the way they conducted themselves. Even if Conroy had been keen, it wouldn't have been the whole gang who would have taken part. Preston might have, but Sean Garvey was an insignificant youth, a follower, never a leader. Individually a coward, and collectively in a group bent on death, standing back, jabbing a knife in the general direction, not using force, probably not breaking the skin.

'We know your gang killed Hector Robinson and Warren Preston, not that we can prove either,' Ross said. 'And quite frankly, that doesn't concern me either way.'

Larry thought Ross's comments unusual.

Ross continued. 'It would have been Conroy on both occasions who would be the guiltiest. Two of your gang are dead, and statistically the chance of you still being alive and free after your twenty-third or twenty-fourth birthday is slim. Time will solve the murders committed by your gang, but we don't have that with the men in the car. Other people have died, more will without your help.

'Now, tell me about the men, and don't try to be smart, not like Wazza was, or it'll be down the police station and me telling the other gangs that you're an informer.'

'You can't do that,' Sean Garvey protested.

'I don't want to. You may prove to be the exception, the one who gets off his arse, finds himself a decent job, settles down, not like your father.'

Over in the armchair, no reaction. The man was asleep, his head on one side, the sound of snoring. Larry took the man's ganja rolled up in cigarette paper and doused it in the man's beer.

'The two men?' Larry said. He was tired of the flat, and the smell of beer, body odour and ganja was unpleasant. He walked over to a window and opened it, a blast of cold air entering the room.

Ross took no notice, the father continued his slumber, and the young Garvey zipped up his jacket, thinking to put the hood up, deciding against it.

'Inspector Hill asked you a question,' Bill Ross reminded him.

'The one with the money spoke well, better than us. The one with the gun didn't speak, only made sure we could see the barrel of a gun.'

'Did they speak to each other?'

'The one with the money did.'

'What did he say?'

'He spoke to the man in the car, told him to be ready if it got nasty.'

'Did the others hear? Neither Conroy nor Preston mentioned it.'

'I was closer to the car.'

Aiming to keep out of sight of the car, displaying his cowardice, or, under the circumstances, showing a degree of wisdom. As Ross had said, maybe Sean Garvey would defy the statistics.

'The two men, what did they say?'

'Only for the man in the car to be ready.'

'Not good enough. People, regardless of whether they intend to, invariably refer to the other by a name. What were they? You were either hiding away or you were smarter than the others. Which is it?'

'The man with the money, he called the other man in the car Gareth.'

'The one with the money?' Does he have a name?'

'I didn't hear one mentioned.'

'The man in the car? Educated, English?'

'An accent, although I wouldn't know what.'

It was a start, but Garvey wasn't going to improve on what he had said. Now, there was a name, not the most common of names, not the most obscure. And if the man in the car had an accent, it was not Ian Naughton.

The two men left the flat, passing the overalled man down on his knees attempting to clean the graffiti from inside the lift.

'Best of luck,' Ross said.

'Get what you wanted?' the maintenance man said.

'Not totally. Are you staying long?'

'Here? Not a chance. We'll be back again next week. We're making plenty, my offsider and me, but our company is on a fixed price contract. They'll not renew next year, and those at the top of the building are stuffed.'

'Do you care?'

'As long as I've got a job, not me.'

It was the same as in other parts of the area, Ross conceded, as he and Larry drove away. Certain parts of London were already deemed neither safe to enter nor to conduct business. The great mass of the lost was growing in size, while in the distance, visible from a high point, were the gleaming towers of the Canary Wharf financial district. Larry left Ross at Canning Town Police Station and headed back to the comparative safety of Challis Street and the adjoining suburbs. The villains were bad enough in his area, but in Canning Town and up into Dagenham, they were another breed.

Chapter 24

Questions were again being asked about why the murder investigations were taking so long, primarily by Chief Superintendent Goddard, but then, as Isaac knew, the man had the commissioner in his ear on a regular basis.

Isaac had long ago decided that worrying about the commissioner served no useful purpose. Before Commissioner Davies had assumed his position as the head of the London Metropolitan Police, his predecessor, a mentor to Richard Goddard, had seen great promise in the tall and urbane junior police officer, seen Isaac as the future of the Met, and on several occasions Isaac had featured in advertising literature for the new look, all-encompassing police force in London.

Isaac was disillusioned the first couple of times that Davies thwarted his advancement, although not more than Richard Goddard when he had confided in him. The chief superintendent should have been two rungs up the promotional ladder by now, and Isaac should have risen by one.

Isaac preferred not to dwell on the negatives, although the house that Jenny had found, close to where they lived, and the mortgage, more than he wanted to pay, but manageable, would have been rendered sweeter by the increased pay that he would have had as a superintendent.

The only two opportunities afforded Homicide to solve the murders were the name of a woman that Mary Wilton had supplied, and a name provided by Sean Garvey. The first of the two had an address, the other was vague and seemed to offer little chance of helping.

Regardless, Larry and Wendy made the trip up the M40 to Oxford, the university city, although Seacourt Road, to the west of the city, was hardly in the surrounds of university buildings and students. Instead, rows of white-painted semi-detached houses, neatly presented, no cars without engines or up on blocks in the street. It was the sort of place where middle managers lived, houses not dissimilar to the one that Isaac had made an offer on in London.

At a house at the end of the street, a Toyota in the driveway, an old cat lying close to the front door, enjoying the weak sun. Isaac leant over and pressed the doorbell.

'What do you reckon?' Wendy said as they waited. 'What do you expect to find out?'

No reply from Isaac, none that he could give. The enquiries so far had twisted and turned, with no straightforward direction. He hoped for better this time.

After what seemed an interminable wait, the door opened. In front of the two police officers stood an Asian woman, a baby in her arms.

'Come in,' she said. 'Don't worry, I know why you're here.' Her accent was the same as Analyn's.

Inside the house, neat and tidy. A baby's cot was in one corner of the living room, a television switched on, a midday soap opera, not in a language that either Isaac or Wendy could understand.

'That's Tagalog, the language of the Philippines,' the woman said as she switched the television off.

'You said you're aware as to why we're here,' Wendy said as the three of them sat down, the baby put on the floor to play with its toys.

'He'll give no trouble, not now. He's just been fed, so if I have to put him down for a nap, you'll understand. I'm Gabbi Gaffney.'

'Mary Wilton was reluctant to tell us about you. Why?' Wendy said.

'She knows my story and the reasons I wanted it left untold. She's a good woman, even if you might think otherwise.'

'Trafficked?' Isaac said.

'One moment. I know how you English like a cup of tea. My husband certainly does.'

The woman went to the kitchen, leaving Isaac and Wendy alone with the baby. Wendy, a sucker for children, leant down close to the infant and played with its toys, much to the delight of the child.

'You've got this to look forward to,' Wendy said, looking over at Isaac.

'I suppose I have,' Isaac's reply, not willing to admit that he was, although it wouldn't be a boy. Jenny had asked and been told that the child she was to deliver would be a girl, which appealed to Isaac.

Gabbi Gaffney returned, poured the tea for all three.

'You seem to have embraced England,' Wendy said.

'Now, but it wasn't always so good, but then, that's why you're here.'

'Analyn?' Isaac said.

'Yes, I know her. But first, my story and how I came to be married and in Oxford.'

'In your own time.'

'Analyn and I are not unique. A lot of women from poor villages with no hope of a good education or a good life are left with only the opportunity of toiling on the land, living a rural life.'

'Prostitution?' Wendy said.

'When life is desperate, people will do what is necessary. The men will turn to crime, the women to selling themselves. It's happened in England in the past.'

'We're not judging,' Isaac said. 'My parents came from Jamaica for a better life; ended up trapped by racketeer landlords, living in slums, labouring at whatever menial jobs they could get.'

'I found a man, an English man. He was older than me, in his late thirties. I was nineteen at the time, almost twenty.'

'Your husband?'

'My husband is much older than me, but it wasn't him. This man, attractive for his age, generous with his money, appealed to me. Some of the women are not so lucky, but financial security other than love is often a reason for marriage. And if the man is not who you wanted, as long as he looks after you and helps your family, then that's fine.'

'And this man did?'

'He came to the Philippines on three occasions, and yes, he was kind, and he did give me money for my family. In the end, I agreed to marry him.'

'And then?'

'There was a delay while he organised the paperwork for me to stay in England permanently.'

'Where is he now?'

'I don't know. Let me continue.'

'Please do,' Wendy said.

'I was in England, a small place in London, a good man for a husband. But after six months, I saw him less and less, and when he came home, he was uncommunicative, not wanting to tell me about where he'd been. Accused me of being the same as English women, always trying to control, whereas he had expected me to be subservient, do what I was told.'

'Not an uncommon story,' Isaac said.

'Anyway, after eighteen months, maybe longer, he tells me that he no longer wants me and I'm to leave.'

'Violent?'

'Not really. I think he was involved in crime, although not sure what sort. There were other women, although he never told me and I never asked, but I used to wash his clothes.'

'Crime?' Isaac asked.

'He kept guns in one of the rooms upstairs. Not that I saw them, nor did I ask. Once or twice he'd take one out with him of a night time.'

'His profession?'

'He told me he was involved in import/export, but I never saw any sign of it. Believe me, all I wanted to be was the dutiful wife, and he was looking after my family. If he had other women, not that I liked it, what could I say? We hadn't married for love, not the sort that you would understand. It wasn't hatred either. I was desperate, he was lonely.'

'As we've said, we're not judging,' Isaac said. 'Why did Mary Wilton give us your name.'

'So I can tell you about Analyn. Her story is similar to mine.'

'You were friends?'

'Not really. We had a similar background, a shared history, that's all. We kept in touch by phone, met up occasionally. England was difficult, and as much as I am glad to be here now, it wasn't always so. In the Philippines, I had my extended family, the weather was

266

hot, not cold and wet. It took time, but now I like the cold nights and rainy days.'

'We were told that Analyn ended up at Mary Wilton's. Did you?'

'Analyn had no option, I did. My husband gave me some money, and I found a job, a bedsit to live. It wasn't a great time, but I managed. Analyn left with nothing, so she took the only option. I told her not to, and I offered to help her out for a few weeks, but she was a proud woman. She had taken charity once from a man; she wasn't going to take it from me.

'I was working in a shop when my present husband came in. He wanted to talk, and he had travelled a lot, been to the Philippines, and he knew where I had lived. I agreed to meet with him, and in time my first husband had divorced me, I found my present husband, Mike's his name, a person to be with. I even grew to love him.'

'What does he do?'

'He's a teacher of geography at the local grammar school. His wife had died young, and his children had left home. I was one of the lucky ones, and we married, and I moved in here with him.'

'Analyn wasn't?'

'She had gone back to her husband.'

'You've heard from her since?'

'Two months ago. She said she was fine.'

'A phone number?'

'On my phone. Is she in trouble?'

'We don't know. Her husband?'

'I never met him. She told me that he rarely socialised, preferring to stay at home. It seemed strange, but as I said, she was an acquaintance more than a friend.

If she was safe and happy, then it wasn't for me to concern myself.'

'Your first husband?' Wendy said. 'What can you tell us about him?'

'I haven't seen him since the day I left. Mike wouldn't want to be reminded of my past, only thankful that I didn't end up in Mary's place.'

'Your first husband's name?' Isaac said.

'Gareth Rees.'

Isaac almost jumped out of his chair; Wendy sat still, not sure how to respond. From one apparently innocent woman, leads to two key people.

'The name of Analyn's husband?' Wendy asked after a pause.

'She never said.'

On the drive back to London, Isaac passed on the details to Bridget – a wedding certificate for Gareth Rees and Gabbi, as well as a photo of the man – and updated Larry as Wendy drove. It was, yet again, going to be a long night.

***

Isaac's long-held belief that if you keep prodding enough, keep asking enough questions, then sooner or later a rabbit would be pulled out of the hat. Now, in the space of twenty-four hours, two rabbits.

Sean Garvey had given the name of Gareth and Mary Wilton had told them of another woman, a fellow countrywoman of Analyn, the mysterious consort of Ian Naughton.

And in a neat and tidy white-painted house, with its wooden fence fronting on the street, a babe in arms, the tie-in had come.

The team in Homicide were elated. For once they had proof positive. Larry had a photo, and he was on his way to Canning Town, Bill Ross waiting for him, and then a visit out to Garvey.

Bridget had a phone number for Analyn and was attempting to track it, but having no success. The number was registered, but no signal was being picked up from the phone, although it was still active, a pay as you go, no address for the owner.

Whether Gabbi Gaffney had avoided the clutches of Mary Wilton, and if, as she had said, she had found work in a shop and Gareth Rees had seen her financially secure, didn't seem important for the moment. Although, if he had, it didn't seem to align with the man who had pointed a gun at Waylon Conroy and his gang.

Gareth Rees, the name on his passport and the dates of his trips to the Philippines confirmed, was an enigma. The man was a blank, with no criminal records against him, no history of employment, although a no longer used bank account and credit cards were found in his name. It was clear that Gareth Rees was the man's respectable name, and that he used aliases for his criminal activities. He was also found to have been born in a small village in the north of the country.

The perplexing part was that Ian Naughton, another alias, had called the gun-holding man Gareth, which indicated a long-term friendship.

It was unfortunate that Sean Garvey, the hoodie with a bad attitude and little parental guidance, had not heard Gareth address the other man by a first name. But Isaac knew that lightning doesn't strike twice in the same spot.

'Find Gareth Rees, bring him in, charge him with murder,' Isaac said to the team.

269

'No evidence,' Larry said, playing the devil's advocate. 'It won't stick.'

'Stick or not, we've got him at the station for twenty-four hours, forty-eight if we're lucky. We lost Naughton and Analyn once, I don't intend to lose anyone else, not at this late stage of the investigation.'

'It would help if we had his aliases,' Bridget said. 'I could run them through the system, see what I can find.'

'Fingerprints, any chance?' Wendy said.

'In the Philippines, it's a probability. Not on the wedding certificate, but Rees must have had to supply them at some stage. If we can get a copy, then we should be able to find if he has a criminal record in the UK,' Bridget said.

'Focus on that, as well as tracking Analyn's movements,' Isaac said.

'When was the last time she used the phone?'

'Thirteen days ago,' Bridget said.

'Holland Park, Godstone?' Larry asked.

'Both. She was the woman in the village on the date that the BMW was taken from the garage.'

Two days passed, two days of frustration as the team sorted through what they had, dealt with paperwork, waited for the opportunity to move forward. It was so quiet that Isaac took time to visit the bank, to sign the mortgage for the new house. He was pleased for Jenny who signed alongside him, frustrated that the crucial stage of the investigation was being hampered. So close, yet so far, he thought.

In the interim, Larry and Ross had visited Sean Garvey, this time at a pub not far from where he lived. The lift that the maintenance man had fixed was broken again, and neither of the police officers felt inclined to climb the stairs, and besides, the young man was preferred on his own, and not with his father.

Garvey had said that the man in the car and in the photo shown to him were probably the same, but couldn't be sure. It was, Larry thought, an honest answer, and Garvey wasn't so keen to talk too much, and as he admitted, the death of Waylon Conroy troubled him. He was frightened, although he had no idea who they were dealing with and where they would strike next.

Wendy visited Brad Robinson and his mother; the youth busy with his homework.

'It's Rose,' the mother said. 'She's told him that she'll never marry someone with no education.'

'Love?' Wendy said.

'At their age, hardly.'

Wendy remembered the love she had felt at Brad's age, the love that Rose felt for Brad, for a farmer's son not far from where she lived on the Yorkshire Moors. She had given herself to him, the same as Rose intended to with Brad. The farmer's son, Wendy knew, was now married with five children, struggling to survive financially, and his health was poor. She had fared better with the man she eventually married, even though he had been singularly unambitious. He had, however, given her two fine sons and grandchildren.

'The Winstons?' Wendy asked of the mother.

'Maeve's still with Rose's father, for her sake more than anything else. That's what she says.'

'She keeps in contact?'

'We meet occasionally, and she's often on the phone. She probably won't forgive her husband, but she's not the type to take off and find another man, and besides, she's got a good life, better than mine.'

'You've got Brad,' Wendy reminded her.

271

'And Jim, soon enough. He's got another five months, and he'll be free.'

'Keep to the straight and narrow?'

'He might want to, but temptation will get in the way. Who's going to give a job to an ex-prisoner, and he's got no skills, other than what he picked up in prison.'

'It's up to Brad to bring respectability to the family,' Wendy said.

'It's too early to know, but I do like Rose. She's the same as her mother, dependable, and Brad's more like Rose's father than his own father.'

'I had some concern that you and Tim…?'

'At school. No, Tim's not Brad's father, even though they look the same in some ways.'

'Janice? Do you think about her?'

'All the time. In time she might have straightened herself out, but it doesn't matter now. She's gone, a plot at the cemetery next to her father.'

'Kensal Green?'

'Not there, too expensive. I find myself talking to Hector. Strange, we get on better now that he's dead than when he was alive. I can pour out my heart, not have to listen to him shouting back at me.'

'We're close,' Wendy said as she sat back in her chair. As rundown as the house was, it was inviting, a place to make yourself comfortable, whereas up at the Winstons, a person felt that they should sit upright, fearful of making the place look untidy.

'Is Brad safe?

'I hope so. We're still troubled by the murders. There's no rhyme or reason for Janice's death, nor for your husband's. And then there are the other women, a Cathy Parkinson and an Amanda Upton.'

'I met Cathy once, not that I can tell you much about her. She was with Janice in Notting Hill. I bumped into them on the street.'

'Prostituting?'

'Not there, not where all the tourists are. But yes, the two were selling themselves, not that Janice would admit to it, not back then.'

'Cathy Parkinson?'

'As I said, I met her, passed the time of day, nothing more. I could see that she was in a bad way. Just hoped that Janice would get through it, not that she did.'

'Are Brad and Rose meeting up?'

'At school. Who knows where else? Tim Winton might be neurotic about protecting his daughter, and Maeve will go along with him, not that she's as severe as him, but Brad's responsible, and Rose won't allow anything to get out of hand. She won't be coming home pregnant, not before marriage, not like with Jim, barely made it to the church in time.'

'Amanda Upton?'

'She was the body at the cemetery, wasn't she?'

'It was the woman that Brad and Rose saw. We know more about her, sold herself, high-class escort, not the sort to tarry on a street corner.'

'Not like my daughter.'

'I'm sorry. Maybe I shouldn't have said that.'

'It was true, nothing to apologise for. I only hope that Brad survives, and he doesn't succumb to drugs and drink.'

'A possibility?'

Gladys Robinson's voice went low. She came over close to Wendy and whispered in her ear. 'He's not Hector's.'

Wendy had seen it before, even commented on it, that Brad was tall for his age and slim, whereas Hector Robinson and the other son, Jim, were short.

'Does he know?'

'Nobody knows. It was one of those times when Hector and I were having difficulties, more often than not if the truth's known.'

'The father?'

'I've told you that confidentially, woman to woman. You see, I have hope for Brad.'

'Wouldn't he benefit from the truth?'

'One day, but not now. He was close to Janice, good friends with Jim. It would destroy Brad to be told.'

'But it would make it easier with Rose's parents.'

'The son of an illicit affair, I doubt it.'

'And he's not Tim's?'

'Not a chance. I know who the father is; let's leave it at that. Nobody needs to know, do they?'

'I can't see it as being relevant,' Wendy said.

Chapter 25

Sean Garvey hadn't been sure that the photo of Gareth Rees was the armed man in the car in Canning Town. However, the waitress at the café in Godstone, as well as the estate agent who had let the house, were certain when Larry showed them the photo. The man they knew was Gareth Rees.

Wendy met up with Meredith Temple at a restaurant close to Meredith's university. The woman was doing well, had just passed some exams and was full of herself.

'I'm planning to move in with my boyfriend,' Meredith said.

'Long-term romance?' Wendy asked.

'I hope so.'

'Does he know?'

'My past? Not yet. Do I need to tell him?'

'The past never leaves us totally. One day, a former client, the wrong word from him and your boyfriend's gone. Men can be unpredictable when faced with reality.'

'Don't I know it. Another man, while I was on the game, he knew, made out that he didn't care, but they all do to some extent. It's natural, I suppose.'

'When you were at Mary Wilton's, did you meet any other women from the Philippines?'

'Some, but I can't say I spoke to them, not that much.'

Wendy pushed a photo across the table. 'Her, for instance?'

'I can't remember her name, or maybe I never asked, but yes, she was there around the same time as Analyn.'

Wendy had hoped that Gabbi Gaffney had been truthful about her past, but Meredith had contradicted her. It had been Gabbi's photo that Wendy had shown.

'Does the name Gareth Rees mean anything to you? Or this photo, do you recognise the man?'

'He came in once, not sure who he saw.'

'Interesting,' Wendy said. She liked Meredith Temple; she hoped she wasn't further involved, as Gabbi Gaffney appeared to be.

The two women ate their meals, drank their glasses of wine, and talked about this and that, nothing in particular. Wendy wasn't anxious to leave; another trip to Oxford didn't appeal that night. It was one of her grandchildren's birthdays, and she wanted to go over to her son and daughter-in-law's house to give the child his present. But, if duty called, then it would have to be another night.

Once out of the restaurant, and not wanting to delay further, Wendy phoned Gabbi, the phone answered by a man with a Glaswegian accent.

Wendy asked for Gabbi, not wanting to elaborate on the reason for the call, not sure how much the husband knew.

'This is about Gareth Rees, I assume,' Mike Gaffney said.

'Yes.'

After a brief interlude, Gabbi picked up the phone. 'Sorry, the baby needed feeding. Always a performance.'

'How much does your husband know?' Wendy asked.

'He knows everything, no secrets between husband and wife, not in this household.'

'But there is. Mary Wilton never told me, but another of her women did. You didn't find a job in a shop straight away. Why didn't you tell me you had worked for Mary Wilton?'

'Shame, I suppose. It wasn't for long, and yes, back in Manila I had done things that I regretted. I thought that Mary Wilton's would tide me over.'

'Gareth Rees visited you there. I know this to be a fact.'

'He was an angry man, and when he had thrown me out, he gave me nothing. The only money I had was in my bag, about five hundred pounds. It wasn't going to last long, not to find somewhere decent to live, and I was at an emotional low, didn't care too much what happened to me.'

'Why the visit?'

'He had felt some remorse. I told you about the guns. I never asked, but I was certain that he used them.'

'Ian Naughton?'

'No.'

'So how come Analyn is with the man we know as Ian Naughton?'

'I don't know. He could have met her through Gareth, but I can't be sure. Gareth was unfaithful, I know that. She could have been one of Gareth's women, or this Ian Naughton.'

'Your husband, Mike?'

'He's listening in. As I said, no secrets. He knows the whole story. Life was tough back in the Philippines, people do what they can to survive. That's what I had done at Mary's.'

'Is that the whole truth? Or do I need to come up to Oxford, slam you in a prison cell and give you the third degree? Lying to the police is a crime, and too many people have died, and Gareth Rees is a strong contender for some of them. A fastidious man?'

'Always well-dressed, aftershave, a freshly-pressed shirt. Yes, he was fastidious.'

'Gabbi, don't lie. People have died for reasons that we don't know, for being connected through Mary Wilton's daughter. It's not over yet, so be careful. We don't know who or what we're dealing with. Gareth? Psychopathic, a sociopath?'

'What's the difference? What do they mean?'

'Anti-social, uncaring, unable to distinguish between right and wrong, lies, deceives, uses false names, unable to make long-term plans.'

'Not Gareth. He was meticulous in arranging the paperwork in the Philippines, and he cared, not always, but he had felt sorry for how he had treated me that day. If he was as bad as you think he might be, I can't say I saw it.'

'I suggest you don't leave the house for a couple of days, nor your husband. I'll phone the local police station, ask them to keep a watch on your house, and I'll text you a couple of numbers for speed dial if you need them,' Wendy said.

Whereas there was no fathomable reason for the other deaths, Gabbi Gaffney had helped the police in the hunt for her first husband. If he was as dangerous as suspected, it was a possibility that he would see his former wife as someone who had betrayed him.

Also, the death of Janice Robinson had been clinical with little blood spatter, the sign of a careful man, like Gareth Rees. Cathy Parkinson's had been messy, which indicated either a master disguise by Rees or a different person.

***

Rees continued to be a conundrum. On the one hand, decent and caring; on the other, violent and quick to anger. And it did appear that his affection for Gabbi had been genuine in that he had applied for permanent residency in the Philippines, and the documentation had required fingerprints.

It had taken longer than expected, the bureaucracy in the Philippines, but Bridget had the prints, and they were in the database. If the man had a criminal record, it would soon be known, a list of aliases used as well.

Wendy visited Tim and Maeve Winston, found the atmosphere in the house chilly, but more for her sake, as well as for Rose, husband and wife chatted amicably. But behind closed doors Wendy doubted if there were any signs of affection between the loyal and dependable Maeve and the philandering Tim. And Janice was probably not the man's first dalliance, even if it came with a deviant attraction, in that he had slept with the mother when she had been younger.

'We're still concerned for Rose,' Tim Winston said. He was sitting in one chair, his wife in another. Rose had excused herself and gone to her room, homework mentioned as the reason, although messaging to Brad had to be considered.

'We believe we've found a significant lead on one of the men,' Wendy said.

'Men?' Maeve Winston said. 'We thought there was only one and the Asian woman.'

279

'So did we, until we came across the other man in Canning Town. We've got a name for him; his birth name, as well as a photo. Although we're certain that he doesn't use that name most of the time.'

'How?'

'The name?'

'Yes.'

'He married a woman from the Philippines, brought her to England, ensured she got permanent residency and then turned her out of the marital house.'

'Charming,' Tim Winston said. 'Not something I could do.'

'I could,' his wife said sneeringly, directing her gaze at her husband.

The underlying tension was palpable, not an ideal environment for the susceptible Rose, a young woman with illusions of perfect love, the result of her sensitive nature and a mind full from reading mushy romance stories.

'This other man,' Tim Winston said, ignoring his wife's aside. 'Did he kill Janice?'

'He's a fastidious man. Her death was clean and tidy, well-executed. Cathy Parkinson's wasn't, so we are tending to rule him out for that one, but Amanda Upton's was neat, clinical.'

'He killed her?'

'Amanda? It's probable. That's why we're leaning toward military training.'

'A trained killer?'

'Trained at the taxpayer's expense and now loose on the street. He could be a gun or a knife for hire, but we have reason to believe that he was on close personal terms with the man we know as Ian Naughton.'

'Cathy Parkinson?' Maeve Winston asked.

'The woman was as low as she could get. A hopeless drug addict, she survived from one hit to the next. Janice Robinson wasn't much better, but she was holding her head above water. With the right care and desire on her part, she might have redeemed herself.'

'Statistically, or is that for Gladys Robinson's benefit? She wasn't the best mother.'

'She was a terrible mother, still is. She means well, but she's weak, besotted with vodka.'

'I still like her, even after all that's happened.'

'So do I,' Wendy said. 'An open book.'

'Is she?' Tim Winston said. 'There are enough skeletons in her cupboard.'

'I'm not sure how much she knew about the abuse of Janice by the men who stayed with her.'

'She must have suspected.'

'Skeletons in the cupboard, as you say. But Brad's almost adult now, no reason to rake over old coals. And besides, I'm Homicide, not social services. They haven't proved anything, not that I'm sure they would have known. Believe me, every house has its demons, even yours.'

It seemed to Wendy that the conversation with the Winstons was glib and of little relevance; as if she was giving them a briefing, getting nothing in return. It wasn't the reason for being in the house.

'Did either of you know Cathy Parkinson or Meredith Temple?' Wendy asked. She didn't expect a direct answer, not from the husband with his wife in the room.

'I don't make it a habit of associating with prostitutes,' Maeve Winston said.

'The names don't mean anything to me,' Tim Winston said.

His response was direct, and to the point, Wendy noted. No determined statement that he didn't know them, that he didn't make a habit of killing women, the response of the usually indignant man. But Winston was impassive, and he looked straight forward, not making eye contact with either his wife or Wendy.

Wendy knew that she wasn't an expert at reading people, but Winston had a sheepish look about him.

'Rose and Brad?' she asked.

'Not if I can help it,' Tim Winston said.

'Tell me about Gladys Robinson. We know that Hector, her husband, was with her on and off, and then he left for good after Jim had given him a good thumping.'

'In particular?'

'The men she went out with; the men who could have abused Janice.'

'Maeve may know something. I certainly don't.'

'I rarely saw her,' Maeve said. 'Sometimes at the school, in the street occasionally, and once or twice we met, had a bite to eat, a cup of coffee. Apart from that, I never saw any of the men, although once Gladys had a bruise on her face.'

'One of them hit her?'

'Not that she'd admit to it. Gladys deserved better than Hector, but she was unable to rise above her lowly origins, condemned to live the life of her parents.'

'She wanted better?'

'She wanted Tim, but he was mine, although I'm not so sure I made the best decision.'

'Rose is your primary concern. It's for you to ensure she grows up in a nurturing environment.'

'We both know that,' Tim Winston said. 'Brad Robinson's not the person for her; his background, his family.'

Wendy wanted to say the genetic encumbrance that the Winstons believed that Brad had, had been diluted, but it was the one secret she knew she would keep.

'Tell me, Mr Winston, are you a fastidious man?'

'Are you inferring that I could have killed Janice? I may be many things, but I'm not a murdcrcr.'

'But you knew one of the other women.' Wendy had tired of skirting around the issues. She hadn't wanted Maeve Winston to be hurt any more than she had been already, but it was a murder enquiry, not a knitting circle, and definitely not the old ladies and their Ouija board that she had chanced on early in the investigation.

'You'd better answer the sergeant,' Maeve said. 'If I'm to forgive you eventually for Janice, then you'd better own up. Two won't be more difficult than the one.'

'I knew Meredith Temple,' Winston admitted.

'At Mary Wilton's?'

'Yes. You realise what you're doing?'

'I do, getting to the truth,' Wendy said. 'I'm sorry, Mrs Winston,' looking over at the wife, 'but this is necessary. I need to know if your husband is capable of murder.'

Both husband and wife were on their feet; both were distraught.

'How dare you?' Maeve Winston said. 'We invite you in, show you courtesy. And you can say that.'

'Good,' Wendy said, adopting an Isaac tactic. 'You're both riled.'

'You want this?'

'Too much beating around the bush. Let's talk honestly. I don't think your husband is a murderer, not yet. But in his defence, he needs to convince you and me that he's telling the truth. I, as an experienced police officer, will know from my training and many murder enquiries; you will know as you are married to him. Sorry to be blunt, but that's the way it is.

'Let's get down to basics. Janice was killed by a fastidious, probably trained killer. And so was Amanda Upton. Which leaves us with Cathy Parkinson. That death was neither professional nor pleasant. Now, either the murderer was inexperienced, or he felt joy in killing her and then stringing her up, or it was professional, made to look as if an amateur had committed it. He had also had sex with her before the murder, whereas Janice's murderer had not.'

'Maybe the man was incapable,' Maeve Winston said.

'If it's Gareth Rees, then we know that he's capable. But we continue to assume there was a different murderer for Cathy Parkinson.'

'Hector Robinson?'

'He was killed by a local gang of hoodies: poorly educated, disenfranchised, the flotsam of society. Not that there will ever be a conviction and two of them are dead; one at the hand of his gang, the other by an unknown assailant, although more than likely a rival gang. Life is tough where they live, and most of them don't live for long, violence and death come too easily. Which leaves Cathy Parkinson. It could be the man we know as Ian Naughton, but so far, we don't know too much about him, other than DCI Cook and DI Hill met the man briefly.'

'Are you trying to pin this Cathy Parkinson's death on Tim?' Maeve said.

'I don't want to. But what I want is the truth. Mr Winston, you knew one of the other women, which indicates that you knew Mary Wilton's premises. Am I correct?'

'You're correct. I knew Meredith. I've told you that already.'

'You paid for her services?'

'I did,' Winston said in a quiet voice.

'Cathy Parkinson?'

'No.'

'Why not?'

'Don't make me out to be a monster. Okay, I slept with Janice and the other woman. If I say I regret it now, it's not going to make any difference. However, I draw the line that I murdered this other woman. I can vaguely remember seeing her, and if it's the same person, she wasn't in good shape.'

'Analyn?'

'Not the name.'

'Gabbi, another Asian woman?'

'A picture?'

Wendy took out her phone, scrolled through the photo gallery, passed it over to Tim Winston.

'Yes, I can remember her, but no, I did not sleep with her. Only with Janice occasionally and Meredith on one occasion. Is she dead? Are you going to try and pin that on me?'

'She's alive and well, no longer lying on her back to make money. She's sorted herself out.'

'Where is she?' Maeve Winston asked.

'At university, doing well.'

One more suspect to consider, Wendy thought, after she left the Winstons' house. Tim Winston's misdemeanours were more than had previously been considered. The man, outwardly portrayed himself as a solid family man, good father, responsible citizen, but there was a dark side to him, a side that enjoyed the company of prostitutes.

Chapter 26

Wendy realised after leaving the Winstons that revealing that Meredith Temple was studying at a university may not have been wise; after all, the apparent lack of connection between the murders, and the unknown motives, might have placed her in jeopardy.

To Wendy, Tim Winston had always seemed to be a decent man, but his rating as a good husband to Maeve had suffered a few too many blows. The revelations of him and Janice Robinson, and now of his having spent time with Meredith Temple, were starting to damn the man. And if she mentioned to her DCI that she hoped it wasn't Tim for the sake of his wife and daughter, Wendy knew that she would receive a gentle rebuke, in that it was murder, and the guilty is the guilty, with no lesser investigation of the upright and decent than of the despicable and criminal.

Wendy had phoned Gabbi Gaffney, checked on Gareth Rees and his sexual appetite; she confirmed that he was normal on that count. That meant that Rees could have killed Cathy Parkinson as well as Janice Robinson.

In the office, on Wendy's return, Larry Hill was briefing Isaac as to what he had found out on the street, although judging by the smell of beer, the discussions with Spanish John, various informers, the destitute and despondent had been conducted in a licensed premise.

'Nobody seems to be able to help much,' Larry said as Wendy passed over a strong mint from her handbag.

'Here, suck on this,' she said.

Isaac remembered when his sergeant had first joined Homicide, and the smell of her smoking. He had had words with her on a few occasions, almost put it in writing once, and now the woman, no longer smoking, was criticising another member of the department for the unpleasant smell.

Larry took the mint, gave an embarrassed grunt in acknowledgement, and placed it in his mouth.

Isaac, choosing not to comment on Wendy's actions, focussed back to the investigation. 'Wendy, Tim Winton? A possibility?'

'Remote, but can't be ruled out. Even so, no motive.'

'But he does,' Larry said. 'His wife and daughter. If the man can't help himself and his wife had him on short rations, who knows? And then Janice is killed, and he knows that it's only a matter of time before we find out about him and her, so he could rationalise, no matter how obscure it seems, that others who know about his needs have to be removed.'

'He's right,' Isaac said, looking over at Wendy.

'I know. It's Cathy Parkinson that concerns me. He said that he hadn't slept with her, only Janice Robinson and Meredith, so why kill her?'

'The man would have been frantic; secrets were about to be revealed.'

'Cathy Parkinson might have spoken, mentioned to someone that she knew about Janice and some of her clients. Her brain was probably addled, functioning on highs and lows, a loose cannon.'

'And one of Janice's clients could have been Gareth Rees or even the mysterious Ian Naughton.'

'Except, that Naughton had Analyn, or so we believe,' Isaac said. 'Why would he have wanted any of the other three? And we met him, remember. He didn't seem the sort of man to go down market.'

'Don't discount someone on what you believe,' Wendy said. 'Your mantra.'

'I can't argue with you, and besides, what we saw might have been a veneer.'

Bridget entered Isaac's office, handed each of the three already there a folder. 'Inside, Gareth Rees, what I could find out.'

'Criminal record?'

'When he was younger, and he used the name of Rees. But as he was a minor, his fingerprints weren't kept on file, a way to give the young man a chance at life, untarnished by a troubled childhood.'

'The précised version,' Isaac said. Larry had opened his folder, so had Wendy. Isaac's sat closed on the desk.

'He was court-martialled out of the military after an incident somewhere in the Middle East. No details and it's unlikely we'll ever find out what it was.'

'Violence?'

'His record in the military had been exemplary. You'll find the usual: where he was assigned, countries overseas, commendations, and so on. But after the court-martial, nothing, not from the military. It seems that he had been found guilty and bundled out of the service, no time in a military prison.'

'Suspicious?' Isaac said.

'Highly,' Larry said, 'but it proves one thing, he would have been capable of murdering Amanda Upton.'

'There's more,' Bridget said. 'I found a fingerprint match. Gareth Rees used an alias, Peter Hood. That name has a criminal conviction against it for grievous bodily harm. This is before he entered the military.'

289

'They recognised raw talent.'

'Gareth Rees in the military; Peter Hood for the GBH. However, his time in prison was short, and soon after release, he was in uniform.'

'As I said, raw talent.'

'The army wouldn't necessarily take a man with a criminal record,' Isaac said.

'Ordinarily, they wouldn't,' Larry agreed. 'But in extreme circumstances, who knows. A naturally-talented and unemotional man might have suited them fine.'

'Gabbi Gaffney told me he was not psychopathic, and that he had treated her with a degree of respect,' Wendy said.

'With the right triggers, he could have been.' Isaac said. 'Behind enemy lines, an assassination, the possibility of collateral damage, innocent people to die in the attempt to get close into the target. It would take a special kind of person, the sort of person who could kill women.'

'The sort of person who could kill a couple of teenagers,' Wendy said.

'This trigger? How would it be switched on and off?' Bridget asked.

'We don't know. All I know is, we need Rees or whatever he calls himself,' Isaac said.

***

Larry made contact with Spanish John, gave him the other name that Gareth Rees had used in the past. Wendy phoned Meredith Temple, told her to make herself scarce for a couple of days, an unknown address, and not to answer her phone unless she was sure of the caller. She also phoned both the Robinsons and Winstons, and told them to take Brad and Rose out of school, and to keep them at home, and that a police presence would be at both houses.

Questions came from all parties contacted; the answer given by Larry and Wendy that the pressure was building up, and persons unknown and known were likely to react irrationally. It wasn't a good explanation, but it was the best they could give.

An APB was issued to all police forces throughout London and England, along with a clear photo. Gareth Rees, also known as Peter Hood, was to be regarded as extremely dangerous. No one was to approach unless armed, and they were to report back to Homicide at Challis Street Police Station.

Ian Naughton still remained the greatest mystery. With the other two that Homicide were looking for, there was, at least, some knowledge. And as to the grave at Kensal Green, a murder site and a cryptic clue to another grave, and Naughton's house in Holland Park – a complete blank.

Three steps forward, two back, Isaac thought. He had the added burden of the sale of his flat and the purchase of a house, as well as Jenny looking to him to go with her to the gynaecologist occasionally. So far, he'd managed it once, and now with the investigation in its closing stages, he couldn't afford to spare his wife the time. It was what he loved about her, the ability to understand, but she didn't like it and they had argued the night before as to how finding a murderer took precedence over his child.

Isaac knew the tension was building on Jenny, with the impending birth, decorating the baby's bedroom, but she was right. It was time for him to back off from the investigation and to deal with family matters. But he needed a couple of days more. He could feel the tension in the department, the excitement building that arrests were to be made; a long-overdue breakthrough.

***

Bill Ross phoned Larry, told him to get over to Canning Town within the hour. It was the last place that Larry wanted to be, but he complied. The information had been clear.

'It's Sean Garvey,' Ross said.

On the street outside the block of flats where Garvey had lived, a tent had been erected in the middle of the road, traffic banking up in each direction, the uniforms doing their best to direct the traffic up side streets; not so easy, Larry knew, as New Barn Street was a major thoroughfare, and it was the middle of the day.

Ross was standing on the side of the road, the father of the dead youth with him. The father was in tears; Larry assumed it was the usual 'he was a good boy', 'never forgot my birthday'. Always, he knew, after the event, the parents who had failed the child remembered the good, omitting the bad.

'Shot,' Bill Ross said as he excused himself from the father.

'A gang?'

'Not likely. A shot from the other side of the road. We're checking CCTV cameras, but there aren't many around here.'

'Professional?'

'The gangs are more into knives, although they're keener on guns than they used to be, but this was daylight, no more than fifty minutes ago. No self-respecting hoodie would contemplate causing trouble in the early morning; they're strictly night time.'

'Any witnesses?'

'The father said he was looking out of the window, saw his son fall to the ground. He couldn't have seen the shooter. What the crime scene team have ascertained, a car was parked on one of the side streets, twenty yards back. There's a fire escape up the side of a building there, a metal structure, the ideal place for a marksman, a clear view of Garvey's flat and the road. The man could have been waiting there for Garvey to come out, or he could have phoned him.'

'The number?'

'Who knows? Slip one of Conroy's gang some money, and they'll tell you anything.'

'We've got an all-points out on Gareth Rees.'

'If it's him, it means he's frightened, making sure that anyone who can connect him to the murders is eliminated.'

'Garvey knew nothing,' Larry said.

'Maybe he didn't, but this Rees character doesn't know that. He's trapped, lashing out, trying to protect himself.'

'Which means others closer in to the murders are under threat.'

Larry took out his phone and called Isaac, conferencing in Wendy. 'It's not a random death; this has been well-executed. And if it's Rees, we're trying to confirm that, then the man's clearly deranged. We need the chief superintendent to authorise protective custody for the Robinsons, the Winstons, and for Meredith Temple. We're dealing with a mad man, a man who knows how to kill.'

'Consider his approval given,' Isaac said. 'If it's Rees, see if you can find out the car he was driving, and then Bridget can work her magic.'

Wendy left the office immediately, her first port of call, the Robinson household. As much as Tim Winston disapproved of Brad Robinson and his mother, as suspicious as Wendy was of the man, the two families would need to be in the one location, and unless anyone objected, not that she intended to let them, they were all to move in at the Winstons'. A patrol car was already on its way to the Winstons'; another was around the corner from the Robinsons'. It wasn't sufficient protection for either of the families.

Meredith Temple had been phoned, but she had lectures to attend, and regardless of Wendy's protestations, study took preference, although the woman promised to be careful.

At the crime scene, possible witnesses were being interviewed. A video copy from a camera at the corner of New Barn Street and the A13 up to Dagenham was with the CCTV officers at Canning Town, and with Bridget, who before joining Homicide had been a CCTV officer.

A uniform came over to where Bill Ross and Larry were standing; at her side a young woman in her twenties, a small child in a pushchair.

'I was taking a picture of her,' the young woman said, her accent thick and Slavic; she stroked the child on the head as she spoke.

'In the background,' the female uniform said. 'A man on the fire escape.' She handed the phone over to Larry, who enlarged the picture as best he could. It was blurry, but it was a good likeness of Gareth Rees.'

'What do you reckon?' Ross said.

'I reckon it's him. I'll forward the photo on to Bridget, see if she can enhance the image.'

'It makes no sense. Why would he still be around? Why kill people on the off-chance?'

'We'll know when he's in custody.'

'Can I keep the phone?' Larry said to the mother. 'It's evidence.'

'I saw the car,' the reply.

'A photo?'

Larry couldn't believe that twice lucky with the same witness was possible.

'It's in the photo.'

Larry looked at the picture again, realised that there was a car, blue in colour, almost certainly a small Toyota.

'The registration number on the plate?'

'I didn't see it. Should I have?'

'No, not at all. It's just that we've been looking for this man for some time. We regard him as dangerous.'

Larry texted Bridget to focus on the car in the photo, to use whatever image-enhancing software was at her command.

'Where do you live?' Bill Ross asked the woman.

'Here,' pointing to the same building that Garvey had lived in. The two police officers understood that not everyone in the building was a criminal or lazy or uneducated. The young woman and her child were well-dressed, very presentable, and no doubt honourable and decent. Larry felt sorry for them that circumstances, the need for a better life than where they had come from, had condemned them to purgatory, although he was sure that in time the woman and her husband would earn their way out of there by hard work and a positive attitude.

***

The net was closing on Gareth Rees, now generally regarded as verging on the psychopathic. It was considered by the team in Homicide and on advice from a phycologist that Rees needed to be handled with a great deal of care. Pressure had been applied by Chief Superintendent Goddard to the military to obtain a transcript of Rees's court-martial and information about his state of mind, but he had had no luck.

A logical mind would have distanced himself from London, and Rees was clearly intelligent and organised, as he had managed to alternate between two names with apparent impunity. There were even two British passports in his name, and if he had left the country, hidden away in a backwater somewhere in the world, then he could have remained at liberty indefinitely.

Bridget had taken the photo from the young woman's phone in Canning Town, enhanced it, proven that Gareth Rees had been on the fire escape and he had at his side a bag, the approximate size of a rifle with telescopic sights, as Sean Garvey had received one bullet to the head, dead before he hit the ground.

The All-Points had been updated with a registration number, more good work from Bridget, and the make of car, a Toyota as believed, as well as its year of manufacture and colour.

Surveillance cameras were scanning for the vehicle, as were cameras in each and every patrol car. It was an automatic sequence; it was bound to give a result, if the car was still visible, its progress after it left Canning Town, and if within the concentration of cameras in the city, a reasonably accurate detail of the location where it had been last seen, good enough for more concentrated enquiries, out on foot and walking the area.

The team knew that Gareth Rees was coming to them; there were just too many factors against him now, although if he was to be taken, armed officers would be needed. Isaac phoned the head of the team that they had used at Naughton's address in Holland Park, assured him that this time it was not a wild goose chase and that Rees was experienced, armed, a murderer, and a crack shot. This was not an amateur that they were dealing with.

Chapter 27

Gareth Rees sat in the interview room at Challis Street. His arrest had been without violence; the man had even been polite as he got out of his car after a patrol car had picked up the registration plate. Isaac had spoken to him briefly on his arrival and could see that he was as Gabbi Gaffney had described. He was well-dressed, an open-necked shirt, a jacket, a pair of grey trousers. He was tall, clearly fit for his age, known to be forty-four.

So far, the man had not had a chance to give his side of the story, although he had been formally cautioned and told that he was in the police station on suspicion of murder. A lawyer of his choice was on the way to the station, and until the man arrived, the interview would not commence.

At eleven-thirty in the morning, the imperious Jacob Jameson entered the station. He was known at Challis Street, a fair-minded man of searing intellect, a cultured accent, the child of affluent parents, and his manner in a courtroom and the eloquence of his speeches for the defence had meant that more than a few villains had walked free. Isaac was determined this was not to happen with Rees.

Isaac went through the formalities in the interview room. Rees sat back on his chair, only sitting upright when stating his name. Jacob Jameson, resplendent in a pin-striped suit, sat firm, his arms folded, only unfolding them to read the case against his client, the murders so far, and the evidence, which, apart from the killing of Sean Garvey, was perilously weak.

'My client reserves comment,' Jameson said. 'Apart from a blurry photo and Mr Rees being in the location of a shooting in Canning Town, and we will contend that he was there on legitimate business, your evidence is based on the circumstantial, and the frustration of the police in failing to find the murderer.'

'Mr Rees,' Isaac said, 'you were in New Barn Street at the time Sean Garvey was shot.'

'I was,' Rees responded. 'I saw a commotion, that's why I left.'

'And you were on a fire escape, with a clear view of the man?'

'I'll not deny it; no point, seeing you have the photo.'

'Your purpose for being up there?'

An interruption from Jameson. 'My client was checking out a property for sale. The prices are depressed in the area, and he was taking the opportunity to evaluate a possible investment.'

Isaac looked over at Larry as if to say, is this true?

Outside the room, Wendy phoned Bridget, asked her to check.

'You were carrying a bag?' Isaac directed his question to Gareth Rees.

'I was.'

It seemed to Isaac and Larry that the forty-five minutes that Rees and his lawyer had spent together before the interview had been time well used. There was no doubt that Rees was Garvey's murderer, but no one had seen the rifle, nor the shot being taken, and the weapon had not been found. Rees was innocent until proven guilty, and Chief Superintendent Goddard, who was listening in from the other room, realised that at this rate the man could still walk free.

Bridget came back within five minutes to state that the building with the fire escape had been up for sale four weeks previously, but had since been withdrawn from sale. Whether Rees knew this wasn't important.

The case against Rees was not cast-iron.

Isaac, struggling to keep the interview going and in the police's favour, tried a different tack.

'Mr Rees, Godstone, a village to the south of London. Do you know it?'

'I do.'

'You rented a house there in the company of an Asian woman.'

'I've driven through it, had a pint of beer in the pub, and as to this Asian woman, I only know of one, and she did a runner as soon as I got her permanent residency in England.'

'Are you in contact with your former wife?' Larry asked.

'No, but I know where she is.'

A veiled threat, Isaac wondered. Rees would have realised that it must have been Gabbi Gaffney who was the primary source of information for the police.

'You are also known as Peter Hood.'

'I am.'

'Why?'

'A man is entitled to call himself what he wants.'

'Your evidence?' Jameson said. He said little, waited his time. Whether Gareth Rees was innocent of the crime that the police alleged was not his concern. His job was to give the best legal advice and expertise that money could buy, and Jameson wasn't cheap, which meant that Rees or someone else had the money to pay him.

'Do you know a Janice Robinson?' Larry said.

Isaac would have preferred that Larry hadn't raised the woman's name, not yet.

'Canning Town, tell us about your time there?' Isaac said, focussing back to the area.

'I prefer to keep out of there as much as possible,' Rees's reply.

'Why?'

'Have you been there? It's not the best part of London, more like Baghdad than Britain.'

'And you've been to Iraq?'

'I have. I was a soldier, enough medals to wallpaper this room.'

'You were a killer.'

'I followed orders. That's what they teach you, and those who join the military hoping for an education and a cushy life are naïve. In the military, you kill or are killed, whether you like it or not.'

'And you, Mr Rees, did you like it?'

'Killing people?'

'Yes.'

'If ordered, I did my duty.'

Jameson was looking over at his client, unsure where the questioning was heading. He leant over, whispered in his ear. 'They're baiting you.'

Rees sat up straight again, rested his arms on the desk. 'Someone had to do it, so you can all sleep safe in your beds at night. And, no, I didn't enjoy it.'

'Sometimes, innocent people were killed.'

'Sometimes.'

'Is that why you were court-martialled?'

'My client's military record,' Jameson interjected, 'is not of relevance here. Whether he had a predilection for killing in a war or not is unimportant. A person is guilty of a crime as a result of proof, not supposition, a muted conscience for right and wrong, moral or amoral. If you are unable to provide further evidence, then it is for the police to terminate this interview and to allow my client to leave.'

'Your client will be formally charged with the murder of Sean Garvey,' Isaac said.

'Without evidence?' Jameson's retort.

'Our investigations are ongoing. Let me ask Mr Rees about his former wife. His understanding of what happened between him and her is contrary to what we've been told.'

'They're all the same. Find a lonely western man, wiggle their asses, get him excited. Once they've got what they want, then it's a changed situation.'

'Analyn?'

'I don't know the woman.'

'She was at Mary Wilton's brothel when you went to see your wife.'

'If she was, I didn't see her.'

'You're not disputing that you visited your wife at a brothel?'

'Why should I? It's what she was doing in the Philippines.'

'You gave her money.'

'I did. It seemed the decent thing to do.'

'Mr Rees, decent and honourable are two words that wouldn't describe you,' Isaac said. 'What we believe happened in Iraq was that you went rogue, exceeded your orders and indiscriminately killed innocent people.'

'It was a war, innocent people die.'

'Collateral damage maybe, but for you to be drummed out of the military is a fair indicator that you care little for life, and that murder comes easily. Why didn't you have sex with Janice Robinson before killing her? Amanda Upton? Why the grave at Kensal Green? It was an assassination of a woman who apart from her choice of a profession doesn't seem to have committed any grievous crime. Who were you protecting? Whose orders were you following?'

'This is ludicrous,' Jameson said.

Isaac chose to ignore him. 'Ian Naughton called you Gareth when the two of you waylaid a gang of hoodies in Canning Town. Why that gang? How did you know that Waylon Conroy was more intelligent than most gang members, more likely to acquiesce and to kill Hector Robinson?'

'I wasn't with an Ian Naughton. I don't even know the name,' Rees said.

'You know him, we know that. What name he uses at other times we don't know, but we met him at a house in Holland Park. He was in the company of Analyn, as you were in Godstone. Witnesses will testify that you are the man in the village, and both Inspector Hill and I know what Analyn looks like. The BMW?'

'What BMW?'

'The BMW in the garage in Godstone and a burnt-out wreck on a vacant block of land in Canning Town are one and the same. Mr Rees, I put it to you that you can act as a rational and decent human being, but as a result of actions you have committed in extremely dangerous situations, you have another side to you.'

'What does that mean?' Jameson said. 'Aspersions have no weight in law, any more than amateur psychology of my client's mental well-being.'

'Post-traumatic stress disorder doesn't seem to be the issue here, but you may have had a prior condition that was invaluable in the military. Not that they should have considered you, and they are not willing to let us know, but with a murder charge, they may be forced to release those details.'

'They won't,' Rees said. 'The Official Secrets Act will keep whatever I and others did under wraps.'

Isaac knew it was true. He had had experience with the secret service before; government-sanctioned assassinations to protect a politician and his indiscretion with a soap opera star when they were both young, a shared son. The son adopted, his later conversion to extremist Islam making him a threat to the government, would have had added power to his voice if his father had become known. In the end, people had died, including the star. Isaac didn't want to have to deal with those who operated in the shadows.

The interview had gone badly, Isaac had to concede. He had tried rapid-fire questioning of Rees, hoping the man would have become confused and blurt out the truth, making a statement contrary to the known facts, indicating knowledge of a person or a location that placed him at a crime scene, but it hadn't worked. Jacob Jameson wanted the man released; Isaac did not.

Gareth Rees, a self-confessed killer under military orders, a killer under the orders of Ian Naughton, whoever he was, or of his own volition, was led down to the holding cells at Challis Street. The team had less than twenty-four hours to come up with more substantive evidence, a possible forty-eight if they could provide proof that the charge against the man for the murder of Sean Garvey was likely to result in a conviction.

***

It was a tense time in Homicide, and Isaac was concerned that the two days he had promised to Jenny before he could focus time on her would not be enough.

Gwen Pritchard was brought back into the team; she would be working with Wendy and Bill Ross out at New Barn Street, looking for people who could have seen the shooter fire the shot, people with smartphones taking selfies, unaware of what was in the background.

Larry was going to follow up on where Gareth Rees was arrested and try to find his home address. Bridget was still trying to find out Rees's mental state from the military, as well as trace the movements of the car that he had been driving, a rental hired by him for the day of Garvey's death.

Isaac wanted to know how Rees would have known that Sean Garvey would leave the building where he lived and walk down the street, not that he got far. The phone that Rees had been carrying did not have Garvey's number on it, which led to two conclusions. The first was that Rees had staked out the area on the off-chance that Garvey would come out, which seemed unlikely. It wasn't the best area, and a well-dressed white male would have stood out, and curious people would have started to ask questions. The second and more probable was that he had used a 'burner', the slang for a throwaway phone favoured by criminals. Used for a day, thrown in a bin at the end of it. Phones were cheap enough and monitoring them, even with the number, was a laborious chore.

As for Isaac, he had to take a couple of hours, go with Jenny to the gynaecologist. His responsibility with Homicide told him that he shouldn't, but his heart told him that he had to. After that, the house in Holland Park where he and Larry had first met Ian Naughton and Analyn.

Wendy phoned the Robinsons and the Winstons back in their respective houses after the threat level had been reduced since the arrest of Gareth Rees. She also called Gabbi Gaffney, told her that her first husband was in custody and her help had been invaluable. The woman was not pleased to hear of the arrest, and there was a sense of fear in her voice.

Meredith Temple had been updated, but still Wendy told her to be careful.

Ian Naughton and Analyn remained at large. Gareth Rees had not admitted to knowing either, but he had definitely been in Godstone with one, in Canning Town with the other, but in English law a man was innocent until proven guilty. And there was no indisputable proof, only a large number of events leading to that conclusion.

Isaac honoured his time with Jenny. There were no problems, and the birth was due in six weeks, long enough to move houses and at least fix up the baby's bedroom. He had even taken Jenny to lunch and then driven her home.

It was just after three in the afternoon when he drew up outside the house in Holland Park. The estate agent had since let the home to a family, the husband transferred to his company's head office in London.

Inside the house, little had changed apart from the family's attempts to make it their own.

'It's only for a short time until we find a place of our own,' the wife said.

'You're aware of why I'm here?' Isaac said. He was on his own; everyone in Homicide was busy, and besides the threat that Naughton would have possibly posed was no longer present.

'Not really.'

'I met a man and a woman here. He was English, she was from the Philippines.'

'They're not here now,' the woman said as she knelt down to pat a small dog that wanted attention.

'I know, and it's unlikely they'll come near here. After we had been here, they soon disappeared. The problem is finding them.'

'I can't help. The place was clean and freshly painted when we moved in, no sign of the previous occupants.'

'No letters addressed to a previous tenant?'

'None.'

Isaac took a seat, looked around him. It was a lot bigger than the house that he and Jenny had just purchased, but Holland Park was a step up from Willesden; it was the suburb of the wealthy and famous, the haunt of celebrities and young upwardly mobile high-flying currency traders. Isaac hadn't the heart to tell the woman that two blocks away Spanish John lived in another equally impressive house. She looked a gentle woman, the sort of person who saw the best in people, who had never experienced life on the edge. Yet now she was living in a house that was inextricably linked with violent deaths. Isaac also knew that the estate agent, when he had shown the house, had not mentioned the police interest in the place.

'The two people I met here are persons of interest in a murder investigation,' Isaac said. The truth couldn't be avoided, although he wasn't sure where the conversation was heading.

'Did they kill anyone?'

'The woman, no. The man we don't think is a murderer either. We already have someone for two of the murders, although one murder is not yet solved. It's proof we need, and the man, he used the name of Ian Naughton, is probably behind the deaths. Yet again, we aren't sure of a motive.'

'I wouldn't have moved in if I had known.'

'No murders were committed here, you're safe on that score. However, a cryptic message led us to this house, which is bizarre. If the people here were involved in wrongdoing, why advertise themselves.'

'The woman in the cemetery? I heard about it on the television.'

'Yes. We know who she is, but not why she died.'

'This Naughton?'

'We don't think so. Amanda Upton did not sell herself in England, not from what we can tell. Any sign of women in the house?'

'Freshly painted. None that I can see.'

'Why this house?' Isaac said.

'A test?'

'That's what we were thinking, an attempt to ensure that the person who deciphered the clues was of suitable calibre, but that's about it. And why was Naughton in this house with the woman?'

'Maybe he knew who was coming. Just wanted to be sure it was that person. Maybe they were watching at the cemetery.'

'If they were, they would have known that the police were coming. It's more than that.'

Isaac left the house, realising that discussing the case with an open mind had raised other possibilities as to why they had been directed to the house, and why Naughton had not moved out immediately.

Chapter 28

Gareth Rees had been picked up close to Kingston upon Thames, nine miles to the south-west of Challis Street Police Station, a street within walking distance of Hampton Court, one of the Royal Palaces in greater London, a residence of Henry VIII in the early sixteenth century.

Larry had visited the impressive palace and its extensive grounds with his parents when he'd been a child, and with his wife and children two years previously.

As impressive as it was, it was the area close to where Rees had been arrested that was of interest. Portsmouth Road fronted the River Thames on its eastern side. It was a busy road with a path on one side of it, a popular walking track of a weekend. The other side of the road was lined with blocks of apartments, most of them upmarket and expensive, which didn't surprise Larry as Kingston upon Thames, close enough to London to commute, was also distant enough not to be part of the hurried life of the metropolis.

Gareth Rees probably wasn't a name that would mean anything to the locals, nor would Peter Hood. So near and yet so far. Rees had managed to live in obscurity, and he wasn't the sort of person to cause trouble where he lived.

In Canning Town and up near Challis Street Police Station, he was a killer, but down in Kingston upon Thames, Larry knew that he would find a different person. But where? That was the problem.

A couple of uniforms had photos of the man, and they were stopping whoever they could, knocking on doors. Rees was in the cells, and the clock was counting down.

Wendy was the expert at finding people, Larry knew that, and her ability to think like the person she was looking for was invaluable. But she was up in Canning Town looking for proof that Rees had fired the shot that had killed Sean Garvey.

Opposite where Rees had been stopped, a gated development. Discreet, out of sight, not easily accessible, the sort of place that ensured anonymity, an environment that would suit a man who wanted to remain unknown.

Larry stood at the entrance to the development, pressed the button for one of the houses inside. He wasn't specific as to which one; he only needed entry. It was a long shot, short on deduction but hopefully longer on luck. A hunch, and even then, it could have been that Rees had only pulled off Portsmouth Road into the side street to stop for a drink at the pub or to buy cigarettes.

The uniforms continued waylaying people, some crossing the road to avoid them, others stopping to say that they didn't recognise the man, or they had left their reading glasses at home, or the face looked familiar, but offering no more.

'Detective Inspector Hill,' Larry said when the second button he had pressed was answered.

'I've done nothing wrong,' the reply.

An instinctive fear of a police officer, Larry knew, the reason people didn't want to get involved.

'I know that. We're trying to find where a Gareth Rees lives.'

'Come in if you want, but the name means nothing.'

Larry didn't expect the name to. A neat three-bedroom house, a large dog that was overly friendly, and a short man, his grey hair and stoop showed that he was probably retired, and the crumpled shirt that he lived on his own. Who walked who, Larry couldn't be sure, but he had his money on the dog.

Larry stood at the front door and showed the photo of Rees. 'Do you know this man?'

'Not to speak to. Is he in trouble?'

'He's under arrest. Are you saying you've seen him?'

'Going in and out, but he doesn't speak, waves sometimes.'

'His car?'

'I'm not sure. He changes them all the time. I thought he was a car dealer, but as I said, I wouldn't know.'

'Where have you seen him?'

'Two houses down, the green door.'

Larry phoned Isaac as he walked to the neat and tidy house with the green door. It was clear that no one was at home.

Isaac was on the way; Larry would wait until he arrived. As he waited, he took a packet of cigarettes out of his pocket. As much as he had told his wife that he had quit, the occasional one gave him respite, a chance for normality. As with his dramatically curtailed alcohol consumption, the need never went away, and at times, good or bad, or as in this case, expectant, a cigarette provided a necessary distraction. He phoned the uniforms, told them to cease their questioning and to join him at the house, and to bring him a hamburger from the fast food place down the road.

The man came over, the dog alongside him. 'I'm taking the dog for a walk. Anything else you want?'

Larry took a phone out of his pocket, scrolled through the photo gallery. 'Tell me to stop when you recognise anyone.'

The dog, sensing that the walk was to be delayed, sat down on the ground. Even though it was big and lumbering, Larry could tell that it had some innate sense, a modicum of intelligence. Not like the dog he had had as a child that would run across a busy road if it saw a cat loitering on the other side. Somehow, the animal had lived till fourteen. Now, the family had a cat, the legacy of the reclusive mother of a murdered man that Wendy had befriended. Before the woman died, she had promised to look after her multitude of cats, Wendy taking one, him taking another, the remainder eventually going to good homes.

'That one,' the man said.

'Are you sure? Anyone else?'

'He wasn't sociable, but I remember her.'

'Why?'

'It was three, maybe four months ago. I was outside of the house, washing my car. She walked past me, said hello. Who is she?'

'A regular visitor?'

'I can't be sure. Probably. I'm not a busybody, and if she came over, then that was up to him and her.'

'A good attitude to adopt,' Larry said. 'It's important.'

'Very well. More than once, but that's all I know. And I only spoke to her once, never to him.'

'His name?'

'He rented the place. I never knew.'

'The estate agent?'

'I don't know.'

Isaac arrived outside the house twenty minutes later. The estate agent had been found by the uniforms who had been into a couple of agencies nearby.

Larry knocked on the door of Rees's house again. There was no reply. Donning nitrile gloves, Isaac and Larry entered through the front door. The estate agent wanted to enter as well, stating that he had a responsibility to the tenant, but Larry blocked his way.

'It's a homicide,' Isaac said, meaning that he wasn't in the mood to deal with the agent's concern, only to prove that the house was Rees's and to see what clues could be found inside.

The neighbour's identification of Amanda Upton had come as something as a shock, and from what had been gained from him so far, she had not popped in for a cup of tea but had spent the night at the house. Which raised questions as to why? Gareth Rees, as had been seen at Challis Street, was a decent-looking man, with a degree of wealth, but not to the extent that Amanda Upton's clients usually had.

Either it was a genuine romance or Rees had been paying, or there was another reason for her presence in the house.

Outside, on the small road inside the gated development, the uniforms kept the neighbour and the estate agent at a distance, ensured that the dog didn't make his mark on the small front garden.

Larry took the room to his left on entering; Isaac the right. The house was in good condition, no rubbish lying around, and in the kitchen at the rear, no dirty dishes in the sink, no sign of recent cooking. In the fridge, a milk carton, some cheese, a packaged pizza to put in the oven. Whatever Rees was, he wasn't a gourmet chef.

Larry was the first to climb the stairs, looking first in the bathroom, confirming that it was a single man who lived there, a toothbrush and toothpaste in a small cup, a couple of rolls of toilet paper to one side of the toilet. None of the obvious womanly touches, no hairdryer or makeup, no towels stacked neatly. The room was functional, fit for purpose.

In the first bedroom, Isaac, who had joined Larry, found a desk and chair, a laptop on top of the desk, its lid folded down.

If Amanda Upton had been in the house, then her fingerprints, as well as Rees's, might be found. He phoned Gordon Windsor, asked two of his people from the crime scene team to get down to Kingston upon Thames as soon as possible.

Windsor's reply, 'as soon as I can', didn't gel with Isaac who repeated his demand, adding, 'within the hour'.

The relationship between Isaac and Windsor was strong, forged over many years and many murders. Windsor took Isaac's insistence in his stride; he would have a couple down at the house within the hour.

In the second bedroom, a single bed. It was just a mattress, and it seemed that it had not been slept on for a long time. In the wardrobe, a row of clothes, all well-pressed and the approximate size to fit Rees. The main bedroom at the front of the house was larger than the other two. It also had an en suite. As before, the bathroom of a man, none of the touches that transposed it from masculine to feminine.

In the wardrobe, more clothes, none female, which indicated that Amanda Upton, if proven that she had been there, may well have spent time at the place, but she hadn't moved in. If she and Rees were sleeping together, and it wasn't professional, then it was casual.

The temptation to lift the lid of the laptop, to attempt to power it up, was almost overwhelming, but neither of the police officers would succumb to the temptation. After all, it would almost certainly have a password, and the only person who could break it was Bridget, and she was in Challis Street.

Larry phoned Bridget, gave her the address and told her to get down to the house; time was of the essence, and she could work at the house as easily as in Challis Street.

The crime scene investigators spent time checking out the house, frustratingly long to Isaac and Larry as they had a deadline. They would need more than they had so far to extend Gareth Rees's temporary incarceration from twenty-four hours to forty-eight; they needed proof of the man's wrongdoing.

After what seemed an eternity, but was only just over ninety minutes, Grant Meston, Gordon Windsor's second-in-charge, delivered the result.

'Amanda Upton was in the house, and it's Gareth Rees's residence.'

'How long ago for Amanda Upton?' Isaac asked.

'Recent, probably within a week or two of her death. I doubt if we can be more precise.'

'The laptop?'

'Gareth Rees's fingerprints.'

'Anyone else?'

'Amanda Upton's. Not as pronounced, but she's used it. It could have been to surf the internet, but that's up to you to find out.'

'Any signs of the two sharing a bed?'

'There are hairs on the bed. Two people, some long strands, some short. We'll pass them over to Forensics, but I'd say a man and a woman. The assumption is that they belong to Rees and the woman; they'll confirm.'

A statement from Meston was good enough for Isaac. The two had shared a bed, and one had murdered the other. Which clarified why there was no struggle at the first murder scene in the cemetery. It did not, however, explain why they were there.

Reasons for the deaths, for the cemetery, for the cryptic message, for Naughton and Analyn being at the house in Holland Park, were unimportant for the present; the evidence to prove that Rees had shot Garvey was the pressing issue.

Solve one murder, and then the pieces would start to fall into place. The jigsaw that had led the department around London was soon to be completed.

Bridget opened the laptop; she knew there would be a password. Not that it concerned her as she had broken many over the years.

'I'm in,' she shouted down the stairs.

Isaac and Larry went up the stairs; the dog, excited by the people in the street, attempted to follow, one of the uniforms grabbing it by its collar and handing it back to its owner.

***

In Canning Town, Wendy was sitting down in an Indian restaurant. They'd spent gruelling and fruitless hours interviewing people, walking up and down the street. Gwen Pritchard was still trying to make headway, and Wendy recognised in the young woman what she had been at that age: indestructible, inexhaustible, with infinite enthusiasm. Mortality concerned Wendy, the realisation that life was finite; she didn't like it, and it wasn't usual for her to feel sorry for herself.

'This place distresses me,' Wendy said, looking over at Bill Ross. 'The futility of their lives.'

'Mapped out from birth for most of them. They don't realise what could be achieved if you got off your backside and applied yourself,' Ross's reply. His transfer was in another week, but he understood where the sergeant was coming from, and besides, he knew that Dagenham, his next posting, wasn't much better, just a change of scenery.

'Narrowed view of the world. They come from other parts of the world, but what do they see? Here, no better than where they had been. Isolated, alone, no longer the extended family,' Ross continued.

'Not all of them.'

'Not all. Certainly not Sean Garvey or the other two gang members. They were born here, and I doubt if any of them had experienced any beauty in their lives. The mind withers with time.'

'DCI Cook said you were a good police officer; he didn't say you understood the people.'

'It was part of the training to work in a deprived area. An understanding of cultural differences, various religions, the inability of them to realise the opportunities afforded them.'

'Some break free?'

'Some do; a lot don't.'

Wendy ordered, hot and spicy for her. Bill Ross went for mild after the Indian that he had taken Larry to before, as he had suffered the queasy stomach as well.

317

Gwen came in with a lady covered from head to toe in black; she was carrying a small child in her arms.

Wendy asked her to take a seat.

'I'm sorry, I can't,' the woman said.

'It's me,' Ross said. 'We're not related, the lady would not feel comfortable sitting at the same table with me.'

'Is that it?' Wendy said, looking up at the woman.

'I hope you'll understand.'

The woman's English was perfect, a London accent. She had been brought up in England, but as Ross had said, criminal intent, unemployment, were generational. And so was a belief in a free society. The idea of equality had not embraced the woman, or maybe it had.

It was wrong, Wendy thought, but she could not solve it, only be polite to the woman.

Ross got up from his seat and walked out of the restaurant.

Gwen beckoned the woman to take a seat.

'It seems we've got an Indian meal going free if you want it,' Wendy said to the black-covered woman.

'That's for Westerners,' she said. 'A true Indian wouldn't eat it.'

'Tea? You'll drink tea?'

'Yes, I would.'

'Gwen, what is it?' Wendy said to the young constable.

'Hania saw the shooting.'

'Proof?'

'She was on Skype to her cousin in Pakistan.'

'A record?'

'I recorded it for my sister,' Hania said. 'Can we move to the rear of the restaurant.'

The three women found a new table. Hania ensured that her face could not be seen by the other patrons as she lifted the veil that covered her face.

Wendy was staggered by her innocent beauty. 'It's a shame that you're covered,' she said.

'It is for my husband. At home, among my sisters and female friends, I would be wearing jeans and a blouse, but out in the street, I must do what I must.'

'Because you want to?'

'It is my religion.'

Gwen, who preferred to go around in as little clothing as possible in summer, didn't understand, but she did like the woman.

'The recording, have you seen it, Gwen?' Wendy asked.

'Hania lives across from the fire escape. It's distant, but it's clear enough. With enhancing, it can be proved.'

'The rifle?' Wendy asked.

'He took it with him,' Hania said.

The baby started to cry; Wendy instinctively lifted it from the mother and rocked it in her arms.

'Thank you,' Hania said. 'Some people wouldn't do that, not around here.' She took her phone and showed the video.

Wendy, distracted by the baby, looked at the video the best she could. It wasn't the best quality, but it would suffice.

'I've passed it on to Bridget,' Gwen said.

'She's busy, out at Rees's house, checking his laptop.'

Wendy handed the baby back to Hania and phoned her DCI. A breakthrough at the last minute from the most unexpected of sources.

Hania's details were taken. She said she would give evidence at a trial if her husband permitted it.

To Gwen, the woman's attitude was perplexing, but Wendy, more worldly, understood that sometimes you don't always agree, but it does not diminish the respect of one for the other.

Chapter 29

Gareth Rees sat in the interview room. Jacob Jameson was at his side. The mood in Homicide was more ebullient than on the previous encounter with the murderer and his lawyer.

Isaac went through the formalities, advised Rees of his rights, his recourse after the interview had concluded. Jameson looked bored; Rees adopted an air of disinterest.

'My client wishes to be out of this police station today,' Jameson said.

Isaac took no notice of the lawyer, only focussed on Rees.

'We've checked where you live,' Isaac said. 'DI Hill found it.'

'So,' the one-word reply from Rees.

'We've found out more about you.'

'Where is this leading?' Jameson said. He had been updated to an extent as to developments. Isaac could see that he was playing for time, attempting to defuse and confuse the police. Isaac had no intention of letting him succeed.

'Mr Rees,' Isaac continued, his gaze focussed on Rees, 'we know by your own admission that you visited Mary Wilton's brothel and that you spoke to your wife, gave her some money.'

'I told you that.'

'You did not tell us that you had a relationship with Amanda Upton.'

'Whoever she is, I didn't.'

Isaac pushed a folder over to Jameson. 'Your client has failed to tell the truth. You'll find a report from Forensics. The analysis of the hairs found on the bed in the front bedroom of the house proves that they belong to Amanda Upton and Gareth Rees.'

Jameson opened the folder, read the front page and pushed it over to his client.

'Maybe I didn't know her name,' Rees said. 'It could just be a coincidence. I live on my own, but sometimes I appreciate the company.'

'There are no hairs from other women in the bedroom,' Larry said. 'It's proof positive that you knew the first woman murdered.'

'My client will not comment,' Jameson said. The previously confident look on his face had gone.

'There was also a laptop in another bedroom,' Isaac said.

'That was private property,' Rees said.

'It's evidence now. Apart from the normal, websites for guns and porn, it appears that you had an interesting sideline.'

'Such as?'

'What do you mean?' Jameson asked. 'Why haven't I received this advice?'

Isaac was not in the mood to discuss semantics or police procedure; he was focussed on breaking Rees.

'Mr Rees, your activities overseas, the reason you were court-martialled out of the military. Was it a military action that went wrong, or were you black-market trading, selling weapons, stealing them, giving away secrets?'

'This is ridiculous,' Jameson said. Isaac was sure he was speaking for effect, not sure about his position. The man's hold on the situation in the interview room was shaky.

'Amanda Upton's fingerprints were on the laptop as well,' Larry said. 'The claim that she could have just been a rented woman for an evening doesn't hold up.'

'Very well. I knew Amanda.'

'How?'

'A club somewhere. If she was related to the brothel owner, I didn't know that.'

'Did you ever visit her place in Marylebone?'

'No. She would never let me go there.'

'And you were aware that she was selling herself?'

'She never made a secret of it, not to me.'

'Were the two of you close?'

'We got on, but it wasn't love. Not for me, anyway.'

'For her?'

'It's probable. She was a moral woman, didn't always like herself for what she did.'

'You were her manager; you set up the clients, which yet again points to places and people you met in the military. We're still trying to get a record of your court-martial.'

'Okay, I looked after her interests. I knew a few people around the world, high-flyers.'

'Men who used you for your expertise in killing; Amanda for her body. It seems that you and she were destined for each other, a match made in heaven,' Isaac said.

Rees leaned over to Jameson, whispered in his ear.

'My client advises you that enquiries about actions committed out of England will run into serious problems.'

'The Official Secrets Act,' Isaac said. 'We've been there before, and whether Mr Rees has conducted actions for the British government or not, it doesn't obviate him from murder in this country.'

'Mr Rees, we have obtained a video of you on the fire escape in Canning Town. Software enhancement of the image will show it to be you,' Larry said.

'I've already admitted that I was there.'

'Not with a rifle, you didn't. It's visible and pointed towards where Sean Garvey died,' Isaac said.

'I'll deny it.'

'Deny all you want, but we have proof. Not only that you were intimately involved with Amanda Upton, but that you were in Canning Town, a rifle at your shoulder, at the time Garvey was shot. Why did you kill Janice Robinson?'

'I didn't. This is ludicrous.'

'It appears, DCI Cook,' Jameson said, 'that you are clutching at straws. I doubt if a video other than professionally made would show the necessary clarity to convince a jury.'

'It wouldn't,' Isaac admitted.

'Then my client will leave this police station today.

'Not so fast,' Larry said as he pushed another folder across the desk. 'Why, Mr Rees, did you keep the house that you shared with your first wife?'

Jameson looked at the photo inside, looked over at his client and then at the two police officers. 'What does this mean?'

'Mr Rees, living a quiet life in Kingston upon Thames, the model neighbour, never intended to act in a manner there that could raise suspicion. That's why he kept his weapons at the old house, not in the bedroom as we expected, but in a concreted pit under the floorboards. As can be seen, there are several weapons: rifles, pistols, and knives. If you look at the photo on the fire escape and the gun that's displayed in the picture, you'll see the similarities.

'Our crime scene investigators are on the way there, and the rifle will be with Forensics within the hour. No doubt, a professional would have cleaned it thoroughly after it had been fired, but we have the bullet that killed Garvey. Within hours, we will know that we have indisputable proof, and all the conjecture as to what was coincidental and what wasn't will be put to rest.'

Jameson looked over at Isaac. 'I will take instructions from my client,' he said.

'Mr Rees will remain in the cells. As far as we are concerned, your client is the murderer of Sean Garvey.'

'I'm innocent,' Rees protested. Jameson took no notice.

'One last question before we terminate this interview.' Isaac said. 'The cells are not the most comfortable. You've been sitting down for a long time. That limp, an old war wound?'

'Serving my country, not like you harassing innocent people.'

'Mr Rees, you are not innocent. We can prove Sean Garvey, and the knives at your house will be checked against the knife wounds inflicted on Amanda Upton and Janice Robinson. What did Amanda Upton have on you? Professing love, found out some secrets about you that you wanted to stay that way?'

'My client will say no more,' Jameson said.

***

Three murders were solved, one of them with enough proof for a conviction.

Rose Winston and her belief that the man had limped had been proven to be accurate, even though almost everyone had discounted the fact.

One avenue that would need to be explored was the possibility of Gareth Rees opening up, telling what he knew, looking to reduce his prison sentence.

Isaac did not feel confident that the man would say much more, and if he had been involved in secret operations overseas, then he might well have people who would prefer him free or dead.

Wendy, after a good night's rest, was at Mary Wilton's. With someone charged with her daughter's murder, it was time to confront her again. Bridget had examined Rees's laptop, found the usual, proof of Amanda's and Rees's business involvement, but little more. And no encrypted files that would lead to Ian Naughton.

Isaac laid out a plan to Chief Superintendent Goddard. Both men had a shrewd idea of how politics and secrecy worked, having felt the brunt of them before.

'Are you sure about this?' Goddard said.

'If Rees was court-martialled, a mock trial possibly, it's because of a major transgression. But the man didn't serve time in a military prison, he acts with impunity afterwards, changing his name at will. And then there are the contacts overseas, the reason he could set up Amanda Upton in business,' Isaac said.

'Are you suggesting that I make it known that if Rees starts talking, he's likely to reveal facts that other people don't want to be known; actions instigated by the British government.'

'We've experienced the neuroses of people in power. Anything, no matter how obscure or trivial that paints them in a bad light, and they're all over it with a veil of secrecy. And as we know, people start to die.'

'We end up with unsolved murders against our record.'

'Even when we know the guilty party. We can get Rees this time for Garvey, not a chance for Amanda Upton unless he decides to talk.'

'Lord Shaw?'

'He was the commissioner of the Met before Davies. He's a man who's guided your career,' Isaac said. 'He's also a man who has the right contacts.'

'Leave it with me,' Goddard said. 'Nothing to lose, not now, and I'm damned sure I'm not about to allow our police records to get another black mark against them for failing to solve a crime.'

***

Mary Wilton sat quietly as Wendy updated her. The events of the last few weeks had aged her. Even though she had been in her mid-seventies when they had first met, she had been well-dressed and lively, but Wendy thought the woman now looked terminal, as though she did not have long for this world. The former brothel was cold and austere.

'I'm selling up,' the woman said. 'What with Amanda and the upcoming court case, I've just had enough.'

'We know who killed your daughter,' Wendy said. 'Not that we can prove it, not yet.'

'Gabbi's former husband?'

'Yes. You knew or you suspected?'

'Suspected.'

It didn't ring true to Wendy; somehow someone had told the woman. It hadn't been reported yet, not officially, and outside of the police station, few people would have known.

'The truth.'

'Gabbi contacted me, told me that Gareth had been arrested and that he was likely to be charged with murder.'

At least that was true, Wendy knew. She had phoned Gabbi herself, told her that her former husband was in custody, yet the case wasn't watertight, not at that time, and the man had figured out that it had been his former wife who had helped the police.

'Gareth Rees and your daughter were more than friends. They had, according to Rees, a casual sexual relationship. Also, he was involved in organising the clients for her, ensuring that the monies were paid in advance.'

'I didn't know that.'

'Which brings up the question as to where they met and why Gabbi gravitated to your brothel after Rees had kicked her out.'

'I always thought it was Analyn who told her about here. It was her that introduced her to me.'

'A natural, Gabbi?'

'I had no complaints. She wasn't here long, though. I liked her, the same as I liked Analyn. None of the coarseness of the others, not like Janice or Cathy.'

'Men haters, Janice and Cathy?'

'Not Janice, but Cathy could have been. Janice could be selective about who she went with; Cathy never was.'

'More money, the more disgusting the act?'

'If the girls negotiated extra, I'd not know.'

'Cathy was more desperate?'

'Always.'

'Let's come back to Rees and Amanda,' Wendy said.

The two women were sat in the sofas that had previously served as platforms for the available women to show their wares when the place had been in business. Back then, scantily-dressed women, voluptuous, bright red lipstick, the suggestion of unbridled passion, the lustful looks of the males. But now, two women discussing the murder of a daughter, and in Mary Wilton's case, the futility of her life.

'If Analyn had known Gabbi, she would have told her about this place,' Mary Wilton repeating what she had said previously.

'Which means either in England or else in the Philippines. We know that Rees was spending time with Amanda. He was also in the company of Analyn in Godstone.'

Wendy was still concerned that Gabbi Gaffney had hidden secrets; something wasn't right.

'I can't help you,' the former madam said.

Wendy was sure that she couldn't. As she left the house, she felt that she would never see the woman again. It was an unsettling feeling, a premonition. It disturbed her.

***

Isaac sat in his office, hunched over his laptop. The worst part of a police officer's life, the paperwork. The paperless office, the automation of processes that had been promised in the new streamlined police force, hadn't eventuated.

Apart from the report on the department's progress in the current murder enquiries, he still had to deal with health and safety, training for his people, preparation of budgets, requests for more personnel; or, more often, a cogent argument as to why he could not manage with fewer people, either as a result of natural attrition or because of the generous retirement packages offered to those approaching the ends of their careers, Wendy, the person most often mentioned as someone who should hand over her badge, receive the customary farewell, a speech from the chief superintendent, a few drinks, and out of the door.

Isaac did not want his sergeant to go, not yet, and on the last three attempts to remove her from Challis Street, he had managed to ensure that she stayed.

Larry spent time with Bill Ross over at Canning Town, attempting to find out more about Ian Naughton, although with three members of the gang that they had paid to kill Hector Robinson dead and gone, the others couldn't be found.

The two men discussed the case, the reason for Hector Robinson's murder, as well as the deaths of Waylon Conroy and Sean Garvey. Murder needs a motive, but motives are often obscure. Jealousy, an argument, money, love, hatred, were all motives, but Sean Garvey, who evoked no emotions other than loathing from Ross, had no reason to die. Not that the area wasn't better off without him, but there were thousands in London living pointless lives.

Ross had admitted to Larry on more than one occasion that even though he had tempered his provocative and racist comments about the majority of the populace in Canning Town, it didn't come easy. Larry knew that the man's stay in Dagenham might be shorter than he would like.

Larry felt that he was wasting time with Ross and that he could not admit to liking his fellow inspector; the man carried too much angst, and too much time in his company was negative. He shook the man's hand, wished him well and returned to Challis Street.

***

It would have required a Herculean effort by Richard Goddard and Lord Charles Shaw, but in the department, a copy of Gareth Rees's military record, a transcript of the man's court-martial.

Both documents, while substantially complete, also had large parts blacked out. However, Homicide, and specifically Isaac, were pleased to have the documents in their possession.

Bridget had photocopied them, given copies to each of the team.

'The salient points,' Isaac said, knowing that Bridget would have separated the wheat from the chaff, the items of interest from the verbiage of a court-martial.

'Gareth Rees, an exemplary record of service, had served in Iraq and Afghanistan, as well as other countries, most of them blacked out, although he had been in Africa on a couple of occasions.'

'To do what?' Wendy asked.

'Unspecified.'

'Which means behind enemy lines, undercover, sanctioned assassinations,' Isaac said.

'There is a name.'

'Of who?'

'It's in the transcript of the court-martial,' Bridget said. 'The charge against Rees is not to do with collateral damage, nor is it the indiscriminate killing of civilians.'

'Then what?' Isaac asked.

'Rees was charged with selling military equipment.'

'Arms trading?'

'That's what it says.'

'And yet he gets kicked out of the military, no time served, even though he's found guilty.'

'Which means?' Wendy said.

'I'd say that favours rendered to a grateful country outweighed the crimes,' Isaac said.

'The sale of weapons, which could have been primarily to rebel groups, and approved by the British Government initially, could have given Rees the idea to make extra money on the side.'

'There's more,' Bridget said. 'It's a doctored document, a lot left out, some left in.'

'Critical.'

'It's in the small print, hidden in the summing up by the prosecution lawyer.'

'What is it?' Isaac asked.

'The man had an accomplice.'

'A name?'

'Only initials, VC, and it's not the medal.'

'Ian Naughton? That would explain the apparent friendliness between him and Rees,' Larry said.

'I've gone through names associated with Rees, names on the public record. VC stands for Vincent Cuthbertson.'

'His service records?'

'Once I had details as to his postings, his rank, his regiment. The man left the military around the time Rees was sentenced.'

'A cover-up?'

'I wouldn't know. What I can tell you is that Cuthbertson is forty-eight years of age, the son of wealthy parents, the father bankrupted when Cuthbertson was in his twenties.'

'A picture?'

Bridget reached over to another folder on the desk, took out three photos and handed one to Isaac, another to Larry, and a third to Wendy.

'It's Naughton,' Larry said. 'Where can we find him?'

'He's a man who appears and disappears at regular intervals. He also has a wife from the Philippines.'

'Analyn?'

'Her name is Leni Ramos.'

Chapter 30

There were, Isaac could see, inconsistencies in the documents that had been procured by Lord Shaw. The most glaring one was that it had been relatively simple for Bridget to find out that VC referred to Vincent Cuthbertson. It was as if the police were being given a hand to arrest Ian Naughton, who may well have outlived his usefulness, and was potentially an embarrassment.

Regardless, it appeared that the potential embarrassment to persons unknown outweighed the short-term expediency of arresting both Rees and Naughton. And now Analyn's part in the sordid affair had been revealed; she was Naughton's wife, not the family maid, nor the nanny of the children.

Cuthbertson's last known address was in Suffolk, a county north-east of London. It was five years since the man had been there, and Bridget had been checking bank accounts, looking for credit cards. There were none, which meant, as with Rees, that the man used different names for different occasions.

Wendy had visited Gabbi Gaffney, still not venturing far from her house, and shown her the photo of Vincent Cuthbertson, asked her why she had lied about her and Analyn in the Philippines. The woman's reply was obtuse and incoherent.

Gabbi was frightened, and she wasn't going to say more, other than Analyn had married the man, although she had only seen him in the Philippines and not in England, and if Analyn knew that he was murdering people indiscriminately, she would be frightened too.

Wendy wanted to believe her, but too many lies had been told by too many people, and Gabbi Gaffney had exceeded her allowance.

The All-Points Bulletin for Ian Naughton, also known as Vincent Cuthbertson, had been upgraded, and now there was a photo, even if it had been taken years previously. An artist aged the picture, a representation of what he would look like now, using both Isaac's and Larry's training in observation to affect a good likeness.

All airports and cross-channel ferries had been notified, as well as the train stations, especially St Pancras International, the departure point for the Eurostar and the continent. If Naughton was in the country, it was only a matter of time before he was apprehended, and Analyn's photo was now available as well.

One or the other would surface soon enough, if only for provisions.

A flurry of activity in Homicide, anticipation that it would soon be over. Bridget busied herself with updating her database. Three murders had a murderer's name against them, although the crimes committed by Naughton weren't known yet. The man had worked behind enemy lines overseas, which meant that he was probably as adept a killer as Rees.

Isaac and Larry visited Rees in prison. The man needed to be updated.

'Vincent Cuthbertson,' Isaac said as Rees sat down.

'I know the name,' Rees's reply.

'We met him in Holland Park. He was using the name of Ian Naughton, and we know now that Analyn, the woman we met and you were in Godstone with, is his wife. Her name in the Philippines was Leni Ramos.'

'Cuthbertson liked them Asian and young.'

'As you do,' Larry said.

'There's no law against it. We used to go there when we had time off, got drunk, got laid, had a great time.'

'A great time, but both of you married women from there. Why?'

'Love.'

'Mr Rees, from what we know, and we do have a copy of your military record as well as an edited transcript of your court-martial, you are not a sentimental man.'

'Your opinion doesn't matter. Gabbi was a good person, and no doubt Leni is. Good luck to Cuthbertson, but we weren't in each other's pocket.'

'We know from your former wife that you knew Naughton's wife, or should I say, Vincent Cuthbertson's wife, in the Philippines.'

'Maybe I did, but where's this going? I've been stitched up for one murder. I'm not likely to see the outside other than from a prison van for a long time. You want my cooperation, although I don't know what for.'

'You were selling weapons.'

'I was following orders.'

'You probably were initially, but you were taking a little extra on the side. Doesn't it irk you that Cuthbertson got an honourable discharge, a pension?'

'No.'

'Is that it? He's walking free, and yet you have been doing his dirty work. And judging by the house in Holland Park and yours in Kingston upon Thames, you were getting the rough end of the stick. You were being shafted by a master manipulator. And why the cryptic message at the grave where you murdered Amanda Upton?'

'Don't make it out to be something it wasn't. We worked together, occasionally screwed each other. It was sex, that's all.'

'But you liked her?'

'Sure, who wouldn't. She was a classy woman, but she was hard, the same as her mother. To your face, she was sweet and coy and desirable, but deep down, she was calculating, able to convince a fat lecher that he was taking her to untold heights of delight.'

'A good actor?'

'She was.'

'With you?'

'We had a good time, no need to pretend with me. I'm as hard as she was, and you would be if you had seen what I had when I was in the military.'

'Done what you had,' Larry said.

'Someone had to do it.'

'You've used that defence before,' Isaac said.

A smug look settled on Rees's face. Isaac didn't like it, as if the man knew something that he didn't.

A curious limbo existed in Homicide; the truth increasingly known but only marginally proved. Larry took the opportunity to catch up on his paperwork, Wendy took the time to rest her weary legs, and Isaac gave more time to Jenny. It was only Bridget who was fully occupied.

Three days after Rees's arrest, a phone call. Isaac was at the gynaecologist with Jenny when he answered his phone.

'Sergeant Bill Dyer, Cardiff Police,' a gruff-voiced man said.

'How can I help you?' Isaac's reply, Jenny casting him a sideways glance, understanding on the one hand, scornful on the other.

'It was one of our young constables, keen as mustard. She was in the supermarket, recognised your Asian woman.'

'Under arrest?'

'I didn't think you'd want that. The constable picked up a plastic container the woman had handled, flashed her warrant card at the cashier and followed her.'

'The prints?'

'You'll need to get your Forensics to check them out, but we're certain they are from Leni Ramos.'

'An address?'

'We've got it staked out. It's in a cul-de-sac. No one's going anywhere.'

'A man?'

'We've not got close enough yet, but the constable's got a team together to make sure that no one leaves the house. They've got photos of both the Asian woman and this Ian Naughton or whatever he calls himself. If either move, we'll pick them up.'

'You've been updated on Naughton?'

'Possibly armed, liable to shoot, handle with extreme caution. We have. We've got an armed response team coming, should be in place within an hour. How soon before you get here?'

'Three hours if we drive, sixty minutes if we can get a helicopter. It depends on the chief superintendent.'

Isaac phoned Goddard, who without hesitation gave his permission. The monthly budget would be blown, but an arrest in Cardiff would outweigh the criticism that the finance department would give him afterwards.

Fifteen minutes later, Isaac and Larry were flying high over London, a police helicopter seconded for the trip.

Larry had been to Cardiff, Isaac hadn't. On arrival, Detective Inspector Everton and the young constable, Catrin Humphreys, met them.

'Constable Humphreys gets the credit for this.'

Isaac instinctively liked the inspector, a fair-minded man who gave credit where credit was due, not like the insufferable Seth Caddick who was always trying to wheedle his way into Challis Street and Homicide.'

'It's not far from here,' Catrin Humphreys said.

'The plan?' Larry asked.

'We were waiting for you. The armed response will go first. Once it's secured, you can go in. It's your arrest,' Everton said.

'Constable Humphreys can do that,' Isaac said. 'Inspector Hill and I have met Naughton and the woman before. The man can charm the birds out of the trees, but his records indicate that he's not the sort of person to get too close to.'

The armed response team reached the front door of the house. It wasn't as impressive as Holland Park, but it was still better than Rees's house.

The door opened. From a distance, Isaac could see that it was the woman that had been with Ian Naughton: Analyn. Not taking chances this time, the woman was secured by one of the men and taken from her side of the door and out through the front garden. She was handed over to Isaac, who asked the young constable to caution her.

Handcuffs were applied to Analyn, and she was placed in the back of a police vehicle.

The armed response team encircled the house, two of them taking positions at the rear, three at the front. The officer in charge shouted out, told anyone in the house to come out with their hands held high.

Naughton walked out, the same smug look that Isaac had seen on Gareth Rees's face at the prison. Isaac decided that even though he had wanted to let the constable caution the man, the seriousness of his crimes and the ensuing trial required him to do it.

'It seems, Chief Inspector, that you are determined to miscalculate the situation,' Naughton said.

As smooth as a knife through butter, Larry thought. The man was good. He was not going to be easy to crack.

'Why the arrogance?' Inspector Everton asked Isaac after the two people in custody had left for the police station.

'Trained killer for Her Majesty's government. Friends in high places, secrets that he knows they'll not want to be known. He thinks he can get out of this,' Isaac said.

'Can he?'

'It's probable. And besides, we can't prove he committed murder, only that he instigated them.'

'Proof of criminal activity?'

'Not strong. His other nefarious activities we can't be so sure about. It depends on his offsider and the woman. If either talk, that is.'

'You don't look confident.'

'We've met his type before.'

***

Wendy sat with Gabbi Gaffney, explaining what was happening in Cardiff, the woman's husband sitting alongside her, holding her hand. It was touching, Wendy thought, but it wasn't going to help if she continued to hold back the full truth.

'We have Analyn in custody. In the Philippines, what name did she use?'

'Analyn,' Gabbi's answer.

Wendy, tired of the charade, turned to Gabbi's husband. 'I suggest you tell your wife to be honest with me. If she was prostituting herself in Manila, I need to know. If she's not told you the full truth, then it's too late. You'll just have to sort it out between the two of you afterwards.'

'I know the whole story,' Mike Gaffney said, squeezing his wife's hand harder.

Wendy wasn't sure he did. There was a sordid underlife that had not been told. According to Gabbi and Mary Wilton, both Gabbi and Analyn were decent women attempting to make the best in an imperfect world.

Wendy had no issues with that, but lying to the police was an offence. She had no desire to deprive the woman of her husband and baby, but if she had to, she would.

'Tell her,' Mike Gaffney said.

'Analyn, although that wasn't her real name, not in the Philippines,' Gabbi said.

'Leni Ramos,' Wendy said.

'Yes, Leni. She had had it rough, a more difficult childhood than mine; poverty, an empty belly. It stunts the brain; makes you do things you'd rather not.'

'Shows for the sex-tourists?'

'Not at first. We came from the same area in the Philippines, although we had not known each other. In Manila, we bonded, dealt with whatever life threw up at us, and, yes, shows, degrading, disgusting. But what option did we have? Our families were suffering.'

'Did they know?'

341

'It wasn't something that was ever spoken about. Mike looks after my family now; it's not a lot of money, and they never cheat him, sit on their backsides waiting for the next cheque. My father is very religious, but not naïve; my mother is. I think my father realised the extent of it more than her.'

'Is any of this a surprise, Mr Gaffney?' Wendy said.

'The past is the past. I judge the person, not their history, no matter how much it might disturb me.'

'And it does?'

'Man's inhumanity to man, or in this case, women, is inexhaustible.'

'Gareth and Naughton. In the audience?'

'We met them on our day off. Gareth never saw me perform, nor did Vincent see Leni, or should I say, Analyn?'

'Either will do,' Wendy said.

'I told Gareth the truth, and he said he'd look after me as long as I didn't return.'

'Out of love?'

'Not then, not for either of us. He was in the country for a few weeks; he wanted a woman to be there for him?'

'For sex?'

'Not only that. He was interested in the culture, wanted me to show him around.'

'And you had no problems with this?'

'It was better than what I had been doing. A good hotel, plenty to eat, clean sheets on the bed. To me, it was a paradise.'

'He married you.'

'He used to have these terrible nightmares; he said that I calmed him. In time and another couple of visits, he asked me to marry him and to go and live in England.'

'The shows, prostituting yourself?'

'Not after I met Gareth. He used to send me money regularly, enough to rent a small place to live and I got a job in a shop selling souvenirs. Life was good; I had a benefactor, and we were married.'

'But he changed?'

'Later, in England. The nightmares never went away, and then he was away more often, and then, one day, I was no longer in the house.'

'He holds you responsible for leading us to him.'

'And you say he kills people.'

'Yes.'

'Which means he could kill me, or Mike or our baby?'

'Not now, he can't. Let's get back to Analyn.'

'Her story is similar to mine. Gareth and Vincent, or Ian, as you call him, were firm friends, inseparable. I went with Gareth; she went with Ian. Ian was better educated than Gareth, and he always seemed to have plenty of money. She fell for him in a big way, and he married her, love at the time for both of them. But...'

'But what does that mean?'

'Both men were secretive, both men had a dark side, but, Ian, sometimes he seemed distant. As though he was calculating the odds, deep thinking. I don't know what it was, but sometimes I felt uncomfortable around him.'

'Analyn?'

'She never saw it, not until she was in England.'

'Mary Wilton's?'

'She had managed to get away from him.'

343

'Violent?'

'Never.'

'He's a charming man, so I'm told,' Wendy said.

'Mike believes it's all a pretence, and that the man's cold and calculating and dangerous.'

'Your husband is right.'

'Is she in trouble?'

'She is probably guilty of a crime, but she may have acted under duress, a fear of her husband.'

'She would have.'

'Then there would be mitigating circumstances. If she's honest with us, then it will go in her favour. She may not know the full extent of what has happened.'

'She would, but fear is a powerful force. So many people have died; she would be frightened for her life.'

'Ian Naughton. Possessive?'

'Not in Manila, and I haven't seen him for a long time. He could have changed. Analyn said he had.'

***

Analyn, although her correct name was Leni Ramos, sat in the interview room. She had been supplied a legal aid lawyer at her request.

Isaac and Larry sat opposite the woman and her lawyer, a man in his fifties, shabbily dressed, a two-day growth of beard. He was, Isaac thought, a poor example of the legal profession. Naughton had organised a top-flight lawyer who was travelling from London.

'Why didn't you take your husband's lawyer?' Isaac asked.

The woman was as he remembered: short, attractive, and easy on the eye.

'I've done nothing wrong.'

'We've spoken to Gabbi. She's updated us on your life in the Philippines, and your subsequent time in England. Is it, as has been said by her, difficult in this country?'

'No. We have been happy. I have a good husband, a good life.'

'According to your friend, your husband controls you. Is that true?'

'No, not Ian.'

'What other names does he use?'

'I don't know. He's self-employed. I don't enquire, not a wife's prerogative.'

'There are many who would disagree with you on that,' Larry said.

'They never grew up hungry, barely enough money for shoes.'

'But now, your husband makes sure that you have both.'

'He does.'

'In the Philippines, you did things that you're not proud of.'

'I survived.'

The woman was proving difficult, putting up an impenetrable barrier between her and the truth.

'Why were you at Mary Wilton's? We know that you sold yourself there.'

'Then why ask? I did what was necessary.'

'Your husband?'

'We had had an argument. I was doing it to spite him.'

'A drastic action.'

'He reminded me of what I had once been. I regret it.'

'Or you had no money.'

Isaac changed tack. 'We know that you were in Kensal Green Cemetery by the grave where Amanda Upton died.'

'I often visit cemeteries, look at the dedications on the headstones.'

The woman, friendly at the house in Holland Park, was anything but in Cardiff.

The legal aid said nothing, just took notes in pencil on a notepad he carried. Isaac could see that he was going to be close to useless for his client.

'Do you prefer Analyn or Leni?' Larry asked.

'Analyn is fine.'

'Analyn,' Isaac said, 'you are either frightened or incredibly naïve. I'm not sure which, but I suspect the first. Am I correct?'

'I didn't kill anyone, nor did I do anything criminal.'

'That is probably true. The house in Godstone, the BMW. Why were you there with Gareth Rees, Gabbi's first husband?'

'He's a friend of Ian's. He asked me to check it out with him.'

'It was you that took the BMW and drove it back to London.'

'It was.'

'That car was subsequently used by Gareth Rees and your husband to meet with a gang of young criminals. Your husband paid them to kill Hector Robinson, Janice's father. Why?'

'Why I drove the car?'

'The car is not the question. Janice Robinson's father, why was he killed?'

'I never knew him, barely knew her. I can't say I liked her much.'

'Why? She wasn't doing anything that you weren't doing. And according to Gabbi, you and she did much worse in Manila.'

'That's the past. Neither of us intended to do it forever, but Janice did.'

The legal aid looked up. 'You have no evidence against my client. You are putting words into her mouth.'

Isaac ignored the man; he had no time for poorly performing professionals.

'Let's be honest here,' Isaac said. 'We know that Gareth Rees is violent and that he had killed in the military and in Canning Town. We can prove Canning Town, but we can't prove that he killed Amanda Upton and probably Janice Robinson. What we believe is that your husband and Rees are involved in the selling of weapons overseas. Some of those trades may be approved by the government, some might not. The case against Rees is watertight for murder, but against your husband, we don't have a lot. He may still walk free.'

'I hope so.'

Isaac knew it to be true, what he had just said. What crime could they pin on Naughton? The man had organised Hector Robinson's death, but who would give evidence. Certainly not Gareth Rees, not unless he was placed in an impossible position. And definitely not Conroy's gang of hoodies. Even if one could be found to testify, what creditability would he have? A competent defence lawyer would have the evidence thrown out in an instance. Naughton was the organiser; Rees was the doer.

'If Rees is free, what do you think he will do about Gabbi?' Isaac asked.

'If he is capable of violence, although he never touched her when they were married, he might do something,' Analyn said.

347

'And if we manage to prove that your husband has been manipulating the murders, removing those who could possibly jeopardise his freedom, what would he do?'

'I don't know.'

'You are married to Naughton; you know him better than anyone else. You may even love him.'

'I…'

'Love or like, hatred, whatever. It doesn't matter. What is of more importance is what will happen to you and Gabbi. Think about it. Janice Robinson is killed because she had heard something at Mary Wilton's. We are certain that Rees killed her, but we can't prove it. Cathy Parkinson, we're not sure about. And then there's Janice's father. What's he got to do with it? Someone who might start causing trouble. And then three gang members. One of them because of Gareth Rees, the other two through a word in the right ear, a rival gang.'

'But why did they kill so many people?' Analyn asked.

'The military mind, trained to kill silently in difficult and dangerous countries. Discretion, paying someone off to keep quiet, doesn't work as well as ensuring the person is dead. If Gabbi gets up in a court and damns her husband, if the woman with the video in Canning Town testifies, what then? What will happen to them? What will happen to you? We can't protect you indefinitely. If either of them goes free, then it's on your own head.'

Analyn sat still for some time before she nodded over to her left. 'I'll need someone better than this man,' she said to both Isaac and Larry.

'Your husband's lawyer?' Isaac said.

'I'm not guilty of any crime. Whatever the outcome, you will have the truth. And yes, I'm frightened for myself and Gabbi. Gareth is a dangerous man, not that I ever knew about him killing people here, but I knew something of what he and Ian had done when they were soldiers.'

'You never suspected when Amanda Upton died?'

'I put it to the back of my mind. I never thought it was Gareth. And I knew it wasn't Ian.'

'Why not your husband?'

'Not on the day she died. He was with me.'

'Why the cryptic message?'

'It was a test for someone else. Ian might tell you, but I doubt if he will. He was surprised when you turned up at the door, calm as he was, but afterwards he downed a few too many stiff drinks, fell asleep in an armchair.'

'Who do you think it was for?'

'I've no idea. One of his devious friends, a test to prove that the man was worthy of being trusted. What you have said about him makes some sense. He scares me, the way he took me back after Mary Wilton's, as if I was a possession, there for his pleasure. I was to him an object, nothing more.'

'The future?'

'If I survive?'

'You will,' Larry said.

'Who else is there? People you don't know of.'

It was true, Isaac knew. It was the tip of an iceberg, a brief sojourn into a world that Naughton and Rees traded weapons to, killed for, and sold Amanda to.

Analyn and Gabbi Gaffney were about to be thrust into the limelight from where there was no coming back.

***

The interview of Ian Naughton was, as expected, of little value. With no need to hide behind a pretence, Jacob Jameson, who represented Gareth Rees, also represented Naughton.

Naughton stated that he and Rees had acted in the past under orders and their current business activities were legal. The only comment of note from Naughton was that if Rees had committed a criminal activity, he had not and that the man would be on his own.

Gareth Rees, two weeks after Naughton's arrest, and on hearing that his long-time friend was willing to sell him down the river if push came to shove, informed Isaac that on instructions from Naughton, his commanding officer in the military, he had committed actions in Iraq that he regretted, and as a result of post-traumatic stress disorder, he might have committed other crimes in England, including the murder of Sean Garvey and possibly his lover, Amanda, not that he remembered committing either. And, if it could be shown that he had been in that bedsit in Sunbeam Crescent, then he couldn't remember that either,

It was a pathetic attempt at absolving himself from criminal responsibility, the chance to be confined to a mental institution until he was deemed safe to re-enter society. There was nothing wrong with the man, but Isaac knew it would form a good defence strategy.

***

Amanda, it had been concluded, after Mary Wilton had told Wendy of a phone conversation she had had with her daughter, had died of love.

Whatever the reason, the woman had fallen for the emotionally-fractured Gareth Rees. And the man, pathologically disturbed as a result of spending time behind enemy lines and emotionally cold, had reacted: he had killed her. Janice Robinson had heard or been told something, although how much would never be known, as had Hector Robinson. The hoodies were collateral damage.

If Rees didn't succeed with the defence of PTSD, it was clear that he still suffered from a mental condition. He deserved to be locked up.

As for Naughton, tests were conducted, showing evident sociopathic traits. The man could be charming, but he was cold, the ideal killing machine. The documents that Lord Shaw had procured were enough to convince Isaac that Naughton and Rees were to be thrown to the wolves.

Only one murder remained unaccounted for, that of Cathy Parkinson. It had been messy, and Gareth Rees could not have committed it. As a professional, his pride would not allow it. One bullet, one knife, no more, and definitely no sex with the victim.

Homicide discussed the murder for over a week, continually drawing a blank. In the end, Wendy and Larry met with Meredith Temple. A model student, she was on her way to a degree, and the boyfriend had been told and had accepted her past.

'Meredith,' Wendy said, as the three of them sat in a pub near to the university. 'Cathy Parkinson, tell us about her?'

'Not much more than I've told you before. She was in a bad way.'

'Did she talk much, threaten to tell wives about husbands, get some extra money?'

351

'She wouldn't have been the first. It usually worked; the men too ashamed not to pay.'

Tim Winston sat in the interview room at Challis Street Police Station. He was reminded that by his own admission he had slept with Janice Robinson and Meredith Temple. He was told that he had lied and he had slept with Cathy Parkinson as well when she had been in one of her most drug-crazed moods.

In the end, he admitted that he hadn't wanted his wife to find out, and after Janice had died, he thought that he could not deal with Cathy's demands for money. The confession came quickly, and the man cried, as did Wendy. Not for Tim Winston, but for his wife and daughter.

Outside the interview room, after Winston had been charged and taken down to the cells, Wendy sat with Maeve Winston.

'I knew about Janice,' she said. 'I would have done anything to keep the family together. He didn't need to kill her.'

'I'm afraid that in time you and Rose will need to make a different life for yourselves.'

'We will, not here, a long way away.'

Wendy knew of only one certainty at the end of a long day and a much longer murder enquiry: the budding romance between Brad Robinson and Rose Winston was doomed.

The End

ALSO BY THE AUTHOR

DI Tremayne Thriller Series

Death Unholy – A DI Tremayne Thriller – Book 1

All that remained were the man's two legs and a chair full of greasy and fetid ash. Little did DI Keith Tremayne know that it was the beginning of a journey into the murky world of paganism and its ancient rituals. And it was going to get very dangerous.

'Do you believe in spontaneous human combustion?' Detective Inspector Keith Tremayne asked.

'Not me. I've read about it. Who hasn't?' Sergeant Clare Yarwood answered.

'I haven't,' Tremayne replied, which did not surprise his young sergeant. In the months they had been working together, she had come to realise that he was a man who had little interest in the world. When he had a cigarette in his mouth, a beer in his hand, and a murder to solve he was about the happiest she ever saw him, but even then he could hardly be regarded as one of life's most sociable people. And as for reading? The most he managed was an occasional police report, an early-morning newspaper, turning first to the back pages for the racing results.

Death and the Assassin's Blade – A DI Tremayne Thriller – Book 2

It was meant to be high drama, not murder, but someone's switched the daggers. The man's death took place in plain view of two serving police officers.

He was not meant to die; the daggers were only theatrical props, plastic and harmless. A summer's night, a production of Julius Caesar amongst the ruins of an Anglo-Saxon fort. Detective Inspector Tremayne is there with his sergeant, Clare Yarwood. In the assassination scene, Caesar collapses to the ground. Brutus defends his actions; Mark Antony rebukes him.

They're a disparate group, the amateur actors. One's an estate agent, another an accountant. And then there is the teenage school student, the gay man, the funeral director. And what about the women? They could be involved.

They've each got a secret, but which of those on the stage wanted Gordon Mason, the actor who had portrayed Caesar, dead?

Death and the Lucky Man – A DI Tremayne Thriller – Book 3

Sixty-eight million pounds and dead. Hardly the outcome expected for the luckiest man in England the day his lottery ticket was drawn out of the barrel. But then, Alan Winters' rags-to-riches story had never been conventional, and some had benefited, but others hadn't.

Death at Coombe Farm – A DI Tremayne Thriller – Book 4

A warring family. A disputed inheritance. A recipe for death.

If it hadn't been for the circumstances, Detective Inspector Keith Tremayne would have said the view was outstanding. Up high, overlooking the farmhouse in the valley below, the panoramic vista of Salisbury Plain stretching out beyond. The only problem was that near where he stood with his sergeant, Clare Yarwood, there was a body, and it wasn't a pleasant sight.

Death by a Dead Man's Hand – A DI Tremayne Thriller – Book 5

A flawed heist of forty gold bars from a security van late at night. One of the perpetrators is killed by his brother as they argue over what they have stolen.

Eighteen years later, the murderer, released after serving his sentence for his brother's murder, waits in a church for a man purporting to be the brother he killed. And then he too is killed.

The threads stretch back a long way, and now more people are dying in the search for the missing gold bars.

Detective Inspector Tremayne, his health causing him concern, and Sergeant Clare Yarwood, still seeking romance, are pushed to the limit solving the murder, attempting to prevent any more.

Death in the Village – A DI Tremayne Thriller – Book 6

Nobody liked Gloria Wiggins, a woman who regarded anyone who did not acquiesce to her jaundiced view of the world with disdain. James Baxter, the previous vicar, had been one of those, and her scurrilous outburst in the church one Sunday had hastened his death.

And now, years later, the woman was dead, hanging from a beam in her garage. Detective Inspector Tremayne and Sergeant Clare Yarwood had seen the body, interviewed the woman's acquaintances, and those who had hated her.

Burial Mound – A DI Tremayne Thriller – Book 7

A Bronze-Age burial mound close to Stonehenge. An archaeological excavation. What they were looking for was an ancient body and historical artefacts. They found the ancient body, but then they found a modern-day body too. And then the police became interested.

It's another case for Detective Inspector Tremayne and Sergeant Yarwood. The more recent body was the brother of the mayor of Salisbury.

Everything seems to point to the victim's brother, the mayor, the upright and serious-minded Clive Grantley. Tremayne's sure that it's him, but Clare Yarwood's not so sure.

But is her belief based on evidence or personal hope?

The Body in the Ditch – A DI Tremayne Thriller – Book 8

A group of children play. Not far away, in the ditch on the other side of the farmyard, lies the body of a troubled young woman.

The nearby village hides as many secrets as the community at the farm, a disparate group of people looking for an alternative to their previous torturous lives. Their leader, idealistic and benevolent, espouses love and kindness, and clearly somebody's not following his dictate.

The second death, an old woman, seems unrelated to the first, but is it? Is it part of the tangled web that connects the farm to the village?

The village, Detective Inspector Tremayne and Sergeant Clare Yarwood find out soon enough, is anything but charming and picturesque. It's an incestuous hotbed of intrigue and wrongdoing. And what of the farm and those who live there? None of them can be ruled out, not yet.

DCI Isaac Cook Thriller Series

Murder is a Tricky Business – A DCI Cook Thriller – Book 1

A television actress is missing, and DCI Isaac Cook, the Senior Investigation Officer of the Murder Investigation Team at Challis Street Police Station in London, is searching for her.

Why has he been taken away from more important crimes to search for the woman? It's not the first time she's gone missing, so why does everyone assume she's been murdered?

There's a secret, that much is certain, but who knows it? The missing woman? The executive producer? His eavesdropping assistant? Or the actor who portrayed her fictional brother in the TV soap opera?

Murder House – A DCI Cook Thriller – Book 2

A corpse in the fireplace of an old house. It's been there for thirty years, but who is it?

It's murder, but who is the victim and what connection does the body have to the previous owners of the house. What is the motive? And why is the body in a fireplace? It was bound to be discovered eventually but was that what the murderer wanted? The main suspects are all old and dying, or already dead.

Isaac Cook and his team have their work cut out, trying to put the pieces together. Those who know are not talking because of an old-fashioned belief that a family's dirty laundry should not be aired in public, and never to a policeman – even if that means the murderer is never brought to justice!

Murder is Only a Number – A DCI Cook Thriller – Book 3

Before she left, she carved a number in blood on his chest. But why the number 2, if this was her first murder?

The woman prowls the streets of London. Her targets are men who have wronged her. Or have they? And why is she keeping count?

DCI Cook and his team finally know who she is, but not before she's murdered four men. The whole team are looking for her, but the woman keeps disappearing in plain sight. The pressure's on to stop her, but she's always one step ahead.

And this time, DCS Goddard can't protect his protégé, Isaac Cook, from the wrath of the new commissioner at the Met.

Murder in Little Venice – A DCI Cook Thriller – Book 4

A dismembered corpse floats in the canal in Little Venice, an upmarket tourist haven in London. Its identity is unknown, but what is its significance?

DCI Isaac Cook is baffled about why it's there. Is it gang-related, or is it something more?

Whatever the reason, it's clearly a warning, and Isaac and his team are sure it's not the last body that they'll have to deal with.

Murder is the Only Option – A DCI Cook Thriller – Book 5

A man thought to be long dead returns to exact revenge against those who had blighted his life. His only concern is to protect his wife and daughter. He will stop at nothing to achieve his aim.

'Big Greg, I never expected to see you around here at this time of night.'

'I've told you enough times.'

'I've no idea what you're talking about,' Robertson replied. He looked up at the man, only to see a metal pole coming down at him. Robertson fell down, cracking his head against a concrete kerb.

Two vagrants, no more than twenty feet away, did not stir and did not even look in the direction of the noise. If they had, they would have seen a dead body, another man walking away.

Murder in Notting Hill – A DCI Cook Thriller – Book 6

One murderer, two bodies, two locations, and the murders have been committed within an hour of each other.

They're separated by a couple of miles, and neither woman has anything in common with the other. One is young and wealthy, the daughter of a famous man; the other is poor, hardworking and unknown.

Isaac Cook and his team at Challis Street Police Station are baffled about why they've been killed. There must be a connection, but what is it?

Murder in Room 346 – A DCI Cook Thriller – Book 7

'Coitus interruptus, that's what it is,' Detective Chief Inspector Isaac Cook said. On the bed, in a downmarket hotel in Bayswater, lay the naked bodies of a man and a woman.

'Bullet in the head's not the way to go,' Larry Hill, Isaac Cook's detective inspector, said. He had not expected such a flippant comment from his senior, not when they were standing near to two people who had, apparently in the final throes of passion, succumbed to what appeared to be a professional assassination.

'You know this will be all over the media within the hour,' Isaac said.

'James Holden, moral crusader, a proponent of the sanctity of the marital bed, man and wife. It's bound to be.'

Murder of a Silent Man – A DCI Cook Thriller – Book 8

A murdered recluse. A property empire. A disinherited family. All the ingredients for murder.

No one gave much credence to the man when he was alive. In fact, most people never knew who he was, although those who had lived in the area for many years recognised the tired-looking and shabbily-dressed man as he shuffled along, regular as clockwork on a Thursday afternoon at seven in the evening to the local off-licence.

361

It was always the same: a bottle of whisky, premium brand, and a packet of cigarettes. He paid his money over the counter, took hold of his plastic bag containing his purchases, and then walked back down the road with the same rhythmic shuffle. He said not one word to anyone on the street or in the shop.

Murder has no Guilt – A DCI Cook Thriller – Book 9

No one knows who the target was or why, but there are eight dead. The men seem the most likely perpetrators, or could have it been one of the two women, the attractive Gillian Dickenson, or even the celebrity-obsessed Sal Maynard?

There's a gang war brewing, and if there are deaths, it doesn't matter to them as long as it's not their death. But to Detective Chief Inspector Isaac Cook, it's his area of London, and it does matter.

It's dirty and unpredictable. Initially it had been the West Indian gangs, but then a more vicious Romanian gangster had usurped them. And now he's being marginalised by the Russians. And the leader of the most vicious Russian mafia organisation is in London, and he's got money and influence, the ear of those in power.

Murder in Hyde Park – A DCI Cook Thriller – Book 10

An early morning jogger is murdered in Hyde Park. It's the centre of London, but no one saw him enter the park, no one saw him die.

He carries no identification, only a water-logged phone. As the pieces unravel, it's clear that the dead man had a history of deception.

Is the murderer one of those that loved him? Or was it someone with a vengeance?

It's proving difficult for DCI Isaac Cook and his team at Challis Street Homicide to find the guilty person – not that they'll cease to search for the truth, not even after one suspect confesses.

Six Years Too Late – A DCI Cook Thriller – Book 11

Always the same questions for Detective Chief Inspector Isaac Cook — Why was Marcus Matthews in that room? And why did he share a bottle of wine with his killer?

It wasn't as if the man had amounted to much in life, apart from the fact that he was the son-in-law of a notorious gangster, the father of the man's grandchildren. Yet, one thing that Hamish McIntyre, feared in London for his violence, rated above anything else, it was his family, especially Samantha, his daughter; although he had never cared for Marcus, her husband.

And then Marcus disappears, only for his body to be found six years later by a couple of young boys who decide that exploring an abandoned house is preferable to school.

Murder Without Reason – A DCI Cook Thriller – Book 12

DCI Cook faces his greatest challenge. The Islamic State is waging war in England, and they are winning.

Not only does Isaac Cook have to contend with finding the perpetrators, but he is also being forced to commit actions contrary to his mandate as a police officer.

And then there is Anne Argento, the prime minister's deputy. The prime minister has shown himself to be a pacifist and is not up to the task. She needs to take his job if the country is to fight back against the Islamists.

Vane and Martin have provided the solution. Will DCI Cook and Anne Argento be willing to follow it through? Are they able to act for the good of England, knowing that a criminal and murderous action is about to take place? Do they have an option?

Standalone Novels

The Haberman Virus

A remote and isolated village in the Hindu Kush mountain range in North Eastern Afghanistan is wiped out by a virus unlike any seen before.

A mysterious visitor clad in a spacesuit checks his handiwork, a female American doctor succumbs to the disease, and the woman sent to trap the person responsible falls in love with him – the man who would cause the deaths of millions.

Hostage of Islam

Three are to die at the Mission in Nigeria: the pastor and his wife in a blazing chapel; another gunned down while trying to defend them from the Islamist fighters.

Kate McDonald, an American, grieving over her boyfriend's death and Helen Campbell, whose life had been troubled by drugs and prostitution, are taken by the attackers.

Kate is sold to a slave trader who intends to sell her virginity to an Arab Prince. Helen, to ensure their survival, gives herself to the murderer of her friends.

Malika's Revenge

Malika, a drug-addicted prostitute, waits in a smugglers' village for the next Afghan tribesman or Tajik gangster to pay her price, a few scraps of heroin.

Yusup Baroyev, a drug lord, enjoys a lifestyle many would envy. An Afghan warlord sees the resurgence of the Taliban. A Russian white-collar criminal portrays himself as a good and honest citizen in Moscow.

All of them are linked to an audacious plan to increase the quantity of heroin shipped out of Afghanistan and into Russia and ultimately the West.

Some will succeed, some will die, some will be rescued from their plight and others will rue the day they became involved.

Prelude to War

Russia and America face each other across the northern border of Afghanistan. World War 3 is about to break out and no one is backing off.

And all because a team of academics in New York postulated how to extract the vast untapped mineral wealth of Afghanistan.

Steve Case is in the middle of it, and his position is looking very precarious. Will the Taliban find him before the Americans get him out? Or is he doomed, as is the rest of the world?

ABOUT THE AUTHOR

Phillip Strang was born in England in the late forties. He was an avid reader of science fiction in his teenage years: Isaac Asimov, Frank Herbert, the masters of the genre. Still an avid reader, the author now mainly reads thrillers.

In his early twenties, the author, with a degree in electronics engineering and a desire to see the world, left England for Sydney, Australia. Now, forty years later, he still resides in Australia, although many intervening years were spent in a myriad of countries, some calm and safe, others no more than war zones.

Printed in Great Britain
by Amazon